W9-AGY-502

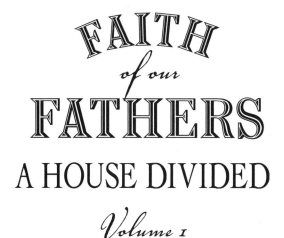

FAITH
of our
FATHERS
A HOUSE DIVIDED
Volume 1

FAITH
of our
FATHERS

A HOUSE DIVIDED

Volume 1

a novel by

N.C. ALLEN

Covenant Communications, Inc.

Cover and interior photographs © Al Thelin
Cover flag illustration by Joe Flores

Cover design copyrighted 2001 by Covenant Communications, Inc.

Published by Covenant Communications, Inc.
American Fork, Utah

Copyright © 2001 by N.C. Allen
All rights reserved. No part of this book may be reproduced in any format or in any medium without the written permission of the publisher, Covenant Communications, Inc., P.O. Box 416, American Fork, UT 84003. The views expressed herein are the responsibility of the author and do not necessarily represent the position of Covenant Communications, Inc.

This is a work of fiction. The characters, names, incidents, places, and dialogue are products of the author's imagination, and are not to be construed as real.

Printed in Canada
First Printing: October 2001

14 13 12 11 10 09 08 07   14 13 12 11 10 9 8 7

ISBN-13. 978-1-59811-489-8
ISBN-10: 1-59811-489-1

Library of Congress Cataloging-in-Publication Data

Allen, Nancy Campbell, 1969-
    Faith of our fathers/N.C.Allen.
        p. cm.
    Includes bibliographical references.
    Contents: v. 1. A house divided.
    ISBN 1-57734-897-4 (v.1)
    1. United States--History--Civil War, 1861-1865--Fiction. 2. Mormon
families--Fiction. 3. Plantation life--Fiction. 4. Southern States--Fiction. 5. Boston
(Mass.)--Fiction. I. Title.

PS3551.L39644 F25 2001
813'.54--dc21   200104761

To Per and Solveig,
Sidney and Maude—
for passing along a worthy gene pool
and a noble heritage.

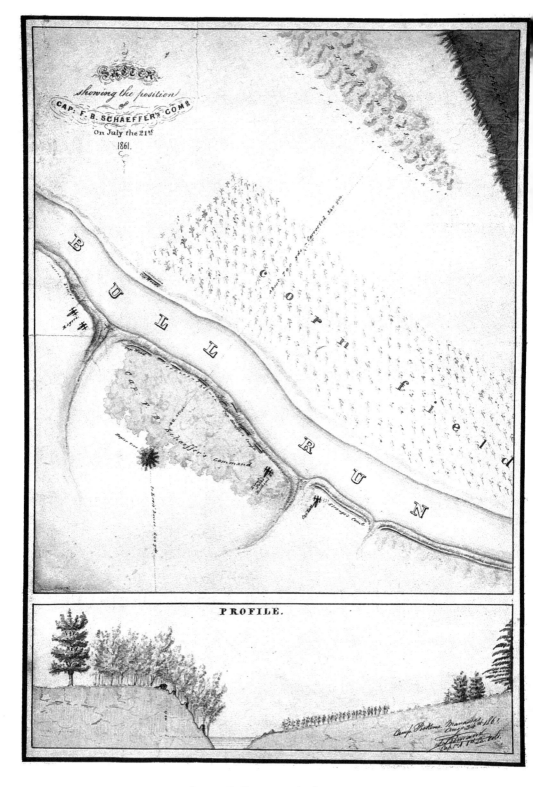

LÉON J. FRÉMAUX'S SKETCH
CAPTAIN F. B. SCHAEFFER'S COMMAND, BULL RUN, JULY 21, 1861

Geography and Map Division, Library of Congress, Washington, D. C.

INTRODUCTION

This novel is the first in a series of four that will follow the lives of six key fictional families during the Civil War. It is my intention with these books to give the reader a varied experience. By placing these characters at various strategic geographic locations and offering key players who are interesting and perhaps a bit unique, I hope to supply the reader with an experience that not only entertains, but educates as well.

My research for these books has been and continues to be enthralling for me. I am fascinated by this piece of United States history, and yet the deeper I delve, the more unsettled my emotions become. If one makes a careful study of the Civil War, one quickly comes to realize that generally speaking, not everyone was all good or all bad—much as life is today. Certainly some were nobler than others, and some were more heinous than others, but it seems that the more layers I peel back, the more complex these issues become.

There is one constant, however, that I have found in the mountain of books and videos currently piling up in my home—and that is that despite many modern opinions to the contrary, this country tore itself in half over the basic issue of race. To be sure, it would be ignorant and simplistic to suggest there were not other contributing factors, but there was only one issue divisive enough to break the proverbial camel's back, and that issue was slavery.

Not everybody owned slaves, though, and not every person in the North was an abolitionist. So why the huge division? Why all the furor over a condition that had existed in the United States from its very inception as a collection of rag-tag colonies?

There are no easy answers, and one thing I've found when discussing this time period with people from all walks of life is that everyone seems to have firm opinions on the Civil War, and emotions still run hot and deep. What I am attempting with this series is to show that there is no simple analysis; there is no black and white, to be trite.

It is not my intention with this book, or with any others that will follow, to create historical fiction with Lincoln or Davis as key players. The reader will see actual, historical people through the eyes of the fictional characters I've created. I do not feel up to the task of taking liberties and putting words and thoughts into Lincoln's head; what the reader will see are fictional characters' honest reactions to events that actually happened. There are a few isolated instances where I have one (or some) of my characters speaking to a person who actually lived, but those scenes are brief and few, and they do not extend to any kind of introspection on the part of real people—in short, the things I have them saying to *my* characters are either actual quotes, recorded in history, or sentiments along the lines of things those people actually did say, at some point.

I do hope, however, that you will come to care for these fictional characters as I have. To me they have taken on a life of their own, and I'm always amazed—often surprised—at the turns they take and the places they lead me. You may find, as you read, that many of these characters seem to be "forward thinkers," that they were not typical of the norm, and in truth, many of them are not typical of the *majority*. History, however, has shown, and continues to show with the perpetual discoveries of diaries and memoirs long lost, that there were people, both in the North and the South, who possessed the light of Christ and had a vision of His will for us. Many of my characters are fashioned after people who were real, and created around those in the minority who were light-years ahead of their times, who knew how life *should* be, and who strove for that ideal.

I hope you will enjoy their adventures, and that as you consider their lives, you will be able to come to your own conclusions about this most momentous period of United States history; because whether or not we realize or acknowledge it, these events shaped the way we look at life today, and the residual effects still echo.

LIST OF CHARACTERS

The Boston, Massachusetts, Birmingham Family

James Birmingham, the father. A wealthy iron magnate.

Elizabeth Stein Birmingham, the mother. Abolitionist descendant of Rhode Island Quakers.

Luke, oldest son. Ardent abolitionist, twenty-five years old.

Anne. Twenty-two years old.

Camille. Eighteen years old.

Robert. Fifteen years old.

Jimmy. Ten years old.

The Charleston, South Carolina, Birmingham Family

Jeffrey, the father. Also James's twin brother, married to plantation heiress.

Sarah Matthews Birmingham, the mother. Plantation owner.

Ben, oldest son, age twenty-five. Left home after joining the Mormon Church.

Charlotte Birmingham Ellis, twenty-three years old. Married to William Ellis.

Richard. Twenty years old.

Emily. Fifteen years old.

Clara. Ten years old.

The Birmingham Slaves

Ruth, head house servant. The "matriarch" of the majority of the slaves.

Joshua, raised as Ben's companion. Twenty-four years old.

Mary, Ruth's granddaughter. Sixteen years old and Joshua's biological sister; close friend to Emily.

Rose, Mary's little sister. Companion to Clara; ten years old.

The O'Shea family, New York
Gavin, the father.
Brenna, the mother.
Daniel, their twenty-seven-year-old son.

The Brissot family, New Orleans
Jean-Pierre, the father.
Genevieve (Jenny) Stein Brissot. The mother; sister to Elizabeth Stein Birmingham.
Marie, their twenty-three-year-old daughter.

The Gundersen family, Cleveland, Ohio
Per, the father.
Amanda, the mother.
Ivar, their twenty-nine-year-old son.
Inger, Ivar's two-year-old daughter.

Isabelle Webb
Dolly and Abigail Van Dyke
Ellen Dobranski and her children

Nonfictional characters to whom reference is made or who play a minor role, interacting with the fictional characters:
President Abraham Lincoln.
William Lloyd Garrison, abolitionist and editor of *The Liberator.*
Jefferson Davis, President of the Confederacy.
Allan Pinkerton, private investigator.
Kate Warne, Pinkerton employee.
Timothy Webster, Pinkerton employee.
Roger Pryor, former Virginia senator.
James Chestnut, former U.S. senator.
Mary Chestnut, his wife and famed diarist.

P. G. T. Beauregard, Confederate General.

Robert E. Lee, Confederate General.

Thomas "Stonewall" Jackson, Confederate General.

Irving McDowell, Union Army General.

George McClellan, Union General.

Winfield Scott, Union General.

William Seward, Union Secretary of State.

Leroy P. Walker, Confederate Secretary of War.

Robert Toombs, Confederate Secretary of State.

George James, fired the signal gun to commence firing on Fort Sumter.

Edmund Ruffin, credited with firing the first shot of the Civil War.

Albert Riddle, Senator from Ohio.

James Mason, Emissary to Great Britain.

John Slidell, Emissary to Great Britain.

"A house divided against itself cannot stand. I believe this government cannot endure, permanently half slave and half free. I do not expect the Union to be dissolved. I do not expect the house to fall. But I do expect it will cease to be divided. It will become all one thing, or all the other."

—Abraham Lincoln

"Suppose there is a division between the North and South, and the fifteen slave States try to form a permanent government, can they do it? I tell you they cannot. How long will it be before some other States, perhaps New York, forms a separate government? And if a State has a right to secede, so has a Territory, so has a county from a State or Territory, and a town from a county, and a family from a neighborhood, and you will have perfect anarchy."

—Brigham Young

PROLOGUE

Charleston, South Carolina
23 August, 1855

The sound of the dogs loomed ever closer, forcing the four shadows deeper into the woods for the third time in less than an hour. Ben Birmingham glanced over his shoulder and drew the matriarch close to his side. With his other hand, he clasped the fingers of the young five-year-old girl, icy cold despite the oppressive summertime heat.

Ben looked into the face of the woman at his side—a woman who had been more of a mother to him than his own. "Ruth," he whispered, "we must go through the river."

The woman nodded, her eyes brimming with a look of defeat that tore at his heart. He gave her shoulders a quick squeeze. "This will work! This will work!"

She blinked once, sending a lone tear from her rich brown eyes and down the smooth chocolate skin of her beautiful face. "I love you, boy," she said, placing a hand alongside his face. "As if you were my own."

"I wish I were your own," he murmured, his own throat aching at the evidence of her emotion. He shook his head and pulled his senses to the fore, attempting to finish the deadly task they'd been planning for months.

"Mary, Rose," he whispered again, "this way." With his arm still about the shoulders of the woman, he led the three slaves toward the gushing sounds of the small river and urged them into the water, hoping desperately to throw off the dogs.

They traveled in silence for another thirty minutes, eventually leaving the water and criss-crossing their way across the landscape and toward the safe house Ben had discovered only weeks before. He had learned of its existence through an elusive grapevine, the members of which were a long time in trusting him, given the pale shade of his skin and his birthright.

There was a light in the attic window of a small house just off in the distance, and Ben leaned over to whisper to the eleven-year-old, "There it is, Mary! A light in the window, just as they said!"

The small group approached the servants' entrance at the back of the moderately sized home. Ruth, Mary, and Rose hid themselves as instructed in a clump of bushes next to the door, and Ben knocked softly, three times.

There was a shuffle of noise on the other side of the door, followed by a muffled cry that had Ben's spine tingling in alarm. He began backing slowly away from the door and was turning to tell the fugitives in his care to run with him for all they were worth, when the door was opened by his family's overseer.

Shock rooted him to the spot and his mouth went slack as he stared at the short, stocky man who had been in the Birmingham family employ for just over a year. The man grinned, his watery blue eyes nearly disappearing into his face. "Well," he rasped, " if it isn't my boss's son. What're ya doing so far from Bentley in the middle of the night, Master Ben?"

Ben clamped his mouth shut, rage boiling from within and making his vision blur. They had been betrayed. Someone had known of their plans and had told Jackson. *How?* They had been so careful! "I might ask the same of you, Jackson," Ben finally muttered between clenched teeth.

Jackson opened the door wider and a shaft of light from a lantern cast its way out onto the dirt path. Behind Jackson stood a man Ben had never met, but whose coffee brown hair and small physical stature matched the description he had been given of the homeowner. Smith was his innocuous name, and from what Ben could gather, the man had been pummeled into submission before Ben's arrival. His face was bloodied and bruised, his right eye beginning to swell shut. The man stood stoically, his shoulders straight.

"I don't know what you think you're doing," Smith said to Jackson, "but you will be hearing from me about this! You have no business coming into my home and assaulting me! And who are you?" he asked Ben. "What are you doing, coming to my house at all hours of the night?"

"I must have knocked on the wrong door," he said to Smith, knowing they were both fighting a losing battle. Smith would no longer be able to operate as a safe house; indeed, he'd probably find himself in jail before morning. "I'll be on my way."

Ben turned from the door, willing Ruth, Mary, and Rose to stay hidden until he could come back for them. He hadn't even turned around before two large white men seized him, on Jackson's orders. "Release me!" he snarled, struggling and breaking free from one of the men. The other, however, had him outweighed by nearly half, and held fast, knocking him on the side of his head with a blow that sent him reeling.

His vision blurred, his head spinning, he watched in numb horror as three more men spilled from the house and began searching the grounds while Jackson shouted, "They're here somewhere! I know they are!" Of course, it took only minutes before the hired bounty hunters searched the bushes nearest the door and pulled forward the three people who meant more to Ben than almost anyone.

"No!" His shout echoed throughout the countryside.

The ride back to Bentley in the back of a rickety wagon while two of the men sat on him after tying and gagging him might have been the worst thing Ben could have imagined for himself, but his mind kept leaping ahead to the fate that surely awaited Ruth, Mary, and Rose once they were returned home.

He wasn't mistaken. After he was unceremoniously dumped in the family library where his parents, wide-eyed and stiff, awaited his arrival, his mother confirmed his worst suspicions. "Of course they'll be punished, Ben," she said in a shaky voice. "What do you suppose would happen if the other servants realized escape attempts were met with mere slaps upon the wrist?"

Sarah paced the length of the library, wringing her hands. He'd never, in all of his twenty years, seen his mother wring her hands. His head ached from the clubbing he'd received at the hands of Jackson's men, and his fear for the slaves' welfare threatened to spill forth the bile rising in his throat.

"Do you suppose," he said to his father in an even tone, "that you could at least untie my hands?"

Jeffrey eyed his son with something akin to sick sympathy. He shook his head once, and made his way to an oak desk in the corner, where he retrieved a small knife. He made short work of the rope knots holding Ben bound, and when released, Ben rubbed his wrists and wandered to the window, his mind working furiously while he tried to maintain an outward calm.

His mother's image was reflected behind him in the glass that looked out into the black night. "Ben, I trusted you," she whispered. "You're my son."

He closed his eyes briefly, wondering why Sarah seemed to feel she had any claim on his emotions. Ruth had raised him, and they both knew it. "I would do it all again, given the chance."

"You would destroy your family? Your own family, your legacy?" Sarah's sharp edge returned, replacing the vulnerable tone that was so unlike her.

Ben finally turned to glance at her over his shoulder, looking at her unmoving features, while his father stood several paces behind her as was his unspoken place. *How did I ever end up here?* he wondered as he looked at the strangers who had given him life. "This is not my legacy, mother," he said.

He might have offered more, but muted cries from outside brought his gaze back again to the window. He squinted into the distance, down the grassy slopes by the slave quarters where torches lit the night. He heard screams, wrenching, pain-filled screams that filled his heart with indescribable agony.

Ben ran to the French doors that led outside and tore them open before his parents could stop him. He ran down the hill toward Ruth, stumbling and nearly falling in his haste to get to her. Finally reaching the spot where Jackson had her arms tied above her head, suspended from a tree, he threw his own body across her naked shoulders and back, a hoarse sob from the depths of his soul escaping his lips.

The angry shouts from Jackson and the crack of the whip upon his own back and shoulders barely registered. The only physical sensation he noticed was the warmth of Ruth's blood as it seeped into the fine lawn of his white shirt. It took his father and several of Jackson's bounty hunters to pry his arms from the woman and they dragged him, shouting and thrashing, back to the mansion.

Ben looked back upon the scene as he struggled to break free—Ruth resigned to her fate and accepting her punishment, the tears coursing in rivulets down her resolute face, Mary and Rose looking on with huge eyes and tear-stained faces, and Joshua, Ben's personal valet and bosom friend from childhood rushing from the main house to gaze at him in horrified shock.

Ben closed his eyes and finally admitted the unthinkable truth.

He had failed.

.

CHAPTER 1

"I am aware that many object to the severity of my language; but is there not cause for severity? I will be as harsh as truth, and as uncompromising as justice. On this subject I do not wish to think, or speak, or write, with moderation . . . I am in earnest—I will not equivocate—I will not excuse—I will not retreat a single inch—and I will be heard."
—William Lloyd Garrison, abolitionist
and editor of The Liberator

***

Boston, Massachusetts
20 December, 1860

The figure of a tall, thin boy darted down the street in the encroaching darkness, dodging deftly between horses and carriages and pedestrians. The sky overhead hung thick with winter clouds that had been threatening all day to dispose of their heavy loads. Such weather was usually welcomed in winter, especially with Christmas approaching, but the people on the street were all abuzz with news that had nothing to do with the pending holidays.

"Did you hear?" the boy heard a man ask his companion as they stood under a nearby street lamp, waiting to hail a passing hack. "South Carolina has seceded!"

The other man's reply was lost to the boy as he continued his journey home. Rounding several more corners on the busy streets of Boston, he approached the quieter section of town on the outskirts that housed his family. Panting, he finally reached his spacious home and quietly skirted the circular driveway, dodging around to the back where the carriage house stood empty. He made his way into the darkened recesses of the building, shucking his hat to reveal a thick head of long, blonde curls.

Running a hand through her hair, the "boy" quickly tried to smooth the tangles with the one hand while she reached inside her overcoat and unbuttoned her shirt with the other. Finally reaching the tiny supply room in the back, she hastily shed the rest of her clothes and donned the garments she'd stashed in the corner—attire more appropriately suited for her gender. She made quick work of the undergarments, petticoats, and the buttons on her gown, patting everything into place as she drew a deep breath.

She had long since learned to choose dresses made of material that weren't prone to an overabundance of wrinkles while lying crumpled in the carriage house as she dashed about town under the guise of a young man. She balled up her boys' clothing and shoved it into a sack that she would retrieve and wash later when nobody was around to see. Twisting her hair hastily behind her head, she gathered up the hairpins she'd placed with her dress and did the best she could in the dark of the carriage house.

Having finally finished her task, she smoothed her skirts one more time before leaving the room. She had nearly made it to the door of the carriage house when a dark figure bumped her from the side, letting out a startled cry. She glanced up in a mild panic, then found herself relaxing.

"George," she said with a smile. "Did I frighten you?"

The head groom laughed when he realized who she was. "Anne Birmingham, one of these days your parents are going to discover what you've been up to. Then what will you do?"

"I'll think of something," she said, still smiling, and left the carriage house, making her way toward the mansion. George was one of her three confidantes. He had been like a favorite uncle to her for as long as she could remember, and he was the one person who wouldn't stand in her way as she traipsed around Boston as a boy, gathering information she would later use in a newspaper column penned under the name, "Adam Jones."

She clutched the notebook she had retrieved from her coat jacket and slipped it into one of the large pockets sewn into her skirts. She would be busy tonight. Jacob would want her finished copy by very early morning.

She walked quietly around to the front door of the house, opened it calmly, then stepped inside. Her eyes took in the wide front foyer, the staircase on the right leading to the second floor, the rich tones of the woodwork and the polished floor. The house had been built in the traditional colonial style, and had looked the same ever since she was a child; and although she enjoyed change, in a world that was constantly evolving, she was grateful for the constancy of home.

Her mother, apparently having heard the front door, appeared from the dining room. Anne smiled at her, grateful also for the stability she found in her family. Elizabeth Birmingham was a beautiful woman in her forty-fifth year, with a head of blonde hair that mirrored Anne's—except for the first signs of gray strands woven in. She was taller than the average woman, her carriage erect and ever unwavering. Her face was pleasant to look at, with even features and an ever-generous smile. But perhaps the feature Anne most admired in her mother was her intellect.

Elizabeth Birmingham returned her daughter's smile, but it faded slightly as she approached her. "Anne, you've been walking without a coat?"

Anne cursed her stupidity. When had she ever missed such a detail? She must be slipping. She had worn a warm overcoat with her boy's clothes, but had neglected to put on her own cloak when she had left to change in the carriage house earlier. "I didn't walk long," she said, making her way toward the staircase. "I think I'll wash up for dinner."

Elizabeth placed a hand on her arm as she walked to the bottom stair. "You've been out for two hours, Anne."

Anne patted her mother's hand and continued up the staircase. "I hardly noticed the cold," she said over her shoulder.

Elizabeth Birmingham stood at the bottom of the stairs, watching her daughter continue her climb to the second floor and disappear around the corner. Anne had grown into a twenty-two-year-old woman, and Elizabeth had to admit that what little sway she had ever held over her daughter was now entirely gone. Her brow wrinkled in a light frown, and she continued toward the kitchen to check on the progress of their dinner. Anne would do what Anne would do. It had always been thus, and Elizabeth knew that nothing she could ever say or do would change it.

***

Anne's twenty-five-year-old brother, Luke Birmingham, sat alone at the breakfast table the following morning spooning eggs into his mouth and reading the paper before going to work at the bank for the day. The full head of short, black hair blended with the tailored perfection of his black business suit, and was in stark contrast to the snowy white shirtfront.

The town was aflame with the news of South Carolina's secession. His green eyes narrowed slightly as he read the various articles offering details about the departure of the Southern state. He knew that South Carolina was only the first. The conflict had been building for decades, and while it was a shock to see it finally happening, he couldn't say he was entirely surprised.

He looked up at the rustle of skirts in the doorway. Anne surveyed the sidebar where the food was sitting on warmers, waiting for the rest of the family to emerge from their bedrooms. It was early yet, and Luke was an early riser.

Luke grinned at his sister. "Why do you leave your bed, Anne? You never look happy about it."

She grunted something unintelligible and filled a plate with food, carrying it to the table and taking a seat across from him. She motioned to the newspaper. "What are they saying?"

He shrugged. "They're saying war is probably imminent, but the president-elect won't say one way or the other what he intends to do."

Anne nodded. "Lincoln's not making any friends by keeping quiet," she commented, picking a small piece of roll apart and taking a bite.

Luke scowled. "He must keep things stable at least until he gets into office. If he angers the Southern states at this point, it will all fall apart before he even reaches Washington!"

Anne held up her hands in mock defense. "I like Lincoln too, Luke. You don't have to defend him to me. In fact, were I allowed to," she added, an edge to her voice, "I would have cast my vote for him. It seems to me, though, that by not taking a firm stance now, people are going to ridicule him. They already are, in fact."

"He'll make it work." Luke continued flipping through the paper, reading intermittently while eating. He paused at a column toward the end. " 'Adam Jones, On the Streets' again."

Anne glanced up from her food. "What of it?"

Luke shook his head absently. "Nothing, really. I like the man, he always seems to know what people are saying, but he never offers an opinion of his own."

She smiled. "He's not supposed to. He's an objective reporter."

"Well, he seems like an intelligent sort. I'd like to know his thoughts about the people he quotes."

Luke went back to his food and missed the gleam in his sister's eye that she hid by ducking her head and thoughtfully placing a forkful of eggs into her mouth. She glanced back up at the sound of someone entering the room. Her sister, Camille, was perusing the sidebar with her pert nose slightly wrinkled.

"Doesn't it seem like we have the same things for breakfast every morning?" she asked nobody in particular.

Luke glanced up from his paper. "Good morning to you as well, Camille."

Camille waved a hand absently in his direction as she proceeded to place a small helping of eggs, sausages, and a roll on a plate. She carried it to the table and sat next to Anne. Anne stole a tired glance at her eighteen-year-old sister, who looked impeccable, as always. Camille was small and trim, with a thick head of chestnut-brown hair she wore piled on top of her head in rich curls. Her skin was smooth and pale, her bone structure small, her eyes large, green, and luminous, and her mouth perfectly shaped, and full. She was presently dressed in a morning gown of soft yellows and blues, the full skirts belling about her in a most attractive fashion and the bodice tightly cinched to show off her trim figure to perfection.

"Honestly, Anne, why *do* you get out of bed in the morning? Your eyes aren't even open yet."

"What are you doing today, Camille?" Anne deflected. "You're up a trifle early yourself."

Camille smothered a yawn. "I have a dress fitting at nine, and then Olivia invited me for an early lunch with her sister."

"The newly married sister?"

"Yes. Did you know that Rebecca's husband was just promoted at the bank? He'll be making fifteen hundred a year, and their new house is beautiful!"

Luke snorted lightly. "He was promoted because he's the grand-nephew of the bank president. He hasn't made many friends among the staff."

Anne cocked a brow, unimpressed with her sister's comments. "I have seen their new house, actually. I find it interesting that you're taken with a place that's relatively small."

"Yes, but Mama and Papa haven't always lived in a house this size! When they were first married, their house was a veritable cottage! Rebecca's starting her new life in grand fashion, and I think that I shan't settle for any less, myself."

Luke raised his glass to Camille in mock salute and downed the rest of his drink, saying as he rose from the table, "I'm sure you'll excuse me, ladies. I have a meeting before work."

"Another abolitionist gathering, Luke?" Camille whined. "It's positively embarrassing to have a brother so outspoken about such things. It was bad enough when it was just Mother!"

Luke's good humor dampened and he glanced at Camille as he made his way to the door. "There are times, Camille, when I think my fondest wish would be granted were I to awaken one morning and find you mute."

Camille rolled her eyes and bristled at the insult, but said nothing further as her brother left the room.

"Do you truly not care, Camille?" Anne's voice was mild, quiet.

Camille sighed. "I do care, but I'm trying to find myself a husband! Luke is so loud with his opinions when he leaves this house, and he's always quoted in the papers with his rhetoric. My friends comment on it and I find myself constantly embarrassed. Many of them have good friends who are Southerners."

"We have close family who are Southerners, Camille." Anne took a swallow of her orange juice and dabbed at her mouth with a crisp, white linen napkin. "That doesn't mean it's right."

Camille scowled. "Uncle Jeffrey is highly respected with his Southern politician friends. All the more reason for Luke to temper his tongue! He doesn't even care about his own family!"

"Ben, himself, left." Anne shot Camille an arch look, then rose from the table. On her way out of the breakfast room, she passed her fifteen-year-old brother, Robert.

"Oh, good, the paper's here," Robert commented as he passed Anne with a brief smile.

Anne heard Camille's plaintive voice as she moved out of the room and down the hallway. "I don't want to hear any of your war opinions today, Robert . . ."

***

James Birmingham stood before the etched-glass mirror in his spacious bedroom. He tied his cravat in a knot, only to fumble and muss his creation. With a mild curse, he untied the fabric and attempted it again.

"Here, let me do that," came a voice from behind his shoulder. He shifted to see his wife coming toward him from the open door that connected their bedrooms, a wry smile upon her face. "You never get it quite right, do you James?" Her tone was light, and not intended to wound.

He smiled and willingly turned the mess over to her capable fingers. "What would I do without you, Lizzie?"

"Well, I'm sure I don't know." She finished tying the cravat and patted it lightly into place. Her face altered slightly, her features suddenly taking on a strained appearance.

"Are you going into the offices, then?"

James nodded.

"Have you seen the papers today?"

He nodded again. "Interesting development, isn't it?" James tried to keep his voice light, but failed. He looked at his wife's face, knowing her strain matched his own. South Carolina had left the Union, and his twin brother, Jeffrey, was a firmly entrenched resident of Charleston. "I've already written to Jeffrey," he told Elizabeth. "I'd like to hear from his own mouth what he has to say about things."

Elizabeth laughed, without mirth. "You know very well what he'll have to say about things, but if you want to know how he feels, you should go straight to the source and ask Sarah."

James shook his head at the thought of his sister-in-law. An admirably strong woman she was, without a doubt, but his brother lacked the strength of character to keep from getting trampled beneath her small, booted feet. He turned back to the mirror, examining his wife's handiwork with the cravat.

He scrutinized his own appearance, taking in the hair that had once been black but was turning to gray, the tall frame that had held its youth fairly well, but had added a few pounds with the years, and the wrinkles alongside his green eyes that had crept up before he realized it. Elizabeth appeared at his side, drawing him close with an arm about his waist. "I'd say you're looking rather well for a man in his fifties," she said with a smile.

He turned and drew her close, resting his chin on the top of her head. In truth, he was not so very different from his twin brother. They had both married women strong of will, and had both come to embrace the opinions and lifestyles of their wives. Of the two, he felt eminently luckier.

He turned at a soft knock upon the bedroom door. "Come in," he called, releasing his hold on his wife. He saw the head of their youngest son, Jimmy, appear around the corner.

"Mama?" Jimmy's voice was usually quiet; today it was doubly so.

"What is it, sweeting?" Elizabeth approached the door and opened it fully to reveal the youngest boy still in his nightclothes.

"I don't feel well," the ten-year-old admitted. Upon closer appearance, James noticed his young son's face did indeed appear flushed under the thick crop of black hair. He joined his wife at the child's side, watching as Elizabeth placed her fingers alongside the boy's cheek and forehead.

"Back to bed with you, young man," she ordered. "I'll bring you some broth in a few minutes." She smiled at the young boy and ruffled his hair.

He turned to go, and then as an apparent afterthought, turned back to his father. "Will the iron still be mined, Papa?"

James raised his brows in question. "The iron, Jimmy?"

"Your iron. Will the business still run with a war coming?"

James and Elizabeth exchanged a glance. "Who told you there was a war coming, sweetheart?" Elizabeth asked.

"Robert. He said there will definitely be a war and he wishes he could fight, but he's not old enough."

James cleared his throat. "We don't know that there will be a war, son. Don't concern yourself over it. And nothing stops my business from running." He said the last with a smile and laid an affectionate hand on the boy's shoulder, sorry that the child was feeling ill. He had considered taking the lad with him to the offices today in an attempt to spend some time with him, hoping to better understand him. Jimmy was a quiet child, who didn't often verbalize his thoughts. He was prone to artwork, and expressed himself through his sketches. That was well and good, James often thought, but the boy would eventually need some kind of vocation. He, perhaps more so than his other two sons, would need some guidance.

CHAPTER 2

". . . A very different-looking class of people are springing up at the south and are now held in slavery, from those originally brought to this country from Africa; and if their increase will do no other good, it will do away the force of the argument that God cursed Ham, and therefore American slavery is right . . . It is certain that slavery at the south must soon become unscriptural; for thousands are ushered into the world, annually, who, like myself, owe their existence to white fathers, and those fathers most frequently their own masters."
—*Frederick Douglass, escaped former slave*

***

Charleston, South Carolina—Bentley Plantation
27 December, 1860

The morning dawned crisp and cold, the air rent with a newborn's first cry. The young baby's mother lay upon her bed in the Birmingham family slave quarters, exhausted from the strain of long labor throughout the night, and emotionally spent at giving birth to a child she hadn't wanted.

Her grandmother, Ruth, performed the afterbirth functions with practiced ease, the only sign of her stress apparent in the subtle creasing of her brow. "Mary?" she asked, when her grand-daughter had collapsed back against the thin sheets.

Mary's eyes fluttered and she glanced at the squirming being in her grandmother's capable hands. "What is it, Mama Ruth?" she asked, in reference to the child.

"It's a boy, child." She paused. "He'll need to eat."

Mary closed her eyes and turned her face to the wall, finally feeling the burning sensation behind her eyelids that she had denied herself through the long, hard night. The tears seeped from their home and rolled downward across her nose and into her ear. She lifted her arms as her grandmother finished her task of cleaning the child, and resigned herself to her fate.

***

The Birmingham family was just beginning to come to life in the spacious plantation home situated up a gradual hill from the slave quarters. The home itself was a grand affair; the porch swept the perimeter of the house, with columns spaced evenly the whole way 'round, bracing a second-floor balcony that mirrored the porch below. The wide, tree-lined drive gave approaching visitors full view of the palatial splendor.

The plantation bore the name of Bentley, a title stretching back two generations to the original Matthews who had purchased the place with an inheritance from a great uncle in England. "Bentley" was the name of his favored childhood dog, and the name naturally transferred itself to Matthews's new American interest.

Sarah Matthews Birmingham sat in her personal parlor, answering correspondence from neighbors. She glanced up from her desk at the entrance of her daughter, Charlotte. Charlotte was a tall woman, certainly taller than her mother, for Sarah was a tiny woman with a trim figure, despite having given birth five times. There were similarities between the two, however; they both shared a full head of rich, dark hair and brown eyes. Charlotte's features were similar to Sarah's, and truth be told, her temperament was much the same, as well.

"I just passed Father in the entrance hall," Charlotte told her mother, without preamble, as she sank gracefully into a chair opposite Sarah's desk.

"Yes?" Sarah's head was again bent over her correspondence.

"He says he's going to speak with Senator Chestnut, probably next week."

"And?"

Charlotte let out a puff of impatient air. "He's forever 'speaking to Senator So and So' but never bothering to run for office himself. Do you not think this could be his opportunity?"

Sarah placed her pen carefully on the desk and folded her hands, giving her daughter the benefit of her total regard. "Opportunity for what, Charlotte?"

"To run! To finally have a voice that means something! Now that we've seceded, the other Southern states are sure to follow, and we'll find ourselves with a whole new government. Father finally has a chance to be someone."

Sarah arched one brow. "Your father *is* someone."

"Someone other than your husband."

The silence lengthened, and Sarah finally chose not to make an issue of her daughter's impertinence. They both knew her words to be true, at any rate, and Charlotte was no longer a young child to be chastised. Indeed, she was now a grown woman of twenty-two, and had a husband of her own. Perhaps out of spite, Sarah chose to toss Charlotte's comments back into her lap.

"And where is William this morning, Charlotte? Upstairs helping the servants arrange your wardrobe?"

"Well, Mother, if he is, it's surely at your direction."

A muscle worked in Sarah's jaw, but otherwise, she gave no outward sign that she was irritated.

Charlotte waved a hand at her. "All I am saying, Mother, is that with things changing so rapidly, now is the time to act. Father could have a very powerful voice and would do well representing our interests, both here and abroad. He is an excellent diplomat, and if you were to encourage him in that direction, he just may listen."

"You're suggesting I tell your father that he run for office?"

"Yes, that is what I'm suggesting."

Sarah picked up her pen again, signing her name to an invitation to dinner. "I will give it some thought, Charlotte." In truth, it was a matter to which she had given much thought through the years, but to no avail. The occasions when she had mentioned it to Jeffrey were the few times in their married life when her husband had managed to find his misplaced backbone. He refused to run for office, preferring instead to pull strings from behind the scenes, offering suggestions and advice to his many friends who were in office. It was a matter of self-preservation, she supposed. He could exert his influence and considerable charm without suffering defeat if his ideas fell short of the mark.

She absently registered her daughter's departure, and looked up impatiently at the sound of someone else in her doorway. Expecting it to be Charlotte, and with a sharp reply at the ready, she held her tongue when she saw, instead, a family servant. This one was Angel, one of the downstairs maids.

"Yes?"

"Ma'am." Angel moved forward with a curtsey. "Miss Ruth was wantin' me to tell you that Mary done had her baby."

Sarah nodded.

As the girl lingered, Sarah probed, "Was there something else?"

"Miss Ruth's also wantin' to know if she can stay with Mary awhile."

Sarah pursed her lips. "You may tell her she may have the morning. I'll need to see her after lunch."

"Yes, ma'am." Angel curtseyed again and quietly left the room.

Sarah sat back in her chair for a moment in quiet reflection. She rose, abruptly, and made her way to the dining room where Charlotte was already seated with her twenty-year-old brother, Richard. Sarah motioned to a young slave who stood at the sidebar.

The girl then busied herself placing food on a plate and bringing it to the head of the table, where Sarah sat and examined her children.

"Good morning, mother," Richard said with a smile meant to charm.

"Good morning, son."

Sarah picked at her food, taking small bites and washing them down with a drink of tea. "Mary gave birth this morning."

Charlotte looked up at her mother's odd pronouncement. "Mother, I can't for the life of me understand why you care so much about that girl!"

Sarah's answering glance was sharp. "And should I not, Charlotte? Mary is an excellent house servant, and now that she's unencumbered, I will have her back at full capacity."

Charlotte waved a hand at her mother's comment. "You've taken an unusual interest her, and I don't understand why her over the countless others here who have had babies."

Sarah glanced at Richard, who was forking food into his mouth, his expression focused behind his sister on the windows that looked down the hill and into the slave quarters. His throat worked in an effort to swallow what, Sarah assumed, probably tasted to him like a mouthful of sawdust. "Aren't you curious about the new baby, Richard?"

He finally made eye contact with his mother. "Should I be?"

Sarah took a sip of juice and eyed him thoughtfully before replying. "Now that Ben is gone, you're next in line to inherit, Richard. I would think you might start taking an avid interest in the business of running Bentley."

He shrugged. "There's time for that, isn't there? You and father are both in the pink of health."

Sarah narrowed her eyes. The impudence her children possessed was wearing on her patience. It didn't help matters much that she had fostered it through the years, herself, without even realizing it. That, coupled with the fact that the bulk of her offspring were now adults, convinced her she would be fighting a losing battle if she pressed the issue at this point.

She continued her perusal of her son, noting the flush that had crept into his cheeks when she mentioned Mary's baby, and that hadn't quite diminished. The fact that her son had fathered a child with a slave was unseemly. It was common enough, she knew, but in genteel society, especially hers, it grated against her well-polished nature. The fact that he had undoubtedly done it without the girl's permission would have had her squirming uncomfortably in her chair, if Sarah had been the kind of woman who stooped to squirming.

It simply wouldn't do to have the newborn remain on the plantation, a constant reminder of her son's weakness and inability to control his baser passions. Her mind cast about for options, coming to rest comfortably on the memory that one of her neighbors to the north had mentioned the need for a child to raise as a playmate for her infant. Perhaps she would consider taking a baby. Sarah couldn't be sure the baby was Richard's—in fact, if she made a concerted effort she might yet be able to convince herself it wasn't, but there was every real possibility that it was.

Yes, without a doubt, the baby would have to be sold.

***

"Still, Jeffrey, I think a fairly influential appointment could be yours for the choosing."

Jeffrey Birmingham eyed his friend and neighbor, Stanley Charlesworth, as they walked the length of Charlesworth's driveway. "I don't know, Stanley. I don't know that I would want it."

"Are you not supportive of the cause?"

Jeffrey's pause was perhaps an answer in itself, but it was at odds with his forthcoming reply. "Of course. But truthfully, friend," he said, halting his progress and looking the man in the eye, "it is either live or die at this point. You do realize this?"

"Life is always live or die, sir!" Stanley laughed, his soft Southern drawl accenting his words. "I fail to see how this is any different."

Jeffrey shook his head slightly and resumed his stroll, Stanley falling into step beside him.

"Perhaps we are alone, all by ourselves in this new venture," Stanley admitted, "but it has been long in coming. It was inevitable."

Jeffrey reluctantly shook his head. "I do not believe we will be by ourselves much longer," he said. "Last night Major Anderson moved his garrison from Moultrie to Fort Sumter."

Stanley glanced up in surprise. "I hadn't heard."

Jeffrey nodded. "Governor Pickens feels it a violation of the Federal promise that the Southern forts will remain as they are. It is my understanding that he will complain to President Buchanan. If the president should allow other seizures of U.S. forts here and with our other Southern sisters, it can't be much longer before we see the secession of other states."

"Why, then this would be a good thing! Bravo to Major Anderson for making our job much easier!" was Charlesworth's joyful response.

Jeffrey ran a finger under the stiff collar of his shirt. He wished he could feel the adulation he'd witnessed in many of his friends and associates over the past week. All he could summon, however, was a sense of doom.

"'Tis ironic, is it not, that had the U.S. government left us alone for awhile we might have come crawling back?" Charlesworth clapped a hand on Jeffrey's shoulder with a laugh. "If they insist on taking the other forts, however, we will be joined in our cause! We will become a mighty nation unto our own, with the very real possibility of gaining support from countries abroad. The English factory mills would shut down without our cotton—this is what I've tried to tell you, friend!" Stanley's eyes lit up with a frenzied excitement. "You could find yourself a diplomat abroad, paving the way for our new nation! But please, you must tell me, what was the mood at the Secession Signing? You were there at the Institute Hall, were you not?"

Jeffrey nodded. He and Sarah had both been in attendance at the ceremonial Secession Signing, along with Charlotte and William, his son-in-law. The place had been resplendent in Christmas décor, the women and men dressed in beautiful apparel to match. The mood had been festive, the conversation animated, and Jeffrey had tried valiantly to summon feelings comparable to those around him.

"It was lively."

"I'm sure it was! I only wish we had been able to attend. My wife plans to visit Sarah later to hear the details."

"I'll be sure to tell Sarah to show Mrs. Charlesworth the knotted palmetto and pen she brought home as mementos of the occasion."

"Oh, she will be green with envy. This turn of events is marvelous, I tell you." Charlesworth clapped Jeffrey brusquely on the shoulder. "I am thrilled at the way things are proceeding! The South will not be mocked! We shall not simply roll over and watch our way of life become extinct!"

Jeffrey's unease mounted with each passing moment. He finally turned to his friend and offered him his hand. "I must be off, Stanley."

"Do consider what I've said. Not often does an opportunity to affect history come along. You're just the gent for the job, Birmingham."

Jeffrey managed a stiff smile. "I will see you again soon."

***

Emily Birmingham sat in the drawing room later that afternoon with her mother, her sister Charlotte, and the Charlesworth women. Mrs. Charlesworth was a large woman; Emily likened her to a ship that sailed the high seas. Her twin daughters, Calista and Clarice, were spoiled and petulant. They batted their eyes in the company of men, and narrowed them in the company of women. They thought they hid their machinations, naturally, but Emily, being an astute judge of character, was not fooled.

Emily herself was bored to tears. She detested afternoon teas with neighbors, hated the balls and dinners she was beginning to be invited to in preparation for her "coming out," although she was not quite yet sixteen, and would much rather have been upstairs in her bedroom, absorbed in a good novel.

She shook herself out of her musings as Mrs. Charlesworth's eyes fell upon her. "Is not all this political change exciting, Emily? You have yet to offer your opinion."

"I think it's idiocy."

Sarah closed her eyes briefly, Charlotte's nostrils flared, and Emily knew she would be on the receiving end of a sharp reprimand from her mother after the women left. She cursed her own stupidity, knowing full well that it was one thing to think radical thoughts. It was quite another to voice them aloud, especially in the company of esteemed guests.

Mrs. Charlesworth sucked in her breath, her jowls aquiver with indignation. The woman glanced at Sarah's pinched expression and Charlotte's disapproving glare, and apparently decided, for decency's sake, to let the matter rest. Calista, however, was not so inclined. "What an odd thing to say, Emily," she murmured, sipping her tea. "But then, you always have been one to scorn popular opinion."

Emily regarded the young woman—-the fat blonde curls that framed the pink, cherubic face, the blue eyes that blinked prettily in the company of men and effectively clouded with dainty tears when the situation demanded. She wanted to give the girl a shove that would send her sprawling backward, chair and all, onto the floor. Her lips twitched at the image of voluminous petticoats and hoop skirts, in all their frothy glory, obscuring the delicate face as she lay on the floor, flopping like a fish out of water.

"You find that amusing, Emily?" Calista prodded.

"Oh, most certainly."

"Emily, I know you had matters to attend to elsewhere; you may be excused," Sarah interjected.

"What matters could Emily possibly have?" she heard Clarice Charlesworth mutter to her twin.

Mrs. Charlesworth cleared her throat, effectively cutting off any further remark.

"Thank you, Mother," Emily said to Sarah's stony face. "Ladies."

She bobbed an insolent curtsey and left the room, head held high. It remained thus until she spied her brother, Richard. He had been passing outside the door, apparently. She turned her face to one side, hoping to avoid conversation with the officious beast.

It was not to be. "Charming the guests again, I see, Emily?" he purred.

"Why, Richard! Still hale and hearty? One would think you'd have contracted the pox by now."

She glanced at his face, feeling a surge of satisfaction when his eyes widened fractionally at her lurid comment. "Tsk tsk," he said, recovering from his obvious shock. "It's no wonder you never last long at tea with the neighbors. It's just as well," he continued, his tone dropping, "with that ridiculous red hair and skinny body, you'll be lucky to find friends, let alone a husband." He yanked on one of her braids, bringing a sting to her eyes she refused to indulge or acknowledge.

"Oh," she said, spinning on her heel. "I forgot to mention something to Calista."

His face took on a sheen of instant panic. "What are you doing?"

Emily quickly ran back to the drawing room, shaking Richard's hand off at the door as he made a desperate attempt to halt her return.

"Excuse me, Mother," she said, "but in my haste, I forgot to mention to Calista that—" she moved closer to the young blonde, lowering her voice and making it impossible for her brother to overhear. "Well, my brother, Richard, has admired you from afar for ever so long, now, and he mentioned to me that he hopes you'll save a dance for him this Friday at the Bedford's New Year's ball."

Calista blushed prettily, her eyes aglow with excitement. She seemed to have forgotten her earlier contempt of the messenger, and thanked Emily for returning to share the news.

Emily left the room without glancing at her mother. She walked past her brother, whose face was red with fury. She made it to the front hall and was near the staircase when he finally dared to vent his anger. Shoving her against the wall near the bottom step between two portraits of dead Matthews ancestors, he glowered in her face. "What . . . did . . . you . . . say?" he muttered between clenched teeth. It was a well-known fact in the Birmingham household that Richard hated Calista Charlesworth, that she drove him batty with her chatter, and that he preferred to shower his affections on women with more maturity, although he never openly admitted as much to his mother.

"I told her I was sorry I had forgotten to bid her good day," Emily answered, frightened, but her fear quickly replaced itself with an anger that would soon match her brother's. She looked at him closely—the full, blonde hair styled off his forehead, the deep blue eyes and chiseled face—how was it that such a handsome person could be so cruel?

"You did not, you little witch," he snarled at her, his fingers biting into her shoulders.

It was with a fair amount of surprise that Emily realized as she looked at her brother that he didn't tower over her nearly as much as he had when she was younger. It had been a long time since he dared physically accost her, and she was empowered with the knowledge that this time, she was older, and more to the point, bigger.

"Release me, Richard," she said, her voice low.

"I should thrash you to within an inch of your life," he said, his face still a mottled red, his fingers leaving impressions that Emily knew would bruise.

"You have to sleep sometime, brother," she answered, her voice dropping to nearly a whisper. "If you persist in tormenting me, you'll find yourself bloodied in your own bed."

"My, my, such big threats from such a little girl."

"They're not threats, Richard. I don't care what you do with your life, but you will leave me alone, and you will leave Clara alone. You also will stay clear of Mary and Rose, or I shall go directly to Mother and tell her everything I know."

His face paled slightly. "And what is it you think you know?"

"I know that you forced yourself on Mary, and that the child she gave birth to is yours!"

His grip again tightened. "Where did you hear such lies?"

She couldn't stop the short bark of laughter, though it was entirely void of mirth. "You fool," she said. "Don't you remember how cold it was last March, and Ruth had taken ill? The other servants were busy preparing for Mother's dinner party so she sent me to take Ruth some medicine. Only she didn't know," Emily continued through clenched teeth, "that Ruth had actually gone up to the cookhouse, but Mary was in their quarters, ill herself. Alone."

Richard's grip slowly relaxed as the pallor in his face increased.

"But she hadn't been alone. By the time I got to her, she was a mess. Her clothes were torn, her lip was bloody and her eye was swelling shut. She was scrubbing herself everywhere with a bloody rag for all she was worth. She wouldn't tell me who had hurt her, but then suddenly," Emily paused, raising a hand to her lip and tapping in mock contemplation as Richard's hands fell from her shoulders, "I remembered passing you as I left the house. You were coming up the hill from the slave quarters and you were in quite a hurry, if I remember, looking nervous and extremely flushed. It wouldn't have meant a thing to me later had I not found Mary in her condition."

Richard backed up a step, his face regaining some of its color, his anger coming again to his defense.

"If you think you can hold this over my head, Emily, you're a greater fool than I thought. Mother doesn't care! What does she care about a slave? Besides, she breeds them! One more baby is a boon to Bentley."

"You are so incredibly stupid, Richard. She sold the baby to the Charlesworths! She doesn't want it here, because I think she suspects, but she may not actually know. When was the last time she sold a baby? Mother doesn't separate families, here. You should know that as well as anyone! She doesn't like the loss of morale, so she keeps them together. And you're wrong, Richard," she added with venom. "Mother does care, in her own odd way. She cares about the servants almost as though they're family. So if she knows for certain that you're the one who raped Mary, you'll pay dearly."

With that, Emily marched up the stairs, satisfied that she'd dared flaunt convention by openly defying her older brother, and leaving him gaping behind her back. She walked on legs that began to tremble, and by the time she reached her spacious blue and white bedroom, she collapsed on her bed after slamming the door behind her.

The fear and frustration had worn her thin. She didn't belong here—she never had. She missed her brother Ben so much it hurt. She was like him. She chafed under a system that she felt instinctively was wrong. Her mind wandered back over that fateful evening in March when she had come upon Mary, bloodied and in agony, and her heart gave a lurch. She had helped Mary clean up as best as she could, wishing the girl would tell her who had attacked her. Mary had kept her lips tightly sealed, but Emily knew.

Throughout the year she had formed a friendship with Mary. It seemed that a mutual disdain and disgust of her brother, Richard, had forged them closer together. Mary's younger sister, Rose, was a constant companion and friend to Emily's youngest sister, ten-year-old Clara; she slept in Clara's room and the two played together daily. Rose had been a gift to Clara from Sarah when the girls were five.

Clara was deaf, and Richard was under the impression that she was, therefore, some kind of freak. He had tormented this young one through the years, behind their mother's back, as much as he had Emily.

The four girls, then—Emily, Mary, Clara and Rose—had formed a small family of their own. Emily had often wondered in her younger years why it was that Ben was so passionately opposed to slavery; she had been only ten years old when he had left the family five years ago, joined the Mormon church and moved west to live with other church members. The pain of his departure had left her grieving as though he had died. But recently, especially in the last year, she had come to understand his reasons. She might not love the Mormons, but she did have one thing in common with him—she abhorred slavery.

And then, there was Joshua. Emily sought Joshua's company whenever she could, finding comfort in the one who had been so close to her brother. He had been a gift to Ben from Jeffrey when the boys were young, and the two had grown up together like brothers. Unbeknownst to his mother, Ben taught Joshua the things he learned in the schoolroom and as a result, Joshua was trapped on a plantation, working in the stables now, with an enlightened mind that yearned for freedom. It didn't always make a difference, though, Emily mused miserably. The uneducated field slaves bore the same haunted expression that Joshua often did. Education might be the key to the possibility of freedom, but its lack didn't rob a person of the same dream.

***

The air was cold that night after dinner as Emily walked quickly down the hill to the slave quarters. She was wrapped in a warm cloak, her step brisk and purposeful. She neared Mary and Ruth's small "home," only to be stopped by Mr. Jackson, the overseer.

Mr. Jackson took his duties seriously. "Miz Emily," he said as she approached. "I hope you don't have a book in that bundle, there."

Emily sighed impatiently. "Mr. Jackson, you know very well that what I do is my own business."

"I also know, Miz Emily, that it's agin' the law to teach nigras to read."

"What goes on in my family is not your concern, sir."

"Y'all should watch yerselves."

"You do like your earnings, do you not, Mr. Jackson?"

The overseer narrowed his eyes a bit, but turned, after insolently tipping his hat, and went to his own quarters.

Releasing a breath of frustration, Emily proceeded to Ruth and Mary's shack, knocking briskly but quietly on the door.

Ruth opened the door a bit, and when she saw Emily, her face relaxed into a smile. "Come in, child," she said.

Emily smiled in return, looking fondly at the woman who was roughly the age of her own mother. Ruth was a tall woman, of medium build, with smooth brown skin that covered a kind face. A frustrated face. A weary face. A resolute face. An enslaved face.

"I have some things for Mary," Emily said. Ruth nodded and bid her sit in one of two chairs situated near a small table. The home was a small, one room affair, with a large bed in the corner that Mary and Ruth shared. Because Sarah liked them, Mary and Ruth were permitted the benefit of the bed, two chairs, and a table. It was luxurious, by slave standards. The floor was actually adorned with rough, wooden planks as opposed to dirt.

Mary was sitting on the side of the bed, her expression blank. Upon feeling Ruth's gentle hand on her shoulder, Mary rose and sat in the chair next to Emily's.

"How are you?" Emily asked her.

"I'm well."

Emily knew better, but didn't pursue the matter. "I brought you some things," she said. She opened the fabric sack she had carried with her from the mansion. "I finally finished this infernal thing," she said, pulling a blue and white crocheted blanket from the sack. "Mother promised that if I finished it, I wouldn't have to do any more handiwork for at least a month."

Mary's mouth twitched in a reluctant smile. Mary was an excellent seamstress, and could create the most beautiful marvels out of nothing. She knit, she crocheted, she sewed—she was beautifully talented and had been since her early childhood when

Ruth had begged Sarah that Mary be allowed to work with her in the main house.

Emily, on the other hand, hated such pursuits, and was not at all gifted with Mary's talents. It had been a standing joke between the two girls that Emily would never finish her crochet project.

"Well done," Mary murmured, running a hand over the blanket.

"Not entirely," Emily admitted, lifting a corner and showing Mary where she'd dropped a few stitches, creating an uneven edge.

Mary laughed a bit. "It has character," she said to her friend.

Emily smiled, relieved to see even a little bit of mirth on Mary's face. "I'd like you to have it," she said.

"Are you sure your mother doesn't want it displayed in your bedroom? It matches the décor."

"I know, but it gets cold at night, and this will help keep you warm. It's nice and heavy—cotton yarn, you know."

"Don't we though," Ruth murmured.

Emily nodded glumly. She looked at the women, her throat aching. "Things are changing," she said quietly.

Ruth looked at her with kindness in her eyes, but said nothing.

"The Southern states refer to the President Elect as 'Black Lincoln.' I take that as a good sign."

"I don't know, child. 'Cotton is King,'" Ruth replied. "The plantation states, if they do eventually form a union, are not going to give up without a fight, no matter what the new president has to say about it."

Emily listened to Ruth's rich voice with affection. She was an intelligent woman who had taken advantage of Joshua's tutelage each day as he had finished his own lessons with Ben. Mary, Ruth, and now Rose, were literate. Sarah couldn't abide ignorance, so it was not to their detriment that they had improved in speech while in her presence, and if she suspected someone had taught them to read and write, she never did comment on it.

Word had a way of spreading along the slave grapevine, however, and it wasn't long before the neighboring plantations were abuzz with the knowledge that Sarah Birmingham had slaves who were educated. Acquaintances who knew of this had chastised Sarah, telling her that educated slaves would eventually revolt. Sarah scoffed at the notion, convinced that she treated her people so well they would never attempt to leave.

She had been proven wrong, however, five years earlier, and at the hands of her own son. At the memory, Emily murmured, "I wish Ben were here. He could at least get the three of you up north."

Ruth smiled in sympathy, patting Emily's shoulder. "He tried, dear child. If he ever came back here, the neighbors'd likely string him up."

Ben had indeed tried, and failed. It had been the final straw that had necessitated the break between him and his family, but Emily knew it would have come regardless. Sarah had been rather naively upset that servants in her possession would want to leave, but it had taught her a valuable lesson she wouldn't soon forget. She might abhor violence, but she had allowed the overseer a liberal hand with his whip ever since.

Ruth and Mary were literate beyond Sarah's comprehension, and thirsting for more. Emily helped when she could, slipping them books and paper on which to write, and she had taught Rose how to read, along with Clara.

With these thoughts swirling in her head, Emily again reached into the sack and pulled forth three books. "Here are some novels for you," she said, turning the spines and reading aloud. "*Pride and Prejudice* and *Sense and Sensibility* by Jane Austen."

Mary's eyes lit up. "Have you read them yet?"

Emily shook her head. "No. You take them first. I'm still reading *Northanger Abbey*."

She was gratified by Mary's response. The young woman took the books, running a hand softly over the covers. "Thank you," she said.

Emily waved a hand. "Just be careful," she said. "Mr. Jackson made a comment outside about me bringing books down here. I reminded him that he should mind his own business, but I'm sure he'll make trouble about it if he can. I assume you still hide the books under the loose plank in the corner?"

Ruth nodded.

"And does Jackson search your quarters regularly?"

"Sometimes," Ruth said. "But I think your mother has told him that she takes care of it, and that he is to leave us alone."

"And does he?"

"Usually."

Emily looked again at the two women, proud, intelligent, with so much potential, and yet shackled. "The day will come when you can leave this place," she vowed. "And more likely than not, I'll want to go with you."

CHAPTER 3

"Utah has not seceded, but is firm for the Constitution and the laws of our once happy country."
—Brigham Young

***

Utah Territory,
26 January, 1861

Benjamin Birmingham stormed down Main Street from the telegraph office in the waning light of the winter evening, his blood roaring in his ears. He felt all of his hopes, the ones he never spoke of to anyone, dissipating. He crushed his fingers into a fist, crumpling the telegram he had just received from his cousin, Luke, and felt a surge of anger so intense he wished someone would challenge him to a fight, just to give him an outlet for his frustration.

He made an attempt to soften his features as he passed people he knew. It wouldn't do to offend the folks who had been so kind to him over the past five years—they had welcomed him when his own family had shunned him. Besides, how would it be at church on Sunday if he were to go on a rage-induced rampage and wreak havoc all over town? Imagine the gossip! He smiled in spite of himself, but it quickly faded as he made his way, without even thinking, to the door of his good friend.

He knocked at the door of Jeremiah Stowe's comfortable home and when the old man answered his rather determined pounding, made his way into the parlor and sank into a chair, staring blankly into the fire. Jeremiah, to his credit, let him sit and stew before finally daring to venture a question.

"There's somethin' wrong, I reckon?"

Ben opened his fist and smoothed the telegram. " 'I suppose you know by now that Mississippi, Florida, Georgia, and Louisiana have all seceded. Stop. It is my belief that Texas will be close on their heels.'" Ben read the words in a flat tone, trying to calm the tremor that lay just beneath the surface.

It had been coming; he had seen it coming. He had known it was inevitable even when he had left home. The country could not keep debating the most primary of issues dividing it without eventually tearing itself asunder. And now that it had, the Confederacy would protect its most vital of interests to the death, if need be. If things had only stayed as they were! There had been so much political and legislative pressure in recent years to put a stop to slavery, or at least halt its progress. It had been Ben's one final hope, and with each successive seceding state, that hope dimmed bit by bit, and his rage grew and grew.

Jeremiah let him sit in silence, leaving him to his thoughts. Ben glanced at his impassive face, grateful for his old friend's support. He tried for a smile he couldn't quite summon, and said, "I apologize for bursting in here uninvited."

Jeremiah merely shrugged in sympathy. "My home's your home, you know that."

There was no other sound in the room save the crackling of the warm fire. Jeremiah lived alone. His two children were grown and lived in houses down the street, and his wife had passed away two years before. The Stowes had been among the first to welcome Ben when he had joined their midst as a young convert, with a brand-new testimony of Christ, and unresolved feelings of anger and frustration toward the family he left behind in the east.

"This bodes no good," Ben finally muttered, still staring into the flickering flames. He gestured with the telegram he held tightly in his hand. "I don't like it. They'll either succeed and keep people in chains forever, or the Yankees will swoop down out of the north and kill them all. I don't like either option."

Jeremiah gave a short laugh. "Are you surprised?"

"No." Ben ran a hand through his hair with a sigh. "I suppose in a way I am surprised that it hasn't happened sooner."

Jeremiah gestured toward the paper. "What else does your telegram say?"

Ben glanced at it, but it wasn't as though his memory needed refreshing. He had received the message, read it once, and it had seared itself into his brain.

Ben shrugged. "Nothing that we haven't already read in the paper, really. I suppose that hearing directly from someone I know . . ." *Someone I know and love who's living right in the middle of it . . .* ". . . somehow is making it seem much more . . . urgent. I feel like I'm trying to stop a speeding train." He paused again, and Jeremiah left him to his thoughts. "It's from my cousin in Boston. He says that people are mocking Lincoln's silence," Ben continued, "and that Buchanan is just biding his time until he can turn over the presidency to someone else."

"I heard that Buchanan finally did take some action; that when the South Carolinian governor complained about the troops in Fort Sumter, he tried to send supplies and reinforcements."

"I think the word 'tried' is debatable." Ben shook his head. "And if you can call it that, then he didn't try hard enough. He sent them on an unarmed civilian steamer! And then it had to turn back because the South Carolinian gunners opened fire on her. I'm amazed that war didn't break out right then! And it means there are no supplies for the troops at the Fort, so they'll either have to eventually surrender or fight their way out."

Jeremiah nodded soberly. "It could get very ugly. Rather makes a man grateful to be far away from it all, wouldn't you say?"

Ben looked at him, opening his mouth to agree, and found that he couldn't. "I feel responsible," he said instead.

Jeremiah gave a short bark of laughter. "Responsible for what? The actions of an entire country? One you're no longer a part of?"

"I left things undone . . . there was something I started and didn't manage to finish . . ."

Jeremiah's answering tone was quiet. "I know, Benjamin; Hannah and I knew there were things at home that you didn't want to discuss, and I made Hannah promise she wouldn't pry—it was in her nature, you know," he said, his eyes misty.

Ben smiled softly. "I'd give anything to have her back right now—I wouldn't mind if she pried."

The older man nodded. "But she's in a good place."

"I know. And I appreciate that you've not wanted to offend me. It's not anything that I intentionally kept to myself; it's only that I'm not proud of my . . . failure."

Jeremiah waited, patient.

"Shortly before I left home to come here, I attempted to help three slaves escape from my family plantation. It was my intention after that to leave, and take my friend, my . . . valet with me and once we were here, and safe, I was going to give him his freedom."

There was a quiet intake of breath, but no response.

Ben paused, his mind wandering over things he had tried to forget. "I arranged all the details, had planned to go with them as far as the Canadian border. The night we left, though, we were caught by my family's overseer and returned to Bentley. Somebody on the plantation knew and had apparently shared the information."

"Were you arrested?"

Ben shook his head slowly, again staring into the fire. "My parents are powerful people. They placed enough money in the right hands to shove the matter under the rug." He remembered as though it were yesterday his mother's reaction when he had tried to protect Ruth from Jackson's beating. Sarah's face had been white with fury—a blend of shock that her own son would contradict a direct order and interfere with a punishment she, herself, deemed necessary, and horror at the fact that because she had followed Ben out of the library and down to the slave quarters, she was being forced to witness that punishment being meted out. Physical violence, for all Sarah's strength and steel, sickened her. She had often shown reluctance to use a heavy hand on her slaves, but gave her approval when she felt it warranted.

Ben often still found himself trying to understand his mother. She cared for her "servants," looked after their well-being, treated most of them as she did her own children, which admittedly didn't always say much in terms of warmth, but she was unwilling to give them the thing they craved the most.

Jeremiah's soft, gruff voice intruded upon Ben's thoughts and brought him to the present. "So that's when you left?"

He nodded. "Yes, after that I couldn't really stay. My mother didn't trust me around the servants; she was afraid I might lead them into servile insurrection," he said, running a hand through his hair and again shaking his head. "Maybe she was afraid I'd let them murder her in her sleep. I don't know what she was thinking, and I couldn't pretend to condone the lifestyle any longer. My uncle James caught wind of things, probably through my father, and offered to let me live with them in Boston. Boston wasn't far enough away, though.

"I couldn't get near Joshua; my parents basically had him under lock and key. They moved him out to the stables and all but threatened me at gunpoint if I tried to talk with him. They threatened to sell him, which would have been his undoing. He loves Ruth and the others—they're his family. Then there were murmurings coming from the general direction of the neighbors that I was a danger to their slaves and their way of life, and rumors of threats on my life started floating around. So I left."

Jeremiah's gaze was also directed at the fire by this time. Ben glanced at him, feeling his stomach clench.

"Are you shocked, then?"

Jeremiah grunted and looked at Ben. "You're a determined young man, Ben Birmingham. My only shock is that you didn't succeed."

"I thought you might not have approved . . ."

"My homes were burned, I saw my beloved leader tarred and feathered and then murdered, I survived an extermination order from a United States governor and was driven from the very borders of the country. But even given all of that, the choice was still mine. I could go with my people, or denounce my religion and stay where I was in relative peace. True, we were denied religious freedom, but I reckon I could have moved somewhere, anywhere, and lived a quiet life had I kept to myself. I can't imagine a worse hell than to be denied that choice. I understand perfectly why you did what you did."

Ben's eyes misted with moisture that he immediately blinked away. "I did break the law."

"Seems to me that's a law that was made to be broken."

***

Ben returned to his home shortly after his visit with Brother Stowe, his angry energy spent. His cabin was a small, two-room dwelling, simple in its furnishings but made warm with the small gifts he had received from Sister Stowe before she died. She had insisted that his home needed a woman's touch, even if he wasn't inclined to find a bride for himself, and had filled the two rooms with small quilt squares, dried flowers, and little fripperies.

It wasn't as though he didn't want a bride, necessarily, but he had a heavy, angry heart, and hadn't been able to shed some of its weight to make room in it for someone else. A wife deserved more attention, gentle attention, than he felt able to give, and so he waited.

He only wished he knew what it was he was waiting for. How long could a person wander about in a frustrated stupor before he finally dropped from the sheer weight of it?

He sat at the small, wooden table situated in a corner near the fireplace and smoothed the telegram with his hand. He missed Luke. He was closer to his cousin in both affection and personality than he was to his own brother. He thought of Luke, in his element at abolitionist meetings, supporting the cause for all the right reasons and not apologizing one whit for it.

It had been seven long years since he'd last seen the Boston Birminghams in person. He had visited them by himself while on break from Harvard. Luke had swept him along in the tide of his abolitionism, and Ben found his heart had been there all along.

It's where my heart still is, he mused while he looked at the wrinkled telegram. He rose and began to pace the small confines of the cabin. Back and forth in front of the hearth he moved, his mind rolling along and taking him in directions he didn't want to travel, and he argued against it.

I've said good-bye to my old life. There's nothing there for me, and I have no desire to return. It's not as though war has been declared, it's just friction that will resolve itself in time. Besides, I've already proven I can't fight that system. I tried and failed.

He was suddenly haunted by the image of a stricken ten-year-old face; when he had left Bentley all those years ago, he had snuck out the servants' entrance near the back pantry like a thief in the night, the blood pounding in his temples and drying in fine lines under the bandages across his back. He had not been aware at first, however, that Emily had wandered into the pantry looking for a midnight snack. Emily—his beloved younger sister. He had sensed a soul kinship with her from the time she was a small girl. It had been the same with young Mary, and as they had grown older, Ben had come to enjoy their company even more. Such sweet young children, with so much potential for greatness.

And he would never see either one of them again.

He had tried to tell Emily that he would be gone for just a short time, but her large green eyes had filled with tears, and he knew better than to try convincing her it was only to be a momentary separation. He had held her close, his hand clasped in the fiery red hair, tears burning a path down his face and onto her head.

And then she had given him a small shove, saying, "Go then, if you must. But I shan't forgive you."

Emily . . . she would be fifteen years old now, almost sixteen. And Mary would be nearly seventeen. How they must have changed in those five short years. He knew *he* had, physically, at least. He had left home a six-foot, one-hundred-sixty-pound, twenty-year-old university student. He had grown two inches, gained twenty pounds, and studied enough with his new friends in Utah at the University of Deseret to make up for the time he'd lost in school. But inside, there were times when the raw emotion felt just as crushing as it always had.

He couldn't shake the self-recrimination, the knowledge that in addition to Ruth, Mary and Rose, he had also failed Joshua, and badly. There should have been something he could have done, some way to get to Joshua that night he had left. He remembered the armed guard standing at the door of Joshua's humble bedroom in the back of the stables, and mused that indubitably, his parents had given the order to shoot him on the spot if he tried anything. Their son's life was not as crucial to them as their way of life.

He hoped life was treating Emily, Mary, Clara, Rose, Ruth, and Joshua well, that they were as happy as they could be. Emily wrote occasionally; those times when she was able to go into town and post the mail herself—mail that would eventually make the trek across country via the Pony Express. She mentioned once that Sarah had forbidden the family any contact with him. Apparently Sarah still feared he could wreak havoc from afar. Charlotte, of course, would echo everything their mother said, and Richard had never been someone to whom he could relate. Richard was a coward, and he preyed on the weak. Charlotte was strong, and she preyed on the strong and weak alike.

Emily's letters of late showed an emerging bitterness for their home life that he recognized in a younger version of himself, and he feared for her well-being. She would either be forced to leave the system entirely, or she would attempt something as rash as he had. He hoped she would choose the former over the latter, if only for her own safety. Emily had always been brave, though, even as a small child, and he knew that if she put her mind to something, she would see it through to its fruition.

His brow creased in a scowl; he halted his pacing. "I'm not going back," he said aloud to the empty room. "Not to Boston, definitely not to South Carolina. I am not going back."

***

Ben sat in church the next morning on the hard, but beautifully shiny wooden pew and sang from the hymnbook with the others in the congregation. His eye roved upward and he examined the neat, curved lines of the ceiling and the richly appointed woodwork along the walls. He marveled again, as he had countless times before, at the amount of work the Saints had managed to achieve in roughly fourteen years. It was amazing. They had created a beautiful oasis in the desert.

He felt the customary tightening in his heart loosen a bit as his mind reviewed the words of the hymn. *O my Father, thou that dwellest in the high and glorious place. When shall I regain thy presence and again behold thy face?* The sweetness of the words was at odds with the monotone rendition of the accompanying melody coming from Ben's immediate left. As he glanced at the young man, Ben's lips twitched involuntarily. Earl Dobranski was nineteen years old, as big as a lumberjack, and absolutely couldn't carry a tune in a bucket.

Earl looked back at Ben, his eyes wide and innocent, as he cocked a brow and raised his volume level a good notch. Ben swallowed a laugh and stumbled through the rest of the hymn, remembering poignantly why he had been drawn to the gospel in the first place. Earl's father was the missionary who had baptized Ben.

Ben glanced again to the side and down the row of young Dobranski boys. They filled the entire pew, each as strapping as the next. There were eight boys in all: Earl, Enos, Edgar, Elam, Evan, Ether, Elijah, and Elisha. They were spaced an even two years apart in age and were so similar in appearance that often passersby and friends would know them by their names only after they had taken a careful assessment of their height. "Ah, yes, the eleven-year-old. You're Evan!" was not an uncommon observation.

The Dobranski matriarch, Ellen, sat at the other end of the pew, her back straight, her dress pressed and nary a hair out of place. She was a tiny woman of five feet, one-half-inch, and perhaps ninety-five pounds dripping wet. She could wield the meanest willow west of the Mississippi, or so the Dobranski brood swore, and many suspected with hidden smiles that therein lay the secret to her disciplinary success.

The family patriarch was conspicuously absent, and had been since before the birth of the youngest, Elisha, five years before. Eli Dobranski had been called to serve a mission, first in the Southern United States, and from there, on to England. Ellen never complained, but Ben couldn't help but wonder what she thought about on those lonely nights when the boys were all settled into bed for the night. On more than one occasion, when Ben had passed by their farmhouse on his way home, he had seen Ellen's profile in the window as she sipped a mug of something warm and stared into the fire, alone.

Ben was startled from his thoughts as he heard his name spoken from the pulpit at the front of the room. " . . . and I was thinking it's been a good five years since we've heard from Brother Birmingham's own lips his story of how he came to be with us," Bishop Montague was saying. "We've had so many others join our midst in recent years, Brother, who haven't heard your testimony. I think we'd all be much obliged if you'd share it with us now."

Ben stared at the man, his mouth slack. Bishop Montague certainly had the right of it. It *had* been years since he'd shared his testimony. It had been awkward then, but he felt he owed it to the people he'd joined to tell them a bit about himself. The thought of rising now and speaking to the gathered assembly made his stomach swim as though leaping frogs had taken up residence.

He finally roused himself when Earl elbowed him sharply in the ribs, and he stood on legs that shook, making his way slowly to the front of the room. Once at the pulpit he cleared his throat gruffly a few times before daring to speak.

"I'm at a loss," he said to the room, his voice echoing oddly into the high ceiling. He registered the pronounced sound of his accent that pegged him for the South Carolinian native that he was. "I hardly know where to begin."

As he began speaking, haltingly at first, then with growing confidence, the memories of his conversion flooded back as though it were yesterday . . .

"What is that book?" a man in the crowd shouted at the two men who stood encircled under the shady trees of a downtown Charleston park. "Is that your gold Bible? I heard of that years ago! My brother knew some crazy boy in New York who said he'd found a gold Bible! Said an angel gave it to him!"

"This book is another testament of Jesus Christ as He appeared to the people living on this, the American continent," one of the men answered without hesitation. He was huge—he was easily the tallest man Ben had ever seen, and extraordinarily broad through the chest and arms. "We offer it to any who would like to learn more."

"Jesus came to the Injuns?" The man cackled his glee and goaded those standing around him into amused laughter. The crowd heckled the pair for a moment longer before slowly dissipating, some waving their hands as though the missionaries were lunatics. Ben watched the church men for a moment, his heart heavy. They looked weary. He knew what it meant to be weary. He was twenty years of age, was planning the preliminary details of an escape attempt that might well mean the end of his life as he knew it, and he felt extremely old. His mind flew involuntarily to the passage of scriptures he had over-heard Ruth reading to little Rose one night at bedtime. "Other sheep

I have which are not of this fold . . ." the Bible verse read, and suddenly Ben glanced at the two men with renewed interested.

"Wait," he called as they turned to leave the park, their shoulders slightly slumped. "What is—that is, what do you have . . ."

The pair turned back in surprise. They approached him cautiously, almost in disbelief. "Are you curious about this book?" the big man asked.

"I suppose . . ." Ben mumbled, wondering why he'd said anything at all.

"Would you like to read it?"

"I . . . yes."

That book had kept him up, reading, through the night. He met with Elder Dobranski and Elder Stevens in the park, first weekly, then semi-weekly, then daily, soaking in every detail of their faith.

It gave him a surge of hope. Everything made sense to him, as though he'd known it all before on a level he couldn't remember. His parents, of course, thought him insane. Why would he want to go chasing after a religion surrounded by controversy and oddity? The Mormons were so strange they had been driven from community to community until they'd been forced to leave the country altogether.

They weren't strange, however. They were a God-worshipping people who wanted to go to church and preach their beliefs without being tarred and feathered, murdered and robbed because of fear and ignorance. Every question Ben posed to the men came back with answers that not only made sense, but also filled his soul with peace. He finished reading the Book of Mormon and immediately began again, learning more each time he read.

A month to the day after initially meeting the Elders, Ben met with them in the park at their customary hour. "I want to be baptized," he told them. "Can you do it today?"

"Have you prayed about this, Ben?" Elder Dobranski asked him, placing his huge hand upon Ben's shoulders. His touch was surprisingly gentle.

"I have. I've never been more certain of anything in my life. And I'd like to do it this afternoon. I have plans tonight, plans . . ." Ben

faltered and fell silent.

    Elder Stevens looked fairly alarmed. "Ben, is everything well? Are you in need of help?"

    "Yes, I am in need of help. Divine help. Should something happen to me . . . I'd, well, I'd like to be baptized."

    Elder Dobranski patted his shoulder once, firmly. "I know of a secluded spot on the river," he said. "We've baptized there before. Is there someone you'd like to be with you?"

    Ben shook his head. "I'm alone."

There was one thing that had changed the moment Ben had cut the ties with his family and moved west. He no longer felt alone. Angry, frustrated, sometimes even enraged at the memories, but not alone. As he looked over the faces of the congregation and registered those who had taken him into the hearts of their families without any prying questions, his eyes burned with unshed tears. Jeremiah Stowe sat with his children, watching him with undisguised pride. Ellen Dobranski nodded at him once, firmly, giving him the same no-nonsense support she offered her own sons.

"Elder Dobranski brought the gift of the gospel into my life, and when I arrived in this valley and introduced myself to his family, they took me in as one of their own." He shared his thoughts on the gospel, willingly offering the details of his conversion, but carefully side-stepped the issue of his failed attempt to free Ruth and the girls. There were some things, after all, that were too painful and private to share with an entire group of people. When he concluded and took his seat next to Earl, he felt the support of his friends in the wet eyes and sniffles that surrounded him. Earl placed an arm about his shoulders and gave him a squeeze that Ben was sure would have his bones snapping.

Dinner following the Church service was the raucous affair that had become familiar to Ben. The Dobranski boys were every bit as loud as they were large, and they consumed, in one meal, quantities of food that would have fed the Bentley plantation for a week. Ben smiled to himself as he forked a bite of roast beef into his mouth. He glanced down the table at Sister Dobranski and felt a familiar pang. Ellen's mother had been a Cherokee, and while her features differed from Ruth's, the golden glow of skin brought to Ben feelings of home. It was also her brisk, efficient manner, Ben knew, that triggered images of Ruth.

His musing were confirmed by Sister Dobranski's next statement. "You've gone back to South Carolina, young Ben," she observed in a quiet tone that he still heard in spite of the lively conversation between the brothers.

"Only for a moment," he said. "I was thinking you remind me of someone I held very dear."

Ellen smiled. "That's a lovely compliment."

"And what do you hear from Brother Dobranski these days?" he asked.

At that, the boys stilled. "He's doing well, and is anticipating his return later this year," Ellen answered.

"Did he give a specific date?"

Elam, the thirteen-year-old, snorted. "He never gives a specific date. He was supposed to come home a year ago."

"Watch your tongue, Elam Dobranski," Ellen said with a sharp glance in his direction. "We've been blessed in your father's absence."

Ben winced for the young boy. Elam would have been only eight years old when his father left home to proselyte. Elijah and Elisha didn't remember him at all; indeed, Elisha had never even been in his father's presence outside the womb. Ben wasn't certain it would be much comfort to Elam that Ben had benefited from the Dobranski's sacrifice. Perhaps there would come an opportune moment to tell the young boy that because of his father, a soul had found a great measure of peace. It was hard to be missing a father, Ben mused over his food. He had wanted a connection with his own for as long as he could remember.

"Besides," Enos said, jabbing Elam in the arm, "we've had Ben!" The noise again erupted and the boys, even Elam, each raised a glass in mock salute to Ben, who lifted his own in response, grinning. Life was good with the Dobranskis. They had filled a void for him, and he for them, that had been mutually beneficial. He knew his spirits would remain high for the remainder of the day until the hour drew so late that he would be forced to go home to his solitary cabin down the street. He wished he could just stay with them forever.

CHAPTER 4

"You dare not make war upon cotton! No power on earth dares make war upon it. Cotton is King."
—*Senator James H. Hammond*

***

New Orleans, Louisiana
27 January, 1860

Marie Brissot urged the horse forward as she maneuvered the small carriage away from the busy streets and onto the more sedate roads leading to the outskirts of town. The place had gone crazy, it seemed, with news of Louisiana's secession. People were everywhere, wanting more news, hoping to hear new details, most ecstatically happy over the turn of events, but some showing signs of reserved enthusiasm.

She had a knot in her stomach, herself. She didn't think secession was a good idea; in fact she considered it suicide. How long could it last? The Union was a powerful nation, and still would be, even with the southern states making a departure. The northern states were those holding the biggest areas of industry and their resources outnumbered those of the southern states in great volume.

Marie snapped the reins, urging the horse forward, and thinking of her father. He owned and operated a small newspaper in the area, the *New Orleans Herald,* and had been too busy last night running the presses to even come home. She had gone with her mother, Jenny Stein Brissot, to visit him and bring him dinner.

"What are you thinking, Jean-Pierre?" Jenny had asked him quietly when Michael, his other employee, had gone home to eat before returning for the long night.

"I am thinking this is madness, Genevieve," he had said, stroking her jaw with his finger before sitting down to his meal.

Marie reflected upon her parents with a tender heart. Her father, a French immigrant, had come to the United States nearly twenty-six years ago to work with an uncle who owned a newspaper in New Orleans. They had taken a business trip to Boston and while there, he had met Genevieve, or "Jenny," Stein, who was living with her sister, Elizabeth Birmingham and Elizabeth's husband, James. Jenny had always told Marie it had been love at first sight, and she had married Jean-Pierre after having known him only a month. She moved to New Orleans so Jean-Pierre could continue working with his uncle, and when the uncle died, the newspaper was given to him.

Marie was their only child, born twenty-three years ago. She was their joy, despite her fallen status in society. As she guided the horse down the dusty road to the schoolhouse, she found her thoughts turning to painful memories now six years old, and she shoved them aside, preferring to dwell on the current political upheaval rather than her own muddled state of affairs.

It had been hard for the Brissots, living in a Southern society. Jenny had been raised in Rhode Island by a family of Quaker descendants. She didn't approve of the South's "Peculiar Institution." However, because she and her husband moved in polite circles, she was obliged to turn her head the other way. Jean-Pierre was no fan of slavery himself, having come from a country where it had been questioned for years, and recently outlawed. But they stayed on in the South, with their faux friends and Jean-Pierre's newspaper, and tried to turn a blind eye to that which they found offensive.

It made Marie angry. She didn't like the fact that in order to maintain their social standing, they had to keep quiet about something against which they were morally opposed. *Tell them!* Marie often thought to herself. *Tell these people that you call friends that what they're doing is wrong!* But they never did, and Marie held her tongue in polite society to keep from upsetting her mother. The wealthy plantation owners befriended Jean-Pierre because they wanted to remain in the good graces of someone who had the potential of putting their names in print, yet he wasn't one of them, and never had been. Because Marie's father was, at the root of things, a mere newspaperman, the Brissots floated somewhere between the genteel society they tolerated and the working-class farmers who scraped to survive.

Marie finally approached the small, one room school house one mile from her home where she taught a group of fifteen students, ranging in age from six to thirteen. They were children of farmers who would probably never have the means to provide their children with any sort of education, and who were willing to part with them daily until the children arrived at a physical stature that could lend itself to work on the farm. Because they barely clung to the lower rungs of the societal ladder themselves, the parents were not bothered by the fact that their children were taught by a woman of dubious reputation.

Marie loved learning, and loved children, so when she had devised the plan the year before to teach the children, her father had donated his time and resources to construct the small schoolhouse, and Jenny had manipulated their wealthy friends into feeling responsible for helping those "less privileged." Their donated funds provided Marie with enough materials to teach a successful class, and she loved it. The children did not judge her.

It was early yet; Marie liked to have time to prepare herself and her lessons before the children arrived. She led the horses to the small stable her papa had erected for her behind the schoolhouse, made sure they had food and water, and let herself in the school building. All was as she had left it the day before, nice and tidy, nary a desk out of line. This was her domain. These children took home each day the things that she taught them, and she slowly and subtly infused them with ideas to contemplate.

Marie possessed a delicate bone structure and violet eyes, was small in stature but fiery in nature. What she lacked in size, she made up for in strength of spirit. She deposited her small bag of belongings on the desk, reaching a finger to the back of her head at a point where the mahogany-colored hair was pulled too tightly into its customary bun. Her hair was long, curly and thick, and she battled it daily into submission. She winced at the pinch until she was able to free the offending hair, and ran a hand over her head to ensure its neatness.

Taking a seat behind her desk, she retrieved the notes she had made for the day's lessons, and reviewed them to be sure she would be ready when her students arrived. She studied in silence, reveling in the peace and quiet she knew would shortly be disturbed, when the sound of the door opening diverted her attention.

She raised her gaze to the other end of the room, slightly frowning in curiosity until the person on the other side of the door made himself known. Her face relaxed into a rueful smile.

"Gustav, what are you doing here?"

The young man walked down the aisle formed by desks, hat in hand, a grin splitting his face. His rich, brown hair was tousled, as though he had recently shoved his hand through it, and his face was bronzed by hours spent in the sun, fishing along the bayous.

She stood as he approached, watching with a smile as he took both of her hands in his and placed a kiss on each.

"I could not wait another minute to see you, Marie."

"Should you not be working? You're usually in your boat by now."

"Ah, but what is work when the most beautiful woman in the world sits nearby, alone?"

Marie laughed and withdrew her hands, slapping at his playfully before resuming her seat. "You are absolutely incorrigible, Gustav. What am I to say to your constant flattery?"

"End my misery, *chérie*, and say you'll marry me."

Marie picked up a pen and after dipping it in the small inkbottle, made an alteration in the margin of one of her lesson plans. "You know I can't do that, Gustav."

"I don't know that at all!" His face took on a serious expression, and the young man knelt on the floor near her chair, leaning on her desk with one elbow. "You constantly refuse, yet you never give me an adequate reason. The wretched sound you hear is that of my heart breaking in two."

She smiled, in spite of herself, and glanced at him. "I am not suitable marriage material. I find that plenty of reason."

"Such a feeble excuse! My own mother wasn't considered 'suitable marriage material,' yet she snared the wealthiest man in the region!"

Marie thought of Gustav's mother with an inward wince. Cecile Deveraux had married young, to a man older than her father, undoubtedly hoping he would pass away while she was still in her prime. Alas, the old man lingered, crotchety as ever and with no inclination of ever leaving the world. Unfortunately, his bad humor was not necessarily associated with his age; he had always been gruff and crass, according to local gossip, and it was rumored that Cecile had often found company elsewhere. To be sure, Gustav looked nothing like his mother or his father.

"But I am not your mother, dear man. I . . ." *I'll never be a suitable wife for any man because of my reputation and besides, if I were to marry, I would want to be married for love, and I find I do not love you.* How could a woman say that to a man who showered her with affection and gifts, and daily declared his never-ending devotion? He did these things in spite of the fact that all of New Orleans believed her to be tainted. Gustav Deveraux was no respecter of persons.

"Is it because I am a fisherman, Marie? For you I would go back home to my parents' plantation—I would!"

This time, the grimace Marie felt inwardly worked its way out and manifested itself on her face. Eventually becoming a plantation mistress was not a scenario she envisioned for herself. She wanted a life with a man she adored, as her mother did her father, and she wanted it free of strife. She didn't want to be constantly holding her tongue, as her parents did, over issues she felt strongly about. She didn't want to run in social circles that required her ever-constant acquiescence and inane chatter. She didn't want to own people. She loved her books, she loved learning, and she wanted to be with someone who wouldn't find her odd because of it.

It was a moot point, at any rate; she would never marry.

Gustav had commented on more than one occasion that she spent too much time studying and not enough time out in society. For all that he had shunned his own birthright, it seemed that he expected her to embrace that life. Perhaps it was for those reasons that she had been unable to return his strong affection.

"Gustav," she finally said, placing her pen carefully on the desk. "The last thing I would want you to do would be to return to the plantation. I like you much better as a fisherman. However, I just can't marry you. Please understand, and you must stop asking me."

He placed a hand theatrically on his heart. "You wound me, lady, but I will never give up! Never!" He rose, and reaching for her hand, he sketched a formal bow and placed another kiss on her knuckles before walking again down the aisle toward the door at the back of the room. She shook her head at his retreating form, noting the crisp line of his brown trousers, the white shirt underneath the plain, but fine brown jacket that would soon be filthy and smelling of fish. Her lips twitching into a smile, she thought of Cecile, who, although severely disappointed that her son had left home to become a fisherman, constantly supplied him with fine apparel in which to do his work.

"Until next time," Gustav said from the back of the room, turning to give her one final grin, and he left the schoolhouse, his step light and a whistle upon his lips.

***

The sky was gray outside and the air slightly chill by the time Marie saw the last of her students out the door. They had been curious about the current political events, and Marie spent the better part of the day trying to explain to them exactly what was taking shape in their state. It was hard to make sense of it in children's terms, especially when she was having a difficult time understanding it in her own.

The ride back through the city streets was uneventful, and she made her way to the respectable neighborhood that surrounded her home. The stately brick house had been her dwelling since birth, and it was familiar and warm. She took her horse around to the back, handing the reins over to the family's aging groom, Winston.

Giving the horse a last, affectionate pat on the neck, she made her way into the house, appreciating the warmth emanating from the hearth in the front parlor. She stood near the fire for a moment, more warmed by the sight of it than the actual increase in temperature.

"And how were the students today, Marie?"

She turned with a smile at the sound of her father's voice. "They were well, Papa. And very curious."

"That seems to be a common affliction today."

"Are you home for the night then, or will you return to the office?"

"I'm home until early morning." He took a seat in one of Jenny's Queen Anne chairs near the fireplace.

"Papa," Marie said with a frown, "why did you and Mama stay here?"

The look of surprise on his face told her he hadn't anticipated her question. "In New Orleans?"

She nodded.

He let out a puff of breath. "Well, because the newspaper was already here, as was my only family."

"Yes, but after Uncle Jean died, you and Mama could have left—moved north or west."

"My work was here, *chérie*. Why would we have left?"

"Because you don't like it here."

His silence was prolonged. "We do like it here," he finally answered, his gentle French accent still prominent, even after so many years away from his homeland, "and this was the closest thing to France I could hope to find in this country. The Acadian culture here is rich, and is familiar to me."

"Why not move back to France, then, if you missed it so much?"

Jean-Pierre laughed. "Marie, this was your mother's home as well. I wasn't about to move her to a foreign country when all of her family was here. The only family I had left after your grandmother died was Uncle Jean. It didn't make sense to go back. Now," he eyed her evenly. "Why all the questions?"

Marie sighed and sank into a chair that matched her father's, facing him across the hearth. "I am frustrated," she admitted. "I love the setting, but I don't belong here."

Jean-Pierre assessed his daughter quietly for a moment, as though attempting to come to a conclusion, before replying. "Your mother and I have talked of the possibility of sending you north, to be with your Aunt Elizabeth."

Marie's eyes widened in surprise. "Why?"

"Because we have sensed your restlessness, of late, and wonder if it might do you good to spend some time away."

Marie leaned her head back on the chair and glanced at the shadows flickering on the walls. Time in Boston? It was something she hadn't considered. She carefully weighed her options. She enjoyed her Aunt Elizabeth and her family, and got on well with her cousins. In Boston nobody knew her —she could actually attend dinners and balls without people whispering behind their fans about her fall from grace. But it wouldn't be the same as being near her precious students, especially with so much in the country changing each day.

She shook her head, looking into her father's beloved face. "Thank you, Papa, but I think I would be happier here. At least for now. I feel responsible for my students, and with the secession—I just wouldn't be comfortable leaving you and Mama right away."

He smiled. "Are you worried about your poor old parents?"

She laughed. "No, it's for my sake, more than yours. I would probably be too homesick."

"And speaking of 'sick,' I saw Gustav today."

At that, she laughed even harder. "You think he's ill?"

"Lovesick, is what I was thinking." Jean-Pierre shook his head, glancing at his daughter with the ghost of a smile. "That young man has been to my print shop every day now for over a month, begging me to influence you in his favor."

"He means well," she said.

"But you still have no interest in marrying him?"

"No."

"You have been friends for years, and he probably knows you almost as well as your mother and I do. Are you sure?"

She nodded, her face tightening almost imperceptibly. "I don't love him, Papa, and I don't think I ever will. He's a good friend, yes, but it's not enough for me. Why, do you think I should? Should I marry a man I don't love simply because no other will have me?"

Her father shook his head, unfazed by her defensive tone. "Not in the least. I'll just keep sending him on his way. Shouldn't you discourage him, though? If you can't start making your 'nos' a bit more convincing, I don't think we'll ever be rid of the poor fool."

Again, she laughed. "I have told him no. He just won't believe me." She glanced about, finally noting the absence of her mother. She commented on it to Jean-Pierre.

"She's upstairs changing her clothes," he replied. "We're having dinner tonight with Mr. Chastain and his wife."

Mr. Chastain was one of the town's more prominent bankers, and lived down the block from the Brissots. Marie scowled slightly. Mr. Chastain had a roving eye, and it usually found its way to Marie's bosom.

Jean-Pierre intercepted before she could comment. "I made your excuses already," he said. "I told them that you were indisposed and needing some rest. The house will be yours alone for a while. Will you mind that?" His tone teased, and she knew he was well aware that she would enjoy an evening of quiet.

"I suppose I can manage some time to myself," she answered with a smile.

***

Jenny Stein Brissot slowly folded her linen handkerchief and placed it neatly alongside the stack of others in the top drawer of her bureau. She then removed her bonnet and gloves, placing them on the surface of her vanity, and studied her reflection in the etched glass of the mirror. She was aging well, she mused objectively, noting that her dark blonde hair still retained much of its former youthful luster, and the wrinkles around her eyes were not as pronounced as others in her acquaintance who looked for every excuse to place themselves above her. Well, try as they may, they could not take her appearance or her bearing, and pride was to her a virtue, where in others it may have been a vice.

She wandered from her bedroom and slowly down the hallway to the stairs, descending with the purpose of heating some milk before bedtime. Jean-Pierre had returned to the office to work on the early-morning edition of his paper, and Marie had turned in for the night before they had returned from dinner with the Chastains.

Jenny was glad her daughter had not been in attendance. Mr. Chastain had been his usual loud self, preaching on eternally about the virtues of his young daughters. That Marie was considered "soiled," continually left a bitter taste in her mouth. The image of a handsome young man's smug face swam in her mind for a moment and she envisioned closing her hands around his throat and squeezing for all she was worth. Someday, on the other side, he would meet his maker and pay for the fact that he had completely ruined a young woman's life, and Jenny would do her best not to jump about in derisive glee while he stammered his apology to her precious daughter. She did not doubt that day would come, she only regretted the Bible verse that proclaimed, "Vengeance is mine." She would have liked to mete out that vengeance herself.

Busying herself in the kitchen, she went about preparing her milk and tried to banish thoughts best left alone. It had been a long, long time, and perhaps with the coming political conflict, things would change enough that people would forget about Marie Brissot's Unfortunate Episode and leave her to live her life in peace without the quiet snubs, the condescending looks.

Jenny sat at the small worktable in the kitchen and sipped her drink, glancing out the window and into the black night sky. Life was good overall, she supposed. Marie was bright and healthy, and seemed with each passing year to come more and more into her own. She was confident and secure in thought and word, and she did so much good for the little children she taught that Jenny couldn't truthfully wish Marie was somewhere else, doing something else. Although she knew her daughter longed for companionship, she also knew that even under optimal circumstances, Marie might have had a hard time finding a proper mate for herself.

Finishing her milk, Jenny washed her cup and placed it back in the cupboard. She made her way upstairs, pausing at Marie's door and peering inside. A shaft of moonlight shot through the white, diaphanous curtains at the window and landed on Marie's face. Jenny's breath caught at the sight of the beautiful woman that was her daughter, and on impulse, she silently crossed the floor and placed a soft kiss on Marie's cheek.

She glanced back once more before leaving the room and closing the door softly behind her. Her daughter was a grown woman. Where had the time gone?

CHAPTER 5

*"Let me tell you what is coming . . . Your fathers and husbands,
your sons and brothers, will be herded at the point of bayonet . . . You
may, after the sacrifice of countless millions of treasure and hundreds
of thousands of lives, as a bare possibility, win Southern independence
. . . But I doubt it . . . When [the Northerners] begin to move in a
given direction . . . they move with the steady momentum and perse-
verance of a mighty avalanche."*
—Sam Houston, Texas Governor

***

New York, New York—Outskirts
1 February, 1861

Daniel O'Shea stood in the comfortable parlor of his parents'
home. He eyed his father in quiet amusement, wondering how
long it would be before the typical Irish temper unleashed itself.

He didn't have long to wait.

"This is absurd!" Gavin O'Shea boomed as he read the newspaper. "It gets worse and worse! How many more states are going
to leave?"

"Supposedly Sam Houston held secession off for as long as he
could," Daniel said, motioning to the paper. "The people of Texas
wouldn't hear of it, though. He was deposed as governor."

Gavin shook his head and sank into his favorite chair. "They're fools then, the whole lot of them. Sam Houston masterminded their independence from Mexico! They should support him—where is their loyalty?"

"With the Confederacy, apparently." Daniel took a seat opposite his father and smiled when he heard his mother's voice coming from the kitchen.

"Gavin, you keep your head about you," she said as she entered the room, carrying a teapot and cups on a tray. "When Louisiana seceded," she said to Daniel, "he broke my favorite vase."

"I just don't understand it," Gavin fumed, again glancing at the paper.

"It's been volatile for generations, Da, since long before we came over. It was bound to happen."

"This will result in bloodshed, you mark my words."

Brenna cast a mildly irritated glance at her husband as she handed him a cup of tea. "That's a bit severe, Gavin, even for you."

"How can it possibly be resolved, Brenna? The Union will never stand for this—Lincoln will not allow the situation to remain as it is."

"Lincoln still hasn't said what he's planning to do," Daniel offered as he accepted the cup of tea his mother handed to him.

"And when is the inauguration?" Brenna asked, settling back into a small sofa with her own cup.

"March fourth, I believe."

"So," Gavin remarked, folding the paper neatly in half and tossing it to the floor by the side of his chair. "You came over to watch your father explode?"

Daniel grinned. "You must admit, your nasty temper has a certain entertaining appeal."

"Hmph."

Brenna turned a wry gaze on her husband. "Doesn't it give you satisfaction, Gavin, to realize you provide us with such joy?"

"No more than Daniel does," he muttered. "I've seen you get mighty feisty a time or two," he said, shaking a finger at his son. He then gestured toward the paper on the floor. "People just don't understand what they're throwing away," he said. "When we came to this country we were starving because of the potato famine, and—"

"And we were welcomed here with open arms. This country gave us opportunities we didn't have in Ireland, and we have all benefited from it," Daniel finished for him. He had heard that speech many a time, and knew it by heart. It had amazed him, however, as he grew older and experienced the prejudice reserved for the Irish and other immigrants, that his father chose to overlook the negative reactions that had actually greeted them, and many like them, when they had sailed into port and attempted to make a new life in the Land of Opportunity. Gavin O'Shea looked at life in America as blessed, and he chose to ignore those who were less than pleased with the increasing immigrant population.

Unfortunately for Daniel, he didn't possess his father's sense of rosy optimism. The prejudice against the Irish ate at him like a burr under a saddle. He grew weary of the comments, the attitude, and the blatant insults.

"Well, it's true," Gavin blustered, looking at his son. "Have we not all benefited from it?"

Daniel nodded reluctantly. "I suppose we have. Truthfully, though, I don't know that my life would be much different in Ireland than it is here." He thought of the small home he owned just down the hill from his parents' own farm where he had been raised. It was a modest affair; it met his needs, and the carpentry business he owned to meet his financial obligations more than filled his daytime hours.

"Surely, it is."

"It is?" Daniel cocked a brow, his question rhetorical. "I could own a carpentry business in Ireland the same as I do here."

"Perhaps," Gavin admitted. "But then you wouldn't be here to witness firsthand the progression of this society!" The gleam in his eye betrayed his inner excitement. This, also, was something Daniel was used to seeing in his father—his zeal for progress and industry.

Daniel smiled. "And I surely wouldn't want to miss that."

"You're just like old Rhys," Gavin muttered. "He refused to leave the Old Country. Watched his children embark on a new life and wouldn't have a bit o' it."

"Well, if old Rhys liked his life simple and uncomplicated, then I'd say I'm proud to be like him," Daniel said.

Brenna stood and took the empty teacups from the men, giving Gavin an affectionate pat on the shoulder as she lifted the tray and turned for the kitchen. "'Tis all right, dearie," she said in her lilting Irish brogue. "At least one of your children shared your obsessions."

She spoke of Daniel's older brother, Colin. Colin had been much like his father in temperament and interests, and had pursued a career working for the railroad. The accident that had taken his life ten years before had left the family reeling in shock.

Gavin sobered at the memory. "Colin was a good boy," he said gruffly.

"Yes, he was," Brenna answered from the kitchen. "He was also reckless. There's something to be said for caution."

"Well, then Danny Boy should be with us for a long time to come, if he can keep that temper in check," he said with a wink as he rose and punched his son lightly on his shoulder. "I have animals to tend to," he said and walked into the kitchen, letting himself out the back door after pausing to kiss his wife.

Daniel walked into the kitchen as well, giving his mother a kiss, and then turned back through the parlor and to the front door.

"Will we be seein' you for dinner tonight?" Brenna called after him.

"Yes, thank you." He closed the door behind him and walked into the brisk winter air, down the hill to his own home. He had furniture to work on in his small shop that was next to his house, and he was glad for it. He appreciated the everyday details of his life, because it kept him busy. The daytime hours usually flew by quickly. The nighttime hours were harder to fill. A man could only sleep so much. Perhaps that was why in all the years since Colin's death, he had engaged in "sport" that would have his mother expiring on the spot if she knew.

The painful ache that had filled his heart six years before at the death of his young fiancée, Alice, had receded into a small pang that struck only once in a while. Even greater than his missing *her*, specifically, was his loneliness at her absence. She had been young, barely seventeen, and he had been but twenty-one years himself. They had met at a church social and he had been taken with her pale blonde hair, the light blue eyes, and the ethereal serenity her soul seemed to exude.

Their courtship had been brief, and his proposal had surprised both her and his family. Alice had accepted, though, and had expressed delight at the thought of living with him in the small home he had recently built. Three short weeks before they were to have wed, she succumbed to a deadly bout of pneumonia that took her life a mere six days later.

And so within a few years' time, he had found himself robbed of his brother and the woman who would have been his wife. He had grieved with his parents, and had kept moving forward, using his forays into the seedy New York nightlife to keep the angry internal wolves at bay. He had been unable, or perhaps unwilling, to find a replacement for Alice, and as time progressed, the path he followed became more and more familiar.

***

Brenna O'Shea busied herself after supper was finished, clearing plates and wrapping the excess food that was salvageable for another meal. She made a mental checklist of neighbors who might enjoy a loaf of bread or perhaps some dessert, knowing full well that more often than not, her sense of thrift and desire to avoid waste often went beyond that which was rational.

She wasn't as excessive as she once was, she told herself defensively. At least she no longer gave half-eaten pieces of pork meat to the neighbors as a gesture of good will. Gavin had convinced her long ago that their neighbors were not in dire straits, and that to give them food that had already been chewed upon would probably be viewed as an insult.

Bread was perfectly acceptable, however, and in preparation for a later delivery, she wrapped a freshly baked loaf in a clean cloth and placed a jar of strawberry preserves next to it on the butcher-block table Gavin had made for her when they first built the house. What a grand day that had been! After living for a year in the slums of New York, the new little farm on the quiet outskirts was a veritable palace. Truth be told, however, the dregs of the city had been preferable to the famine and devastation they had left behind in Ireland. She and Gavin had been so desperate to provide for their children that they had worked their fingers to the bone and hadn't looked back.

Well, Brenna had to admit with a sigh as she washed the dishes with the pump that was attached to the deep stone sink, every time she was forced to clear uneaten food from a supper plate, she looked back. It went against her every instinct to throw perfectly good food into the compost heap out back for the pigs when, on the fringes of her memory, were the faces of her two boys, their young faces pale with the pain of hunger.

"But Brenna," Gavin had told her with a warm arm about her shoulders the first time she had balked at giving the pigs something she would have nearly killed for a mere few years earlier, "we feed the pigs, they grow nice 'n fat, and then we eat *them!*" She had laughed at his cheerful expression and marveled at his inexhaustible ability to make her smile.

They were well off now, at least in comparison to their former life, and there wasn't a day that went by that Brenna wasn't on her knees, thanking a gracious Father for her blessings. She prayed daily for Colin's eternal soul, hoping that he was in the realms above, perhaps with a nice Catholic girl, and she prayed for

Daniel, hoping much of the same for him. "Please, though," she often prayed, "let me have Danny a bit longer, yes? He's not yet lived a full life."

No indeed, she mused as she wiped her hands on a snowy white towel and looked out of the kitchen doorway and into the parlor where Daniel sat sprawled in front of the fire, again goading his father into a political debate, a smile of devilment playing about his lips. *Daniel hasn't lived a full life, yet. Colin did, because he took life by the throat and lived it to its fullest. Daniel's pursuits might yet get him killed, but he has never really enjoyed himself.*

Brenna knew full well that when Daniel went to town he associated with people that he wouldn't have dared bring home for Sunday dinner. His occasional bruises and scrapes were evidence of the fact that he lived a life that was separate from the facade he tried to present to his parents. Figuring he perhaps tipped the bottle back a bit too far, she assumed the evidence of his fighting was due to a dependence on drink. It worried her.

She sighed as she returned to the kitchen. Daniel was his own person now, a man, and she couldn't very well tell him what to do anymore. She wished she could, however. Oh, how she wished she could.

***

Daniel shook his head at the bartender between fights when the man offered him a bottle. He knew his mother assumed he drank too much, and that therein lay the periodic evidence of his brawling. If she only knew the truth, she might be relieved. He never touched a drop. It wasn't the alcohol that drew him back to this place each Saturday night. It was the fights themselves.

Daniel was a prizefighter. He had made money for hard-working Irishmen all over New York, showing them confidence when they placed their bets on him and following through with victory after victory, week after week. Nobody ever beat Daniel O'Shea, and though they tried, he was determined that they never would.

It was Daniel's one victory over all those who looked at his Irish heritage and scorned him for it. It was his way of beating a system that was determined to keep him from succeeding. The rage was channeled through his controlled fighting, and it kept him from hurting other people, "respectable" people, who wandered about town in the light of day, dressed in finery and thumbing their noses at the immigrant population.

Stripped to the waist, he stepped to the center of the shabby tavern at the signal, and faced another nameless opponent. Dodging flying fists, moving with the quick speed that was his trademark, he landed blows with an accuracy that had the rough crowd cheering. It wasn't long before the man he fought lay prostrate at his feet, and Daniel raised a fist in victory as money changed hands and the tavern owner handed him a rough towel.

Wiping his face with it, he stepped to one side and watched as people gleefully took each other's hard-earned money. The tavern owner himself would hand Daniel a bag full of coins for his efforts in bringing business to the establishment that had been virtually uninhabited before Daniel O'Shea began fighting there. He moved from place to place, acknowledging the following he was building, but never mixing with the crowds beyond the occasional casual conversation.

"Seems t'me you're gonna find yourself bored before long if we can't find ye some good competition," the tavern owner was saying to Daniel over the din of the crowd.

Daniel shrugged. "I've been doing this for a long time, Smitts," he answered. "I'm not bored yet."

"Still . . ." Smitts put a grubby hand to his rough-shaven chin in contemplation. "Lemme see what I can dig up. We'll make things interesting around here. Getcha some good competition."

Daniel clapped a hand on the man's shoulder and handed him the towel. "You do what you feel you must do, Smitts. I'm not worried about it."

He walked to the corner and retrieved his shirt, thrusting his arms into the sleeves and buttoning it while Smitts ambled over to a spot behind the bar and pulled a bag of gold coins from its recesses. Daniel accepted the bag from Smitts with a half smile and a promise to be present one week hence.

Making his way to the door, Daniel waved at those who cheered for him in gratitude for their current good fortunes, and laughed at those who grumbled at their losses, threatening to kill him in his sleep. "I'll be waiting," he called to one man who threatened to hunt him down like a dog.

He was nearly through the threshold when he was stopped, as he was each week, by a woman in a dress of purple satin that sported black lace trim and a plunging neckline. She was a pretty woman, with lines on her face that bore the evidence of a hard life.

"Company tonight, Daniel?"

"No thank you, Lavender." He softened the refusal with a gentle smile.

"You always say no, Daniel O'Shea," she pouted. "One of these days, you'll say yes."

"I can't do that, lovey. My mama raised a good Catholic boy."

Leaving the disappointed woman behind, Daniel walked out into the night air, grateful that it was cold. Not only had his mama raised a good Catholic boy, he mused grimly, she'd also raised a smart one who knew to avoid the pox. Lavender was a kind woman, he knew, but she was also a professional. Time spent intimately with her or with the countless others he had met through the years could well mean a man's death, and it was an ugly one.

Daniel retrieved his horse and buggy and began the two-mile trek back to his small home. Nobody knew where he lived; to date nobody had tried to actually do him harm, although they always threatened, and Daniel liked it that way. The regulars who followed his fights assumed he lived in the city, and that suited him fine. His nightlife was separate from his daytime life, and he preferred the division. It was as though he had two selves, and he couldn't manage to convince the two to join in a constructive way. Until he found something (*or someone,* his mind whispered), that would be interesting enough to keep him home at night, he'd keep doing what he was doing and be grateful for the outlet.

CHAPTER 6

"Where slavery is, there liberty cannot be; and where liberty is, there slavery cannot be."
—*Senator Charles Sumner*

***

Cleveland, Ohio
5 February, 1861

Ivar Gundersen finished milking the second of his two cows, glancing at the window and out into the approaching dark. The stars above were just beginning to twinkle, and the air was clear. It meant another cold night, and Ivar was thankful that his genes were a gift from ancestors accustomed to climes significantly more northward than Ohio.

He saw to the security of his chickens, the cows, and the pigs, one of which was nearly ready for slaughter. Taking the two pails of milk in his hands, he left the small barn and walked the distance across his two acres and onto the adjoining land that was his parents' farm. The light was on in the kitchen, and he smiled, anticipating the feel of two-year-old arms encircling his neck.

Sure enough, as soon as he entered his mother's kitchen, his little daughter, Inger, leaped from his mother's arms and with a squeal, threw herself at his legs. He laughed, and handing the pails of milk to Amanda, he plucked his child from the floor, and tossed her high before holding her in a tight squeeze.

"And how's my little sugarplum doing?" he asked, tweaking her nose.

"Do you have candy?" the little one asked, patting his face between her hands.

He laughed. "Is that all you ever want from me, Inger?" He reached into his pocket and pulled forth a peppermint. She took it with a laugh of delight and popped it into her mouth as he set her down on the floor.

"Papa is still outside, then?" Ivar asked his mother in Norwegian.

She nodded. "Yes. I told him to wait for you, but you know how he is."

Ivar frowned and walked out the kitchen door and into the yard. The light in the barn told him his father was insisting on milking his own cows, again. He approached the barn after calling to Inger that he would return shortly, and went in search of his father.

"How's the leg today?" he asked when he found his father inside the barn.

"It's doing just fine," Per grunted.

Ivar looked at his father's left leg, outstretched, and shook his head. Per Gundersen was a stubborn man, and wouldn't admit to the fact that he needed help. His leg had been injured in a plowing accident several years before, and had caused him considerable and increasing pain ever since.

"I'm sure it is," Ivar answered, "but all the same, I've promised Mama that I would finish this for you. She shoved me right out the door and said to send you in for supper," he lied.

Per shook his head. "Your mother thinks I am a child," he said, but rose awkwardly from the stool and shuffled his way over to Ivar. He gripped his son's shoulder and patted it briefly before making his way slowly to the door where his cherry-wood cane stood propped. "I mustn't keep her waiting, though. Amanda takes her supper very seriously."

Ivar thoughtfully watched Per's retreating back before settling down to finish the task his father had abandoned, not feeling one whit of remorse for his white lie. His father would move heaven and earth for his mother, and if it meant using that against him, well, it was for his own good.

Ivar inhaled deeply, appreciating the feel of the crisp air in his lungs, and the smell of animals and hay. They had been scents he remembered from childhood, even from before his parents had moved him, at ten years of age, to the new country. His father's brother had already emigrated from Norway, marrying a woman from Ohio and settling near her family, and Per and Amanda were soon to follow, lured by the promise of much land for the taking. They hadn't regretted the move, as far as Ivar knew, although sometimes at Christmas each year he noticed a faraway look in his mother's eye that told him she was elsewhere—most likely home with her mother and sisters.

Ivar turned at the sound of the barn door opening a crack. His mother moved quickly into the barn, bundled tightly in a coat, scarf, mittens, and boots.

"Is something wrong?"

"No, no," she answered, clapping her hands together lightly to keep them warm. "I just wanted to ask you something about your father."

Ivar watched her as she slowly walked to one of the cows, placing her mittened hand upon the beast's head, and waited patiently for her to speak.

"His leg is worse, you know," she said.

"I do know."

"I've spoken with Doctor Child—he seems to think there's nothing more we can do for it."

Ivar looked at his mother, taking in the salt-and-pepper graying hair, the sturdy frame, the brown eyes that had looked so often on him in compassion or reproof. Where was she going with her current musings? Was there something about his father's condition of which he was unaware?

"What are you thinking, Mama?"

Amanda let a puff of breath out and again patted the cow's head before dropping her hand and turning to him. "I'm worried."

"We'll take care of him. He'll be fine."

She looked at him for a moment without comment. "I know," she finally said. "I suppose . . ."

"You suppose?" he finally prompted when the prolonged silence stretched interminably.

"It's foolish, I know, but Inger asked me today if Bestefar won't soon join Berit in heaven."

Ivar's eyebrows shot up in surprise. "She was talking about Berit?" It had been ages since Inger had mentioned her mother.

"She said that since Bestefar isn't walking well, that he might soon die and join Berit in heaven."

"Mama." Ivar smiled a bit. "Inger also thinks the pigs in our barn will eventually learn to fly like the ducks."

Amanda laughed, the sound rising through the rafters and into the night. "I told you it was foolish." She shook her head and walked toward the door, her step taking on the brisk stride she usually employed. "I'll keep supper warm for you inside. Your father is in there now with Inger on his lap, trying to eat his meal while she chatters."

Ivar smiled again as his mother left the barn. Inger did indeed chatter—an odd mixture of English and Norwegian. It was delightful.

That night, back in the coziness of his own small home, Ivar tucked his daughter snugly into her bed under the thick, fluffy down blanket. He reflected on the conversation with his mother in the barn, and he gazed into the little face that looked, ironically enough, so much like Amanda's.

"Have you been thinking about your mama, Inger?"

The little one nodded. "Sometimes I see her in my dreams."

"Hmm. And does she say anything to you?"

"No. She smiles."

Heaven must have done wonders for Berit, then, because she had rarely smiled while with them on earth. Ivar shook his head slightly and leaned to kiss his daughter's forehead. He ruffled her blonde curls and positioned her small stuffed doll closely underneath her chin.

"Sov godt, venin min." *Sleep well, my little one.*

"Sov godt, Papa."

Ivar wandered into his bedroom, running a hand through his thick, blonde hair and down around the back of his neck, doubting he *could* sleep, let alone well. Talk of Berit had him agitated, and he wished he had never met the woman. Truthfully, he had to admit, as he wandered to the window and stared out into the night sky, his hands shoved deep into the pockets of his pants, that wasn't the case. He was glad he had married Berit because Inger had been the result, and Inger was his life.

He wished he could tell his daughter wonderful things about her mother, when she came of age to understand, but he would be hard-pressed to find any admirable qualities about the woman who had been his wife. He had met her in his late teens, had admired her from afar, but assumed his infatuation would never amount to anything when she had spurned the few attempts he had made to speak with her.

They lived in the same small community through the years, Berit going away to visit family in Chicago and sweeping back into town again like a princess, with Ivar watching her and wishing she would pay him some notice. He had his pride, however, and was not about to be made a fool of, so he kept his distance.

As time progressed, Ivar entertained the notion of moving to New York and studying architecture. Berit discovered his ambitions through a mutual friend, and suddenly began showing an interest in him that caught him completely, delightfully, by surprise. She said she had always loved him, that he was an admirable man of immense character, and that she would be proud to be courted by him.

Utterly besotted, he trailed around after her, catering to her every whim. He expressed a continued interest to live in New York, and had her complete and total support. She loved the big city life, she said, and couldn't abide the thought of living on a farm forever.

They married before long, and moved to New York on Ivar's meager savings, setting up house in a hovel of an apartment with Ivar promising his crying wife every night that it wouldn't be long before he would be finished with his apprenticeship and would be earning money that would have them living well.

And then had come Per's accident. Ivar was beside himself at the thought of his mother trying to run the farm by herself, and so the move back home to Ohio had been swift and without any heart-wrenching contemplation. Berit, however, had kicked and screamed the entire way. By the time Ivar realized he had made a horrid mistake in tying himself to the woman, it was too late.

Berit determined to make his life miserable once he purchased the land adjacent to his parents, and she succeeded. She had conceived while still in New York, and complained while carrying the baby, complained once she was born, and complained every time Inger cried. The baby was a mere six months when Berit returned to New York, leaving her young family with a note that said she was in love with another who could provide for her as she deserved.

It was understandable, then, that the Gundersen's felt shock, perhaps, but no remorse upon learning of Berit's death a year later of consumption. Inger was told that her mother died when she was a baby, and that was that. The little family moved forward with life and tried to forget the pain. There were times, though, when Ivar found himself laying awake at night, wondering how he had ever let himself be so stupid, and vowing to never again be taken in by a deceitful woman.

***

Amanda glanced once at her sleeping husband before leaving the bedroom and making her way down the stairs in the dark. Try as she might, she couldn't block the voice of her young grandchild from her mind.

Will Bestefar die and be with my mama and Jesus?

Not if Amanda had anything to say about matters, and Amanda usually willed things her way. Work was always the answer, and ignoring the fact that she was in her nightdress, she filled a small bucket with water and soap, and bending over on her hands and knees, began to scrub the kitchen floor.

It wasn't as though the floor needed scrubbing; it had been cleaned the day before. Amanda didn't like to be plagued with foolish thoughts, however, and always found solace in keeping busy. She would pay for it in the morning, she knew, when Inger would occupy her time while Ivar worked the farms, but she couldn't bear to go back into the bedroom and listen to Per's uneven breathing. He was in pain, even in his sleep.

She had forged a new life in a new country for her small family, and had done it well. There wasn't anything she couldn't handle; there wasn't anything she couldn't fix. Perhaps that was why her husband's pain had her grasping at straws. She couldn't make the pain go away, and she couldn't restore her husband to his former health. It chafed at her in ways she couldn't explain.

Work was always the answer!

It was a lesson she had learned from her own parents, and from their parents. If a person worked hard enough, anything could be achieved. She scrubbed the clean floor, ignoring the burning sensation in her eyes and throat that had nothing to do with the strong lye in the soap. If she worked hard enough, everything would be fine.

Ivar awoke the following morning to find his father again going about the chores on his farm with a decidedly slow step. Ivar had finished his own business and had taken Inger to his mother. Now, as he watched Per attempt to do things that should have been simple for him, he felt himself frown. He remembered Amanda's words from the night before and shook them off, chiding himself for worrying overmuch.

"May I help you with that?" Ivar asked his father, gesturing to the pitchfork.

Per glanced up in surprise, apparently startled. "I didn't hear you come in," he admitted.

"You were somewhere far away."

"I was thinking about this secession business."

"Ah." Ivar took a feed bucket from the wall and began dispensing the contents to the chickens. "And what do you think of it?"

Per paused for a moment and looked into the distance. "I'm thinking it's none of my business," he finally commented. "I live here, but often find my heart back home."

Ivar smiled slightly. American politics may not be his father's business, but by virtue of the fact that Ivar was now a U.S. citizen, it certainly made it his. "Do you not find one side or the other at fault?"

Per shrugged slightly. "Fault is subjective. You ask a person on either side whose fault it is and of course he will blame the other."

"But what do you think?"

"I think," again, he paused. "I think a man's life is his own business, regardless of what color he is."

"So you favor abolition, then?"

Per nodded. "I suppose I do. A man should be paid for his work, and should be able to keep that pay. I know I would not care to have my life dictated for me. I can't imagine any person would." He shook his head slightly. "Norwegians would never do something like this."

Ivar smiled. "There's very little variance in skin color in Norway, Papa."

"No, but we haven't enslaved the Swedes, now, have we?" Per's expression remained bland, but his blue eyes twinkled with mischief.

Ivar laughed out loud. "That's hard to do when the Swedes are in power." He clapped his father lightly on the back, and after the chickens were fed, he replaced the feed bucket and made his way outside and across the field. The trees in the small orchard that connected his parents' farm with his own were bare and cold, their branches retaining an inch of snow that had fallen in the night. The ground was hard beneath the snow, and his breath formed around his head in a fog.

The cold invigorated him. It kept his senses sharp and alert. He mused over the things his father had said and wondered at them himself. Would all this secession business lead to a larger conflict? Would the Union be content to allow the rebel states their departure and not pursue the matter further? In his lifetime in the U.S., he had seen the states battle at issues wide and varied, and opinions grow heated and hostile, but never had any of the states actually severed their ties, although they had certainly threatened.

Apparently the issue of a state's right to allow ownership of human property was one over which compromise had finally failed. Ivar reviewed his father's words in his mind and had to agree. A man's life should be his own. The question was, he supposed, how would it directly affect Ivar and his family? They had blended into a country that had given them little resistance and left them in peace to farm their new land. What would it require of them in return?

CHAPTER 7

"There is nothing going wrong . . . nobody is suffering anything . . . there shall be no blood shed unless it is forced upon the Government."
—Abraham Lincoln

"If Mr. Lincoln has nothing better to offer upon this fearful crisis, let him say nothing at all."
—The New York Herald

***

Montgomery, Alabama
18 February, 1861

Jeffrey Birmingham stood outside the state capitol with the bustling crowd, watching as Jefferson Davis took his oath of office. He cast an eye about at the people gathered on the lawn, the small, sloping grass hill leading down to carriages standing still in the street. People crowded the two balconies of the capitol building, watching the proceedings from their lofty vantage points.

Upon taking the oath, Davis then turned to address the crowd. "Our present political position has been achieved in a manner unprecedented in the history of nations," he said in a loud, firm voice. Mrs. Varina Davis had confided to Jeffrey only the night before that upon receiving the telegram informing him of his new position as President of the Provisional Government of the Confederate States of America, her husband had looked as though he had received a sentence of death. The strength present in his speech disguised the man's apparent inner misgivings.

"It illustrates the American idea that the government rests on the consent of the governed, and that it is the right of the governed, and that it is the right of the people to alter or abolish them at will whenever they become destructive of the ends for which they were established . . . Obstacles may retard, but they can not long prevent the progress of a movement sanctified by its justice and sustained by a virtuous people," Davis continued.

The people about Jeffrey cried and cheered, singing "Farewell to the Star-Spangled Banner" with joy and much obvious emotion. He glanced toward his right at Mary Chestnut, wife of former U.S. senator James Chestnut, Jr., of South Carolina. She had an inscrutable expression on her face; he found himself wondering what she was thinking.

He moved closer to her and said with a friendly smile, "You don't join in the singing, Mrs. Chestnut?"

She smiled in return, if in a slightly reserved manner, and replied, "I find myself cautiously optimistic about these proceedings, Mr. Birmingham." She would have commented further, but Alexander Stephens, the newly elected vice president, was taking his turn at speech.

"Our new government is founded on the opposite idea of the equality of races," he was loudly proclaiming. "Its cornerstone rests upon the great truth that the Negro is not equal to the white man; that slavery, subordination to the superior race, is his natural and moral condition. This, our new Government is the first in the history of the world, based upon this great physical, philosophical, and moral truth."

Amidst the cheers and further shouts of excitement and adulation, Jeffrey shifted uncomfortably. His son, Ben, was again infesting his thoughts. Jeffrey's life had been relatively simple before Ben had come to the conclusion that slavery was morally wrong, that there were no differences in class between the races, and that to enslave a person was an affront not only to that person, but to God.

For all his oddity in thought and expression, for all that he basically ostracized himself from the only life he'd ever known, Jeffrey had to wonder if his son was right. Now, listening to the new vice president of the Confederacy, he found himself wincing.

Jeffrey again glanced at Mary Chestnut. Her expression was troubled and he wondered at it; he knew her to be a South Carolinian native, a Rebel born to a man who had been governor during the Nullification Crisis.

He touched her arm lightly, and watched as her strained expression gently eased. "Do write to Sarah again soon, won't you?" he asked of her. "She does so love hearing from you."

"Indeed I will, Mr. Birmingham. It would be my pleasure." She gathered her skirts in her hands and wandered off toward the direction of the capitol, doubtless moving to join their common circle of friends that currently formed the basis of the new Confederate government.

Jeffrey moved forward as well, shaking hands as he walked and tossing back well-wishes from varied acquaintances. He reflected on the new Confederate Constitution, the details of which he had learned from a colleague the night before upon his arrival. The new constitution was very like the old one they had left behind. There were a few explicit differences, however. The new constitution extended the term of the office of presidency to six years, it granted each member of the cabinet a seat on the floor of Congress, and expressly guaranteed the right to own slaves, although it did forbid international slave trade.

He shook his head slightly at the rhetoric bouncing about as he walked. In theory, the concepts were well and good. But without a strong, central government, what was to keep the Confederate states from seceding from their new union on a whim? He was in favor of stronger states' rights, to be sure, but he couldn't squelch the uneasy feeling in the pit of his stomach at the joy of the revelers. He sensed impending doom.

The next few days were occupied solely with forming the new government. Davis appointed people to his cabinet as fairly as possible, choosing one from each state in an effort to be diplomatic. Diplomacy wasn't a feat that came easily for the new president; he was exceedingly formal, a bit nervous, as evidenced by a recurring twitch in his cheek, and according to his wife, had been hoping for a military command as opposed to a political position.

Jeffrey Birmingham walked down a hallway of the hotel where the new cabinet was attempting to conduct its business. He paused outside the door bearing a piece of stationery proclaiming that the President's office lay within. He stood there, studying the paper for a moment before turning at the rustle of skirts.

Smiling grimly, Mary Chestnut approached him. "A bit primitive, isn't it?" she asked.

Jeffrey nodded. "They'll need money, soon. I'm happy to donate to the cause."

"And I'm sure they'll gladly accept it. I suspect they'll move the capitol before long. I don't imagine it will remain here in Montgomery. I think most are hoping Virginia will join with us. A Confederate capitol in Richmond would be strategically sound, being so close to Washington." She paused for a moment, her head tipped slightly to one side. "I'm surprised you didn't clamor for a cabinet or diplomatic position as have the rest of our associates, Mr. Birmingham."

He shrugged lightly. "My interests lie with my plantation, Mrs. Chestnut. I enjoy my associations with our political friends, but choose to avoid the stresses of actually filling such a political position. I fear that must make me a coward," he finished on a smile.

"Nonsense," she said, tapping her closed fan against his arm. "It makes you intelligent. I do wish, however, we had more young blood in these offices," she murmured, motioning to the hotel rooms that housed the Confederacy's newly appointed officers.

"These men are afraid to capitalize on our younger strengths and resources. Instead we keep the old, who are wearing down! I am nervous about this entire endeavor."

He had to agree. They were interrupted by the approach of the new Secretary of State, Robert Toombs. He had nearly reached them when another young man with whom Jeffrey was not acquainted overtook him.

"Where might I find the State Department?" the stranger inquired.

"In my hat, sir," Toombs answered the gentleman. "And the archives in my coat pocket."

Jeffrey glanced at Mary Chestnut with a wry, if apprehensive, smile, and with a certain amount of resignation she shook her head subtly in return. Yes indeed, he agreed with the good lady. Nervous was an apt, if understated, description of his feelings.

***

Charleston, South Carolina—Bentley Plantation
20 February, 1861

Mary sat on the edge of her bed, holding an empty blanket. It was small and threadbare, and had been wrapped around her newborn son for two short days. When she held the blanket to her nose, she could still smell the distinctive scent of new baby.

She stared at the thing; it was an ugly blanket, really—it had once been white, but had faded to gray through the years. What made it special was that it had been hers as a child. She had held the thing to her when the dreams at night were frightening, and had wrapped it around the doll Mama Ruth made for her longer ago than she could remember.

Mary's feelings these days were so confusing she hardly knew what to think. Her usual feelings of depression at her lot in life, in general, had become heightened to an extent she would never have dreamed possible. She hadn't even wanted the child! Heaven help her, then why was she grieving?

Those two days she'd had with her son were now nothing but a blur. She had awoken when he needed to eat, held him as close as necessity demanded, and then, before Mary had even fully regained her strength, Miz Sarah had sold the baby to the neighbors. The only reason Mary even knew of the child's whereabouts was due to Emily.

Mary had been unable to look at the child without remembering the horrible night he had been conceived. Had she been well, she might have been able to fend off the attack, but she had been extremely ill, and her feeble physical protestations had been useless. For one insane moment the next morning, Mary had actually considered approaching Miz Sarah with the information that her son was a rapist, but common sense prevailed, and she had kept her mouth closed. It wasn't as though society considered it a crime for a white man to force himself on a slave. It was an issue that simply wasn't discussed in polite circles.

She had to wonder now, however, if Miz Sarah knew who had sired the child. The mistress had sold the baby much too quickly for Mary to believe otherwise, and the breaking apart of families was something Miz Sarah rarely did. It flew in the face of conventional Southern wisdom to allow the families to remain together, but Miz Sarah was in favor of high morale among her property.

There were times when Mary so despised her mistress she felt she'd surely be sick with it. Sarah Birmingham treated her slaves, especially the house slaves, with something that dangerously resembled reserved affection. Yet she refused them the one thing they all craved almost as badly as they needed the very air in their lungs. The hypocrisy was disgusting, and Mary hated it.

But Mary was mild in temperament, and wasn't in danger of losing her house privileges due to an outburst of impertinent anger. She kept her temper, and shared intimacies of private thought only with Emily and Ruth.

There were some things, though, that she shared with nobody. She moved to the window, noting Ruth, who stood in front of the shack next door, speaking with one of the few women at Bentley who had lived to see fifty years. They conversed in hushed tones, and Mary was comforted by the murmur of her grandmother's voice, muffled and unintelligible from her position inside the house, but soothing, nonetheless. She was doubtless giving the woman advice; as the head house servant, Ruth was a woman of considerable consequence amongst the slaves. She was also good for morale. Mary smiled as the old woman with Ruth burst into spontaneous laughter, cackling, "Laws a mercy, Ruthie! If you just don' beat all!"

Mary gazed up at the stars, her thoughts shifting inward, wondering if *he* was, perhaps, looking at the very same constellation as was she. She loved him. She always had. It was cruel to taunt herself with dreams of the impossible, but sometimes it was only those dreams that managed to help keep her sane.

Had it been he, instead of his brother who had fathered her child, she would have rejoiced—would have been a willing participant. As a child she had harbored a silly dream of someday being his bride. A harsh reality, however, had soon asserted itself upon her senses, convincing her of the painful truth.

White men did not marry black women, especially their slaves.

Except he had never thought of her as a slave, had never given her any indication that he held her in any different regard than he would one of his white neighbors down the street. She had always been careful to hide her childlike adoration of him, but after he had gone and as she had grown older, the adoration had transformed into something painfully more substantial—made all the more painful because he was gone, and had been for years.

The blanket slipped from her grasp, and she glanced down at it, the present again coming to the fore. She picked it up and held it briefly to her nose, inhaling the soft scent and trying to ignore the sting in her eyes.

True, the child had been Richard's.

But it had also been hers.

***

Utah Territory
20 February, 1861

Ben Birmingham stepped out onto the Clark family porch for a breath of crisp, fresh air. Sister Clark meant well, but she was in such desperate straits trying to marry off her oldest daughter that her attentions were becoming a bit suffocating. It was painfully clear that the daughter wasn't altogether interested, and who could blame her? Ben was moody and hard to read, and it was common knowledge, even to him, that he wasn't exactly looked upon as prize husband material. The mamas were the only ones who seemed to be interested, and that was usually because he was handsome, he still possessed some measure of Southern charm when he put his mind to sharing it, and he was financially sound because he had learned to work hard and hoard his resources like a miser for the past five years.

His eye found the North star and he stared at it, willing it to speak to him from its lofty perch in the heavens; to give him some advice he would find useful. Advice on how to calm a churning stomach, and quiet an angry mind.

The world was spinning at a faster rate, and nothing he could do would make it slow down. To date, six states had left the Union, and in his heart he knew there would be serious conflict to follow. He tried repeating to himself that it wasn't his affair—that his life was in a different place—but nothing seemed to work. He couldn't shake the premonition that, try as he may, his old country would suck him back in and make him finish what he'd started.

He turned at the sound of the opening door, and smiled grimly at Chloe, who ventured out into the cold. "I know you're not feeling well, Brother Birmingham," she said. "Truly, I will not be offended if you would like to go home."

"But isn't your mother planning a lively round of charades?"

"Are you really interested in staying here for a lively round of charades?" The smile was wry, and not unkind.

"Truthfully, I think I could use some rest."

"Then rest you must. I'll tell my mother you've taken ill, and we will see you at church on Sunday."

He took Chloe's hand in his own and pressed it gratefully. "Please tell your mother that dinner was wonderful. You're a treasure of a woman, Miss Clark."

She inclined her head. "It's kind of you to say so."

He left the home after she went back inside, acknowledging his own cowardice. He was more than happy to let Chloe make his excuses for him, and even more pathetic was the fact that he knew his excuse of "needing rest" was a farce. Rest was the last thing he needed, and was most likely the last thing he'd find until he came to some sort of resolution concerning his future.

When he had arrived in the Utah valley, he'd thought to never leave again. Now, it was as though a giant hand was pulling him eastward, and he didn't want to go. When he arrived at his home, a short two-block distance from the Clark cabin, he sat down at the table within. Shrugging out of his winter coat, he draped it over the back of the chair and picked up his pen, determined to finish the letter he'd begun earlier in the day.

He read over what he'd already written:

Luke,

I received your letter, and am glad to hear that all is well with the Boston Birminghams. It's nice to know that some things stay the same—Anne is still her usual, mysterious self, Camille is keeping the suitors at bay until they're worthy of her, and Robert is still dreaming of eventual military glory. I'm sorry to hear that Jimmy has been ill, but glad he's on the mend.

Ben dipped his pen in the ink bottle and continued:

Cousin, now that the niceties are covered, I must admit to feeling a severe amount of trepidation over recent political events. I'm glad to know things are still progressing along with the movement—once again I urge you to use caution when out with Garrison and the others (fine advice coming from me, is it not?). You know full well that The Cause is not one embraced by the majority. Please do not misunderstand me—I support you wholeheartedly, but this is a dangerous business you are about, believe it from one who knows only too well.

I feel restless, Luke, and angry, and am at a loss to explain it. Sometimes I feel as though I've been angry my whole life. I feel a sense of urgency that I cannot define, and it will not let me sleep at night . . .

He put the pen down, unable to form the words that adequately described his turbulent emotions. Finally, growing frustrated, he gripped the pen again and finished the letter:

I hope this letter finds you still well, and that you will write again soon. You mentioned hearing Frederick Douglass speak again—I should love to hear the details, if you can remember. I know I shall never forget the time I visited you in Boston and was privileged to meet the man. It set me on a path that changed my life, and although it has been drastic, I'd do it all again, without second thought. My only regret is that I failed.

Sincerely, Ben.

He placed the pen carefully next to the inkwell and pursed his lips in thought. He couldn't put his finger on the source of his discontent, but he knew that he would shortly be a candidate for bedlam if he wasn't soon able to banish it. The trouble was, it had been so long since he had felt at peace that he couldn't determine when it had been. He had never been happy at Bentley, he had felt a small measure of contentment upon his arrival in Utah, but ghosts from the past still dogged his footsteps.

He rose from the table and ground the heels of his hands into his tired eyes. Pulling his shirt from his breeches, he made his way into the small bedroom that adjoined the living room. Perhaps, tonight, he would find some peace in sleep.

***

Ruth sat by her mama's side as she worked the cotton. "But why ain't we in the big house anymo', Mama?"

Her mother shrugged her shoulders, her fine-featured face void of expression. "Ain't no concern of yours, Ruthie. Hush now."

"But mama, I likes it best inside! It ain't so bloomin' hot in there!"

"Massah takin' a likin' to your ma, that's why, little Ruthie," offered Ruth's aunt, Iris. "The mistress don' like it none."

Ruth's mother glared at her sister. "Iris, hold your tongue!"

Iris shrugged. "It be true, Lily, and you know it. You be lucky if you don' get up and sold . . ."

How prophetic those words had been, Ruth thought as she rose wearily from her bed, shaking the last dregs of the dream. Her heart hurt. It was as though she had been a child again, safe at her mother's side. Not one week after that ill-fated conversation, Lily had been sold from the cotton plantation in Louisiana, where Ruth was forced to stay behind, to a plantation in Georgia, belonging to her master's brother.

Ruth never saw her mother again. A year after her separation from her mother, she, herself, was placed on the auction block and purchased by one Percy Matthews from Charleston, South Carolina, as a gift for his daughter, Sarah. *So close and yet so far away,* Ruth mused as she pulled her work dress over her head and settled it into place, reaching for her pinafore and donning it as well. Only one state separated Ruth from her mother, and in all the years since she had been Matthews property, she had never seen her mother or any other family members, for that matter.

Ruth made her way to the main house to see that the fires were stoked in the parlors the Birminghams would first occupy when they arose; she gave instructions to the house slaves as to which carpets needed to be beaten and which rooms were next on the list for dusting. She passed a slave girl who was heavy with child and envied the younger woman's relationship with her husband, whom Sarah had allowed her to marry not a year before. Ruth's memories of her own love were painful, and watching the girl was like looking into a mirror of the past.

She had loved once, had married one of the field hands with Sarah's blessing, only to lose him a scant month before the birth of their daughter to a deadly fever that swept through the plantation like wildfire. That she had been spared death seemed a mockery. Only her love for her child, whom Sarah had allowed her to name Lily, after her mother, had kept her from taking her own life.

It was destined to be a day of painful memories, Ruth supposed as she straightened young Angel's pinafore and instructed her to dust the library. Lily had died while giving birth to Rose, a second unwanted child, fathered by a white overseer who was also to die not a year later from malaria. Ruth had harbored no love at all for Mary and Rose's father, that much was true, but after losing Lily, her two little granddaughters became Ruth's strength, just as their mother had in her infancy.

And now here they were, years later, with Mary turning seventeen and Rose eleven. Ruth cast an eye about her as she left the main house and walked the short distance to the cookhouse. She wished, with all her heart for a moment, that she were in possession of her own little patch of land. She didn't need the splendor of the Birmingham mansion, didn't care for the meadows or rice fields—all she really wanted was a patch of earth to call her own, to plant vegetables and flowers, perhaps alongside a small, white-washed cottage furnished with comfortable chairs and beds. She wished to be paid for her work. She wished her husband were still alive.

Shaking her head, she chided herself. *Ruth, you know better than to let your thoughts get the best of you. Get hold of yourself now, girl!* She would never know the freedom her brothers and sisters to the North enjoyed, would never know the joy of admitting to literacy, of tending her own garden patch and dusting her precious fripperies. She had tried escape once, and paid the price. She would never again endanger Mary and Rose with an attempt at escape, and the thought of leaving them behind tore at her heart.

She would live as she always had, tending to someone else's needs, someone else's home, someone else's life, and never her own.

CHAPTER 8

"I now leave, not knowing when, or whether ever, I may return, with a task before me greater than that which rested upon Washington. Without the assistance of that Divine Being who ever attended him, I cannot succeed. With that assistance, I cannot fail. Trusting in Him who can go with me and remain with you and be everywhere for good, let us confidently hope that all will yet be well. To His care commending you, as I hope in your prayers you will commend me, I bid you an affectionate farewell."
—Abraham Lincoln, embarking for Washington, D.C., from Illinois

***

Washington, D.C.
4 March, 1861

The morning was cold and windy. Hundreds of people, however, flocked to the front lawn of the capitol building, the dome of which was still incomplete. "Adam Jones" was in attendance, wishing for the hundredth time that her hair wasn't always an issue. There was simply too much of it, and she wished she dared lop off the long tresses that were pinned tightly to her head, causing her undue discomfort.

Bringing herself back to the task at hand, she surveyed the crowd, jotting notes in a small book and trying to gauge the mood of those gathered. Adding to her strain on this particular day was the fact that her family was gathered on the capitol lawn as well, and she'd had a devil of a time trying to make her excuses earlier as to why she couldn't just leave the hotel with the rest of them to attend the inauguration. "Because I must dress like a boy" was an explanation she didn't think would be welcomed.

As she wandered among the people, she noted faces she'd only seen from afar or in photos in newspapers and books. Everyone in Washington was out to hear what the new president would finally have to say about the current state of affairs in the country, and Anne noted with interest the comments she overheard as she milled around the throng.

There were sharpshooters positioned in every window and upon the neighboring rooftops, and cannon placed on the front lawn in anticipation of trouble. Lincoln had as many enemies in the capitol as he had supporters, and the precautions were an obvious reminder. She passed the overweight, gout-stricken Mexican war hero Winfield Scott and choked back a horrified laugh at his comments. "I'll manure the slopes of Arlington with the blood of any who dares disrupt the proceedings here today," he stated with unequivocal, duty-bound fervor to those in close earshot. Anne jotted another note to herself with a satisfied smile. Her column would be rich with quotes and sentiments from the day's events.

The inauguration eventually found itself underway, and Anne observed with the objective eye of a reporter. She moved slowly, quietly through the crowd, observing not only the citizens, but the principal players as well.

Lincoln began to speak to the gathered crowd. He spoke first of his determination to hold the Union together, and then specifically addressed the South.

"In your hands, my dissatisfied countrymen, and not in mine, is the momentous issue of civil war . . .We are not enemies, but friends. We must not be enemies. Though passion may have strained, it must not break our bonds of affection. The mystic chords of memory, stretching from every battlefield and patriot grave, to every living heart and hearthstone, all over this broad land, will yet swell the chorus of the Union, when again touched, as surely they will be, by the better angels of our nature."

Anne scribbled as quickly as she could while the tall man spoke, wishing he would go back a bit and repeat what he'd said so she could be sure she transcribed it correctly. He was clearly a gifted speaker, and his eloquence rang forth not only in the words themselves, but also in the tone with which they were delivered.

When Lincoln finished speaking, Chief Justice Roger Taney rose to stand with him and swore him in as the sixteenth President of the United States. Ironic, Anne mused, that the very man who had handed down the controversial Dred Scott decision, which had sparked dismay and outrage in the North, should be the man to swear in the first U.S. president who openly admitted abhorring slavery, and who had vowed in times past to stop its expansion, if not demand its immediate expulsion from all states.

Anne worked her way toward the front of the crowd to get as good a look at the two men as possible. Taney was aging, his jowls hanging from his thin face. Lincoln himself was every bit as peculiar as folks had made him out to be. He was tall and thin, his nose and brow prominent, his eyes penetrating, even from a distance. It was impossible from her vantage point down on the lawn for Anne to see with complete clarity, but the air about her was charged, both from the presence of the tall man on the stand, as well as the energy of the crowd behind her back. It was an occasion of momentous import; she felt it in her bones.

When Lincoln completed the oath, Anne was jostled from behind by a person who had stumbled forward by mistake. She glanced over her shoulder to see her brother, Luke, who had apparently pushed forward, as she had, for a better view of Lincoln. Turning her head to one side, she waved a hand absently at his quick apology for having bumped her, and moved to her left, allowing the crowd to swallow her as she walked.

What were the odds she'd encounter her own brother, for heaven's sake? Her luck was running short, and she knew it. She had managed her charade for quite awhile, and it was only a matter of time before someone in her family discovered her activities. Would they mind so terribly much? After all, her mother was a bright woman, determined that her daughters use their brains as well as their feminine wiles (for all the good that tutelage had done Camille), so perhaps she wouldn't fall apart with a fit of the vapors should she discover that her oldest daughter routinely dressed as a boy and went running about town. Anne snorted lightly at the thought of her mother falling prostrate with a fit of vapors over anything, and shifted her thoughts to her father.

He might not look with as much patience on her disguise, she concluded with a slight wince. He was fairly traditional, and had mentioned on more than one occasion that she could have her pick of Boston's finest suitors if she would but choose one. The problem was, however, not one she cared to explain to her father. How should a young woman tell her sire that of all the men in a very large city, she hadn't yet met one she wouldn't run roughshod all over? And that she found herself unable to respect a man she could trample underfoot? His response would most likely be that she should soften her personality and attempt to become a bit more demure. As if such a thing were possible.

Anne shook her head clear of her musings and again glanced about the crowd, hoping to avoid any further collisions with her family members. When she actually did spot a familiar face a few moments later, she did so with a small exclamation of surprise. She had come across the one person, other than her editor, and George, the family groom, who knew of her disguise.

Isabelle Webb was an employee of the famed Allan Pinkerton, private investigator. His first female employee, Kate Warne, had come to him looking for work, and promised him that she would be able to breech certain social fortresses that he, as a man, could not. Indeed, her words proved true, and he had hired a few other women as well. He was radical in that he employed women to aid in his work, but his willingness to gamble had paid off, and handsomely.

One of those women now stood before Anne, grinning broadly. "Why, Adam Jones! I hardly recognized you!" She looped her arm through Anne's and began to stroll toward the left of the capitol moving into a less densely populated area.

"It's good to see you too, Isabelle!" Anne smiled at her friend, wanting to throw her arms around the other woman in surprised glee, but suppressed the impulse for fear of giving away her masculine disguise. She glanced at her friend, whose eyes were dancing in delight, and her heart registered the warmth she had always associated with the young woman. They had been classmates together at a prominent girls' school in Boston, and Isabelle was one she knew she could trust with the knowledge of her clandestine career.

When they moved away from the crowd, Isabelle murmured in an undertone, "I've never seen you in your work attire, Anne. It suits you." Her smile was infectious.

"I'm a bit dismayed that you recognized me so readily, though," Anne admitted. "If you knew me on sight, and you haven't seen me for three years, then my family will know me for certain!"

"Then you must take care to keep your distance." She laughed. "If you were anyone else, I might worry. I hardly need to caution you, that's for certain. I keep telling you that you should move to Chicago and work with me for Pinkerton. He's really very agreeable, you know."

"I'm sure he is. Luckily for me, however, Jacob is every bit as agreeable."

"Is he still letting you write your column as you choose?"

"Yes, thankfully. He edits very little."

"Imagine that. And you a woman." Isabelle's tone was dry.

Anne laughed. "Luke likes to keep the family abreast of the American Anti-Slavery Society's newest members, and he mentioned that Jacob attended the weekly meeting and that he stayed later for the Women's Rights Society meeting that followed."

"Well, then, I suppose you're no worse off for the wear with him. Funny, isn't it, Anne—the lengths to which we must go in order to maintain our professions? Your brother mentions your employer in passing, having no idea how closely associated you are with the man!" Isabelle huffed a sigh. "Well, should you decide you ever would like a different experience, I'll whisper good things about you in Pinkerton's ear."

"Speaking of Pinkerton, he's here, I assume? I had heard he was hired to escort Lincoln into Washington."

"Yes, well, actually, he was hired originally by one of our clients, the Philadelphia, Wilmington, and Baltimore Railroad. They suspected secessionists were planning to cut the tracks in Baltimore in order to isolate the capitol. What Pinkerton discovered instead was an assassination plot." She dropped her voice to a barely audible whisper. "You wouldn't believe how many Southern sympathizers there are right here in the North. It's rabid with anti-Lincoln sentiment, and the man's lucky to be alive. Kate, herself, played a huge part in getting him into the city unscathed."

"Shawl and all, eh?" Anne's smile was sympathetic. The papers had virtually crucified Lincoln for entering the Union capitol posing as an invalid, wearing a shawl. Southern political cartoonists, and several Northern ones as well, took great delight in portraying the new president as a weak grandmother.

"Yes, shawl and all. That shawl saved his life." Isabelle scowled. "They can mock him all they want to, but it would have been lunacy to try it any other way."

"How on earth did Pinkerton uncover the assassination plot?"

Isabelle cast Anne a sidelong glance. "Confidentially?"

Anne grinned. "Of course."

At Isabelle's dubious expression, Anne added, "I promise."

"Well, the railroad's master mechanic told Pinkerton that he heard that the son of a 'distinguished citizen' had taken an oath with some others to assassinate Lincoln before he got to Washington. This person lives in Baltimore, where Lincoln was to have changed trains, going by carriage from the Calvert Street depot to Camden Station.

"Pinkerton did what he does best, and working with Timothy Webster, found that the plot was designed for Lincoln to be shot at the Camden Station as a prelude to a wondrous rebel invasion of Washington. So Allan sent Kate Warne to New York to warn Lincoln's advisors of the planned attack."

"Was Kate in Chicago at the time?"

"No, she had been in Baltimore with Pinkerton and Webster. The president, meanwhile, had been on a tour of several cities on his way from Illinois. I'm assuming you've been reading about that in the papers?"

At Anne's nod, Isabelle continued. "So the president was told of the assassination plot when he reached Philadelphia, and Pinkerton told us later that Lincoln appeared more sad than frightened. He insisted on completing a couple of the scheduled activities in Harrisburg the following afternoon, but agreed that afterward he would follow Pinkerton's advice.

"So rather than take the train from Harrisburg to Baltimore, which was what the conspirators were expecting, Pinkerton escorted Lincoln back to Philadelphia, and from there, they made plans to board a train for Baltimore. Kate, meanwhile, had secured an entire train car to transport her 'invalid brother' to Maryland. Allan escorted the president from dinner and they met Kate at the train station, where she acted as his sister in a loud voice, in case any should overhear. Once in Baltimore, they were able to get Lincoln to Washington, despite a two-hour delay, and I say it was extremely well done, and showed wisdom on Lincoln's part that he took their advice. He would most certainly already be dead if he hadn't."

"You'll get no argument from me," Anne remarked, her tone grim as she looked about them, again taking in the presence of the sharpshooters and cannon. "He'd best watch his back at all times. I'm beginning to wonder if he doesn't have more enemies than friends."

"I'd be inclined to agree, if he hadn't just won a national election. You can't emerge victorious if you have nothing but enemies. He has many, to be sure, but I have to hope his supporters will rally, now that he's actually here."

"I wouldn't say he has nothing but enemies, but the only reason he won this election was because the Democratic party was so split. I wonder if he understands what he faces."

"Oh, I daresay he does. I met with him briefly when he arrived. He's very intense in his regard, extremely focused in his thoughts. His gaze is at once penetrating and yet somehow very tender."

Anne halted their progress and looked at her friend. "You like him then? He gives you a sense of hope?"

"Yes, I like him very much," Isabelle answered without hesitation. "He gives me much hope. For all that he said little after the election was over, his words here today, and my earlier meeting with him have lifted my spirits immensely. I trust his commitment to the country."

"And did you meet Mrs. Lincoln? How did you find her?"

"Yes, I did meet her, and I found her snooty. It may be a rush to judgment on my part, but Kate told me Lincoln was once overheard to say that the Todds like themselves so much, that while God made do with one "d," the Todds demanded two. I fear that that anecdote, coupled with my brief meeting with her the other night, left me with few positive feelings for the woman."

"And where do the Todds call home?"

"Lexington, Kentucky. Prominent slaveholders, they are. Interesting, isn't it?"

"Indeed."

"Still, if she can support her husband in his frightful task, I'll not besmirch her character. Overmuch, anyway." The engaging grin was back, and Anne found one of her own to match.

"Your profession has made you cynical, Isabelle."

"I'm afraid it has. One can witness mankind's idiocy for only so long before a jaded view of the world begins to emerge."

The women were still strolling, when Anne stopped short, halting Isabelle's forward momentum as well. "That bodes no good," Anne murmured, nodding forward.

On the ground, waiting to be hoisted into place once the capitol was complete, was a statue of a blindfolded woman, holding the scales of justice and mercy.

Isabelle raised a brow. "Rather fitting that she's prostrate on her back, given the current state of affairs, wouldn't you say?"

***

Utah Territory
4 March, 1861

Half a world away, Ben Birmingham stood on South Temple in Salt Lake City in front of the Beehive House and watched the grand processional parade up the street. The street was filled with horses and carriages, and people joyfully celebrating the inauguration of the new president.

The parade was a mile long and consisted of both military and civilian folk marching and giving speeches, interspersed with ceremonial artillery firing. Ben eyed the proceedings with a sense of hope. It was the first inkling of such he'd had since Christmas. Perhaps his recent sense of gloom and doom was misplaced. If the current mood of the crowd was any indication, there was much to be hopeful for.

Ben turned as someone jostled against his elbow. It was Sister Clark. "Now, young man," she said, her breath coming out in a puff against the cold air, "when are you going to come over and join us again for dinner? You know that invitation has been extended for two weeks, now."

Ben smiled at the woman. Sister Clark had not given up on her intentions for Chloe. "I haven't wanted to impose," he said.

"Nonsense! A body wouldn't issue an invitation if it were an imposition! Now, I insist. This Friday, you simply must join us."

"Well, good lady, you are most persuasive. You propose a time and I shall be at your front door."

The woman beamed. "Wonderful! Oh, how I do love that southern drawl of yours!" she exclaimed with a small clap of her gloved hands. "We shall plan on seeing you at six o'clock. Oh, and do you plan to stay here today for the fireworks?"

"Of course. I would hate to miss the fireworks." He had to smile at the woman's enthusiasm.

"They are going to be quite spectacular, you know. I have it on good authority that . . ."

Ben listened with half an ear as Sister Clark filled him in on the firework details that supposedly nobody else was privy to, his mind wandering to places far away, places he hoped would see safety under the watch of a new president.

CHAPTER 9

"... I understood the pathway from slavery to freedom ...
Though conscious of the difficulty of learning without a teacher, I set
out with high hope, and a fixed purpose, at whatever cost of trouble,
to learn how to read. The very decided manner with which [my
master] spoke ... served to convince me that he was deeply sensible of
the truths he was uttering. It gave me the best assurance that I might
rely with the utmost confidence on the results which, he said, would
flow from teaching me to read."
—*Frederick Douglass*

***

Charleston, South Carolina—Bentley Plantation
4 March, 1861

Joshua Birmingham sat outside his small shack and watched
the proceedings with a blank expression on his face. The Bentley
slaves were taking a moment to quietly revel in the inauguration
of Abraham Lincoln. The small bonfire on which they roasted
their rabbit supper, (a treat, to be sure!) flickered in the darkness,
drawing Joshua's gaze to it again and again. He had obtained the
rabbits by trading his services for a week at the Charlesworth's
plantation, with Miz Sarah's approval. The only other time the
slaves ever enjoyed such a rich repast was once a year at hog
slaughtering time.

If one were to climb a tree and look down upon all of the
Bentley slave quarters, he would see this very scene repeated
several times down the rows of shacks the slaves called home. Mr.
Jackson, the overseer, had already demanded an explanation for
the small celebrations; Joshua had told him that they were again
glorying in the fact that South Carolina had seceded from her
oppressors and formed a new and wondrous country. The white
man was not stupid, and he had eyed Joshua with a look of
distaste so intense that Joshua had almost given into an insane
impulse to laugh in Jackson's face. If they were on any plantation
but this one, perhaps, Jackson would have taken his whip to
Joshua's bare back for daring such impertinence with his outright
sarcasm. Miz Sarah was very firm in her insistence that she be told
if the slaves were whipped, and why. She demanded that they not
be harshly disciplined on a whim, and the overseer apparently
found enjoyment from his employ. He contented himself with
shaking a finger once in Joshua's face before turning his back on
the celebrations and heading for his own cabin.

Joshua knew his days with the man were numbered. It
wouldn't be long before Jackson's temper finally snapped and he
threw Mistress Birmingham's admonitions overboard. He would
attempt to flay the skin from Joshua's hide, and Joshua knew that
he would fight back. It might mean his death, but so be it.

The sound of full voices rose in harmony, echoing similar
songs heard throughout the slave quarters. *We are climbing Jacob's
ladder* . . . Joshua's heart ached. This life was no life at all. He
looked at the people around him, people with whom he had
shared his earthly years (he supposed them to be twenty-four but
he couldn't be sure) and felt all the emotions he saw daily in their
eyes. Anger. Frustration. Sorrow. Joy at the quaint antics of a
child, only to be quickly replaced with a weary resignation and
acknowledgement that all happiness found in slave life was super-
ficial and fleeting.

The election of Black Lincoln had given many of the Bentley
slaves hope for the future. Hope that someday their lot might not

be as it currently was, as it had been for their parents and grandparents—that all the rhetoric in the New England North might somehow find its way south and offer the oppressed that which they sought above all else. Joshua clamped his lips together each time one of his fellow brothers or sisters dared whisper of such hope. It was empty. Lincoln hadn't promised to free the slaves; indeed, he had promised leaders in the South that he wouldn't interfere with slavery where it already existed. Rather, his purpose was to preserve the Union and still keep slavery from spreading into new territories that would eventually join the Union as states.

It was true, Lincoln had gone on record in his days as a senator and before that, stating unequivocally his abhorrence of slavery; however, the new President's recent stance on prohibiting the expansion of slavery did Joshua Birmingham no good. All it meant to him was that if Jeffrey and Sarah Birmingham at some future point were possessed with an idiotic notion to leave their wealthy plantation and venture west into untamed territory, they would not be permitted to own slaves once there.

Of course, there was always Dred Scott to consider. Joshua shook his head slightly and moved his gaze away from the flames and into the dirt at his feet. Dred Scott had lived for years in a free state, and was still denied his freedom, in the end, by the same man who had sworn in the new President that very morning. The Birminghams could, in theory, take their slaves west, and, given the precedent set in the Scott case, Joshua still might not be a free man.

He spied Ruth coming toward him in the darkness, her features silhouetted by the light from the fire. He smiled. Ruth's good nature and wisdom were often his salvation.

"Now, why would a handsome young man be sittin' here all alone, I wonder?"

"Just waiting for my good aunt to spare me some attention."

"And what are you thinking about, Joshua?" Ruth sat next to him on the step, shaking her faded brown skirts lightly to dislodge the dust that had gathered about the hem.

"Nothing much, I suppose."

Her voice dropped to a low murmur. "Well, I did want to mention that if a person were looking to get his hands on some new reading material, he ought to look in the usual place."

Joshua nodded. "I appreciate that, Aunt Ruth. Very much."

She nodded back, once, in reply. "You're still minding your tongue with the others, I hope?"

"Yes, ma'am. When I's in the stables and fields, I's just a po' slave." The shifting in language was a necessity for Joshua. When he spoke to his fellow slaves in the literate manner he had learned while raised by the side of the master's son, he was often met with a wide variety of reactions, spanning from amused, to irritated, to jealous, to fearful. The Bentley slaves were not allowed to learn to read and write. Joshua had once been an insider, however, and had learned from the master's child. But those days were long since past, and Joshua now worked outside with the rest, who often resented him his many years in the main house, and thought he was seeking to place himself above his station.

Things might have been different if Ben had been able to stay. Once the boys had grown into men, Joshua had become Ben's personal valet. He had watched Ben's friction with his family escalate into unmanageable proportions, until circumstances forced him far from Bentley's borders. He missed his old friend, but what was worse—he envied him with a passion that nearly ate him alive. Ben had planned to take Joshua with him when he left, but by that time, Jeffrey and Sarah Birmingham anticipated his movements and had guarded Joshua like dogs, neatly preventing his departure with their oldest son.

"You must be thinking of Ben," Ruth observed when Joshua fell quiet.

"And how is it that you read minds, Aunt?"

"You always look like that when you think of him." She patted his hand softly. "Perhaps you will join him someday in that wild, untamed west."

"Please, dear woman, don't tell me you believe this nonsense." He gestured to the others, milling about and exchanging expressions of hope. "I expect it of the others, but you?"

She shrugged. "It helps me sleep at night. Proverbs 13:12, Joshua. 'Hope deferred maketh the heart sick.'"

"Then I fear my heart must be as dead as a horseshoe."

"That's unfortunate. Even young Emily has been cautiously optimistic."

Joshua smiled. "That does say something significant, then." The world had never seen a bigger cynic than Emily Birmingham. She had mourned her brother's loss for years, probably mourned him even still. He knew she managed to get letters to him on occasion, but he also knew, because she had told him herself, that she was so angry with Ben that with each letter she sent, she was filled with a resentment so profound it kept her awake at night.

Emily had found Joshua in the stables, grooming the horses, not quite two weeks ago, and had sought him out as the company she missed in her brother. It had often been thus in the past five years; Emily and Joshua found comfort in conversation because each reminded the other of Ben. Of course, if Sarah had known of their odd friendship through the years, she would have locked Emily in her room.

"It wasn't really his fault, you know," Joshua had said to her that day in the stables. "He had to leave. He burned the bridge behind himself so thoroughly that he had no choice."

"He could have taken us with him," she insisted stubbornly.

Joshua had laughed then, though he tried to soften it when he took a good look at her face. "You know very well he couldn't. Your parents would have had him arrested for kidnapping and theft."

She grabbed a pitchfork then, and for a moment he feared she meant to run him through with the thing. Instead, she stabbed it into the stack of hay he was distributing throughout the stalls and began doing his job for him. He wasn't surprised. It wasn't the first time she had insisted on helping him with his duties; he shrugged, knowing it wouldn't do any good to tell her it was unseemly, and taking hold of another fork, began working along-side in silence, content to let her fume in peace. After watching her for a moment, he tried another angle.

"You're an intelligent young woman, Emily. You *must* be rational."

She stopped her furious movements with a sigh and jammed the pitchfork into the earth, still clutching the handle. "I can't, Joshua. I simply cannot. He was the only one in this family who understood me—who was like me." Her eyes filmed over and she clenched her jaw, apparently angry at her display of emotion.

He sought to ease her discomfort with humor. "Aw, come now Miz Emily! You—"

"Don't you dare to call me that, Joshua! That's not funny!"

He should have known it wouldn't make her laugh. Not long ago, Emily insisted that Joshua stop calling her "Miz," or "Miss." When he had argued that even the young white men of her acquaintance addressed her with some form of respect when they socialized, she had replied, "But they don't *have* to, Joshua. You do. It isn't right."

As her irritation with his jest eased, he murmured, "You have Clara," hoping to give her a smidgen of comfort. "You must keep your head about you for her sake. You are to her what Ben was to you. Not to mention Rose. Do you know what would become of her if you weren't here to help her? She wouldn't have nearly the opportunities for learning that she does now."

"For all the good it might do her! You were educated as well as Ben, and look at where you are now!" Emily gestured with her arms outstretched, still clutching the handle of the pitchfork. "In the stable! You should be up north with Frederick Douglass! You're every bit as articulate as is he, and think of the good you could do!"

"Emily."

"Truly!" Her eyes took on a wild glow. "Perhaps I can help you get to him!"

He cast a nervous glance over his shoulder. "Emily, lower your voice." He looked into her eyes, hoping to find some semblance of reason within.

She finally met his direct gaze and he glimpsed a flicker of defeat. He breathed an inaudible sigh of relief. She still harbored the impetuousness of youth. When she was able to shed it, and instead adopt the wisdom and rationale of an adult, she would be a force with which to be reckoned. Then her rashness would be tempered with sound judgment and he wouldn't have to worry that she would get herself into trouble. Ben, for all that his brave plan had failed, had attempted it with vision and with a great deal of knowledge and careful planning. He had failed only because he had been betrayed from within. Who had known of his plan, and had told Sarah, was still a mystery, although Joshua had his suspicions.

He brought his thoughts to the present, and his "Aunt." He gestured toward the people still situated around the fire, singing. "There are those who would defend slavery on the grounds that the slaves sing. 'They sing because they are happy with their lot in life.'"

Ruth smiled. "Look at what a little education will do for a man, Joshua. I'd say it's made you mighty frustrated."

He glanced at her sharply. "Would you rather that I had remained ignorant? Would I be any happier?"

She patted his knee. "Don't go workin' yourself into a lather, dear boy. I was making a simple observation."

"How do you stand it, Aunt Ruth?" His voice was barely audible. "How can we stand this? For how many more years? Until we are freed only in death?"

Her expression was troubled. "I don't know. But what I do know is that morning comes quickly, and there are many of us with chores still to do." With that, she rose, and wandered to the others gathered around the fire, gently reminding them of the washing and mending that must be done before bed. There was no time during the day to tend to such tasks, and it often meant that the slaves worked late into the night and were afforded little of their much-needed rest.

Joshua glanced down the row of slave quarters, each shack looking just like the next. He supposed he should be grateful.

There was at least a cot or marginally comfortable pallet to be found in each shack, although how many had to share those cots and pallets was another story altogether. Still, many slaves on other plantations were not allowed even that much. Ah, yes, Bentley was a veritable slave paradise.

***

Emily stood on the balcony just off her bedroom and turned her face toward the evening breeze, appreciating the fresh air upon her skin. Looking out over the vast plantation, her vantage point afforded her a view of Bentley in its entirety. The firelight flickered in the slave quarters, and Emily wondered what Mary, Ruth, and Joshua were doing.

She shook her head with a wince. More likely than not, they were washing their meager clothing and doing chores when they would have liked to settle down for the night. She turned her gaze to the far end of the plantation and the vast rice fields, the grassy meadows, and the plethora of small buildings surrounding the house that served to keep the plantation in full operation.

The cookhouse was closest to the main house where Emily stood. She glanced down upon it, recalling the many hours of her life spent in it by Ruth's side, dogging her footsteps and chattering at her endlessly, asking questions—so many questions. She looked out to the stables where Joshua's humble quarters were, now that he was no longer privileged to be the valet and companion to the master's firstborn. Her heart ached. Emily envisioned Joshua's handsome face and large, muscular frame, and cursed the fates that had brought him into the world as someone's property.

She tipped her head to one side, thinking about the young man. She loved Joshua, easily as much as she loved Ben. Each time her mother spoke of Emily's impending quests for suitors, Emily could think of no man she would rather spend time with than Joshua. Her lips twisted into a pained smirk, as she envisioned sharing those feelings with Sarah.

Reaching her hands upward to release her long braids, she ran her fingers through the tangled hair and again turned her face into the breeze, her gaze following the turn of her head and falling upon the smithing shack, the tool and drying sheds, and the smokehouse. Lastly, she looked at the slave quarters that stood in neat rows, a path running down the middle and snaking its way around like a small road that connected all of the plantation buildings.

It was like a small town, really, entirely self-sufficient and entirely lucrative. The Birminghams were wealthy people. Looking upon the whole of it, Emily wished with all her heart for a moment that it belonged to her, Ruth, Mary, Rose, and Joshua. Then they could pay people to live and work there as they chose, in houses that were comfortable and well stocked, and she could appreciate the beauty that was her family legacy.

Her eyes smarted with tears, and her gaze again fell to the slave shacks. She wanted to love her home. It was beautiful, genteel, and moved at a slow, leisurely pace. She loved taking her books into the gardens and finding shade under the beauty of a lush tree, losing herself in the pages, surrounded by the warmth of the sun and the coolness of the shade.

She hadn't always been so discontent. Ben's leaving was the catalyst for a maelstrom of emotion that had her questioning everything she was surrounded by. Ben had wanted the gift of freedom for people both he and Emily loved very much, and despite her youth, she had begun to see their world through his eyes.

Clearing her throat, she straightened her shoulders and her resolve. The place may well have been beautiful, but the people who owned it were not. It wasn't right, and Emily knew it to the marrow of her bones. She turned her back on the lush tapestry of the plantation and returned to her bedroom, clicking the French doors firmly in place behind her.

CHAPTER 10

"I pray you, abolitionists, still to adhere to the truth. Do not get impatient; do not become exasperated . . . do not make yourselves familiar with the idea that blood must flow. Perhaps blood will flow—God knows, I do not: but it shall not flow through any counsel of mine."
—*William Lloyd Garrison*

***

Boston, Massachusetts
10 March, 1861

Luke Birmingham walked the streets of Boston's commercial center on his lunch hour, his gaze raised toward the tops of the buildings. The country's current state of affairs was on the mind of nearly every person he passed. People could be heard discussing the new president, the seceding Southern states, and their own perceptions of the whole affair while on the streets, in the shops, and in places of business.

It had often been thus; the entire country boasted of several newspapers and periodicals that continually espoused the virtues held by their owners and editors. As a result, the populace was provided with plenty of fodder for thought, and more often than not, when people thought, their opinions were soon to follow via their mouths.

Luke always found it pleasurable to hear those who may not have formerly been advocates for abolitionism speak in favor of it. It was with a certain amount of discouragement, however, that he often heard people say that they chose to respect their Southern friends' rights and wished to simply leave things as they were.

He eventually found himself standing at 221 Washington Street, the home of the abolitionist paper, *The Liberator*. Making his way inside, he sought out the presence of the paper's creator and editor, William Lloyd Garrison. When the man came forward, he greeted Luke with his ready smile.

"How are you feeling today, sir?" Luke asked as he warmly shook Garrison's hand.

"Never better," was the reply.

Luke knew better. Garrison suffered from chronic bronchitis and had been forced to cancel his speaking engagements of late. Indeed, he hadn't spoken publicly for months, and Luke had missed it. Perhaps he was not the greatest orator the country had seen, but Garrison still was Luke's personal favorite. Possibly it was the look of utter conviction in the man's eye, representing the fervor he held for the things he preached. There could be no doubt in a person's mind that Garrison believed every word he spoke and wrote. More to the point, Luke believed he was right.

"Will we be hearing from you again soon, then?"

"Well, perhaps in a while. I've been advised to save my strength for the editorials, so this has been much of my domain, of late." Garrison gestured to the office behind him with a smile.

He was balding, thin in the face, roughly sixty years in age, and had an intensity of gaze that was at once riveting and intimidating. His countenance was softened, however, by a tenderness that at times belied his straightforward speech. He was, quite possibly, the man that Luke admired most of any he could think of.

As they chatted and walked among the presses that delivered the weekly anti-slavery paper to thousands of subscribers, Luke was again struck, as he had been many times before, with the goodness and integrity of the man. Garrison had always preached the necessity of maintaining peace, while appealing to the conscience of greater America as it regarded the issue of slavery, and had veered from that course but once, and that was on the occasion of John Brown's death, when the country had been in an uproar, divided in opinion, over his execution.

Fearing that the abolition community, which he had helped shape, would think him weakening in his stance on slavery, he had acknowledged the fact that oftimes, issues with a valid moral base, such as the country's own Revolution, are justifiably resolved in bloodshed, but he hadn't repeated his words since, instead reverting to his former and longtime stance of achieving abolition peacefully.

It was that stance that Luke most admired. Although Garrison himself, and other prominent leaders of the day were justifiably frustrated with a political party that claimed to be anti-slavery yet continued to offer compromises that did little, if anything, to force an eventual end to the abomination, they kept their dignity, and their heads, about them.

Luke watched Garrison's expressive face as they chatted, finding it hard to believe that nearly twenty-five years before, Garrison had been hustled through the streets and nearly lynched by a mob that had opposed the gathering of a female anti-slavery society. Garrison had been in support of the women, and the mob had attempted to use him as a sacrificial lamb when the women had been escorted to safety. Saved by two muscular, unlikely rescuers who took pity on him in his plight, he found safety that night in the city jail.

Garrison and *The Liberator*, aside from the influence of his own mother, were largely the reasons Luke had joined the American Anti-Slavery Society, and held such stringent views on the topic. Luke had found it ironic, when learning of Garrison's brush with death, that his life had been threatened by the very descendants of the patriots who witnessed the Boston Massacre; yet they threatened Garrison for upholding the views that their ancestors had espoused: that all men were created equal.

"Well, sir," Luke finally said upon parting, "I need to let you be about your work. I hope we see you out again frequently, and soon."

Garrison shook his hand warmly in return. "It's good to see you, Luke. Do come by the house again soon. I'm sure Franky would love to see you," he said in reference to his twelve-year-old son. "He helps me proofread, you know. He's actually getting to be quite good at it!"

Luke smiled and said his good-byes, making his way back onto the street with much on his mind. It was with some surprise that he found his musings interrupted by a soft, feminine voice.

"Did you know that Mr. Birmingham attended our last Female Anti-Slavery Society meeting?" the woman was saying to her walking companion in a stage whisper, the corner of her mouth lifted in a smile.

"Scandalous!" the woman's mother answered. "What would the rest of the menfolk have to say about that?"

Luke laughed and sketched a courtly bow to the pair. "Ladies, it's a pleasure."

Abigail Van Dyke laughed with him and smiled as he placed the ghost of a kiss first on her mother's gloved hand, then upon hers.

"And might I say I missed the pleasure of your company at that meeting, Mrs. Van Dyke."

The older woman's brow wrinkled in disappointment. "I was ill, regrettably. I shall be at the next meeting, for certain." Dolly Van Dyke's physical appearance was much like her name; she was beautifully complexioned, her facial features pleasing to the masculine eye, her stature small. Upon preliminary introduction, most would judge her delicate. Once she opened her mouth, however, and her straightforward, opinionated intellect ventured forth, that judgment invariably altered. Women like Luke's mother found Dolly to be delightful. Women like his sister, Camille, found her bookish, outspoken, and irritating. He suspected it was because Mrs. Van Dyke used words with which

Camille was unfamiliar. He tried to hide a smile at his sister's expense, but failed.

"I'm glad you're feeling better," he said to Mrs. Van Dyke, disguising the reason for his amusement. "The meeting wasn't the same without you."

Abigail, a twenty-year-younger version of her mother, tucked a stray, coffee-colored strand of hair back into her fashionable green velvet bonnet and held her hand out to Luke. "Well, since you're here, Mr. Birmingham, you may have the honor of escorting us to the bookshop. We are on a quest."

He raised a brow and stepped alongside the younger Van Dyke, offering her his arm, on which she placed a small, gloved hand. "What kind of quest?"

They proceeded at a pleasant pace, enjoying the feel of the springtime air and the clopping sound of horses' hooves on the street. "We are looking for early issues of *The Liberator*," Abigail answered.

"Have you asked Mr. Garrison?" Luke gestured back at the building they had just passed. "I'm certain he has some copies."

"Oh, he does," Dolly Van Dyke responded. "But I'm sure he'd like to keep them, and we're not interested in borrowing any issues. We'd like the old issues for our collection."

"Ah." The Van Dyke book and periodical collection was legendary amongst the American Anti-Slavery Society members. The women themselves were definitely "originals," and those who knew them well loved them for it. Mrs. Van Dyke's husband had passed away when Abigail was still an infant, and the women didn't consider themselves much worse for the wear without him. He had been controlling in the extreme, by all accounts, and upon his death, Dolly had joined the general American Anti-Slavery Society and Female Anti-Slavery Society, merely to spite the ghost of her late husband, which she was convinced still loomed heavy in the house. One week of attending the meetings, she claimed, and the oppressive presence had vanished.

"He couldn't bear to be around it," Dolly often claimed.

"Drove him plain out of what little mind he had." It was a wonder, beautiful as she was, that Dolly had never remarried. She wasn't inclined to do so, she said, and the one thing that her husband had managed to leave her, other than nerves stretched taut to the breaking point, was a substantial amount of money on which to live a comfortable existence with her young daughter.

Abigail wasn't in a hurry to get married either, it seemed, although it wasn't for want of attention from the male portion of the population. She flirted in a friendly way, but never encouraged overmuch the attention of one she definitely didn't care for. She had taken a page from her mother's book, it seemed, and was determined to avoid the kind of marriage her parents had had.

As for Luke—he had watched Abigail at Society meetings for some time now, growing more and more enchanted with her. She was a friendly young woman, though, and he couldn't assume her current banter and stroll to the bookshop meant anything significant. He certainly wouldn't mind if it did, however.

***

Not far from Luke's current position on the street below, his father sat in his offices meeting with an acquaintance who happened to run in some very influential circles in Washington, D.C.

"I'm telling you, James, you're about to see wealth like you've never imagined."

James smiled. "I *have* wealth like I've never imagined." And it was true. Growing up as the son of a poor, upstate New York farmer, James Birmingham and his brother Jeffrey never dreamed, when they were young, of the wealth they would both someday possess—one through his own efforts and a lot of good luck, and the other by marriage.

"By the time this conflict is over, you'll be able to buy and sell Boston."

James sighed a bit and leaned back in his chair, growing tired of his friend's theatrics. "Samuel, what is it you're trying not to tell me?"

Samuel Jones smiled. "You know I've been appointed aid to Senator Frankle."

James nodded.

"That means I hear a substantial amount of news."

Don't we all? James wanted to answer. With the advent of the telegraph and numerous newspapers dotting the country, the populace was informed as it had never been before. News was transmitted and printed sometimes the very day it happened, the next, at the latest.

"So what is this news you've heard?"

Samuel leaned forward in his chair, tapping the ash from the end of his cigar into an ashtray on James's desk. "The day after Lincoln took office, he received word from Major Anderson at Sumter that they have only six weeks of provisions left."

James drew in a long breath. The implications were huge. Samuel leaned back in his chair, noting the comprehension dawning on James's features. "Yes. You see? War is looming; mark my words. If Lincoln attempts to reinforce Sumter with provisions, South Carolina will fire on whatever craft they use to bring those supplies. Buchanan may have stood for it, but Lincoln won't."

James was quiet.

"And war means iron. Iron for ships, iron for guns, tools and machinery, iron for railroad tracks and cars. And you, my friend, are iron."

James nodded slowly. He had purchased, through the years, two iron pits and two foundries, and had transformed them into huge operations. In recent decades, his pits and foundries had seen an immense increase in work because of the demand for more iron and his business had quadrupled in size. He had more money that he knew what to do with. If war was indeed looming, as Samuel suggested, it would mean even more.

The problem was, James didn't necessarily feel he needed more, and he was unable to find any joy at the thought of more wealth if the reason for that increase was due to a war that would assuredly wreak havoc in his homeland. He glanced at the smug face of his friend and suddenly resented his presence in his office.

"You don't look happy, my friend! I bring you news that is of a most fortuitous good nature to you!"

"Forgive me if I find the prospect of war unappealing."

"Bah. The 'war' will not last long. What do the Southerners have but a bunch of cotton? It will not take long to squash the rebellion, I assure you. South Carolina will never know what hit her."

"I have a brother in South Carolina."

Jones had the grace to look chagrined. "Pity," he said.

"Yes."

Once Samuel Jones had finally left, in the face of James's dampened mood, James decided his business could wait. He made his way outside, located his carriage, and went home.

Once in the house, he wandered about looking for his wife. The home was running at its usual level of quiet precision, and for once he found it irritating. The children were grown, and there was no noise of running feet and boisterous laughter. Elizabeth no longer had to spend her time running after them, looking harried. Even when they had begun to make respectable money, Lizzie had insisted on caring for the children herself. "My mother did just fine without nannies," she told him once, and that was the end of it.

Where was his wife? He climbed the stairs to his bedroom, walking in to find it in its usual, pristine state, and wandered down the hallway, poking his head in and out of doorways, hoping to see someone. When he finally did, it was one of the young upstairs maids who was in the process of changing the bedding in Camille's bedroom.

"Nina," he said when the maid noticed his presence. "Have you seen Mrs. Birmingham?"

"She went into town, sir, with Miss Camille and Master Jimmy. He said he wasn't quite well enough yet for school today, so Mrs. Birmingham let him stay home."

"Do you know when they will return?"

"No, sir."

James left and went downstairs to his office and sat behind his desk, feeling despondent. When the front door finally opened some twenty minutes later, he strolled out to the entrance hall, trying to appear nonchalant.

"James! You're home already?" Elizabeth untied her bonnet and handed it, along with her light spring cloak, to Griffen, their aging butler. She took a closer look at her husband's face, her own registering an expression of mild alarm. "What's wrong? Did something happen?"

"No." He moved forward, placing a hand about his young son's shoulders. "No, I just thought it might be nice to spend some leisure time today."

"Why?" Her voice was laced with suspicion and he had to laugh.

"Is it such a surprise, Lizzie?"

"Yes, James, it is! I can't remember the last time you came home in the middle of the day."

He glanced down at his son. "Where should we go today, Jimmy?"

The boy looked up at his father in confusion. "I . . . I don't know."

"Can you think of something you would like to do that we haven't done for a long time? Or something we've never done that you'd like to try?"

Jimmy shrugged slightly. "My throat is still a bit sore . . . I was thinking it would be nice to have an ice from that store downtown . . ."

"An ice it is, then! Where is your sister?"

"She's having tea at the Sylvesters's," Elizabeth answered.

"And Robert?"

"He's in school, James."

"Well then, it's the three of us." James glanced at his wife. "Will you come?"

She stared at him for a moment. "Of course. If you'll tell me what is transpiring in that brain of yours."

"Just a sense of my own mortality, I suppose."

"Now you're frightening me."

"Nonsense." He put an arm about her shoulders and propelled her, along with Jimmy, back to the door. Calling over his shoulder to Griffen, who materialized again with the bonnet and cloak Elizabeth had just discarded, they made their way out into the sunshine.

CHAPTER 11

"God forgive us, but ours is a monstrous system."
—Mary Chestnut

***

Charleston, South Carolina—-Bentley Plantation
5 April, 1861

Emily stared at the political cartoon with huge eyes, trying valiantly to hold back a snort of laughter. She eventually lost the battle, and guffawed out loud, to the irritation of her older sister.

"I can't imagine anything that funny, Emily," Charlotte muttered with a scowl, between bites of her breakfast.

"I'm sure you can't." Emily smothered her laughter and tried to eat. She folded the paper and put it to the side of her plate.

"May I?" William, Charlotte's husband, gestured toward the paper.

"Of course," Emily replied, with an inner flicker of unease. She was easily the only member of the family who would find humor in the piece.

William studied the cartoon with a bland expression, and Emily tried to see it through his eyes. It was an image of the Governor of South Carolina and the former U.S. President, James Buchanan. The Governor was preparing to light a cannon, with a threat to do so if the President didn't withdraw federal troops from Sumter. The president was responding with a plea to please wait until he was out of office before taking action. The humor of the piece came from the fact that the cannon was pointing directly at the Governor's groin, suggesting that the artist considered any kind of action on the part of the rebel state to be suicidal.

William cleared his throat without comment and folded the paper, setting it again next to Emily's plate. "It's a bit dated, isn't it?" he finally offered.

Emily nodded. "It was run quite awhile ago in some of the major papers—before Lincoln took office, obviously. I only just received it today."

William raised one brow and tore a bite from a small roll, placing it into his mouth. "I'd wager it wasn't run in any Southern papers. I know I didn't see it."

She shrugged. "It may have been run outside the state—it's probably safe to say it didn't see the light of day in South Carolina."

"So which paper is that?" Charlotte asked, pointing a fork at the folded pages.

"It's from Boston," Emily answered.

"What are you doing receiving papers from Boston? Did you subscribe? I'm sure Mother didn't."

"She didn't. I receive things periodically from Anne."

"Cousin Anne?"

"Yes."

Charlotte scrutinized Emily with a look that had the younger girl bristling. "May I see that paper?"

"That all depends on what you plan to do with it."

"Emily, hand me the paper."

"It's mine, Charlotte."

"William."

Emily's brother-in-law glanced at her, almost apologetically, before finally gathering the folded paper and handing it across the table to his wife.

Charlotte looked at the political drawing with the same bland expression as had her husband before finally tossing it back to Emily. It landed with a small thud and skidded to a stop next to her plate. "Why would cousin Anne think you would find that interesting, Emily?"

Probably because cousin Anne knows I hate this place. "I like to keep abreast of events that occur on that end of the world as well as this. She sends me papers periodically to give me a sense of the mood in Boston."

"One might question your loyalty, Emily."

"One might."

Charlotte glanced up, her expression sharp. "You watch yourself, young lady. I'm sure Mother would find it interesting that you're receiving inflammatory nonsense from our sweet Boston relatives."

"Do you think for one minute that Mother doesn't know what goes in and out of this house, Charlotte?" Disgusted, Emily rose from her chair, leaving the remainder of her breakfast untouched. She picked up her paper and left the room without another word. The truth of the matter was, her mother didn't really know the extent of her relationship with Anne Birmingham. Emily had kept up a casual correspondence with her older cousin for nearly six months now, ever since she had received a letter from Anne asking her to describe the mood in South Carolina. Anne knew Emily to be a bright girl, the letter had stated, and she needed to pass the information on to a friend who wrote a newspaper column. She wanted feedback from the citizens who were living the transformations as they happened.

As a result, they had struck up a correspondence, and Emily had found a kindred spirit in Anne, and gladly received humorous bits of information and rhetoric in small packages, along with letters detailing the current state of affairs, both in Washington and in Anne's hometown of Boston. Sarah knew about the letters, and she hadn't said a word to Emily regarding them, but she didn't know of the nature of the relationship developing between the cousins. She didn't know that with each letter Anne sent south, she was more and more firmly aligning her young cousin's ideals with those of the New England North, both politically and morally.

Emily made her way to her bedroom, deciding that in the future, she would be sure to keep anything she received from Anne hidden well. She would also do well to mind her tongue around Charlotte, she realized with a grimace. Her efforts to be blasé and mild around her mother would get her nowhere if she bungled matters by her consistent insolence with the rest of the family.

In the dining room, Charlotte and William were continuing their meal in silence. William finally broke it by asking his wife, "Don't you think you should be careful not to alienate your sister?"

Charlotte gave him a long-suffering sigh. "And why would I care about that, William?"

"Because she reminds me of stories I've heard about Ben."

That gave Charlotte pause. She quickly brushed it off with a slight shake of her head. "She's only fifteen."

"She's almost sixteen. She's nearly ready for her coming out, and she has the soul of an adult."

Charlotte stared at her husband for a moment before her mouth quirked into a smile decidedly lacking in warmth, but carrying an overabundance of sardonic amusement. "Waxing poetic, William? How very original of you."

He shrugged and cut a small bite of sausage, forking it into his mouth. "You can say what you like, dear, but you might not want to entirely alienate yourself from that girl. If you do, she may one day catch y'all by surprise."

"'Y'all'? I find it interesting you don't include yourself in that statement, William."

At that, he laughed. "When have I ever warranted a place in this family, Charlotte? I'm nothing but your stud horse, bought and paid for, for all the good it's done."

Her cheeks flamed. "Mind your mouth!"

Again, he shrugged. "It's true, is it not?"

She stood, jostling her chair. "I refuse to sit here and be abused, William. You entered into this relationship with your eyes wide open. If you'll recall, *I* was the one who was surprised by the ugly truth!"

With that, she left the room. William continued eating his food, his natural inclination to be disturbed by angry outbursts and harsh words long since blunted. It had been poor form, he had to admit, to have behaved so crudely, and at the table, on top of it all, but perhaps had his wife been a lady, he might have tried to curb his tongue. She was more suited to be an overseer than a wife.

He had met Charlotte Birmingham after first making the acquaintance of her father, who felt they might make a suitable match. William had courted her for only a short time before he realized they had as much in common as oil and water, but her father seemed to feel differently.

William had acquired a staggering amount of gaming debts that, despite appearances to the contrary, he was never going to be able to pay. Jeffrey Birmingham somehow discovered that fact, and offered to not only pay his debts but provide a life of luxury for him as well if he would marry Charlotte.

William had to suspect that much of the pressure had come from his future mother-in-law. Charlotte had tried and failed at courtship with any one of a number of wealthy plantation owners' sons; since they couldn't get Charlotte away from Bentley, the next step, as far as Sarah was concerned, was to find someone who had nothing to lose and could therefore be controlled. Someone who would be forced into eternal gratitude and therefore be willing to play a silent puppet and sire children.

The silent puppet part he was growing accustomed to. The fatherhood issue was a bit more complicated considering the fact that his wife wouldn't let him into her bedroom. The fault was his alone, however. One night, with entirely too much bourbon in his system, he had opened his mouth and let the truth fly.

***

Charlotte walked back and forth in her sitting room, trying to bottle the rage so it wouldn't take on the form of tears and humiliate her further. That he would throw the conditions of their marriage so harshly in her face was beyond the pale! It was all well and good for him; he wasn't the one who had discovered that his love match was a sham!

He had courted her, wooed her, soothed her wounded pride when she had expressed dismay over the fact that her other suitors had spent time with her and found her lacking. When she married William, she did so thinking he truly loved her. And then one night (on their honeymoon!) he confessed, stupidly, that her father had paid off all of his debts. She might not have thought a thing of it—might have considered it a dowry, in fact, if it hadn't been for the thoughtless comment her brother, Richard, had made to one of his friends the day of her wedding.

"Nobody else would have her, so father had to buy her a wastrel," Richard had chortled, not realizing she was within earshot.

The comment had stung, but she had dismissed it, because William had pledged his undying love for her. But when she had heard from her husband's own lips that her father had paid him, and quite handsomely, from the sounds of it, she had pushed him to admit that he wouldn't have married her, otherwise.

To his credit, he never did admit it, but his silence and slow response to the contrary were all the evidence she needed. From that point forward, she had denied him her good graces and her bed. Had he held his tongue, she might never have known and she could have treated him with the affection she had felt upon their union. But that would have been a lie, and Charlotte despised lies, and to be made a fool of was the worst possible imagining. She should be grateful, she supposed. Had he never told her the truth, she would have lived a lifetime of embarrassing fawning over a man who didn't care to be with her.

She actually considered playing that role at first, just to spite her parents, but realized that if Jeffrey and Sarah saw her happy in her marriage, they would congratulate themselves on a match well made, and be altogether too pleased that not only had they shifted responsibility of their daughter onto another man, but they had done it well. They hadn't done it well—they had humiliated her, and from the moment Charlotte and William Ellis returned to Bentley from their honeymoon trip, Charlotte became the embodiment of her mother, ruling over her husband in comment, gesture, and expression, exactly as she had seen her mother do all the years of her life. Charlotte took great pleasure in mocking her mother with it.

William, himself, was pathetic. He had nowhere to go, no family to support him, nothing to his credit but charm and a handsome face. He was trapped at Bentley and they all knew it. As a result, Charlotte took great delight in making his life miserable.

Much to her dismay, one lone tear escaped and slid down her cheek as she continued traversing the length of her sitting room. Enough! she admonished herself. He was easily enough handled.

All thoughts of her Northern-loving sister had been pushed to the back of her mind.

***

Next door in the cookhouse, unaware of her oldest daughter's turmoil, Sarah Birmingham sat with Ruth as they planned the week's menus. Ruth was the head house-servant and was in charge of coordinating efforts, overseeing each slave's responsibilities, and keeping the home running smoothly; and she was more than competent with her responsibilities. Perhaps it was for this reason that Sarah always discussed the many details of the plantation with Ruth, making sure the household knew who was still in control; it would have been unthinkable for Sarah to turn so much responsibility for her domain over to another woman, especially a slave.

"And Tuesday evening we will be having the Charlesworths for dinner again, so we need to be sure we avoid the salmon. We know by now that Calista swells up like a hot-air balloon when she eats it." Sarah glanced up at Ruth and saw the corners of the woman's mouth twitch. Her own followed, and the two exchanged an amused smile that Sarah knew she would later regret. Too much familiarity with a slave was not a good thing. It led to impertinence and insubordination.

"So's I done tol' him, boy, I'll wallup your hide a good 'un if you don' stop messin' wid the pantry!" came a voice from across the kitchen. Nan, Bentley's head chef, was gossiping again with her underlings.

Sarah kept the woman, in spite of her chattering mouth, because of her excellent culinary skills. Emitting a soft, long-suffering sigh, she said, "Nan, I don't suppose this is something of which I need to be aware?"

The ample black woman turned to Sarah, as though surprised by her presence in the cookhouse. "Well, no'm, I don't suppose so. Jus' young David again, messin' wid my bidness."

"Would you like me to speak with him about it?"

"Oh, no'm. I can handle it jes' fine."

Sarah nodded once, curtly, and returned to her papers. "Keep your finger on things," she murmured to Ruth. "The last thing we need is more food disappearing from the pantry."

Ruth nodded. She had never been impertinent; she knew her place. As Sarah finished the menu and left Ruth to coordinate efforts with Nan, she wandered slowly back to the main house and her downstairs parlor where she conducted her correspondence, her thoughts focusing with more intensity on Ruth than was comfortable.

Ruth had been with her since childhood. When Sarah's father had passed away and left her Bentley, it had been only too natural to raise Ruth through the ranks and eventually put her in a position of some power in the household. Ruth had delivered each of Sarah's children, as well as numerous slave babies born through the years. Sarah had even gone so far as to turn her head the other way when she knew that Joshua and even Ben were teaching her to read, and now, especially now, she wondered if she had made a mistake. There were times when Sarah looked at Ruth, knowing there wasn't a thing Sarah could learn that Ruth also couldn't, and she felt a stab of panic.

Sometimes Ruth looked at her with such pain in her eyes that Sarah usually found herself sniping at the woman—finding fault with some little thing or other if for no other reason than to make Ruth drop her gaze. On those occasions, Sarah often felt a twinge of conscience, which she quickly replaced with relief. As long as Ruth remained respectful, she might not try to leave again. If Ruth found a way to leave, then the rest might think they had a right to try also. If the slaves were gone, so too, was Sarah's whole way of life.

It was unthinkable! Plantation life had always been thus, and it was worth protecting. The Northerners had no idea what they were suggesting when they spewed forth their abolition talk. They, too, were beneficiaries of the Southern system, and they were hypocrites for trying to exclude themselves from it! Their clothing mills—they were filled with Southern cotton. The material and clothing they imported from England also used Southern cotton! They ate Southern rice and smoked Southern tobacco. They could moralize all they chose, but when it came down to it, the North would be hurting if they listened to the radicals who were clamoring for the total and complete abolition of slavery. Sarah could stomach limits on the expansion of it, but they had darn well better leave it as it already stood. Besides, slavery was a kindness! What on earth would the Negroes do if left to their own devices? How would they sustain themselves if they didn't have a more experienced, intelligent race telling them what to do? They would be at a loss!

Ruth wouldn't be at a loss. She shoved the thought aside.

Sarah eventually reached her parlor, lost in her thoughts, when she spied a letter on her desk that bore handwriting so familiar her heart skipped a beat. It was from Ben. She stood for a long moment, rooted to the spot.

Emily must have missed this one.

Sarah knew that Emily often ran to intercept the mail before Sarah could get to it, and although Sarah had given the servants instructions to destroy all mail coming from Ben Birmingham, she suspected they often gave it to Emily instead. The thought rankled, and she would have been well within her rights to call them on it and have the servants punished, but she was, if nothing else, a fair woman. She wasn't about to go accusing her people of crimes they may not have committed. She was a fair mistress, after all.

Her hand reached, of its own volition, for the envelope, and rather than toss it into the wastebasket, as she had intended, she broke the seal instead, and opened it. She began reading, her heart aching at the familiar "voice" behind the letter.

Dearest Emily,

I don't know if you will receive this letter, as you have accused me of not answering some of your past letters to me; please believe me that I most assuredly answer every letter you send. If Mother has forbidden that you speak of me, or receive my mail, it is to be understood. Things will never be the same again, I hardly need to tell you that much, I'm sure.

My life is going well. My little home here is familiar, and people here have been so good to me. I have friends, I have a routine—I even have new employment. I am now working in the telegraph office, so I receive news as soon as it is transmitted.

I must admit, it was with some dismay that I heard of events transpiring in the States these days—or rather, what WAS the States. I worry for your safety and that of our family—this business will get nasty before it gets better. This is my opinion, at any rate.

I hope this letter finds you well, and that Mary, Rose, Clara, Ruth, and Joshua are well also. I would ask you to give my best to Mother and Father, but they might take exception to the message and

wreak havoc on the messenger. In the interests of your own good
health, you probably ought not mention my felicitations.
Please take care, dear sister, and know I will see you again, if not
in this life, then in the next.
My love forever,
Ben.

Sarah sank onto her chair behind the desk, barely registering
the moisture on her cheeks. Her son, her Ben, was alive and well,
and thriving, from the sounds of it. Not that she cared, of course.

For one brief moment, she allowed a sob to escape and she felt
the grief all over again—the deep sorrow, first at his betrayal, then
at his absence. There had been so much terrible, soul wrenching
rage in the house that night. She could still hear Ben's screams
echoing as first Ruth, and then even little Mary and Rose had
been punished for running away. He had looked at her with such
hatred in his eyes that she had actually taken a step back,
although he had been beaten into submission on the floor of the
library and had been tied in ropes for the second time that night,
and posed her no physical threat.

She had always been secretly proud of her son as he had grown
into a young man. Angry at him, frustrated with his bull-headed
attacks on their way of life, but proud nonetheless of his fortitude.
It was unfair, she had often thought, that so much compassion,
intelligence and charm had been poured into her first son, leaving
very little for the rest.

Well, not entirely, she had to amend now as she glanced at the
letter. Ben's correspondence with Emily led her thoughts to her
fourth child; Emily did seem to share his spirit, and that thought
both warmed and worried her. If she wasn't careful, she would
turn her back and find Emily leading the slaves right into open
rebellion. Emily had never given any indication to Sarah that she
felt the same way her brother had—the girl was almost too quiet
sometimes—but there was an edge to her, a look in her eye,
perhaps, that Sarah found unsettling. Perhaps because Emily

spent so much time with Ruth and Mary, Sarah was assuming Emily shared her brother's insane political views, but then, perhaps she was merely overreacting. Still, it was undoubtedly time to focus more on Emily's upcoming position as a new debutante. It would force her beyond the borders of Bentley and instigate possibilities for marriage.

Ben's letter was harmless enough, she supposed, as she glanced down at the missive, and she knew he possessed more wisdom than to give Emily slave-freeing guidance from afar—at least not when anybody could intercept it, as she had. Still, it made her nervous, and she was left to wonder exactly what kind of gumption her young redheaded daughter possessed.

Mulling over these thoughts, she folded the letter and prepared to tear it asunder, when she was gripped with a momentary stab of compassion, not for Emily, but for Jeffrey. Taking the letter, she walked the length of the hallway, past the dining and ballrooms and into Jeffrey's study. He was away on business, still, with Davis and the newly appointed cabinet in Montgomery, Alabama. She knew he was exerting his influence with his friends and she didn't fault his absence; he would represent well the plantation and their holdings, and it might be a good thing for the newly elected to be reminded exactly by whom they were chosen to serve.

Placing the letter on his massive oak desk, she took a blank piece of parchment from the top drawer and dipping a pen in an ink well and dating the paper, wrote: *This letter came today. I thought you might like to know.* She then placed Ben's letter on top of the paper, just beneath her own careful script. She replaced the pen and, straightening, looked again at the handwriting she recognized so well.

Finally releasing a breath that sounded suspiciously like a sigh, even to her own ears, she turned from the desk and left the room without a backward glance.

CHAPTER 12

"This country will be drenched in blood, and God only knows how it will end. It is all folly, madness, a crime against civilization! You people speak so lightly of war; you don't know what you're talking about. War is a terrible thing!"
—*William Tecumseh Sherman*

***

Montgomery, Alabama
7 April, 1861

Jeffrey Birmingham sat in the outer office, ears straining against his better intentions. His good friend, Senator James Chestnut, Mary's husband, was within, discussing current matters with Confederate President Davis and other members of the cabinet. Jeffrey had graciously accepted the invitation to wait for Chestnut in this other room, although he dearly would have loved to be discussing issues himself. Perhaps he should have petitioned Davis for a position. Time would tell if the opportunity would arise again.

As it was currently, however, Jeffrey might as well have been in the room with the men; the walls were no barrier, and the French doors separating the rooms were ajar anyway. He was given clear access to the voices within.

"Lincoln sent word on the sixth that he will provision Sumter, but won't send additional troops or munitions, so long as the fort isn't attacked." Davis's voice was strong, and at its usual resolute best.

Jeffrey heard James Chestnut chuckle. "And that after Seward assured us privately that Lincoln would order that Sumter be abandoned. He was certain he could bend Lincoln to his will."

Jeffrey shook his head. What Lincoln had been thinking when he appointed William Seward his Secretary of State was anybody's guess. It was no secret that Seward had hoped to be president himself; indeed, he had been the front-runner for the Republican nomination that Lincoln had won. Seward was openly derisive of the new president and had seemed to think that he would be controlling Lincoln from behind the scenes like a puppet. Apparently the new president had other ideas.

"Well, then I'd say our course is firmly defined," Secretary of War, Leroy P. Walker replied. "Our Alabama friend Gilchrist seems to think that unless we sprinkle blood in the face of the people of Alabama, they will be back in the old Union in less than ten days. I think an attack on Sumter would be the surest way to not only retain the others who have joined with us, but convince Virginia to join in as well."

Jeffrey heard Secretary of State Toombs jump into the conversation. "Mr. President, at this time it is suicide, murder, and will lose us every friend at the North. You will wantonly strike a hornet's nest which extends from mountain to ocean, and legions now quiet will swarm out and sting us to death. It is unnecessary; it puts us in the wrong; it is fatal."

The cacophony of voices raised in denial at Toombs's suggestion was aggressive. It seemed the better part of the cabinet was fired for war. Jeffrey's brow creased in thought as he listened. He was of a mind to agree with Toombs. Firing on Sumter meant the death of the South, and he knew it in his bones.

And am I a Southerner? The question rose, unbidden, like a specter out of the fog. Yes, he supposed that by now, he was. Raised with his family in the North, he and his brother James had grown up in some of the most severe poverty the world had seen, and they had both vowed, while still young, to rise above it. James had found his success in iron, and Jeffrey had found his at a dance one night while visiting a school friend from Charleston. His success had come in the form of Sarah Matthews, and it had been a high price. It had meant his life, and the sale of his soul to a woman so set in her ways and so unwilling to shed even the slightest bit of compassion on him that he often found himself loathe to return home at the end of his little journeys.

He supposed she cared for him, on some level, but he recognized the reasons she chose him for her husband, and he supposed he'd *always* known. He had wanted to escape his life of poverty, and she had been the key to a life of riches, indulgence, and a lifestyle he had imagined only in his wildest dreams. He never realized that he might want more; that his male pride might, at some point, yearn for some respect or at least a measure of mutual friendship. It was fortunate, for his sake, that he had been able to form significant political relationships. They were his only personal accomplishments, acquired without her direct help, and they were the only things that had given him even a measure of stature in Sarah's eyes. The only other emotion he'd truly felt from his wife was a sense of derision. He'd sold himself to her, and they both knew it.

It wasn't so unlike his daughter Charlotte's union with William. It was unfortunate that history was to continually repeat itself, and he felt guilty for his part in it. His only regret was that Charlotte seemed to have lost the happiness he'd witnessed in her on her wedding day. She had come home from her honeymoon the very image of her mother, but with an edge that seemed even more pronounced.

Jeffrey pulled his thoughts to the present and stood as he heard chairs rustling in the other room. He examined some landscape paintings on the wall as the other men moved through the room and out into the hallway, some shaking their heads, others still engaging in heated debate. He turned at the feel of a hand on his shoulder.

"It seems I am to pay a visit to Major Anderson at Sumter," James Chestnut said, his expression serious. "As it's in your own back yard, would you care to join me?"

***

Charleston, South Carolina
11 April, 1861

Jeffrey examined the line of guns aimed at the small fort out in Charleston Harbor. It was surrounded on all sides; there were batteries at Morris, James, and Sullivan islands, the forts of Moultrie and Johnson, where Jeffrey currently stood, and the town of Mount Pleasant. Bombardment would commence in the early hours of the morning if Anderson didn't immediately surrender.

Jeffrey stole a glance at the man of the hour—the Confederate Louisianan General Pierre Gustave Toutant Beauregard, dashing in his military finery, who was organizing the forthcoming attack. He was a handsome man; his angular face and light brown hair and moustache gave him a dapper appearance, commanding the respect of those working around him. He spoke a few words with James Chestnut, who nodded once, accepting a piece of paper from the man.

Chestnut made his way to Jeffrey's side, glancing down at the note in his hand. "Beauregard delivered an ultimatum to Anderson. This was the reply." He held the paper forward, and Jeffrey strained to read it in the waning light of evening.

"*Gentlemen, I will await the first shot and if you do not batter the fort to pieces about us, we shall be starved out in a few days.*"

Jeffrey glanced up at Chestnut after reading the message. "So what does Beauregard plan to do?"

"He wants me to give Anderson one last warning. We'll go out by boat in a couple of hours. Will you join me?"

Jeffrey nodded.

The midnight hour approached and passed, darkness became an absolute, and the small rowboat carried the four men ever closer to Sumter's front door. Jeffrey was quiet, listening to the lap of the oars against the water. Chestnut's expression could best be described as solemn.

"Did you know that General Beauregard had an artillery instructor at West Point who liked him so much that he went against convention and hired him as his assistant for two years in a row?"

Jeffrey shook his head. "I wasn't aware."

"You won't believe who the instructor was."

Jeffrey shrugged lightly, awaiting an answer.

"Major Anderson."

Jeffrey sat in shocked silence. "*This* Major Anderson?" he finally managed, pointing a finger in the direction of the fort they were approaching.

"This very one. General Beauregard is about to open fire on his former instructor."

The enormity of the situation struck Jeffrey with a force that nearly took his breath. It was unthinkable. The nation was about to go to war upon itself. *Well*, he grimly amended, *actually the rebels are about to declare war upon the United States of America.* Their Revolutionary ancestors would more likely than not roll about in their graves if they knew. Of course, much of the Confederacy believed themselves to be fighting the second American Revolution. Many of those forebears had predicted such an outcome, and had even hoped to prevent it. Jefferson himself had been a slave-holder who had longed to be rid of the institution, continually drafting legislation in hopes of seeing an end to it, but was never able to turn his back on his own way of life and release the slaves he, himself, owned. It would have taken an enormous amount of courage, and Jeffrey knew that he, personally, didn't possess it.

His son did, however. As Sumter loomed ever closer, Jeffrey's thoughts drifted to Ben, living half a world away because he'd had the strength to turn his back on a system he didn't believe in. Jeffrey knew that even if he ever came to feel as strongly about slavery as did Ben, he still wouldn't have the strength to leave it all behind. He was weak, and he knew it, Sarah knew it—the whole family probably knew it.

He watched, feeling numb, as they reached the fort and Major Anderson was summoned. When the man finally appeared, Jeffrey felt an enormous stab of pity for him. He was tall, had once probably been of medium-to-large build, but the stress of the past several weeks, combined with insufficient nourishment, had left him with gaunt cheeks and dark circles under his eyes.

"Sir," James Chestnut began, "I am here to inform you that you are about to be bombarded."

Anderson looked weary and resigned. "Unless I receive further orders or supplies from my government, it is still my intention to evacuate the fort on April fifteenth."

"I'm afraid that will not do. You will be fired upon in one hour."

As the men turned to go, Anderson offered his hand to James Chestnut. "If we never meet in this world again," he said to the senator, "I hope that we may meet in the next."

James nodded, a muscle working in his cheek. Jeffrey followed him back to the rowboat and they slowly moved away from the fortress that loomed high in the darkness. He watched it as they left; it was an impressive fort, really. It was entirely its own island, having been begun during peacetime in the 1820s, built upon a slab of New England granite and towed to the harbor. Ironically enough, it still wasn't completely constructed. They were about to fire upon a fort that wasn't even finished.

Jeffrey mulled over Major Anderson's parting words. "What do you know of Anderson?" he asked Chestnut.

"I think he's a good man," James replied. "He's in an odd place, to be sure. He was a slave-owning Kentuckian, himself, yet is very loyal to the Union." He was quiet for a moment. "One can't help but admire loyalty," he murmured.

***

Charleston, South Carolina
12 April, 1861, 4:30 A.M.

"Well, 'Senator' Pryor," General Beauregard said in his heavy Louisianan drawl to the Virginian who had resigned his U.S. senate seat in March to join the Confederate Army, "given the fact that you told the Confederacy to 'strike a blow!' and Virginia would join us, I suppose you might like to be given the honor of firing the first shot?"

Jeffrey watched with interest as Roger Pryor paled visibly, even in the darkness. They all stared at the man, waiting for him to back his earlier inflammatory bravado with action. He eventually shook his head, saying in a weak voice, "I can't fire the first gun of the war."

Jeffrey turned to James Chestnut, who stood close by. "I thought Pryor was a rabid fire-eater."

"He was," Chestnut scoffed. "Where are the strong words now?"

Beauregard had shifted his attention, motioning for a Captain, George James, to fire a signal gun, at which point Edmund Ruffin, a radical sixty-seven-year-old Virginia newspaper editor with long, wild white hair, whom Jeffrey had met on a few earlier occasions, gladly took Pryor's place and fired, with relish, the first official shot upon Fort Sumter.

The barrage that followed was deafening. It was as though the heavens had opened and let forth an onslaught of thunder so intense Jeffrey felt it reverberating in his heart. The black sky was bright with flame as arc after arc of gunfire found its way to the island fort in the middle of the harbor.

Emily awoke with a start. It sounded as though the world were falling down about her bedroom. She leapt from her bed in the family townhouse in downtown Charleston where the Birminghams were vacationing for a few weeks, quickly donning her double gown and shawl, and raced into the hallway. There was much confusion about the entire house as people scurried from room to room. Charlotte was at the end of the hallway, looking out the window and into the night.

"They're all on the rooftops," she said to William, who rushed into the hallway from his own bedroom.

Emily followed the pair, and her mother soon joined them as they raced to the rooftop. Once outside, the four stood still in shock, viewing the chaos that abounded in the night sky. From their elevated view, they could see what was undoubtedly bombardment on Fort Sumter, out in the harbor.

Emily finally found her voice. "Well, now, here's a way to spend an evening."

Her mother glanced at her with an ashen face. "Oh, Emily," she murmured, "hold your tongue and say your prayers instead."

It seemed that Sarah's thoughts were not entirely original; Emily glanced out at the other rooftops, all holding Charleston residents, many of whom were screaming with wild, joyous abandon, but many still who had fallen to their knees and appeared to be petitioning Deity. Sarah, herself, took up the cause. "Please, God, help us," Emily heard her mother plead, her hands clasped at her breast as she watched the flames fly over the harbor.

Help us what? Emily wondered. Help us not to die? Help us to win the war we've just started? Help us preserve slavery? She would have asked Sarah exactly what it was she was praying for, but took her mother's advice and held her tongue.

Instead, she moved to the edge of the roof and watched the scene unfold with fascination. It was more intense than any fireworks display she'd ever seen, and the noise was thunderous. *It's happening*, she mused with a sense of morbid excitement as the shells exploded with fury over the water, and were occasionally answered back with some from the fort under attack. *It's finally happening. If there was ever a cause more lost, this is surely it! Lincoln will swoop down upon us and put an end to centuries of madness.* Well, she had to admit, perhaps that was a bit of a stretch. Lincoln had said that his aim was not total abolition, but preservation of the nation. Still, she mused, it was the start of something big, this folly of firing on the fort, and she knew as she watched her neighbors jumping up and down for joy that she shared their euphoria, although the purpose for her emotion was different than was theirs. They were ecstatic at the thought of Southern independence. She was ecstatic at her own intuition that they would fail.

What do I care anyway? This legacy isn't mine by choice—there's nothing here I wish to inherit. I'm heading north as soon as I'm old enough. I'd be happy to see this place rot. Emily turned about, viewing the entire scene from three hundred sixty degrees, and tried to dredge up some surge of pity at the results of the decimation she felt sure would soon visit itself upon the countryside, and was almost alarmed to feel nothing. She glanced to the north, in the direction of Bentley, where she knew Mary, Rose, Ruth, and Joshua were sleeping in their humble beds, and finally did feel something.

Anger. The need for vengeance. She glanced again out over the harbor and felt a sense of satisfaction.

Fine, then. Let it begin.

***

Bentley Plantation

Joshua stood outside in front of his shack, his eye catching the glow on the horizon. It had finally begun, it seemed, and he had to wonder at his own fate. He turned slightly at a presence to his right. Ruth and Mary had joined him, shawls thrown about their threadbare brown nightdresses.

Mary's expression bore the confused emotions he was certain were displayed upon his own face. He threw an arm about her shoulders, pulling her close for a quick hug. He and Mary were similar of feature. Rumor had it amongst the slaves, and it had been verified by Ruth herself years ago, that the Bentley overseer who had been so fond of Mary's mother had also been fond of Joshua's mother. Joshua would find it highly surprising if he and Mary were not siblings.

At any rate, blood or not, he viewed her as his sister, and he placed a kiss atop her head. "What do you think?" he asked her and Ruth.

Ruth shook her head. "Don't know what to think," she murmured. "I'm at a loss."

"It could mean great things, or it could mean the end of all hope."

He felt Mary nod her agreement against his chest. "Emily seems to think something fantastic will happen, in the end."

Joshua shook his head, a reluctant smile tugging on the corners of his mouth. "I'm beginning to wonder if Emily isn't slightly batty."

"Oh, she is." Mary's soft laughter found its way to his heart, and he was glad to hear her sounding like a measure of her former self. That a slave could speak in such a teasing, flippant manner about her mistress spoke volumes about the friendship Mary enjoyed with Emily.

The sound of cannon in the distance echoed and reverberated through the air, drawing his thoughts to the uncertain future. What would happen from that point on was anybody's guess.

***

Four thousand rounds and thirty-four hours later, Jeffrey Birmingham returned to James Chestnut's side at the battlements to see the stars and stripes over Sumter lowered and a white flag raised in its place. Jeffrey had returned to the townhouse for rest and to speak with Sarah concerning recent events, only to have his son, Richard, beg to be allowed to accompany him back to Beauregard's men. Jeffrey watched now as Richard sauntered amongst the men, finally stopping to speak with Roger Pryor, who seemed to have regained his former zeal.

Chestnut gestured toward the man. "I think Beauregard is going to send him into the fort to act as emissary. More likely than not, I'll go with him. Would you like to come along?"

Jeffrey nodded, still watching his son. Richard was a disappointment, and it was a bitter pill for a father to swallow. Richard was forever trying to ingratiate himself into the good graces of others in power, usually hoping for something in return. Perhaps more troubling, however, was the fact that he was untrustworthy. Jeffrey would trust his life to his son, Ben, who had all but tried to undermine their entire system, before he would to Richard, who would defend that system to the death.

Richard laughed out loud at something Pryor said, and when it came time to board the boats and head out to the beleaguered fort, Jeffrey suffered a pang of disappointment when he realized that Pryor was bringing Richard along, as well. "It'll be good for you, boy," Pryor was saying to Richard as they boarded. "You can learn from the best how things work."

Jeffrey glanced at James Chestnut, who was eyeing the pair dubiously. Mercifully, however, his friend refrained from comment. They traveled back to the fort in silence, and Jeffrey noted the appearance of the place in its current condition as opposed to the last time he'd seen it. Closer inspection once within the walls showed it as basically sound, but with huge chunks of the walls missing. The fires had been put out, and before long, the white bed sheet was lowered and the new Confederate flag was raised in its place. "The Stars and Bars" it was called, looking much like the United States flag, but bearing a circle of seven stars and three stripes, or bars. It whipped smartly in the breeze, and Jeffrey noted the expressions of the Union soldiers within the fort as they looked upon it.

He couldn't help but pity them; they were hungry, exhausted, and beaten. He followed Pryor and the others as they made their way into the fort's hospital so that Pryor, acting as General Beauregard's emissary, could dictate the terms of the surrender. Major Anderson was there, looking as exhausted as his men, as were a handful of other Federal troops and the fort's surgeon.

"Did you sustain any casualties?" James Chestnut asked Major Anderson, and he was rewarded with a negative response. Jeffrey released a breath he hadn't realized he'd been holding. It was a relief. As impossible as it now was, he wanted the conflict to resolve itself without loss of life.

Pryor took a seat at a table, and with relish, began to dictate the terms of the surrender. "I'm thirsty," he muttered mid-sentence, and grabbed the nearest bottle, taking a swig before bothering to read the label. "Iodine of Potassium," he muttered as he finally glanced at the bottle, swiping a hand across his mouth. The surgeon spun around, looking at Pryor with narrowed eyes.

"Did you just *drink* that?"

Pryor nodded dumbly, a look of panic crossing his features. The surgeon hauled him from his seat and took him forcibly outside. The men crowded about as the surgeon pumped Pryor's stomach, saving his life.

"Now there's something a man doesn't see every day," Jeffrey muttered to himself, and as he looked at Pryor, the word "fool" sketched itself indelibly across his conscious thought. He glanced at James Chestnut, who viewed the whole scene with an air of disgust. He rolled his eyes at Jeffrey, and turned back to the men still gathered in the fort's hospital.

"Gentlemen, shall we?"

CHAPTER 13

"Woe to those who began this war if they were not in bitter earnest."
—*Mary Chestnut*

***

New York, New York
20 April, 1861

Daniel O'Shea stood among the 100,000 people who were crowding Manhattan's Union Square. The flag taken from the fallen Fort Sumter now proudly waved from the statue of George Washington, situated high above the crowd and placed there by Major Anderson himself.

Daniel glanced at his father, gauging his mood. Gavin was euphoric, as Daniel had known he would be. The current festivities spoke to the man's patriotic heart, and in truth, Daniel couldn't help but be swept along with the tide. Never, in his life, had he been witness to such a show of nationalism. The people about him were reveling in unabashed joy at the thought of war with their Southern brethren. The flag placed high atop the statue was a symbol, to the masses, of the new cause.

Daniel looked about himself, watching the people with interest. There were bodies as far as the eye could see, and Daniel wondered at the sudden sense of oneness they all seemed to feel.

Some of these were undoubtedly the same who had often looked at him in disdain, despising his Irish roots and his imposition on U.S. hospitality. Yet now, here they all were, singing the praises of the Union and vowing to crush those who had dared raise a fist in treason.

"Don't be lookin' so grim, Danny-boy!" Gavin bellowed at him, his grin splitting his handsome face. "'Tis a time for celebration!"

"Since when is the prospect of war a cause for celebration?" Danny answered back, raising his voice to be heard above the roar of the crowd.

"It's not just the war, it's the principle!"

"Hmm."

Gavin shook his head at his son. He appeared to be searching for words, then finally shook his head and instead, placed an arm about Daniel's shoulders. "All will be well, my boy," he said close to Daniel's ear. "You'll see."

It was with a sense of relief that Daniel finally convinced his father to leave the throng at Union Square and go in pursuit of that for which they had come into the city. Daniel was in need of more wood from his supplier. He had a dining room table and six chairs on order from a long-time customer, and had run short of wood the day before.

The two men climbed into Daniel's open wagon and made their way along the streets, which grew less congested as they moved away from the square, but were still crowded by normal standards. The entire city was out to celebrate, it seemed, and while their movement wasn't impeded, necessarily, Daniel found himself impatient at those who crossed the streets at a leisurely pace, or who stopped their carriages in the middle of the streets to chat with friends who passed on the other side.

He finally directed his team of horses to the store where he purchased his supplies, and leaving the reins with Gavin, set the brake on the wagon and went inside.

"Hello," he greeted Mr. Swanson, the shop proprietor.

"Mr. O'Shea!" The man greeted him with some enthusiasm. "Here to retrieve your supplies?"

"Yes, sir, I am."

"And have you noticed the streets today? It's quite a celebration, isn't it?"

"I did indeed notice."

Mr. Swanson left the room and made his way toward the back of the large shop, still talking over his shoulder as he went. "I almost considered closing the store today, but business has been brisk, so I kept the doors open." Daniel heard rustling sounds and the clanking of wood. The shopkeeper momentarily returned to the front of the store.

"Here are some of the finer pieces you ordered," the man stated. "For the larger ones, I suppose you'll pull your wagon around back to the lumber yard?" Swanson jerked a thumb over his shoulder.

Daniel nodded and retrieved his money, paying the man for the supplies.

"So, did you hear that Lincoln has put out a call for the states to raise 75,000 volunteers to fight the rebels?" Swanson's face was glowing with his enthusiasm.

Daniel nodded. "I saw the papers this morning."

"Looks like that call to arms pushed Virginia over the edge. She's joined the Confederacy."

Gavin had had much to say about *that* most recent turn of events. Daniel recalled with a smile his father's verbally explosive tirade. Swanson apparently mistook his expression to be a reflection of his own feelings on the matter.

"I agree!" the man stated. "Let them leave—it will be worse for them in the end. They'll be sorry! So, are you going to enlist, then?"

Enlist? The thought hadn't even entered his mind. "I don't think so."

Swanson stared at him, his mouth slack. "But . . . but how can you not?"

Easily. Why would I want to fight for a country that would be happier without me in it? "I have obligations with my parents that are my primary concern." Truly, it was quite a stretch, and Swanson probably knew it. Anybody who knew Gavin and Brenna O'Shea knew they were about as capable a couple as there was. They didn't need help with anything.

Swanson's face took on a smug expression that he appeared to try to mask with false compassion. "Ah, but of course your feelings of patriotism probably wouldn't run as deeply as others who were born in this country. I imagine it's hard to summon any feelings of loyalty, being as you're Irish, and all."

Daniel studied the man quietly, his teeth aching in the effort it took to keep his mouth closed. His face felt hot. *Not here, not now,* he told himself. Swanson was a good source for quality supplies at an amazingly low cost. He couldn't afford to ostracize the man with comments that would set him in his place, to be sure, but would also effectively cut off any future good will. Daniel had his business to consider.

"Good day, sir," he muttered. Making his way out of the front door with the smaller pieces of wood in his arms, he reached his wagon and carefully deposited the supplies inside. He climbed up to sit beside his father, and taking the reins and disabling the brake, guided the team and wagon around to the back of the establishment and into the large lumber yard. One of the workers recognized his face and motioned toward him with his hand. Daniel followed the young man and, at his signal, again stopped the horses and climbed down to help load the wood. Gavin followed, exchanging a pleasant greeting with the worker.

"Have you been downtown today, Tommy?" Gavin asked the young man.

"Not as of yet," Tommy answered in a thick, Irish brogue. "Too busy here."

"'Tis a sight to behold," Gavin said as he and the young Irishman loaded large pieces of wood into the back of the wagon. "The whole city must be outside!"

They exchanged banter and pleasantries that Daniel barely registered. When they finally finished loading the wagon, he again took the reins and made his way through the streets with his mouth closed and his thoughts churning about in angry disarray.

"Alright, boy-o, let's hear it," Gavin finally said when his attempts at conversation had yielded nothing from Daniel.

"How do you do it, Da? How do you feel so much support for a country that spits on us? Swanson asked me if I'm going to enlist and it was all I could do not to laugh in the man's face!"

Gavin was quiet for a moment, and Daniel felt himself begin to fidget under his father's regard. He hadn't fidgeted for a good many years, and he wondered at it. His father was still his father, he supposed, no matter how old he grew. "People will be people wherever you are, son," Gavin finally said.

"But in Ireland, at least we were with our own."

"And we were starving."

"But—"

"You were younger, Dan, and you don't remember as well. We had no choice, and this land was the best o' the lot to consider. What good do you suppose it would do me," he continued, "if I listened to all the things people have to say about me? How does that help me live my life? And the truth of the matter is," he said, holding his hand up to forestall Daniel's interruption, "that not every person in this country hates Irishmen."

"Hmph."

"Think about it, son. There are 383,000 immigrants in New York County alone. That makes 383,000 people who probably don't hate Gavin O'Shea and his family."

Daniel stole a sidelong glance at his father and finally laughed out loud. "I suppose that's one way to consider things," he said.

"Indeed it is!" Gavin slapped Daniel hard on the back, and with a smile, Daniel guided the wagon through the crowded city streets and began the two-mile trek home.

***

New Orleans, Louisiana
April 20, 1861

"If you'll look at the map," Marie said to her students who were crowded close around her desk, "you can see exactly which states are now part of the Confederacy."

She watched the young children absorb the information as she pointed to the states in order of secession. "South Carolina, Florida, Mississippi, Alabama, Georgia, Louisiana." She trailed her finger along the map, noting the recognition on the children's faces when she pointed to their home state. "Texas, and lastly, Virginia."

"Is that all, then?" Constance, a young twelve-year-old girl with light brown braids, spectacles, and a perpetually serious expression, pointed to the upper two-thirds of the map. "All the rest of these are the United States now?"

"Well, in a manner of speaking. Most of them. Except for Arkansas, North Carolina, Tennessee, Delaware, Maryland, Kentucky, and Missouri," Marie answered, pointing to each state as she named them. "They haven't yet joined the Confederacy, although there are many who think they might, and they are called 'Border States.'"

Constance nodded. "And do you think they will join the Confederacy, Miss Brissot?"

Marie nodded. "I think maybe a few of them will most likely join before long. It's difficult to predict, though."

Peter, Constance's thirteen-year-old brother, was the oldest student in the class. He gestured toward the northern expanse of the map. "And now that we've fired on Fort Sumter, what will they do?"

Marie swallowed. *Destroy us all, most likely.* "Well, there will be some conflict now, Peter, but I'm not sure I can tell you exactly what will happen. President Lincoln hasn't declared a state of war, necessarily, but he is calling it an 'insurrection.'"

"What's Fort Sumter?" The question came from a dark-headed little six-year-old. Jonathan was probably the least privileged of all the students in the class. The only reason he had shoes on his feet was because Marie had purchased them for him. His mother was a widow, trying desperately to keep her small farm running, and Jonathan was her only child she could spare for education, because he was too small yet to be of significant use around the farm. Her two older children were twelve and fourteen, and worked alongside their mother from sunup to sundown.

Marie gestured toward Charleston Harbor on the map and explained what had happened to the fort.

Jonathan gazed at her with enormous brown eyes. "Were the people inside bad, then?"

"No, Jonathan, they weren't bad. They were just . . ." Just what? Marie had never had to explain war to a child before. She found it increasingly difficult to paint the "enemy" as a true enemy, when she felt little loyalty to her own side. "They didn't agree on who should be inside the fort."

Jonathan nodded seriously. "That happened to me, once. I wanted to climb the tree next to my bedroom window, and I was there first, and my brother made me climb down because he wanted to be in the tree."

Marie nodded, her eyes stinging. It almost sounded that childish, the whole of it. Boys spoiling for a fight. She cleared her throat and stood, urging the children back into their seats. "Please retrieve your slates now, and we'll practice our arithmetic." She suppressed a smile at the light chorus of groans from some of the older students, remembering a time when she had been in that very position, herself. She enjoyed reading, history, and geography, but hadn't ever looked forward to working her sums.

She taught through the rest of the day with one half of her brain on the task at hand, and the other half on the map that still lay stretched across her desk. The tan parchment and black lines kept drawing her gaze until she wanted to take the thing and hurl it out of the window. She was tired of worrying over what would happen, and tired of the anxiety she felt on behalf of her father.

The Confederacy had begun amassing an army as soon as it had declared its independence from the mother country, even before the incident in Charleston Harbor. She hoped the number of overzealous men who had already hastened to answer the call would suffice; she couldn't bear the thought of her father going off to fight.

When the school day finally drew to its close, Marie was tidying her desk and belongings and was surprised to see that Constance stood beside her desk, looking a degree more solemn than usual.

"Aren't you walking home with Peter today, Connie?" Marie asked, giving a playful tug on one of the child's braids.

"I told him to walk on ahead of me. I'll catch up with him later," the young girl replied, and began to chew on her lip.

At this sign of distress, Marie straightened and stilled her busy hands, deciding that her own tasks could wait. Constance was a serious child, it was true, and very bright, but one thing she was not, was nervous. In all the time Marie had known the child, she had never seen her fidget, even a bit.

"What is it, Constance?" she asked, taking a seat in her chair and pulling the girl to her side.

"I . . . I . . ."

Marie watched the girl with narrowed eyes, her anxiety level rising at the stammer. When Constance paused uncomfortably, Marie ran a soft hand along her elbow. "What is it?" she repeated in a whisper.

"I would like your opinion on a . . . certain . . . matter," the girl finally admitted.

"Of course. Anything."

"Do you—do you think that everybody has a right to an education?"

This was what was bothering her? Marie's eyebrows shot up in surprise, but she endeavored to keep her voice level so that Constance wouldn't be embarrassed. "Yes, Connie, I do. I think everybody should have the right to education and schooling."

"Everybody?"

What was the young girl trying to say? "Certainly," Marie

replied, her curiosity growing with each passing moment.

Constance nodded, once. "I thought you would say that." She smiled, although it was a fleeting thing that was gone almost before it materialized. "I had hoped you would say that."

"Why do you ask?"

Constance shrugged. "I was just curious." Her solemn, assured manner had returned, but Marie noted with interest that the girl wouldn't look her in the eye.

"Hmm. And was there any particular reason you were curious about that?"

"No." She gathered her books close to her chest and turned toward the door. "Not really," she said over her shoulder as she walked down the aisle of desks. "I need to catch Peter now—he's going to wonder what's become of me."

"Of course," Marie murmured in confusion. "I'll see you tomorrow then, Connie."

"Yes, ma'am." The door closed behind her, and Marie was left to wonder over the child's cryptic questions.

***

"Jean-Pierre, please! You must be insane to want to print such an inflammatory editorial!"

Jean-Pierre Brissot looked at his assistant and smiled. "You worry too much, Michael. I must tell the truth as I see it, and nobody in this town expects any less of me. Indeed, I think they would be disappointed if I held my tongue."

"You are suicidal, you crazy young fool!" Michael's face was white with concern. "The people here in this city are not interested in a viewpoint that will make the Confederacy seem less than perfect! You will alienate yourself from those in power, and then heaven help us all."

"Michael." Jean-Pierre wiped his ink-stained hands on his apron and placed them on the older man's shoulders. "I feel compelled to give people an alternate viewpoint. Perhaps I see things differently because this is not the land of my birth. I come from the outside, and my thoughts are often, well, different. People may have opposed my editorials in the past, but it has never resulted in bodily harm. I don't believe it will in this case, either."

Michael shook his head in weary resignation. "You will do what you will do, it is true," he said in heavily accented English. His native French often got the best of him, and more often than not his and Jean-Pierre's conversations were an odd mixture of English and French. "But I fear this will take things too far." Michael turned his eyes heavenward, clasping his hands in a simulated prayer. "Mon Dieu," he said mournfully, "talk sense into the boy!"

Jean-Pierre waited as the silence lengthened, the smile on his face growing in affection as he watched Michael beseech the heavens for, apparently, some sort of angelic visitation. This man had been his uncle's friend and his own right hand since he had taken over the paper.

When no heavenly visitor appeared, Jean-Pierre clapped his friend on the shoulder and said, "It is a sign. I must go forward with this editorial."

Michael shook his head. "I am older than you, foolish boy. Years older. Why do you not listen to me? You're as crazy as was your uncle. He was always looking to fight."

"Ah, but my uncle looked for fights because he enjoyed the fighting. I merely like to make people think."

"Oh, they will think, for sure," Michael muttered as he walked slowly to the larger of the two presses and eyed it with an unmistakable expression of nostalgia. "They will think they need to burn this place to the ground."

"Nonsense. Freedom of speech did not disappear with the dissolution of the old country. The new constitution guarantees me my right to speak my mind, and thus I shall."

"Even if it means speaking out against your 'new' country?"

Jean-Pierre paused, rubbing a finger alongside his temple in thought. "It's not so much speaking out as it is bringing to light facts that people may not have considered." He sobered, looking at his old friend. "I feel it is my duty, Michael. I mustn't do any less."

Michael heaved a sigh. "Then you do what you must. And heaven help us all."

The world was sleeping by the time Jean-Pierre made his way home that night. He was weary and concerned, his fatigue causing him to give way to Michael's earlier fears. Perhaps he was a fool. Maybe people didn't care one whit for his version of the truth. He glanced at the front of his house as he approached on horseback, smiling at the light in the parlor window. Somebody was still awake, and he had to admit he was glad for it.

After personally seeing to the comfort of his horse, saving his aging groom the trouble of rising from his bed, he made his way into the house and wandered slowly to the parlor, his steps sounding tired, even to his own ears.

"Ah," he said as he spied the room's occupants. "Both of my girls."

Jenny and Marie both sat beside the fire, each cradling a mug of something warm.

"You're tired," Jenny said immediately, her brow creasing in concern.

"It's near midnight." He sank down next to her on the small couch. "It's been a long day, that's all."

"But you're never affected by lack of sleep. Something has you troubled."

He nodded. "You always were too astute, *chére*, by far." He withdrew a piece of paper from the inner pocket of his coat and unfolded it. "This is my most recent collection of rambling thoughts," he said. He handed the paper to his wife. "It runs in tomorrow's paper."

Jenny took the paper and read the editorial from start to finish without making any comments. She handed it to her daughter, who did likewise. When Marie finished reading, she eyed her father evenly.

"Are you thinking the locals will support this?"

"Not necessarily." He shrugged, striving for a nonchalance he didn't feel. "They need to think, though. We are all having momentous decisions made for us, sometimes without our consent. Issues that affect us all should be carefully considered. People are not doing that."

"Yes, but you've tried so diligently through the years to culti-vate good relationships with the influential of this city. They are among those of whom you speak here," Marie said, waving the paper she still held in her hand, "who have made some of those momentous decisions. They will not be happy to think you are questioning their judgment or their integrity."

"So you think I shouldn't run the piece?" He looked to his wife, then his daughter and back again.

Jenny sighed. "I think you should run it, Jean-Pierre. I think you should run it and we'll see what people say."

"Marie?"

His daughter sighed as well. "I think you should run it too, Papa. I just don't want people angry with you. That would make me angry."

Jean-Pierre chuckled. "You always were protective of your dear old papa. What father needs a champion when he has a daughter who loves him?"

"'The Confederacy, it seems, was formed by a few influential men who would speak for the masses living in the South,'" Marie read aloud from the paper she still held in her hand. "'The state legislatures of those seceded states sent representatives to their respective state conventions, and when one takes careful stock, one will see that basically seven hundred wealthy men have made the decision for secession, and made it for nine million people who did not elect them.

"'The voters of Tennessee rejected a secession convention by nearly ten thousand votes, but one hears it whispered on the wind that the governor of Tennessee is not happy with this result. How long before said governor finds a way to join his state with our ranks, without the approval of the citizens of Tennessee? How deep will this conflict become? Are we willing to sustain the loss of life? Are we content as a people to let a small fraction make decisions for the whole?'"

Marie stopped reading and lowered the paper to her lap. "You are a brave man, Papa. But you know, those in power are finding a way to sway those masses to their way of thinking."

Jean-Pierre nodded. The politicians and wealthy plantation owners were working long hours, it seemed, spreading the word to the middle class and the poor that if the Union were to persist on her current course, the South would see an end to slavery, and those same slaves would take their jobs, their lifestyles, even their women. More to the point, the people believed it. He shook his head.

"I know, Marie. They think to frighten them with myths. I suppose I was hoping to suggest, in a very subtle way, that we need to be thinking for ourselves, and not allowing a few select to be the voice for all."

"And you say it well, Papa, but it is too late. The states have seceded, the course is set, and the people are breathing fire! Even Gustav, who is the silliest, most peaceful person I know is thinking he might like to have an opportunity to kill some 'Yankees,' he says. If someone like Gustav can be turned into a fire-eater, I fear for the rest."

Jenny placed an arm about her husband's back and laid her head upon his shoulder. "I am proud of you, my sweet," she said softly, and Jean-Pierre was left to wonder whether she referred to him or her daughter. Knowing Jenny, more likely than not, she meant both.

Marie left her parents in the comfort of the parlor and climbed the stairs leading to the bedrooms on the second floor. The image of the contented couple stayed with her as she readied herself for bed and climbed beneath the crisp, white sheets. She wanted that image for herself, and it was a bitter thing to realize it would never be.

She had been so young, so foolish. He had said he loved her, that he wanted to marry her, and he couldn't bear to be away from her. She closed her eyes as she remembered herself as a naïve young eighteen-year-old child, allowing him to take her into the gardens of the home of a mutual friend while the festivities clamored about inside the house.

He hadn't debauched her completely, and in truth, she had trusted him enough to allow it, but by the time the matron of the home found them together in the gardens, Marie's hair coming loose from its elegant coiffure and her dress in a decided state of dishabille, her reputation was finished before it had begun. After that, Marie had gone, in the space of a few weeks, from being innocent and happy to leery and more than a bit cynical.

Society was fickle, and quick to condemn. At least three of Marie's friends, with whom she had attended a prestigious finishing school, were forced to rush to the altar with their beaux. If one counted back the months from the birth of each first child, one came to the obvious conclusion that the children were conceived before the vows were uttered. Yet those friends had snared young men willing to commit, and because the girls married, the influential society matrons forgave them. Marie knew that had Gregory decided he loved her enough to "do right by her," the tongues would have stopped wagging and she would not now be looked upon as a harlot.

She settled back into her fluffy pillows with a sigh. Perhaps it was just as well. She didn't want to be married to a man who didn't love her, and Gregory had certainly proved he didn't. Their clandestine stroll through the gardens that fateful night, she later discovered through a vicious, jealous neighbor, had been nothing more than a wager between Gregory and his friends. Marie never did tell her parents. She had no wish to see her father imprisoned for murder.

Turning on her side and tucking her heavy quilt and sheets tight under her chin, she gazed out the window and into the night sky. Truly, she couldn't complain. She enjoyed her life, she felt a tug on her heart each time she thought of her school and her students, and she truly felt useful. Her one wish, to be most likely forever unfulfilled, was to find a man who wouldn't judge her for her past lapse in judgment, and find her a worthy companion. A man whose affection she could return.

CHAPTER 14

"There has been a serious disturbance in Baltimore. Regiments from Massachusetts assailed by a mob that was repulsed by shot and steel . . . It's a notable coincidence that the first blood in this great struggle is drawn by Massachusetts men on the anniversary of Lexington. This is a continuation of the war that Lexington opened—a war of democracy against oligarchy."
—George Templeton Strong, New York Diarist

***

7 May, 1861
Boston, Massachusetts

Anne Birmingham sat in a chair near the small hearth in her bedroom, her eyes flying with interest over the words written on a paper she held in her hand. It was a letter from Isabelle Webb, postmarked from Washington, D.C.

Dearest Anne, the letter began:
I cannot begin to tell you about the odd situation our capitol faces. There is nobody here to trust! The city is swarming with spies; people who held office and entertained foreign diplomats in their homes are now sending covert messages to the Confederate Government, first to Alabama, and then to Richmond, Virginia, now that the Confederate capitol has been moved. The entire city is

surrounded on all sides by Southern sympathizers, and the President was waiting on pins and needles for reinforcements to arrive from the other Northern states to defend the capitol.

Surely you must have heard by now of the incident in Baltimore—I was still there with Pinkerton, Kate Warne, and Timothy Webster when it occurred, and I must tell you, it was awful. The 6th Massachusetts Militia was traveling through Baltimore on its way to Washington when a crowd of Southern sympathizers that the locals call 'Plug Uglies' (called thusly because of the hats they wear, and the spikes situated in the front of their boots, meant to inflict harm on any they choose to kick!), attacked the soldiers by throwing bricks and rocks at them. The soldiers fired into the crowd, killing twelve civilians and wounding others, and four soldiers died as well.

The Plug Uglies wander about, terrorizing those they please even still, and on the night of the debacle with the militia, the citizens took it upon themselves to burn the railroad bridges leading to Washington to prevent further militias or regiments from moving through the area on their way to the capitol. The governor has begged Lincoln to keep any more troops from moving through Baltimore, but Lincoln refused. Lincoln's argument is that the men can't fly, or worm their way underground like moles; how are they supposed to reach the capitol if not on rails and through the streets? It is my understanding, however, that the president has made other arrangements for further traveling troops and plans to keep them away from Baltimore.

I tell you, Anne, Baltimore is in a state of anarchy. People have evacuated the city in hopes of keeping their families safe, and the situation here in D.C. is not much different. There are boards over some shop windows where shopkeepers have left town. Federal office windows are covered with iron bars for protection. City and government officials defect to the Confederacy every day! And when we awoke on the morning of April 20, we found that pro-Confederate Baltimoreans had blockaded the railroads and taken control of the telegraph office. We were entirely cut off from the North. I had never seen anything like it.

The city itself has since taken on a new appearance; Lincoln's reinforcements have arrived from various states and set up camp *everywhere! The soldiers are stationed in the Patent Office, the floor of the chamber of the House of Representatives—even in the cellar! The people of this city who are more prone to 'dignified' behavior are, of course, scandalized. I hear women daily expressing their disgust with the current state of affairs. I am often tempted to suggest they pack their china and move to Richmond, where their true sympathies obviously lie, but am forced to hold my tongue, because the role I am currently playing requires me to pretend to be one of them.*

Anne paused in her reading, a smile on her face as she envisioned Isabelle giving the prim Southern sympathizers an earful of her strong opinions.

I daresay Washington, D.C., is the most efficiently protected city on the face of the earth, now. There are twenty-two batteries and seventy-four forts encircling the place. I think Lincoln can breathe a sigh of relief that, should the Rebels attempt a takeover of the capitol, they would be met with a good show of resistance.

Anne stood and began pacing the length of her bedroom, restlessly tapping the paper against her skirt, her brow creased in a frown. The "insurrection," as the president was calling it, was occurring well south of Boston. "Adam Jones" could only accomplish so much on his home soil. The action was elsewhere, and as she paced, a tiny seed of an idea took root in Anne's head.

She stopped still.

And why not?! she mused as she continued her movements about the room, this time with a pace that was decidedly quicker than it had been before. *I've already proven I can pose as a man— the rest is just a matter of detail.*

As details were not usually a problem for Anne, she sat at her desk with a smile and picked up a pen. Dipping it in her inkwell, she began a return letter to her friend.

Dearest Belle . . .

***

"I'm half inclined to be disgusted, but the man's shown amazing military brilliance in the past," Robert Birmingham said as he ate his breakfast.

James smiled at Elizabeth when Robert's head was turned down toward his plate.

"It's true, he's seventy-five, gouty, and too fat to ride a horse, but I'm of the opinion that his judgment is still sound."

Camille clanked her spoon against her fruit bowl in annoyance. "Honestly, Robert, one would think you were raised in a barn! Surely you can think of more appropriate meal-time conversation?"

Robert glanced up at his sister with a grin. "Certainly. I'll tell you all about Scott's Anaconda plan."

"What's an Anaconda?" Jimmy asked from the far end of the table.

"It's a South American snake that squeezes its victims to death."

"Mother!"

Elizabeth calmly spooned a small piece of grapefruit into her mouth with a slight smile and a glance at her husband.

"The Army is going to go after the Rebels with snakes?" Jimmy's brow creased in confusion.

"Not quite." Robert looked at his younger brother, a gleam forming in his eye that his parents had long come to recognize as his unabashed fascination with all things military. He placed his fork and knife alongside his plate, impatiently brushing a lock of coffee-brown hair off his forehead. "Winfield Scott is the general-in-chief of the U.S. Army. He's old, but can still think."

"Amazing, isn't it, Lizzie, that a person can still think, even when old?"

Robert glanced in mild annoyance at his father's smiling face. "As I was saying, Scott has devised a plan that will surely ruin the Confederacy. He proposes to send gunboats down the Mississippi to take New Orleans, and to blockade all Southern ports and the coastline. Without New Orleans, the South loses one of its richest cities, and by imposing a blockade on all its ports, the Rebs will be unable to export their cotton or import other goods. And by taking control of the Mississippi, we effectively deny the Confederacy any help from states or territories west of the river." He picked up his fork and resumed his meal. "It will take time, but I, for one, find it brilliant."

Camille snorted elegantly as she placed a grape in her mouth. "Too much coastline," she said after she swallowed.

Robert paused, fork poised midair. "I beg your pardon?"

"The Confederacy has in excess of thirty-five hundred miles of coastline, and our navy is in possession of a total of forty-two ships, most of which are abroad. We don't have enough ships, and the ones we have aren't even here."

James, Elizabeth, Robert, and even little Jimmy stared at Camille, openmouthed. Robert was the first to find his voice. "And how, might I ask, do you know this?" he squeaked.

Camille flushed. "Olivia's sister, Rebecca, thinks it's wise for a woman to be aware of her surroundings. She's challenged us all to read the newspaper. One has to wonder, however, how secure the nation's capitol is when military secrets are leaked to the press."

When her statement was met with still more stunned silence, her expression grew increasingly defensive. "You don't all need to stare at me so! I do know how to read, you know!"

Elizabeth shook her head slightly as though pulling herself out of a deep reverie. "Remind me to thank Olivia's sister," she murmured, resuming her breakfast.

"So it's suddenly fashionable for a woman to be informed, then?" Robert asked. "Well, you're years behind mother and Anne, but with dedication, I'm sure you'll catch them in no time."

"Clear that smirk from your face, Robert Birmingham," Camille retorted. "I, personally, find it blasé to talk politics all day, but Rebecca seems to find it important. As I value Rebecca's opinion, I saw it prudent to follow suit."

"So, you're saying then, with this new-found wisdom you've acquired, that you find the Anaconda Plan folly?"

"Yes, I do. And I'm not the only one. I've seen several drawings that mock this supposedly brilliant plan—they show an ugly snake with Lincoln's head on top, or sometimes with Winfield Scott's head. People think the whole idea is lunacy."

Robert had seen those same drawings himself, and it had made him angry that the general public was so willing to discount and ridicule what he, himself, considered to be a sound plan to economically cripple the South. "You know, it will only be a matter of time before the Naval fleet is more substantial. Already they are busy building new ships, steam-powered ships, and are purchasing commercial vessels as quickly as they can. True, there are miles of coastline, but not so much that the Union can't handle it."

James smiled at the pride evident in his son's voice. Robert had been a fan of history, especially military history, since his early youth. He had learned all there was to know of the American Revolution, the war with Britain in 1812, the Indian wars and the Mexican War, of which Winfield Scott, the current subject under discussion, had been a hero.

"Camille's right—you're one of the few who support the plan," James mentioned to Robert. "You and Lincoln. Most Northerners find it timid and inglorious. They feel this 'insurrection' can be put down in a matter of a few weeks with a decisive battle or two."

"Not only that," Camille interjected, "but Winfield Scott is a Virginia native. He even suggested withdrawal of Sumter before it was fired upon. I wonder if he isn't actually a Southern sympathizer." She sniffed.

"That's insanity! He's old, yes, but he's loyal to his duties and the Union!"

"Robert, I find it disconcerting you equate age with possible idiocy." Elizabeth's voice was mild, and held an unmistakable edge of subtly veiled amusement.

He waved a hand dismissively. "You know what I mean."

"Not exactly."

This time, he ignored his mother altogether. "And Camille, one might have taken you for a Southern sympathizer lately, yourself!"

Camille flushed again. "I'm not a Rebel," she grumbled. "I just . . . I don't know."

"It's confusing, isn't it?" Elizabeth glanced at her daughter in sympathy. "Things are changing quickly. But you know, it's been happening for a long time."

"Robert?" Jimmy ventured.

"Yes?"

"What's gout?"

***

Later that night in the privacy of his own room, Robert sat at his desk, absently tapping his pen against the wooden surface. There had to be a way to convince his parents to let him go, but he was at a loss as to how it should be accomplished. The tapping of the pen grew firmer and more insistent until the noise finally penetrated the fog around his brain and irritated him into dropping the pen on the desk.

I wonder . . . Camille had shown a remarkable amount of insight earlier that morning, especially for her, and he mused over the fact that he might have a possible ally if he played things just right. She was a bit flighty, it was true, but she was also older than he was, and she did enjoy a certain amount of freedom because of it.

Making a decision he wasn't sure he wouldn't later regret, he left his bedroom and made his way down the hallway to hers. He tapped lightly on the door, and heard a rustling sound from within. "Just a moment," came a muffled response, and moments later, Camille's face appeared at the door. She was wearing a wrapper over her bedclothes, clearly surprised to find Robert standing in the hallway.

"May I come in?"

She cocked a brow. "Why?"

He glanced down the length of the hall, hoping to avoid his parents. "Please!"

She opened the door wider and allowed him entrance into her pink, frilly world. "What do you want?" she asked as he glanced about at the trimmings and lace evident in every corner of the room. "Are you coming to mock my opinions again? Because I'll tell you again, not only is your Winfield Scott fat and gouty, he's also slow-witted! And 'Old Fuss and Feathers?' What kind of nickname is that? Is it supposed to inspire confidence in the hearts of his troops?"

Robert closed his eyes briefly. "I thought you were opposed to the words 'fat' and 'gout'."

"Only when we're eating."

"Camille, I came to make you a proposition."

She said nothing, but waited expectantly, one hand on her slender hip. Her hair was down from its customary elaborate daytime configuration and had undoubtedly been brushed with one hundred firm strokes. She was beautiful, his sister, and Robert didn't have to wonder why so many suitors were constantly at the family door.

"You mentioned Olivia Sylvester earlier today," said Robert. "She has a younger brother, Nathaniel, who is my age." He waited for some sign of recognition from her, but her face remained blank. "Do you not even know that Olivia has a brother?"

"I know she has a brother! I didn't remember his name, though—believe it or not, Robert, my friends and I have more important things to discuss than our siblings. At least the younger ones, anyway."

Robert ground his teeth together. "It doesn't matter. At any rate, Nathaniel was telling me today that his parents are planning a trip to Washington this summer."

"Washington! Are they insane? Olivia never mentioned it to me."

"Olivia may not know about it yet. Nathaniel overheard his parents talking last night, and they are planning a trip to the city to visit Mrs. Sylvester's sister, who lives there with her husband and children."

Camille's pretty brow wrinkled. "It would make more sense for the sister to come here. Why on earth would anyone go to Washington now?"

"Because things are happening in Washington! Nothing is happening here."

"It doesn't make sense to me," she repeated. "The Sylvester's aren't exactly adventure seekers."

"It doesn't matter whether they are or not! The point is they're going to Washington! Nathaniel plans on asking them if he can go along, and he's going to see if I can go, too."

At that, Camille laughed. It might have been a delightfully happy sound if Robert hadn't wanted to choke her for it. When she finally sobered enough to respond, she did so with the very sentiments that he had feared, himself. "Mother and Father will never let you go to Washington now, Robert. Surely you can't be that idiotic."

He ignored her bluntness, although he secretly wondered if she wasn't right. "I was thinking the Sylvesters might allow Olivia to accompany them. I happen to know they are not nearly as stringent about pesky details as are our own parents."

Camille raised a skeptical brow. "Pesky details like personal safety?"

Robert waved a hand. "Washington is probably the safest city in the country these days. It's more heavily fortified now than it's ever been in history."

"So why do you want to go?"

"I can't legally enlist for another three years, and the 'insurrection' is sure to have come and gone by then! Besides, I'm tired of sitting around here." Robert caught the flicker of concurrence that crossed his sister's features, and it gave him hope. "You could come along if Olivia does," he murmured.

"Now why would I want to do that?"

"Because there are still many wealthy citizens in Washington—people who run in the same circles you hope to live in all the days of your life. You never know; you might just find yourself a husband."

She was weakening, he could feel it, but she appeared to be stubbornly clinging to what she undoubtedly regarded as one last shred of common sense. "People know our parents in Washington. All we have to do is mention our last name and the game is finished."

He shrugged. "Who says it has to be a game? If we get father's permission, we won't be hiding who we are."

She almost laughed again. "Robert, the prospect of our father giving us permission to go to Washington, D.C., is slim, at best. And even if he did, Mother would definitely not allow it." She sighed. "It was a noble effort, foolish boy, but I'm afraid you're going to have to abandon it."

"Oh, Camille! You won't even try to ask?"

"Robert, first of all, the Sylvesters haven't invited us! And secondly, their own children aren't even supposed to know about this trip, apparently. If they don't take Olivia and . . . and . . ."

"Nathaniel!"

"Yes, Nathaniel, then they won't take us either. I see no point in asking permission for something that isn't even a reality."

"I'm not telling you to ask now, for heaven's sake! But if they do take Olivia and Nathaniel, and if Nathaniel can convince them to take us along, then will you go to our parents with it?"

Camille heaved a huge, theatrically dramatic sigh. "I suppose. But Robert," she said, holding up a hand when he moved to clasp her shoulders in glee, "don't imagine that this may actually happen. The odds are not in our favor."

CHAPTER 15

"We sat down at the table. Grandma wanted to know what was the trouble. Father told her and she began to cry. 'Oh my poor children in the South. Now they will suffer! God knows how they will suffer! I knew it would come . . . Oh to think that I should have lived to see the day when Brother should rise against Brother.' She and mother were crying. I lit out for the barn. Oh I do hate to see women cry."
—*Theodore Upson, sixteen-year-old Indiana farm boy*

***

Cleveland, Ohio
10 May, 1861

The schoolhouse was crowded beyond capacity as townsfolk clamored close together, attempting to hear one another over the din. Ivar lifted Inger high in his arms so that she wouldn't be trampled underfoot. The child looked about with unabashed interest, apparently not the least bit intimidated by the crowd.

The town was in the process of pooling their resources in hopes of helping the families of those who were enlisting. Money and other necessities were generously offered, and a good many men were planning to, or had already enlisted. Ivar looked at the faces he had known since childhood and felt a surge of wonderment at the sense of community that the current political state had brought about.

Ever since Sumter, entire towns across the country had seen
an explosion of patriotic activity: fundraisers were being held to
raise money for the soldiers, women were sewing uniforms as
fast as their fingers could manage it, parades were being held,
patriotic decorations and flags were prominently displayed in
every nook and cranny—it was as though both regions, North
and South alike, finally experienced a sense of unity and causes
worthy of life and death. Each side, of course, considered its
cause to be supported by God. Ivar shook his head slightly in
wonderment when he considered it. Each was convinced it was
in the right.

Their town was not unlike countless others across the Union
and Confederacy. Whole towns were enlisting to fight for their
respective causes. Neighbors were now fellow soldiers; young
boys who had grown up and gone to school together were now
drilling side by side, each hoping for a glorious opportunity to
defend his country. Physicians who had brought those boys into
the world were now serving as regimental surgeons and doctors.
The sense of family was enormous, and as Ivar considered those
in the schoolroom, he could pick out many men with whom he
would trust his life.

The majority of enlistees across the board were young men
eager to do their worst on the enemy. The average enlistee age,
Ivar noted, not only in his town but according to newspaper
reports of other towns as well, was between eighteen and twenty-
nine. This knowledge had put him in a bit of a quandary for the
past weeks that had him feeling torn.

He had responsibilities at home that money alone couldn't care
for. His father's health had declined in the past weeks and he was
less able to handle his responsibilities around the farm. Ivar had
taken to quickly finishing his own work and then rushing to help
Per, who always brushed him aside with a dark look and a grunt.
But Per could grunt all he wanted; the fact of the matter was that
he was favoring his aching leg more obviously each day, and the
pain seemed to be depleting his energy and strength.

Ivar glanced at his father, who stood next to him, leaning heavily on his cane, having refused a seat upon entrance although there were many who had offered him one.

Per still looked to the old country as his "home." It had been so long since they had left that Ivar could hardly remember it, and this new country had taken its place in his heart. He felt a loyalty to it that he was hard-pressed to define or explain.

There was much at stake, as well. Ivar had been reading articles in the newspaper that quoted some of Lincoln's many concerns in the matter, not the least of which was the fact that if the United States of America failed as a new young democracy, her European counterparts who had insisted all along that such a system could never hold itself together would be correct in their assertions. If a minority were permitted to simply leave at will, according to Lincoln, they would prove to all those who had jeered and mocked the notion of democracy that a self-governed people could not hold themselves together.

Ivar found himself in favor of the freedoms he enjoyed as a citizen of his adoptive land, and felt a tugging on his heart at the thought of defending the system. One glance at his father, however, with his face strained and white with the effort of standing, and he knew where his first loyalties lay.

Per turned to him, as if reading his thoughts, and said, "So when will you enlist, then?"

Ivar shook his head and leaned in close to his father. "There are enough already without me; Ohio has more than exceeded Lincoln's call for seventy-five thousand by itself. Besides, the call was for a ninety-day tour of duty. One month of that has already passed."

Per scrutinized Ivar's face, and the son wondered if his father could indeed read his thoughts. "But you would like to enlist," he said astutely.

Ivar shrugged and nuzzled his nose against Inger's cheek. "I have much to keep me home," he answered.

Per didn't respond, but he looked at Ivar for a few more intense moments before finally turning his gaze back over the room at large, where people were still making arrangements and preparations for war.

The night pressed onward with feelings and emotions still running at a high level. Just as the meeting was drawing to a close, a young woman Ivar had known since childhood approached him with a smile. "And how is little Inger doing these days?" she asked.

When Inger made no move to respond, but instead ducked her head in the crook of her father's neck, he nudged her a bit and said, "Will you tell Miss Harrison how you are faring, Inger?"

The little girl shook her head, bumping it against Ivar's jaw. He rolled his eyes a bit and said, "She's doing well, Elsa. She must just be feeling a bit shy today."

"Ooh," the young woman crooned, "that's fine, Inger. Sometimes I feel a bit shy myself. You have a good evening, Ivar," she said with a nod, and turning to go, cast one last appreciative glance over Ivar's muscular frame before joining her party at the other side of the room.

"Shy?" Per grunted, watching the young woman retreat. He glanced at his son. "Elsa Harrison is a nice enough young woman. She might welcome a visit sometime."

Ivar watched the young woman interact with her family and friends, his gaze passive and inscrutable. "I don't think so."

"You've known her for years."

"I knew Berit for years."

The conversation died a natural death at that point, and the subject of Elsa Harrison was dropped. The two men eventually left the schoolhouse and made their way home in Ivar's wagon, with Inger asleep, tucked close against her grandfather's lap. She didn't stir an inch when Per was returned to his home, and her custody transferred to her father's strong arms. Ivar carried her from the wagon to the house, where he placed her in her warm little bed with a kiss upon her forehead.

After seeing to the security of the animals and settling the house for the night, Ivar took his gold-rimmed spectacles and a book of Norse mythology from the mantle. He sank gratefully into the large wooden rocking chair that had once belonged to his grandfather and slowly tipped back, enjoying the rest and gazing into the fire for a moment.

He placed the spectacles on his face and opened his book, for a moment considering the momentous issue of the war, and the minor issue of one Elsa Harrison. One was infinitely more complex than the other, and as he had decided to avoid enlistment for the present, he turned his thoughts instead to the woman. She was beautiful, to be sure, and still available. Shaking his head slightly, he flipped through the pages of his book until he found the place he had finished reading the night before. His was a solitary life, and he preferred it that way. Better to be alone than to be hurt again.

***

Per Gundersen stretched his leg painfully before the fire and sat back in the chair, allowing himself the luxury of a wince. If Amanda had been in the room, he would have kept his expression carefully blank. She worried too much, his wife, and she always assumed there was nothing on God's green earth she couldn't take care of, if she worked hard enough. He feared she'd work herself into an early grave if she thought it would heal his leg.

And then, there was the matter of his son. Ivar wanted to enlist, Per mused, and he wouldn't because he was of the same mind as his mother. He was duty-bound and loyal, and determined to help his parents with their responsibilities since Per was now but a shadow of his former self. Per mentally cursed his wounded leg for the millionth time.

He glanced up as his wife entered the room and took the seat opposite his in front of the fire. She gathered her knitting into her lap with a contented sigh.

"What are you making this week?" he asked.

"New stockings for Inger. Her feet grow bigger by the day."

"Mmm." Per took his pipe from the drawer of the small table at his elbow and packing the sweet-smelling tobacco into it, lit it and settled back into his chair. He puffed for a moment before voicing his thoughts to his wife. "Ivar wants to enlist."

Amanda glanced up in surprise. "Did he tell you that?"

"No. He didn't say it aloud, but I read it in his face."

She shook her head and looked back down at her knitting. "He feels a connection to this country, you know. It's his sense of loyalty that will have him enlisting."

"He comes by that sense of loyalty through no fault of his own." Per puffed on his pipe and gazed into the fire, his expression bland.

She glanced up and stilled her hands, dropping them into her lap. "Are you blaming me for his loyalty?"

Per glanced at his wife with a smile, and removing the pipe from his teeth, pointed it at her. "I know you well."

Amanda bristled and resumed her knitting. "You're a clever one, aren't you, teasing your wife?" She sniffed. "Besides, loyalty is not a faulty quality."

"No," he admitted, "it isn't. But a father rather hopes it won't get his son killed." Danger or no, however, Per had seen Ivar's face, and had known even before the town meeting that his son would want to contribute his time and resources to the Union cause. Ivar's friends from childhood, grown with families of their own now, were already enlisted and drilling at a camp near Cincinnati.

"We can manage without him," Per mused aloud. "And we can care for Inger. She stays with us during the day, anyway. We'll just make a room for her in Ivar's old bedroom."

Amanda glanced up again, her expression tight. "I don't want him to go."

"I don't want him to, either. But he feels he needs to. He's a man now, and can make his own choices. I would hate for him to look back on his life feeling regret that he didn't do his duty. Regret is an unpleasant thing."

Amanda's features softened. "Surely you don't have regrets, Per."

"I ought to have been more careful."

She placed her knitting into her basket beside the chair and walked the two steps separating her chair from her husband's. He surprised her by pulling her downward and holding her close in his lap. She placed her hands around his neck and cradled his head close under her chin. "It was an accident. You couldn't have done anything to be more careful."

"It doesn't matter. It's done. I would like to talk to Ivar, however, and tell him to enlist. We'll be fine here."

"Yes, we will." Amanda felt a tear burn in her eye and fall down her cheek. "I'll talk to him first thing tomorrow morning."

***

Utah Territory
10 May, 1861

Ben's dreams took him back again to Bentley. He was spending time with Luke, who was visiting with his family for a month in the summer. The boys bellowed with laughter as they ran about the immense plantation property, playing a game of tag that had usually lasted the full afternoon in years past. The amazing thing was, that as long as it lasted, the boys rarely ended up in the same place twice. The plantation was gargantuan, and was filled with lawn and forest that a young child could lose himself in for days. The weather was usually pleasant, the vegetation lush and green, and the willows swaying constantly in the breezes looked like giant fairies, ready to grant one's fondest wish.

Ben looked back at Luke, who was rapidly closing the gap between them. Ben's eleven-year-old legs had grown over the summer, and he had been happy over that fact, but unfortunately Luke's legs had grown as well, and Ben was as evenly matched now as he ever had been. He groaned with a laugh at the feel of his cousin's fingertips as they brushed the back of his fine linen shirt that had been pristine when he had donned it that morning, but was now sweaty and spattered with mud. Acknowledging defeat, he slowed his pace to a walk, his breath coming in uneven gasps.

"You're it," Luke said, grinning, his black hair tousled, intense green eyes flashing.

"You're doing well, for a Boston pretty-boy," Ben laughed, still breathing hard. Looking at his cousin was like looking into a mirror. Folks often mistook the boys for brothers. The Birmingham black hair and green eyes were sprinkled liberally throughout the family, but none with such startling repetition as with the two cousins.

Luke punched him in the arm, but his face maintained its pleasant expression.

The boys turned at a shout from near the house. Luke squinted. "Who is that?" he asked.

"It's Joshua. He was a birthday present from my father this year. I like him very much! He can run even faster than I can and he's quite good at building things."

Luke glanced at Ben, but said nothing. Ben felt his face grow warm, this time not owing to the excessive South Carolinian heat. "I know," he began, and then stopped. "Does your mother still . . . does she still think that . . ."

"—that it's a 'sinful abomination?'" Luke finished for him. He nodded a bit stiffly. "Yes, she does. I think that's why she stayed home this time." Luke kicked at the dirt with the toe of his once-shiny shoe.

Ben watched as Joshua approached them, his jaw tightening. "You don't live here, Luke, you don't know how it is."

Luke shrugged but held his tongue. When the slave boy finally reached them, Luke extended his hand. "Luke Birmingham," he said, sounding and looking ridiculously adult—like his father when he met with business associates. "I'm Ben's cousin."

Joshua looked at Luke as though he were a fish flapping out of water. He finally took the proffered hand and shook it awkwardly.

"Joshua Birmingham," the young boy answered.

"I was thinking of looking for that tree house we made last year," Luke said to Ben. "Is it still there?"

Ben nodded. "My mother almost made me tear it down—she fears it'll collapse."

"Never! It could withstand a hurricane!" Luke grinned, and walked toward the edge of trees on the northern border of the Birmingham plantation. "Come along?" he asked Joshua over his shoulder.

When the boys located the platform situated nearly twelve feet off the ground, Luke laughed in surprise. "It looks as good as new! Just like when we built it."

They scrambled up the branches and finally perched, the three of them, atop the platform that probably wasn't suitable for even two. Taking turns standing and surveying the view, they imagined they could see enemy ships out in the harbor.

The resounding crack that split the platform caught them all by surprise. Landing on the ground below with a rush of expelled air, the three lay prostrate for a moment before they were able to emit groans of dismay. "I'll be darned," Luke muttered as he rolled to one side and into a sitting position, cradling an arm that had been pierced by a small chunk of shattered wood. "Your mother was right."

The battered trio hopped and pulled their way toward the plantation house, wondering at the best course of action. "If we go in there," Ben said, swiping at a trickle of blood that ran down one temple and toward his eye, "I'll have to tell my mother what happened."

"Well, we can't just sit here bleedin' all day," Joshua commented painfully, his hand clamped on blood oozing from his jaw where he'd struck a rock upon landing. His eyes brightened. "We'll go to Ruth!" he said.

Ben shook his head, wincing. "Ruth's probably in the house."

"She ain't," said Joshua. She was on her way to her shack to check on Mary when I left the house to find you."

Ben nodded and turned toward the slave quarters, situated down a gentle slope from the big house. "What's wrong with Mary?"

"She gots the fever, or somethin,'" Joshua murmured as they dragged their pathetic selves down the hill.

Ben eyed the faces of the slaves as they ventured toward Ruth's door. The expressions were often distrustful, resentful, or perhaps apprehensive when they met his face before casting their gazes downward. Thoughts of Northern rhetoric that he was only just beginning to hear from his cousin and his Aunt Elizabeth swirled about in his head as he studied the scene.

Finally, Ben knocked on a door that was identical to all the rest along a row of small shack-like houses. Ruth's face was as familiar to him as his own mother's, and he suddenly doubted the wisdom of going to her for help. She was a kind woman, but very no-nonsense, and he found himself wishing he could look away from her knowing expression.

"Well, Mastah Benjamin," she murmured, "what've you boys gotten yourselves into?"

Ben cleared his throat, stammering about for the right word.

Joshua finally intervened. "We was climbin' a tree, Auntie Ruth, and we done fell out of it."

"And this here tree? Did it have a tree house attached?"

The boys suddenly found themselves extremely interested in the toes of their shoes. Ruth finally caught sight of the wood protruding from Luke's arm. "Oh, you crazy boys," she moaned and gestured for the three of them to enter.

Ruth bustled about inside, going through a few jars and fabric bags situated on a shelf, while a young girl of two slept on a bed in the corner. An older child, probably six or seven, sat by the baby's side, watching her sleep.

"Are you Mary?" Luke asked the older girl in quiet tones, not wishing to disturb the sleeping toddler.

The girl shook her head and pointed to the baby. "That be Mary," she mouthed. "I's just takin' care of her."

Luke eyed the crudity of the small house and Ben knew his cousin was seeing it for the first time. He had known Ruth since before he could remember, but had never before set foot in her shack. Ben tried to see the shack through Luke's eyes, and that new perspective made him intensely uncomfortable. Ruth was smart and kind, and the house somehow didn't fit her.

Luke turned his attention to Joshua, who was still holding a hand along his jaw. "So Ruth is your aunt?"

"Naw. That just be what we all calls her. She's like ever'body's aunt, and she's mighty fine at doctorin'."

"Good thing," Luke murmured and watched as Ruth finally collected whatever it was she had been looking for, and approached them with rags and a few jars of who knew what.

"Now," the woman said as she took Luke's hand in her own and extended his aching arm. "Why didn't you three head up to the big house?" The smile in her voice suggested she already knew the answer.

"Oh, Aunt Ruth," Ben said. "You know what my mother would say."

"I does indeed. And she'd be right." The soft, rich tones of her voice were soothing despite her censure.

Luke winced as Ruth gently pulled the small piece of wood from his arm and angled him toward the light from a small window, making sure she'd retrieved all of the splinters. She then wiped his arm with a damp cloth and rubbed some horrible smelling salve onto it before wrapping it in a strip of bandage.

As she applied her ministrations to the other two boys, Ben noticed she took care to serve Luke and him first—caring for Joshua, whose wound was by far the nastiest, last.

"Interestin', ain't it, boys?" She finished with Joshua and gathered the rags she'd used on the three of them, holding them up to the light for comparison. "Y'all bleed the same."

Ben awoke with a start, his body damp with sweat, his throat raw. His breath came in quick gasps as he tried to orient himself in the bedroom of his small home. The dream had been so real, the memories so fresh it was as though he had lived it all over again. He placed a trembling hand to his forehead, almost expecting to feel the bandage Ruth had placed there those many years ago.

He mentally cursed as he felt a burning behind his eyes and wished the tears away, although they paid him no heed and fell down his face. Rising from his bed, he ran a hand through his disheveled hair and paced the room for a bit, eventually coming to a stop beside his bed and falling to his knees.

"Please," he whispered aloud, "please, wilt Thou not simply let me forget?"

CHAPTER 16

"Lincoln may bring his 75,000 troops against us. We fight for our homes, our fathers and mothers, our wives, brothers, sisters, sons and daughters! . . . We can call out a million of peoples if need be, and when they are cut down we can call another, and still another."
—*Confederate Vice President Alexander Stephens*

***

Charleston, South Carolina
15 May, 1861

Richard Birmingham strolled down the street on the way to the family townhouse where he had been staying since the attack on Fort Sumter. Town life was much more exciting than the plantation; his friends were all at their townhouses as well, and with the state of things in the Confederacy, he wasn't willing to miss one exhilarating moment. Besides which, he mused with a scowl, Emily had all but made his life a living nightmare with her continued veiled accusations about the fatherhood of the slave girl's child. Ever since that girl had given birth and Emily had first implicated him in the hallway after her visit with those Charlesworth women, Emily seemed to have made it her mission to drive him from Bentley.

She had succeeded, but he told himself it wasn't because he was afraid of the recriminations. He knew he was the child's father, and he also knew that almost every one of his friends and their fathers had sired children by their slaves, some of them more than one each. He drew himself up as he walked, shoving his bitterness at his stupid sister and their mother out of his mind.

It was true, Sarah would not have taken it well had he actually admitted to fathering Mary's child. It made him angry. Who was she to tell him what he could and couldn't do? He wasn't a child anymore, and besides, it was unseemly the way Sarah ran their homes and their lives. His father had not one ounce of say in anything transpiring at Bentley, not that Richard had ever heard him try, and Richard found it humiliating that his friends all had conventional parents; fathers who were in charge of the plantation and its business, and mothers who took care of the parties and the general running of the household.

He longed for it to be thus in his own family—then he could hold his head up with pride—but no, Sarah not only supervised the household, she also supervised the field work, the amount of rice produced, the details concerning the produce grown on the plantation. She negotiated the sale of the produce—she did everything! All Jeffrey ever did was run about the country with his politician friends. It would have been one thing if his father had run for and secured an office of his own, but he was too pathetic for even that. He "advised" his friends. He sometimes acted as a liaison between disagreeing parties. But he never took the bull by the horns and claimed a position of his own.

Richard shook his head as he entered the front door, opened by a Negro servant who stood at the door day and night to watch for his comings and goings, and pondered on the one good thing that had come from his father's associations with influential people. Because of Jeffrey, Richard had been on hand when Sumter was fired upon, and had met Roger Pryor.

Pryor was the key to everything Richard wanted. He wanted a commission in the Confederate Army, and he wanted to be stationed as soon as possible in Virginia, across the Potomac from Black Lincoln's capitol. He wanted to be part of an attack on the tyrannical city, and he wanted in on the glory that was sure to follow. According to information he had amassed from his friends in recent weeks, the "Palmetto Guards" were on their way to Richmond to be mustered into Confederate service, and he wanted to be part of that Company. It was Company I of the Second South Carolina Volunteer Infantry that had been in place on Morris Island when Sumter was attacked. Now they were on their way to become part of Robert E. Lee's Army of Northern Virginia. Richard determined then that he would be one of them, or die trying.

His abrupt dismissal from West Point the year before had been a humiliation almost beyond bearing and was not something the family ever discussed. He had old scores to settle and could accomplish those ends if he were actively employed and engaged with the new Army. His superiors at school had contested that his grades and scholastic performance were substandard, and that he was not fit West Point material. They had also asserted that he had a problem with authority—that he was unwilling to follow the orders of his superiors and that he was insolent and impertinent.

He! Impertinent! Did they not know that his family owned hundreds of slaves, that they produced more rice each year than many of the other plantations combined, and that he was as wealthy as Midas? They had no idea of the Birmingham wealth and power, even if it was spearheaded by his mother, of all people, and hadn't a clue who they were dealing with.

Richard knew that Roger Pryor was an influential Virginian, and being Jeffrey Birmingham's son had its advantages. Most Confederate officers and politicians knew of Jeffrey and admired his cool head. Richard had decided the night Sumter was bombed that he would use it to his advantage and shake the dust of Bentley from his feet. Maybe when he was done living his life he would settle down on the plantation that was now his since Ben, the fool, was no longer around. And when he did claim Bentley for his own, the first thing he would do would be to give Jackson liberal permission with the whip, and then he'd teach Mary a thing or two about sharing secrets with the plantation master's sister.

Smiling at his own bright future, he walked with a firm step into the study and sat at his father's massive oak desk. Casting an appreciative eye over the masculine appointments evident in the color and décor of the room, he took a piece of paper from a drawer, dipped Jeffrey's pen in an inkwell, and drafted a letter to Roger Pryor in Virginia.

***

Utah Territory
20 May, 1861

Ben Birmingham sat in the telegraph office receiving the incoming message. When it was final, and he glanced down at the words he'd written himself, he placed his elbow upon the desk and rested his head in his hand. Massaging his forehead against the pain he felt building behind his eyes, he surrendered to the inevitable.

North Carolina had just seceded. Earlier in the month, Arkansas and Tennessee had joined the Confederacy as well. That made a grand total of eleven states—eleven—that were preparing to wage war on their mother country. There were other states still on the "border" that were volatile, many split in half, with one side favoring the Union, the other the Confederacy, and it was anybody's guess as to which way they would fall.

Lincoln tread very carefully, his movements measured and cautious, yet he was uncompromising in his commitment to preserve the nation. While Lincoln had one plan, however, Ben had been mulling over a plan of his own.

There was a chance, a chance, that with the nation's state of affairs, he might be able to finish what he'd started before leaving South Carolina. Lincoln's current goals might not include the total abolition of slavery, but they did include the prevention of slavery expansion into the new territories and states. Lincoln had said on more than one occasion that he didn't feel it was his constitutional right to interfere with slavery where it already existed, but it was rumored in the press that he was beginning to doubt the constitutionality of slavery altogether. He had long called it "abhorrent"; Ben had to hope that in time, and if the North prevailed, the country would follow suit with its European contemporaries and abolish the enslavement of people.

Given his newfound hope, Ben didn't see any recourse other than to do that which he had been avoiding all along. He had to go back. Not to Bentley, but to Boston. It was one small thing that he could do to not only help preserve a nation that was crumbling at the seams, but also fight against a system he had learned to mistrust when exposed to the opinions of his abolitionist relatives, and then hated as those opinions had become his own.

The door to the telegraph office opened, and Ben emitted a low groan at the person who stepped inside. It was Earl Dobranski. He brandished two pair of over-sized gloves as he entered, gleefully stating, "Look at what just came by Pony Express! Now we can fight and not worry about breaking our knuckles!"

Ben just stared at the young man, the corners of his mouth twitching involuntarily into a grin. Earl continually egged Ben into wrestling and fighting matches that often left both of them bruised, bloody, and sore.

"And I suppose you'll be wanting to try those gloves immediately?" Ben mused with a shake of his head.

"Well, if you're finished here, that is."

Ben glanced at his pocket watch and nodded, rising from his stool and taking the most recently transmitted message into the inner office where his boss sat, hard at work transcribing news for the paper. "This just came over the wires," he said to Douglas O'Brian.

O'Brian scanned the contents, his features grim. "Another one," he sighed. "I'm glad I'm here and not there," the man murmured, adding the paper to a large stack on his desk. He glanced at the clock on the wall, which had begun to chime the five o'clock hour. "That means you're finished for the day," he said to Ben. "Have a good evening."

Ben offered the man a sympathetic smile and thought of Earl, on the other side of the door, with those enormous gloves. "Are you sure you don't want me to stay a bit longer tonight? I really don't mind."

O'Brian waved a hand at him. "You go. Enjoy your night. I'm sure we'll be plenty busy tomorrow." The telegraph was brand new, the wires having just that year been strung and connected, and the flow of information from the East coast was staggering and, at the same time, miraculous. News that before was weeks old, at best, was now available the very day it happened. People were ecstatic.

Ben took a closer look at his boss. The man was tired. He was young, perhaps barely into his forties, and had a wife and seven children waiting at home for him.

"Truly, sir," he said, sincerely this time, "I don't mind staying if you'd like to go home."

O'Brian sat back in his chair and yawned. "No," he finally said. "You go. Perhaps I'll accept that offer tomorrow night."

Ben joined Earl in the front office, warily eyeing the gloves. "Well," he told the young man, "I don't suppose you're going to just let me go home peacefully?"

"Definitely not."

"Somehow I figured as much." Ben accepted the pair of gloves from Earl and the two made their way outside. "My house this time, or yours?"

"Let's do it at yours. My mother will box my ears herself if she sees these."

"And with good reason."

"Rubbish! These are safer than regular fists!"

"Boy, I think you are just plumb crazy," Ben muttered as they strolled down the street toward his house.

"When are you going to lose that funny-sounding accent of yours? You been here a good five years!"

"I suppose some things just don't go away, now matter how much you wish they would."

***

Cleveland, Ohio
20 May, 1861

Ivar Gundersen paced back and forth in front of the enlistment office, waging an internal battle about whether or not he was going to go inside. His mother had spoken with him over a week before, telling him that she knew he was feeling he needed to support the cause and enlist, but that he had felt reservations about leaving the family. She had drawn herself up, then, and told him in a voice that brooked no argument that the family would be fine, that she would help with Per's farm duties, as well as Ivar's. "And besides," she had added, "Inger spends most of her time with us anyway. It won't be much different for her than it would be if you were here."

He wasn't sure how he had felt about that, but his mother had been right about one thing—he was feeling a certain amount of something . . . perhaps it was just guilt, but he had watched as all of his friends enlisted and left and wondered if he shouldn't have followed suit. He was a man, after all, and a Gundersen at that. Gundersens didn't shirk their responsibilities, and he felt Uncle Sam tugging on his shirttails.

Ivar muttered a curse and finally entered the building, his decision made. A cheery clerk, roughly fifty years old, greeted him. Once Ivar stated the reason for his visit, the man's smile grew even bigger, something Ivar wouldn't have believed possible upon his entry.

"You've come just at the right time, then, my friend!" the man boomed. "Last week I would have told you we had too many, but as it happens, we just received word yesterday of a bad measles outbreak at Camp Dennison. In case those poor sick ones don't fare too well, we're sending a few more in, just to have as reserve."

"Camp Dennison? Where is that?"

"Cincinnati."

Ivar took a deep breath. It was only ninety days, after all. Ninety days passed quickly, and if people's optimistic projections proved to be accurate, he would be home in no time. "Sign me up," he said to the man behind the counter.

"Right you are! Son, welcome to the Seventh Ohio Volunteer Infantry!"

***

New Orleans
21 May, 1861

Jean-Pierre sat at the desk in his office, grateful that the swelling in his left eye had diminished enough that it was no longer an effort to see through it. Marie had been right. Nobody in New Orleans had been happy with his editorial, and under the cover of darkness, he had been mobbed on his way home the day the article had run.

Now, he faced another dilemma. He sat, pen poised over paper, reviewing his latest editorial. Part of him had written the thing for spite; he was not about to be bullied into censoring his own thoughts just because the majority demanded it! And yet he had to wonder at the wisdom of actually printing it.

North Carolina had seceded the day before, bringing the grand total of Confederate states to eleven. He had taken the information he possessed on each of those states, and arranged, on paper, some interesting numbers. To date, the South enjoyed the ownership of nearly 20,000 factories, employing 100,000 people. The problem, however, in terms of comparison, was that the North boasted 100,000 factories, employing over one million workers. The huge disparities did not stop there; the North possessed 20,000 miles of uniform gauge railroad track, to the South's mere 9,000 miles of track that differed in width, necessitating numerous stops and starts, and the emptying of goods from one train and loading onto another in order to continue along the journey.

When one looked at the sheer numbers in population, Jean-Pierre wondered if he were the only person in the South considering the vast differences. The population of the Northern states was twenty-two million people. The South held approximately nine million, four million of which were slaves. Jean-Pierre rubbed his sore eye and shook his head. The more information he amassed, the more alarmed he became. The Union possessed eighty-one percent of the country's bank deposits, placing Northern wealth amazingly beyond what the South laid claim to.

The South had cotton.

The Confederacy pinned the bulk of its hope on cotton, its value to European buyers, and the morale of a South willing to defend its way of life. The Confederacy had even begun withholding shipments, which, given the preliminary efforts of Lincoln's blockade was actually a fortuitous thing, in hopes that European markets would panic without it, officially recognize the Confederacy, and aid its war efforts.

In Jean-Pierre's opinion, it was all a hopelessly lost cause. Wise purchasing decisions and good prices had allowed Europeans, especially the British, to stockpile cotton in prior years, leaving them with nearly a two-year supply on hand. Added to that fact was that Egypt and India, areas in which the British currently held a vested interest, were producing cotton on their own. To bring that fact to light, however, might just be Jean-Pierre's demise. He shifted in his seat, wincing at the pain in his left side. The pain stirred him into angry action, and he began setting the letters for the article despite a warning voice inside his head that bid him stop. Hurriedly, almost blindly, he stacked the words side by side, glancing at the paper on which he had written his thoughts but hardly needing to; he had already committed the brief article to memory.

Finally, the thing was finished and ready for printing. He stood back to view his handiwork and carried the tray to the press. He set it down and paused, resting his hands on his hips, his hot temper finally retreating and cooler reasoning taking its place.

It would be suicide to print the article. The influential members of Confederate society would not appreciate having their enormous disadvantages thrown out for all to see, and the underprivileged, working class laborers and farmers had bought into the myth that Southern society worked to their advantage by keeping its thumb on the Negro. Nobody seemed to care or agree that the Confederacy was doomed to failure, if for no other reason than the fact that its purse was too small. And Jean-Pierre found himself wishing, for the first time in many a year, that he were home in France. France was not perfect, but it was far away from the current chaos that had become his reality.

Smiling grimly, Jean-Pierre printed one sheet of his article and held it up, blowing gently on the ink. With a sigh of resignation, he mulled over the fact that the two most precious things in his life, his wife and daughter, were more important to him than speaking his mind to the New Orleans general populace. He didn't want further injury, nor did he want to place Jenny and Marie in danger.

He left the article on a nearby table and took the typeset, dismantling the letters and placing them back into their proper trays. Perhaps if he didn't have quite so much to live for, he could afford to be reckless. The potential outcome simply wasn't worth the risk.

Going about his duties of setting other, less inflammatory articles for the paper occupied the rest of his time, and he worked steadily until Michael entered the shop early in the evening. "It is my turn, boy," the older man said without preamble. "You go home to your wife."

That Jean-Pierre didn't argue spoke volumes about the level of his fatigue. He gathered his belongings, showed Michael the work that had been accomplished to that point, and turned to go. As he walked toward the front door, the lone paper containing his article caught his eye. He retrieved it from the table as he passed, folding it in four and placing it in his coat pocket.

He fetched his horse and open carriage wearily, preparing them for the short trip home. He glanced at the front of the newspaper office, his home away from home for so many years, and felt a surge of pride at his successes. He loved that newspaper, and realized it meant almost as much to him as did his family. His features pensive, he climbed into the carriage and gathered the reins, not noticing that a piece of folded paper fell from his pocket as he clutched his left side, inside his overcoat. The pain was subsiding, he noticed, but was an ever-present reminder of the nature of his "friends."

He snapped the reins and made his way toward home, unaware of the piece of paper, subtly blowing in the breeze as it lay innocently on the dusty street in front of the newspaper office.

CHAPTER 17

"In the untimely loss of your noble son, our affliction here is scarcely less than your own. So much of promised usefulness to one's country, and of bright hopes for one's self and friends, have rarely been so suddenly dashed as in his fall."
—*Letter from Abraham Lincoln to the parents of Colonel Elmer Ellsworth*

***

*Boston, Massachusetts
24 May, 1861*

Luke picked up the newly delivered paper and took a seat in his father's office, across the desk from him. He sat back in his chair, one ankle slung over the other leg, his foot bouncing until his eyes snagged on the headline.

"And the killing has begun," he murmured to James, who gave a small start of surprise.

"Where?"

"Alexandria, Virginia. Across the Potomac from the capitol."

"What does it say?"

Luke leaned forward and spread the paper sideways on the large desk so that James could read along with him. Apparently, Lincoln had decided that the Virginians, in his own words, having "thus allowed this giant insurrection to make its nest within her borders . . . this government has no choice but to deal with it, where it finds it."

There was a perfunctory knock on the door before it opened and Elizabeth stepped inside. "Am I going to dine by myself this morning, then?" she asked, then stopped short when she noticed the men, their heads nearly touching over the desk, scanning the contents of the paper.

"What is it?" She fairly flew to the desk.

Luke sighed. "Apparently Lincoln sent troops across the river, thinking to occupy Alexandria, and a Colonel Elmer Ellsworth made to remove a Rebel flag flying above a hotel. He climbed the stairs, removed the thing, and on his way back down was shot by the hotelkeeper."

"What happened to the hotelkeeper?" Elizabeth's face was white.

"Ellsworth's aide shot him," James murmured, still reading over the article.

"Well," he finally said when he finished. "It appears we have our first martyr. And the Confederacy has theirs."

Elizabeth picked up the newspaper and read the article herself. "Ellsworth was a personal friend of the president; his body is now lying in state in the White House," she murmured as she read. "People have been carving out chunks of the staircase where he died as souvenirs." She shook her head as she walked from the room, still reading the story, her full skirts making a soft rustling sound as she moved.

She stopped short in the hall, James bumping into her from behind, as she viewed Anne who was rushing into the house with Robert close on her heels. Robert dashed around his sister, his eyes enormous. "The flags outside are at half-staff! Have you heard the news? Those dirty Rebels have killed a Colonel! I wish I could go take care of them myself!"

Anne, meanwhile, was smoothing her hand over a decidedly wrinkled day dress of periwinkle blue. Her hair was coming lose from its pins, making her appear as though she had been running around outside.

"James," Elizabeth said in a deceptively calm voice. "What

time is it?"

James consulted his pocket-watch. "Seven-thirty."

"Seven-thirty. Now why is it my children are running about town so early in the morning before they've even had breakfast? How is it, I wonder, that they leave and I'm not even aware of it?"

Anne, Robert, Luke, and James all eyed her warily. The voice might be calm, but beneath it was a strain they knew all too well. When Elizabeth was irritated, the family usually ran for the figurative hills—not because she was explosive, but because the arctic blast from her formidable stare was their collective undoing.

"I was out with Nathaniel," Robert stammered. "He sent a note around early this morning saying something big had happened, and the paper wasn't here yet, so we went out to see for ourselves . . ."

Elizabeth pointed at the breakfast room, and Robert grinned sheepishly, making his way through the open doors.

"But isn't it amazing?" he stuck his head back through the doorway to ask. "They've shot and killed an Army colonel!"

"Eat!" Elizabeth responded. "And you," she said, looking at Anne. She approached her oldest daughter, creasing the newspaper and folding it under her arm, taking in Anne's appearance with a slight shake of her head. "Anne, I won't even pretend to know what you've been up to lately, and I know you're well past the age where I can tell you what to do, but as you're still living in my house, don't you think you at least owe me the courtesy of keeping me informed?"

Anne had the grace to look chagrined. Two spots of color appeared on her high cheekbones and she tucked a wayward strand of hair back into its bun. "Mother," she said finally on a sigh, "I've been . . . working."

Elizabeth cocked a brow. "And this 'work' of yours sends you home with wrinkled clothing and mussed hair?"

Anne snorted. "It's respectable work, entirely. It's only that . . ." She paused, glancing at her father, who had moved to stand next to his wife and was also eyeing his daughter with interest.

"Yes?" he prompted.

"It's not exactly conventional," she muttered.

"Have you been working down at the docks?" he asked.

"No, sir."

"Are you a stonemason?"

"No, sir."

"A bricklayer?"

"No."

"And we've already established that you're not frequenting seedy taverns for entertainment purposes."

"Correct." Her color mounted.

"Well, then," he concluded, "how dire can your straits possibly be?"

Her mouth twitched. "You, father dear, are toying with me."

"Indeed I am."

She sighed, an expression of resolution crossing her face. "Have you ever heard of Adam Jones?"

Elizabeth's brow wrinkled. "The name sounds familiar."

"The newspaper reporter?" James asked.

"Yes." Anne paused. "He's me. I'm Adam Jones."

The stunned silence that met her announcement echoed in the foyer. "You're a man?" her father finally choked out.

Anne's laughter burst forth in genuine amusement, but there was an edge to it that belied the true state of her nerves. "I write under the name of Adam Jones—I simply go about the city, listen to people's conversations, and write my observations. It really is as simple as that."

"Then why," Elizabeth countered, "do you come home looking as though you've been in a fight?"

"I like to hurry . . ." Anne trailed off lamely.

Her parents scrutinized her without comment.

"Oh, very well," she huffed. "I dress as a boy."

This time, the silence fairly roared.

"That is," Anne continued in a hurry when they could do nothing but stare at her in disbelief, "I have access to many more places when I'm dressed in unobtrusive, yet *respectable* boy clothing, and nobody really questions what I'm about. If they ask, I tell them exactly what I'm doing and more often than not, they're altogether too willing to speak to someone who may have the power to place their names in print." She spread her hands wide. "It's not as awful as it sounds."

Anne glanced to her right, where her brothers, all three, stood in the doorway to the breakfast room. Each wore an expression of shock so similar, even young Jimmy, that had she been less worried she would have laughed aloud. James opened and closed his mouth three times before finally clamping it shut altogether and retreating to his study with a firm step. To her right, Anne heard Robert whisper to Luke, "Get the smelling salts."

"Why?" Luke whispered in kind.

"Because I'm going to go tell Camille!"

***

Luke left the house after eating breakfast, still shaking his head over his sister's revelation. He supposed he should be scandalized, but he was secretly so proud of Anne that he wanted to tell everyone that "Adam Jones" was his sister. He was only one of a million people, though, who would find that fact impressive. If patrons of the paper knew that one of their favorite columnists was actually a woman daring to venture into male territory, they would find it appalling. The men would find it insulting. Luke knew, himself, of perhaps a handful of female newspaper columnists across the country, and to his knowledge, none of them had posed as a man in order to get a story.

Anne was a bright woman, as was his mother, and now according to Robert, Camille was actually showing signs of substantial intellect. Luke had tried for weeks now to draw Anne into not only the Abolition Society meetings, but the women's rights meetings as well, but she had claimed to be too busy. He had felt she had been making excuses that were unfounded.

He smiled and whistled a sprightly tune as he strolled the last few feet to the entrance to the bank. Now he knew she had been legitimately engaged in something far more time consuming than he would have ever imagined. He entered the building and spied, almost immediately, the president of the bank with whom he was on fairly friendly terms.

"You're looking chipper this morning, Birmingham. Perhaps you've not heard the news."

Luke immediately sobered. In his adulation over Anne, he had forgotten there was a war on. "Actually, sir, I have heard. It's tragic."

Mr. Strickland offered Luke his hand. "It is indeed tragic. But even worse, we have trouble brewing in the New York office. I'd like you to come upstairs with me for a moment to discuss it."

Luke agreed; what could he do? He couldn't very well mention to the man that he had a stack of work waiting for him at his desk. He was a loan officer, and it was almost a surprise daily that despite events occurring to the south, the world still revolved, and loans still needed processing; people still purchased buildings for businesses and lots for new homes.

When they reached Mr. Strickland's office, Luke was offered a seat across from a massive desk. He tried not to stare at the enormous room, which was easily as large as his father's office down the street. It was a fresh experience; Luke had never had a personal visit with the bank president.

"Mr. Norman tells me that you've had some experience in smoothing ruffled feathers for the bank before. Last year, wasn't it?" Mr. Strickland asked, his fingers steepled, elbows resting on the desk.

"Yes, sir, but it really wasn't much . . ."

Strickland waved his comment aside. "It was enough, apparently, to stave off a riot. Those immigrants and tradesmen are never content with their lot; they want to make life miserable for the rest of us who work hard to achieve our positions."

They work harder than most of us ever will, and won't receive a fraction of what we have! Luke clamped his jaw so tightly it hurt. He had his own job to think of. It wouldn't do to insult the president of the institution. It was true; he had prevented a problem the year before, but it hadn't been because he was defending the bank. He had listened to the complaints and predicaments of a handful of tradesmen when they had applied for a loan to launch their own business. The bank had been prepared to turn them away, but Luke had rescued the application from the garbage can and met with them, working through weaknesses in the bank's stringent requirements to find a way for them to receive the money they needed. He hadn't regretted it for a moment, either. The payments were always in full and timely.

So what, exactly was the point of the current discussion? He couldn't imagine what Strickland wanted from him. The man responded as though reading his thoughts.

"How would you feel about a trip to New York?"

"Now? But sir, I have so much work to do here—"

"I'll have your work reassigned." Strickland sighed and rubbed the bridge of his nose with his forefinger. "I received word from my brother this morning that they are in need of someone who can act in a . . . diplomatic capacity. The Irish in New York are on the verge of explosion. We need a bank representative who can cool some tempers. I thought you might be the man for that job."

"Because of one small instance last year? Forgive me sir, but I don't understand why you're choosing me." He might be killing his chances for movement through the ranks at the bank, but Luke was wary of the man's motives. Aside from that, he hadn't risen to his current level by merely being complacent. He watched his own back, and very carefully. "I might think you would send your nephew, instead. He seems to hold much more influence than I do, at this point."

Strickland stared at him as though he were insane. "Do you not appreciate what I'm offering you, Birmingham?"

"I do, sir, I just don't understand it."

Strickland sighed and leaned back in his chair. "My nephew couldn't talk his way out of an argument with an infant."

Luke suppressed a smile. He'd have to pass that along to Camille. Her precious Olivia's sister's husband's bank promotion had indeed been an act of familial kindness.

"And," Strickland continued, "my brother's branch has gone through several changes in recent months that have left them with very inexperienced leadership. Feelings in New York right now are also running high against the immigrant population, and while my brother is disgusted, and justifiably so, it won't do to have the ragamuffin lot of them tear the building down, brick by brick.

"Last year, when you worked your magic for that loan application, Mr. Norman wasn't happy. In fact, he came to me complaining about it." Strickland smiled grimly. "I let it go, because I wanted to see what would happen with it. Had they defaulted on that loan, it would have meant your job, Birmingham. Were you aware of that?"

Luke hoped the surprise he felt wasn't obvious on his face. He'd have to be sure to thank the borrowers for making their payments on time! "No sir, but I do remember Mr. Norman being angry about it."

Strickland nodded. "Well, basically, you're my last hope."

Finally, a shred of honesty. "I can appreciate that, sir, and I'll go to New York. I'm not entirely sure what you'd like me to accomplish, however."

"We'll talk about that. Let me send for Norman and I'll have your other work reassigned."

Luke bit back a protest. Much of the work he had waiting for him concerned applications much like the one Strickland had made reference to; the one that had nearly cost him his job. Luke knew of only one other person in the entire department who might give the applications a fighting chance.

"Please, sir," he interjected. "Would you see if Mr. Norman won't give my work to Leonard Goldwell?"

Strickland looked at him closely, but in the end, agreed. He then spent the bulk of the day instructing Luke on the business of the New York office, and exactly what they hoped would transpire with his visit.

When the workday finally drew to a close, Luke made a quick

trip to his office and apologized to Goldwell for his excess work-load. The man grinned good-naturedly and told Luke he would one day call in his favors. Luke left the building, his brain taxing itself with trying to sort his thoughts. He passed the enlistment office and paused, his heart giving a leap.

Ever since Lincoln's call for men, he had felt torn. His first impulse had been to rush downtown and sign up immediately. He had held back, however, for reasons he couldn't understand. Now the quota had been more than filled, and everyone waited to see if the South's little rebellion would be squashed immediately or prolonged. It was the general consensus of those in the North that the insurrection would be resolved in a very short matter of time.

Luke continued walking, his eyes cast downward as he lost himself in his thoughts. He had much to do before leaving for New York. Tonight there was another Society meeting, followed by a women's rights meeting, where he was hoping to see Abigail Van Dyke again. His heart jumped a bit at the thought, and he smiled for the first time in hours.

He made the mile walk to his home in a short time and strode through the front doors, going immediately to check the mail left on a side table. He flipped through his personal correspondence, stopping with a smile at a letter from Ben. It was what he had been hoping for; he missed his cousin immensely.

The house was relatively quiet for the evening and he wondered where everyone had gone. He asked Griffen when he passed through the hallway, and was told the bulk of the family was attending a charity dinner for the local hospital. Luke wandered into the empty parlor and sat on the sofa with a sigh, looking about at the home that had been his refuge for so many years. It really was past time he purchase a home of his own; he had been dragging his feet because he knew, silly as it sounded, that he would miss the daily association with his family.

He propped his feet on a nearby ottoman, crossing them comfortably at the ankles, and after loosening his tie, opened the letter from Ben.

Luke,

I find myself thinking of home every waking hour, I dream of home when I sleep, and of the business I left unintentionally unfinished. I am haunted by memories and faces, and I know I'll not rest until I return to do my part to help set things right.

I don't know of your plans for the future, but I think my first step must be to join you in Boston. I have sufficient funds to see me through the journey and support myself once there. I don't know how long this conflict will continue; I have read the papers and correspondence we receive from your end of the country, and I know people seem to think it will be over quickly. I have my doubts, however. If the North thinks to vanquish the petulant child with a quick whipping, I would tell every northern citizen that they do not know what they're facing.

They're facing a people who will bleed and die before willingly sacrificing their way of life, and what they see as their "freedom." That this freedom holds as its main component and supporter the enslavement of others is of no consequence. The ideology is at odds with logic, but it is reality, and will not change. The armies of the North will be forced to charge their way South and completely destroy the whole of it before Southern aristocracy will admit defeat.

At any rate, cousin, I will see you as soon as I can. I'm making arrangements here for someone to care for my home and few belongings, and will join you shortly. I have one request: please do not enlist without me.

Always,

Ben.

Luke reread the letter two, and then three times before setting it gently in his lap and leaning his head back against the sofa. He stared at the ceiling, knowing with a sinking surety that Ben was right. Those who felt the conflict would resolve itself in a matter of weeks were living a fantasy that would soon be destroyed. The war would last as long as the Confederacy could hold out, and he supposed that length of time remained to be seen.

As for enlistment, it was as though his earlier pause outside the enlistment office downtown had been somehow prophetic. Ben wanted to enlist, and was going to raise up arms against his homeland. Suppose Ben's brother, Richard, enlisted? What then? Brother fighting against brother? Would they someday meet on a battlefield? Be forced to shoot each other? It was insane!

The contents of the letter on his lap swirled with his thoughts of the trouble he would soon be facing in New York, and he wondered when his life had suddenly become so complex. He had been happy going to work, attending Society meetings and spending time with his quirky family.

Change was on the horizon.

CHAPTER 18

"I've got the best suit of clothes that I [ever] had in my life."
—*Private Peter Wilson, 1st Iowa Volunteers*

***

Camp Dennison, Cincinnati, Ohio
4 June, 1861

Ivar sat in the barracks, looking outside at the sheet of rain that cascaded to the earth in a flood unlike anything he'd ever witnessed. He had been at the camp with his new regiment, the 7th Ohio, for just over a week, and when it wasn't raining, it was instead hot and humid.

He wallowed in self-pity for a moment, wondering what Inger was doing at that very moment and hoping she was happy. Of course, his mother had been right—Inger's routine hadn't been greatly changed.

It wasn't as though camp life was so horribly bad—the time of the day not occupied with drills was filled with letter writing to those at home, personal quiet time, and of late a camp favorite—trying to deal with the leaking barracks. By the time he arrived in camp, rumors about possible movement toward Virginia had begun to spread, and he wondered how much longer the troops would stay at Dennison.

The sheer number of men was impressive. Even before he had arrived, the 5th, 9th and 13th Ohio Volunteers had joined the

7th. The level of enthusiasm and expectations for success were high. Upon his arrival, Ivar had been greeted by two of his long-time friends, and he had been grateful for their presence. The camaraderie amongst the troops he daily observed was unparalleled, and he was glad for it. There were moments of frustration with the demands of drill, the confusion of marching, formation and necessary memorization of scores of differing bugle calls, but the underlying feel of the camp was one of optimism.

The cross section of men stationed at the camp was a good reflection of the state of Ohio itself, Ivar mused as he watched those souls who were daring enough to brave the deluge of rain run from place to place outside. There were lawyers, farmers, teachers and tradesmen all serving together, and Ivar appreciated the mix. It couldn't hurt to approach the current situation with a wide variety of perspectives, and the regiments surrounding him definitely had that.

He glanced up as the door opened and then slammed, admitting his good friend, Mark Stephenson, who shuddered and shook the rain from his coat much as would a dog. "It's wet out there," Mark said with a grin.

"It's wet in here too," Ivar stated, turning an unenthusiastic eye toward the tin pails that were situated throughout the room, catching the rain as it cascaded through the roof.

"I'm the bearer of good tidings," Mark said as he made his way into the room, and reaching into his coat pocket, he pulled forth mail that seemed to have escaped any major damage. "Letters from home!"

Ivar stood quickly and gratefully accepted the letter Mark handed him. "Looks like I got one from the wife and one from the folks," Mark said in unabashed glee, and he sat down on his cot, tearing into one of the letters.

Ivar sat again on his cot and after retrieving his spectacles and placing them on the bridge of his nose, opened the letter that had been addressed to him in his mother's neat hand. Inside were several pieces of paper—apparently the whole family had taken the time to write him a little something. He glanced through the pages, his heart nearly coming to a stop at the last. Inger had drawn a picture of herself and her father. True, Ivar's legs extended directly from an overly large head and had no body to speak of, but to him it might well have been a priceless museum piece. He smiled and traced his finger along the drawing, taking comfort from the fact that Inger's little hands had touched that very paper only days before. He closed his eyes briefly, hoping the time would not be far-gone before he would see her again.

The door opened and slammed again, bringing with it a gust of wind and rain from outside. A young corporal that Ivar hadn't known before enlisting rushed inside, stamping his feet and shaking the water from his overcoat. "It's almost suppertime!" the lad exclaimed enthusiastically, and Ivar had to smile. Mealtime broke the tedium of drill, rain, and sheer boredom. The food itself, however, could be defined as such only in the loosest of terms, and Ivar found himself daily missing his mother's good Norwegian cooking.

"Well, that's good news indeed," Mark said from his cot as he looked up from his mail. "Nothing like a good batch of teeth-dullers to fill a man's belly."

"Better teeth-dullers than nothing," the young boy said, maintaining his cheer. "Soak 'em in coffee and they're not half bad."

Ivar reflected on the hard tack, or "biscuits" of which the men spoke with an inward wince. His mind took him home to the farm, envisioning a plate full of new potatoes and halibut. He smiled.

"You see?" the young boy, Sam, said with a glance at Ivar. "The Norwegian agrees with me. You soak your sheet-iron crackers in coffee, too?"

Ivar brought his thoughts to the present and removed his spectacles from his face, folding them carefully and placing them in his haversack. "I will now, Sam. And I'll pretend they're fish."

***

Washington, D.C.
1 June, 1861

Isabelle Webb sat in the hotel room that had become her temporary home in recent weeks, her eyes flying with horrified amazement over a letter from Anne Birmingham. The letter had been mailed nearly a month before, but faulty communications around the city had caused a delay in its arrival.

Dearest Belle, it began:
I have an idea. You may not agree with me, but as you are adventurous, I am in hopes that you will support my plans. I'm going to enlist. Adam Jones has seen all there is to see of Boston, and it's time he spread his wings a bit. I've heard before of soldiers of independent means who sign on with the Army, and as an "independent," I believe I would have the option of transferring into and out of various regiments; it would be the perfect way to gain a broad view of the current conflict.

Only a fool would believe this will soon be over, Belle. It will last beyond Lincoln's ninety-day tour, to be sure. In fact, I heard recently of his call for an additional 45,000 to sign on for three years. I cannot let an opportunity like this pass by and not take it. I have the details carefully arranged in my head, and the reason for my letter to you at this point is to request your help.

As you might assume, my parents are not likely to support me in this endeavor. I plan to tell them that you have relocated back to Chicago and that I am going to work with you for Pinkerton. There is no need to inform Pinkerton himself; I sincerely doubt that my parents will ever cross his path. All I would need of you is this; I will send my correspondence to you and ask that you forward it on to my parents in Boston, postmarked from Chicago. If you are not returning there any time soon, do you happen to know of someone currently stationed in Chicago who would be willing to commit this small act of subterfuge on my behalf? I only ask for someone trust-

worthy who is not overly curious. I'm more than willing to pay for this service.

I have access to my trust fund, and have since my twenty-first year. Money will not be an issue for me, and at any rate, I'll be earning an Army salary! And I'm sure that worthy amount will keep me living the fine life. (If you were here, now, you would hear me laughing!)

Please, Belle, don't judge me harshly concerning this. You and I are cut from the same cloth, and while I know you will tell me 'tis idiotic folly, you know I must do this.

Will you help me?

Much love,
Anne.

Isabelle sat back in her chair with a gusty sigh. Anne was correct about one thing, for certain. Her plan was definitely "idiotic folly." Yet, she was also correct about something else; they *were* cut from the same cloth, the two of them, and she knew without a doubt if she were in Anne's shoes, she would attempt the same thing.

There were two reasons Isabelle hadn't enlisted herself. The first was that she had never attempted to pass herself off as a man, and she wasn't sure she could master it. The second was that her adventurous spirit received all it craved working with Pinkerton and acting as a spy and detective. She didn't feel a pressing need to go into battle.

Isabelle shook her head slightly, leaned forward, and slid her chair closer to the small desk in the corner. Retrieving paper and pen, she began her reply to Anne.

Dear, idiotic friend,
You have my full support . . .

***
Boston, Massachusetts
8 June, 1861

Jacob Taylor read over the paper in his hand while Anne sat in one of the many hard, unforgiving wooden chairs adorning the man's cluttered office. "Honestly, Jacob, as often as I'm in here, one would think you'd supply me with a comfortable corner."

The man grunted a noncommittal reply and was silent until he reached the end of the article she'd given him. "This is good, Anne. It'll run in tonight's edition." He glanced up with a smile. "What are you going to work on next?"

"I think I'll be a war correspondent."

"What?" His tone was flat. His smile faded and he sank into a chair next to hers.

"I think it's time Adam Jones enlisted." Anne watched her employer's face carefully, knowing he was the final obstacle. Her parents were a non-issue; they would never find out. Isabelle was a potential problem, and Anne had yet to hear from her friend regarding the letter she had sent nearly a month before. Jacob was the only other person who might resist, and if he did, she had to admit that she would feel defeated. She could still enlist, but if Jacob refused to support her and discontinued printing "Adam's" observations of life, she knew there would be a void she probably wouldn't be able to fill.

Anne loved reporting, but more to the point, she loved the kind of reporting Jacob had hired her for. She thoroughly enjoyed watching people, and she lived to transfer her observations into the printed word. She had tried her hand at fiction, but was dissatisfied with the result. She wanted the hard, fast truth, and newspaper reporting was the only way to sate the craving.

Jacob scrutinized her face, his brows drawn into a fierce frown as though he couldn't comprehend what he was seeing. With a nearly imperceptible shake of his head, he leaned back in his chair, legs crossed at the ankles, assuming the comfortable sprawl that Anne had come to identify with him. If he wasn't standing or pacing, he was sprawling.

"That's a stretch, Annabelle, even for me," he finally said, still looking at her as though she were an oddity he couldn't define.

Anything else he might have said was interrupted by voices in the hall. Anne looked with irritation over her shoulder and rose to close the door. Resuming her seat, she looked at Jacob with what she hoped was an earnest expression.

"It makes perfect sense, truly. You need someone in the field, and why not someone the readers already know?"

He shook his head. "You just told me your whole family now knows what you've been doing. If they start seeing articles by 'Adam Jones' from the battlefield, don't you think they'll react rather strongly?"

Anne chewed on her bottom lip. There was that to consider, she supposed, and cursed the day she had divulged her alter-identity to her parents. Her mother had been so intense in her scrutiny! Anne had felt the woman was reading into her very thoughts. And her father—he hadn't spoken to her since. It had been over a week, and he was still so incensed at the thought of his daughter running about town in boy's clothing that he hadn't been able to form a complete sentence if she was in the room.

"I've tried not to think about that," she admitted, "but perhaps we could do this; I'll tell my parents I'm going to Chicago to work with Isabelle for Pinkerton. They won't be expecting to see any more 'Adam Jones' articles in the paper, and you could even print something small that would say, in effect, 'Adam Jones has retired, and replacing him is our new war correspondent,' followed by whatever new name I'll choose." She relaxed a bit in the hard chair. "I think that might take care of it."

Jacob rested his elbows on the arms of his chair, one forefinger absently rubbing the bridge of his nose. He was handsome as sin, Anne had to admit, and she had wondered through the years if they might eventually form some sort of permanent attachment. The problem as she saw it, however, was that there didn't seem to be a "spark" between them. She wanted to feel some kind of thrill, and although the man's stature was large and masculine, and he had a thick head of dark brown hair and pleasing features, she couldn't quite envision herself on intimate terms with him.

She called herself a dozen kinds of fool over the lack of attraction—she was not likely to find another man who would be so accepting of her independence and radical personality, let alone an eligible bachelor of independent means, in his early thirties, who approved of the fact that she ran about town in boy's clothing, pursuing a man's profession. It wasn't enough, however, to just *like* someone, she had long ago decided. For herself, she wanted something special.

"Anne," Jacob finally said, dropping his hand. "You're insane."

"I know."

"Your parents will eventually find out."

"They won't. And if they do, what can they do? Drag me back home by my hair? I'm not a minor anymore—many women are married with children by my age."

"But you're still a woman. There's not a man in this country who would find fault with your father for marching onto whichever battlefield you find yourself and hog-tying you into submission. It's only a matter of time." He shook a finger slightly in her direction. "They will find out."

She lifted her chin a notch. "I'm telling you, they won't. Once I have Isabelle's support and am sure I have someone in Chicago to handle my correspondence with the family, I'll be in a position to move forward with this. The only way my parents would discover my activities is if someone were to tell them."

Jacob shot her an expression of mock surprise. "And you think I would do such a thing?"

"Would you?"

He sighed. "No, Anne, I won't." He looked genuinely troubled for the first time in their association. "I don't quite know what to think of this, however."

"You wouldn't hesitate to send one of the male columnists."

"You're right," he admitted blandly. "That's different."

"Because they're men?"

He looked at her, his head cocked to one side. "Anne, what happens if the men in your regiment discover that you're a woman? Do you think they'll all be chivalrous? Do you know that the 6th New York Regiment is full of Bowery toughs so hardened by life that the current joke is that in order to be a member of that regiment, one must have done prison time?"

"You're forgetting the 7th, who are nothing if not elite and have set out with all the amenities comfort dictates, including velvet-covered camp stools."

He threw his hands into the air. "So you're going to make sure you end up in a regiment that sports velvet-covered camp stools? It may not be that simple! And what about your hair?"

"I'm going to cut it off."

"And your, your . . ." He made vague motions at the feminine curves hidden beneath the soft fabric of her green dress.

She felt herself flush. For all that she and Jacob were good friends, they had never before discussed matters on such a personal level.

"I'll do what I always do when I'm Adam," she said. "Binding works quite nicely."

"Perhaps, but this will be different. You'll be sleeping next to these men, and dealing with private . . . functions . . ."

She finally laughed. "Jake, I can take care of myself. I have options, a certain amount of freedom given the way I plan to enlist, and I'll choose my regiment with care. If problems arise, I'll request a transfer. The 'private functions' I will deal with."

He was quiet for a moment. "I don't like it," he finally said.

She studied his stubborn features. "But will you still publish me?" She hated that it came out on a whisper.

He slowly nodded. "I will. But you must promise me you'll take care. If something happens to you, I'll go to the grave with this on my conscience."

Anne experienced a huge sense of triumph she was hard-pressed to hide. "I'll be careful," she said.

Victory!

***

Anne arrived home a few hours later to find a letter from Isabelle waiting for her on the side table by the front door. She snatched it up and hurried upstairs to her bedroom, hoping nobody would stop her. She reached her room unmolested and tore into the letter, smiling at her friend's response.

Isabelle was to stay in Washington a bit longer, it seemed, but she had a younger sister in Chicago who, Isabelle was sure, would gladly forward Anne's mail to her family, especially if Anne paid the younger woman. "Monica is nothing if not resourceful," the letter said, "and she is always on the lookout for money-making ventures. Her fiancé left her six months ago, taking a large portion of Monica's savings, and she's working odd jobs to recover the loss . . ."

Anne frowned at the news, remembering meeting Monica once, years ago. She had been quite young then, and vivacious. Anne determined to pay the younger woman twice what she had originally planned—she knew that Monica couldn't expect help from any quarter other than Isabelle, as their parents had died nearly four years earlier.

However concerned Anne felt for Monica, she couldn't suppress the lift in her spirits that the final link to her plans had fallen neatly into place. She looked at the bottom of the letter where Isabelle had scrawled Monica's address, and committed it to memory.

Yes, indeed. Things were progressing swimmingly.

CHAPTER 19

"The die was cast; war was declared . . . every person, almost, was eager for the war, and we were all afraid it would be over and we not be in the fight."
—Private Sam Watkins

***

16 June, 1861
Charleston, South Carolina

"I don't care what he says, I don't believe a word of it." Emily snapped a bed-sheet and folded it neatly in half. The Bentley linen closet was more like a small bedroom; as closets went, the thing was enormous. She worked alongside Mary, folding the bedding that had just been brought into the house from out on the lines. The material was crisp and smelled fresh. Emily placed her nose next to the folded sheet in her hands and inhaled deeply before setting it on its proper shelf.

"He seems to think he'll be made general before the month is out," Mary commented in a dry tone that was barely more than a whisper. If any in the house, other than Emily, heard her speaking ill of the master's family, Sarah would undoubtedly be forced to punish her harshly.

Emily snorted. "He's an idiot. My guess is he'll be dead before the month's out."

Mary paused in her work and looked closely at her young friend. "Do you harbor no love for him in your heart at all?"

Emily returned Mary's gaze, squarely. "Do you?"

"No," Mary admitted, "but he's not my brother."

"He's not mine, either. No brother of mine would rape a woman. If I were Jewish, I would rent my clothes and declare him destroyed and living in the afterlife with Beelzebub himself." Emily paused, her throat thick. "My brother, my true brother, is thousands of miles away living in the desert."

Mary fumbled and dropped a snowy-white pillowcase on the floor. Emily reached down and quickly scooped it up, shaking it firmly. "There," she said, folding it herself after a cursory examination, "no worse for the wear." She glanced at Mary, who looked slightly chagrined.

"I'm sorry," Mary murmured.

"Why? It was a simple mistake." Emily looked more closely at Mary's face. "What's wrong?"

"Nothing."

Emily briefly closed her eyes. "It was Richard, wasn't it? I'm so sorry." She put her arms about Mary's shoulders for a hug. "We won't speak of him anymore. He can go off to Virginia and march with Mr. Kershaw and we'll just forget he ever existed. Yes?"

Mary nodded, her chin bumping against Emily's shoulder. Emily pulled back and smoothed Mary's long, black hair, which was fastened in a twist at the back of her head.

"Is there something else?"

Mary shook her head. "No. It's nothing."

"I don't believe you."

Mary only shrugged, so Emily did likewise. "Well, then," the young redhead said, "if you won't tell me now I'll just have to drag it out of you later." She turned back to the folding table. "Let's get these sheets finished or you'll be too tired tonight for the new book I gave you."

Mary shook her head. "Emily, you know I appreciate the help, but if your mother finds you in here again . . ."

"Nonsense. My mother is too busy making herself feel superior to your grandmother. Besides—"

As though the conversation itself had produced her, Sarah appeared at the doorway. "Emily! There you are—I have been looking all over this house for you!"

Emily jumped in surprise and dropped the sheet she was folding.

"I told you last week I wanted this stopped. What are you doing in here again?"

"Instructing Mary on the finer points of being effective human chattel."

"Out. Now." Sarah's face was white, her lips pinched in fury.

Mary stared at Emily, her mouth momentarily slack, eyes huge. For all that Emily spoke her irreverent mind with her and Ruth, she *never* sassed her mother.

Emily spared Mary a quick glance and passed her mother in the doorway, feeling the woman's anger radiating from her frame. She followed Sarah's clipped command to go to the front parlor and once there, sank into one of two well-cushioned window seats. Her mother stood before her, looking nothing short of combustible.

"Emily Elizabeth," she said through clenched teeth in a voice that shook, "if you ever, ever speak to me in that tone again, especially in front of a Negro, you will lose the privilege of spending time with that girl forever. Am . . . I . . . clear?"

Emily took a deep breath and looked out the window at the sprawling lawns that were her family legacy. She knew she had overstepped her bounds with her mother the moment the words had left her mouth, but found she didn't regret them for the reasons she probably should. She should respect her mother, but found that the older she grew, the less she was able to call forward the natural instincts of reverence one should normally feel for a parent.

"Yes," she finally said in a wooden tone.

"Look at me."

Emily reluctantly dragged her gaze from the window and made it rest on the beautiful woman who had given her life.

"If I find you helping Mary with the laundry, or hear you speaking with her in an insolent manner again, I'll take the whip to that girl, myself. I'll not have you putting ideas in her head."

Emily gasped in outrage. "You wouldn't!"

"I would, Emily. If for no other reason than to teach you a lesson."

Emily's eyes narrowed. "You would bloody another human being, innocent of any wrongdoing, merely to prove a point to someone else? You would do that, Mother?"

Sarah's eyes flickered with a brief expression of unease that Emily wondered if she had only imagined, before the older woman replied, "I would do it in a thrice, Daughter." She paused, her lips pursed. "Charlotte and I are going to the Charlesworths for tea in thirty minutes. I was going to make your excuses, but in light of this little altercation, I think you'll be coming with us."

Emily groaned. "Mother, I will go to my room and stay there until you come home—I won't even think Mary's name if you'll let me stay here."

"No. Go upstairs and change your dress into something more appropriate for tea. I'll meet you in the foyer in half an hour. In fact, you'll be appearing in public more with your father and me from now on. Your debut is not far off; I think it's time you started thinking about your future. Specifically about finding a husband."

Sarah turned, her skirts rustling. She reached the doorway when Emily called out to her in a voice that shook, whether from fear or anger, Sarah couldn't discern. "You know he did it, don't you, Mother?"

Sarah paused, and slowly swung around. "Who did what, Emily?"

"Richard. You know what happened. You are aware that you sold your own grandchild to the neighbors, aren't you?"

Sarah's face looked as though it were cut from stone, and she remained frozen in shocked silenced.

"Oh, and here I go being insolent again," Emily murmured, her eyes narrowed and complexion flushed. "By all means, go beat the mother of your grandchild in order to punish me."

Emily watched in sick triumph as her mother's face took on an ashen expression, and she knew in that moment that Mary was safe from the whip. Her mother might hold to the lifestyle of generations of slaveholders, but Emily knew that Sarah *knew*. Sarah knew it was wrong, and while Emily pitied the position her mother was in, she despised her all the more for the life she continued to lead.

***

Sarah left the parlor and walked on legs that felt like lead up the stairs and into her apartments on the second floor. Entering her sitting room and closing the door weakly behind her, she leaned against it and gasped for breath. Of course she had known, but how humiliating that her daughter knew and actually held her in contempt! Her fifteen, nearly sixteen-year-old daughter thought herself morally superior to her mother and dared to stand in judgment! Her insolence was beyond the pale. The girl would have to be married off, and soon.

She rubbed her temples with fingers that shook and drew as deep a breath as her tightly drawn corset would allow. How crass of Emily to speak of things that polite society swiftly swept under the proverbial rug. Still, she had verbalized the one thought that Sarah had refused to confront; the fact that Richard's child was, of course, her grandchild.

She felt a burning in her eyes and closed her eyelids, pushing her fingertips angrily against them. That infant living not even a mile away might very well be the only grandchild she would ever have. Ben lived a world away, and had willingly turned his back on his birthright. Charlotte never shared a bed with her husband, and Sarah suspected it was a form of revenge not only on William, but her parents, as well. Richard was about to enlist in the Confederate Army, of all things, and would most likely get himself killed. Emily would leave as soon as she was able and would never return because she apparently hated them all—well, Sarah amended with despair, all except the slaves. Clara was a young deaf child and who knew if she would ever enter society normally enough to actually bring suitors 'round? Sarah barely knew the girl, herself. Emily knew Clara, however. Emily had been a mother to the child when Sarah, herself, had refused.

It was a bitter thing, she learned, standing alone in the opulent splendor of her home, to realize that she had failed so dismally as a parent. None of her children liked either her or Jeffrey. The sole passion, nay obsession of her entire life had been Bentley, and insuring that it pass on to the next generation in the full glory and majesty in which she had received it. There may well not be a next generation, and Emily had been right. Her own flesh and blood lived down the lane and in quarters that were not nearly as accommodating as those at Bentley. Sarah knew that to be a fact.

Sarah moved to the divan and sank upon it, for one brief moment considering the unthinkable—she could buy the child back and raise it as her own! After all, Mary was half-white herself, and with Richard as the biological father, the child would most likely grow to maturity with a very light complexion.

As soon as the thought materialized, Sarah realized it was doomed to failure. She could never claim the child now that the neighbors knew it had been born as a slave. It was unthinkable. The child would never be accepted, and to leave the Bentley legacy to a slave, a *slave*—she must be daft!

Sarah pulled herself together and brushed at the lingering moisture in her eyes, angry that she doubted herself for even a moment. Society was society, she was a Matthews, for heaven's sake, and she would prevail, grandchildren or no. She would deal with her children and take care of Bentley. Bentley was the one thing that never failed her. People would come and go. Bentley was her rock.

***

Joshua watched from the stables as the carriage bearing the Birmingham women pulled away from the house and down the long, tree-lined drive. He had seen Emily's angry strides as she had approached the vehicle; that she was unhappy undoubtedly meant she had been coerced into tea with the neighbors.

The carriage eventually disappeared from sight and he watched the now-empty drive with his brows drawn. Emily was never happy anymore. He was hard-pressed to remember the last time he'd seen her smile when in the company of her family. The only times she ever seemed at peace were when she was with her sister, Clara, or Ruth, or Mary or with him. For a white girl, that was dangerous.

He shook his musings and busied himself in the stable, uninterrupted until the overseer darkened the doorway. "You," the man said, pointing at him. "The pantry supply wagon just rolled in. Go help them unload it."

Joshua nodded once to the man and placed the saddle he was polishing to one side, immediately walking to the back of the main house where the outer door was open. What little supplies in terms of food and other household staples that were not produced directly on the plantation were carried in by wagon, and it was often Joshua's task, on occasions such as this, to help unload and carry things into the house.

While the task itself wasn't daunting or complicated, Joshua often resented those few trips back into the mansion. While on the one hand he enjoyed his memories of Ben, he didn't like the empty feel of the house without him. And there was also the issue of his own education; Joshua had had the world opened to him within the walls of this very home. For that, he would always be grateful, in an odd, complex way, to Miz Sarah. He suspected she knew Ben had taught him all he learned from his tutors, and had she been like so many others of her acquaintance, he never would have been allowed to stay in the main house. To him, that education had been like coming out of darkness and stepping into the light.

And yet, Joshua despised Sarah, because she denied it to other Bentley slaves who, in her opinion, would never have a use for it. They were left to wither in an intellectual desert. Bright, fertile minds that could have accomplished great things! It sickened him to dwell upon it, and yet with so many hours in the day at his disposal to think, he was unable to avoid it. He had often considered putting his own skills to the test and using them to escape northward, but he continually held himself back. He knew it was because of his attachment to Ruth, Mary and Rose. They were the only family he knew, and he couldn't bear the thought of leaving without them. When he finally was able to leave (and it would have to come to that or he would surely die!), he would do so with them by his side.

He wished things could have been different. He had known of Ben's plans to take him with him when he moved out West, and it was for that reason that Joshua hadn't attempted escape with Mary, Ruth, and Rose that fateful night. It had seemed the most logical course of action, although the thought of being separated from the three, for even a short time, had been one he had wrestled with. Once escaped and free, however, then he would have been able to travel! He could have visited them wherever they had settled—perhaps moved to live near them, even.

Those had been his thoughts, anyway, and he tortured himself with the notion that maybe, if he had gone along when Ben made the daring attempt that somehow they could have all made it to safety. He knew it was ridiculous; it undoubtedly would have been bad for all of them, especially him. Sarah would have sold him, at the very least.

He hefted a large sack of flour onto his shoulder and made his way into the house. He passed a group of housemaids who were whispering in a corner of the kitchen, and he slowed his step so that he might overhear their conversation. Joshua catalogued information in his brain for later use; he never turned a deaf ear to anything.

". . . girl at the Charlesworths was caught taking a jar of

molasses from the pantry because she liked it so much, and she wanted to put it away for a treat, later," one of the young women was saying.

"And what happened?" came a response from another.

"Her massah make her sit down and eat the whole jar all at once! She got so sick, o' course, she tossed it all back up. Massah says that'll teach her . . ."

Joshua gritted his teeth and quickened his step. There were times he felt he would choke on the indignity! Treated like children, all of them! Even those who managed to reach old age, who should have been afforded the luxury of looking back on a life of pleasure and trials and time spent with loved ones, wrapped in the freedom of one's choices, were treated as the dullest, naughtiest of children.

Nearly half the Southern population was enslaved, and as he walked down the hallway to place the flour sack in its proper pantry, Joshua reflected on his worn copy of Frederick Douglass's slave narrative that he kept hidden in the stables. Mr. Douglass had the right of it. How did a region enslave nearly half of its population?

They didn't allow them an education.

That, coupled with the fact that those in power spread panic amongst their fellow, less fortunate whites regarding the "evil, inherent nature of the black man," served to keep an entire people in chains quite effectively. Joshua gently dumped the flour bag on top of several others already in place in the pantry and turned to leave when Ruth appeared in the doorway.

She smiled at him, and it warmed his heart. "And how are you today?" she asked, with all the concern of a mother.

Given the current depth of his troubled thoughts, her sympathy and kindness were nearly his undoing. Fighting tears and feeling foolish, he mustered a smile for her in return. "I couldn't be better, Aunt Ruth. How about yourself?"

"Well, I'm right as rain, Joshua." She moved a bit closer to him and glanced over her shoulder. "Mary spoke to me earlier," she said quickly and in an undertone. "Emily is . . . she's going to get herself in trouble. That girl has a mouth . . . apparently she's decided to use it on her mother." Ruth shook her head and was silent for a moment. "I'm going to talk to her about being more careful—I'm afraid she'll not only harm herself, but might involve Mary as well, although she would never intend it."

Joshua glanced at her in surprise. "You think the mistress would use Mary as the 'whipping boy'?"

Ruth shook her head. "I don't think to that extent, but she would definitely forbid contact, and that would be hard on both of those girls. They need each other like plants need sun. I also worry that Mrs. Birmingham would separate Clara and Rose, and the situation there is the same. It wouldn't be good."

Joshua nodded, wondering exactly what it was Ruth intended by telling him, other than perhaps for his own information. Surely she didn't think he could actually do something about it? Talking sense into Emily was often like trying to converse with a sheep. You could open your mouth and let the words out, but there was a good chance the creature hearing the noise wasn't processing it.

"Did you want something from me?"

"Well, if you have an opportunity, perhaps—I know she sneaks into the stables to see you. I think that maybe, if enough of us tell her to calm down, she might."

He nodded again, and slipped past the older woman, receiving her quick squeeze on his arm for the affection it was. It wouldn't do to be seen or heard talking with her about the family of the house. He finished helping the others unload the wagon and made his way back to the stables. He passed the overseer on his way, keeping his gaze downward and answering immediately when the man asked where he was headed.

The man eventually let him pass, and Joshua released a pent-up sigh when he was out of earshot. He was on Jackson's bad side, and it was in his own best interest to avoid the man as much as possible. He knew that if he looked him in the eye, his contempt would be so obvious that he'd find himself punished, without a doubt. The lashes weren't a deterrent. He would undoubtedly fight back, but it wasn't as though he feared the pain. And if it actually came to death, well, that would be mercy. His greatest fear, however, was that he would be sold. To be sold would be as unthinkable, to him, as trying to escape to a life of freedom without Ruth, Mary, and Rose. What light and color he had in his life would be snuffed, and he would mourn the loss of their association forever.

CHAPTER 20

"During the whole of that time [served in the Army]—more than a quarter of a century—I have experienced nothing but kindness from my superiors and a most cordial friendship from my comrades. To no one, General, have I been as much indebted as to yourself for uniform kindness and consideration, and it has always been my ardent desire to merit your approbation. I shall carry to the grave the most grateful recollections of your kind consideration, and your name and fame shall always be dear to me.

Save in defense of my native State, I never desire again to draw my sword."

—Resignation letter from Robert E. Lee to General Winfield Scott, following the secession of Virginia

***

Richmond, Virginia
18 June, 1861

Jeffrey took a few moments in the quiet of his Richmond hotel room to pen a quick letter to his wife. It was true, their marriage was an odd one, but they maintained the pretenses and kept each other more or less informed of their whereabouts. He reflected back, for a moment, on the letter Sarah had left on his desk at Bentley—the one from Ben. It had taken him by surprise; first of all, the letter itself was a shock, as though a son who might as well have been dead had risen from the grave, and secondly, the fact that Sarah thought to leave it for him was a courtesy he hadn't expected from her.

He began his letter with his brow furrowed in thought. So much was happening, so quickly, that he hardly knew where to begin. He glanced at the late hour on his pocket watch, and smothering a yawn, began to write.

Dear Sarah;

I'm beginning to think I've had enough of politics to last a lifetime. I find myself exhausted each day with all that must happen in order to form a new government and make it work. I fear that we may have all jumped into the water a bit too soon, but I suppose that is neither here nor there. The new president and his cabinet are hellbent on seeing this cause through to a quick and decisive end, and have Southern society's best interests at heart.

Troops arrive here and about in the region, by the hundreds, daily. They come from all varieties of Southern towns and cities. Many are fresh young farmers not any larger in stature than our own Richard. They are ready and willing to fight for the cause, and yet at times I fear for them because of their innocence. The great majority of these young men have never fired a shot at another human being.

On to more optimistic topics; we have ourselves, as I'm sure you've heard by now, a wonderful new commander for Virginia's state forces, a Robert E. Lee—he has been in place since late April, and the general sentiment is that this man is worth his salt. In fact, Lincoln wanted him first! Working through Winfield Scott, Lincoln offered command of the U.S. Army to Robert Lee at Scott's hearty endorsement of the man, but Lee turned it down in favor of going with his home state of Virginia. Lee has an impressive military history and was loyal to the Union, the story goes, but his first loyalty is to his home state. I'm certain that had Virginia remained loyal to the Union, Lee would have, as well, and we'd find ourselves on opposite sides of the fence.

Jeffrey paused in his writing for a moment and considered Robert E. Lee. He had met the man not quite a month before when James Chestnut had asked Jeffrey if he'd like to accompany him to the site where the Confederate troops were drilling. Lee had held a commanding field presence, drilling men who were not soldiers by profession, but now by passion. They hadn't spoken long, but Jeffrey felt a sense of resolution in the man; that although in the past he had spoken quite well of the U.S. Army that had given him his livelihood, he would fight to the death to defend the state that had been his family's home for generations.

Jeffrey shook his head. It was odd—that was the only way he could find to describe the current set of circumstances. Men who had, mere years before, fought alongside each other against foreign powers were now taking up arms against each other. How would the scene present itself, he wondered, when those former comrades faced each other on opposite sides of the battlefield? It was coming as surely as the sun rose each morning. There was no avoiding it.

He finished his letter to Sarah and sealed it, dropping it onto the desk. He would post it tomorrow with his other correspondence, and then see where the day would lead. He knew he was avoiding Bentley, and he wondered how long he could legitimately continue to socialize with Chestnut and the rest of Davis's cabinet before he made a nuisance of himself. Truthfully, he acknowledged without guile, he could probably stay as long as he wished. They seemed to value his levelheaded input, and nobody seemed in a hurry to be rid of him.

There was one person whose contact he had avoided, and he knew it was past time he wrote to the man. It was his brother, James, in Boston. James had sent him numerous letters since the South Carolinian secession, and Jeffrey had avoided answering him. The letters themselves were always solicitous and expressed concern for the welfare of his family, but in recent years, a rift had arisen between the two brothers—that, Jeffrey knew was largely his own doing.

When Jeffrey had met Sarah, James and Elizabeth were already married, and Elizabeth had already begun to assert her upbringing on her husband. James and Jeffrey had been raised largely without any particular political or social leanings one way or another, other than they both nurtured a fervent desire for money. When James and Elizabeth were married, however, Jeffrey noticed a decided sway in his brother's opinions against Southern society. He immersed himself not only in iron mining, which had started small and blossomed into a huge industry, but also in his wife's Quaker roots, which held an unquestionably unfavorable view of the Southern institution of slavery. It had been banned in Rhode Island since the 1700s, and Elizabeth was of the opinion that it ought to be thus throughout the country.

The families, however, even after Jeffrey and Sarah were wed, still managed to spend time together, usually long periods of time during the summer months. Their children had virtually grown up together, and it had often been a source of amusement between the two families that the Birmingham men seemed destined for "sameness," their entire lives, from their appearances to the number of children they each sired.

They weren't the same, though, and as the years progressed, those differences began to manifest themselves in large ways. The families, as the children grew toward adulthood, spent less time together—where Elizabeth and Sarah had formed a casual friendship of sorts in the beginning, now they could barely stand to be in the same room together. Polite conversation was not enough to sustain vital ideological differences, and the two wives were representative of everything that was different about the families themselves.

When Ben had taken his cousin Luke's philosophies to heart, it had nearly been Sarah's undoing. She viewed it as the ultimate betrayal, and knowing of her feelings concerning her son, Jeffrey's surprise at the letter on his desk from Ben had been doubled. His wife undoubtedly still harbored love for the boy—well, he supposed, the *man* he must be, by now—and part of him hurt for

Sarah as much as it did for himself that they had not even shreds of a relationship left with their firstborn.

Jeffrey sighed and took a fresh piece of paper from the desk drawer, and drafted a short letter to his brother. He hardly knew what to say—they were now literally at war. How to begin such a letter? "So, James, I understand that now your industry will make a fortune supplying the weapons that will most likely kill my children?" It hardly seemed friendly.

In the end, he decided on measured honesty.

Dear James,

I apologize for the lapse in time between my letters; I find myself extremely busy. There is much to be done in forming a new government, and although you undoubtedly disagree with recent proceedings, I hope in my heart that you will not come to hate my family and me. Things have been strained between us, brother, and I fear that will never change. The paths we have chosen have led us far from each other, and I mourn the loss of our former friendship.

Things must be as they must be, however, and I do want you to know we are well, we are all healthy, and I hope, God willing, this conflict between our countries will soon be resolved.

Yours,
Jeffrey.

"There," he said aloud as he sealed the letter. Now, perhaps, his conscience would let him rest and he would be able to put James from his mind for a while. It was hardly likely, he had to admit to himself, but it was certainly worth a try. If he mused overlong on the fact that Luke might well enlist, that if the conflict raged for long then young Robert might even become involved, his stomach would certainly tie itself into knots not easily undone. He didn't want to think of his young nephews brandishing weapons any more than he relished the thought of his son doing so. He knew he ought to view Richard's zeal as refreshingly patriotic, but he couldn't bring himself to find joy in it. These boys could well end up dead, and it weighed heavily on his mind.

Sarah had written him the week before that Roger Pryor had secured a place for Richard in Kershaw's 2nd South Carolina, with the "Palmetto Guard." Richard had become a rabid fire-eater, it seemed, and was eager to take up arms across the Potomac from the United Stated capitol. Any other father would be immensely proud, and perhaps had Richard been a son he would have found pride in anyway, it would have been easier. But perhaps not. He had to presume that if his relationship with Richard were a better one, it would be even harder to send him off to war.

Jeffrey readied for bed, his head pounding with thoughts that wouldn't leave him at peace. He suddenly wished he were far, far away from everything.

***

Nebraska Territory
18 June, 1861

Ben sat under a blanket of stars, cradling his scriptures in his lap and flipping through them in a desperate attempt for some comfort. He had made arrangements for the care of his small home in Salt Lake, terminated his job, said good-bye to his friends and the good people who had embraced him as one of their own, and was now heading back into hell.

It was the only way he could describe it, and each mile closer to his destiny, he felt his heart grow ever more oppressed. It was right, though, and he knew it. It was time to have things resolved, one way or another.

He currently traveled with two riders of the Pony Express, and would stay with them as far as Minnesota, where the rail lines began that would carry him to Boston. The pace was swift and he envisioned reaching Boston in a few weeks. His companions were friendly enough, but didn't ask too many questions, which served Ben quite well. They knew him to be "one of them Mormons," and left him alone each night when he retrieved his scriptures from his saddle bags, probably fearing he would preach to them if they sat too close. He had to smile.

Ben angled the book so that it caught the best of the firelight and searched for a section he had been reading earlier in the month. Where was it? He turned page after page, noting his own markings and passages he had underlined; things that had significance for him. He would know the passage when he found it, for he had placed a large star next to it.

There it was. Section 87. It amazed him now, as it had back in December of the prior year, that he was alive to see a prophecy come to pass. Joseph Smith, in December of 1832, had received revelation that the United States would eventually wage war upon itself. It had come, according to the scriptures, at a time when Joseph and the brethren were pondering upon African slavery on the American continent, and slavery throughout the world.

Verily, thus saith the Lord concerning the wars that will shortly come to pass, beginning at the rebellion of South Carolina, which will eventually terminate in the death and misery of many souls;

And the time will come that war will be poured out upon all nations, beginning at this place.

For behold, the Southern States shall be divided against the Northern States, and the Southern States will call on other nations, even the nation of Great Britain, as it is called, and they shall also call upon other nations, in order to defend themselves against other nations; and then war shall be poured out upon all nations.

It was further testimony to Ben, every time he read it, of the divine calling of Joseph Smith. How had he known those things would transpire? Truly, he had been a prophet, and Ben wished he could have known the man, himself.

Ben turned his thoughts eastward, and to his family. How were they faring, he wondered? How were the relationships? Had they changed since he had gone? According to the few letters he had received from Emily through the years, they had changed, and greatly. Charlotte was no longer her mother's puppet, it seemed, but was apparently hell-bent on making her parents pay for her unhappy marriage. Richard, apparently, had become a monster if Emily were to be believed, continually harassing her and Clara, not to mention the slaves. Emily had hinted at something heinous but hadn't actually gone into any detail, and it had left him wondering what Richard had done.

Emily, herself, sounded miserable. She was growing, though, and for that he was grateful. Perhaps, if she were so inclined, she might be rescued from home by marriage, but he had to admit that the tone of her letters lately sounded as though she were interested in anything but solidifying her position in Southern society. It seemed she and he were kindred spirits after all, exactly as he had suspected all along.

Little Clara—he wondered how she was. Was she happy? Were people kind? Did she have many friends?

So many questions—so much frustration at his impotence. He turned his thoughts northward and considered the family he was about to visit. They had a closeness about them, his uncle James's family, that Ben's had never been able to achieve. He suspected it was because as it concerned things of import, they were all of the same mind. They agreed where it mattered most, and therein lay the key to their familial success.

He wished it could have been like that for his own family. The Southern Birminghams were basically a group of strangers sharing a common heredity and ancestry. It wasn't enough on which to build unity. It was sad, really, that when Ben thought of the term "father," he felt in his case it applied more strongly to Jeremiah Stowe than to Jeffrey Birmingham. Jeremiah had shown more interest in Ben's life and opinions than his own father ever had, and Ben wondered at it. What was it that made his father so indifferent to the comings and goings of his children? Had he truly been so emasculated by Sarah's strong influence that he felt he needed to absent himself from everything that fell under her realm? Wasn't that realm also his? It had never made sense to Ben. His uncle James had a fairly close relationship with each of his children, and his wife was as strong-willed as was Sarah. Why the difference?

He supposed it was the marriages themselves. Elizabeth had always treated James with affection. Sarah had often treated Jeffrey with indifference, if with anything at all. Jeffrey had been her stud horse, and Ben shook his head at the crudity of the thought, even as he knew it to be true. He had to wonder if Jeffrey didn't have more in common with his son-in-law, William, than with any of his own sons.

Ben shuddered to think that he might still be living in their system. As much as he regretted all that had happened and the fact that he'd left behind people he loved, he knew that it had been inevitable. He never could have stayed.

His musings were interrupted when his two traveling companions hesitantly approached. Their reluctance to speak with him was at odds with the air in which they both carried themselves. They were both hardened frontier men; one identified himself as "Jameson," the other, simply as "Slim."

Jameson sat close to the fire and gestured toward the book Ben held in his lap. "Yer readin' yer Bible again?"

Ben nodded with a shrug. "It helps to pass the time."

Slim took a seat next to Jameson on a large log. "You sound mighty Southern, ya know," he said as he sipped something from a tin cup. "What're ya doin' so far from home?"

"After I joined my faith with those living in Utah, it made sense to live with them there, at least for awhile."

Jameson nodded. "So why're ya goin' back?"

"I'm going back to fight."

Slim started in surprise. "What on earth for? Why wouldn't ya stay where it's safe?"

"I'm hoping for a certain outcome to this war," Ben said. "Seems only right that I try to help bring it about."

Slim nodded sagely. "Ya wanna drive back those invading Yanks?"

Ben laughed without humor. "No. I want to help them."

The two men stared at him, slack-jawed. "Yer fightin' against your own kind?" Slim finally managed to get out.

"Yes, sir, I am."

Jameson narrowed his eyes. "What kind of man fights against his own family?"

"The kind who is nearly killed by his own family."

The men's mouths formed small "O"s, and they sat in quiet contemplation for a moment. "So that's why you went out west?" Jameson finally asked.

"Basically, yes."

He looked slightly confused. "But you were already one of them Mormons?"

"Yes."

"Why?"

Ben tried hard not to laugh at the man's earnest expression. "Because I believed the message presented to me by a missionary; I prayed about it and I felt good about it. I joined the Church and have never regretted it."

The men nodded, again silent. "Well," Slim said after a pause, "we'd best get some shut-eye. Mornin' comes early."

Ben nodded and bid the men goodnight, spreading his bedding on the ground close to the tree where his horse was tied. There was nothing like sleeping under the stars to give a man proper perspective of his place in the universe.

CHAPTER 21

"It takes a raw recruit some time to learn that he is not to think or suggest, but to obey. Some never do learn."
—*Warren Lee Goss, Massachusetts soldier*

***

New York, New York
22 June, 1861

Daniel O'Shea stood impatiently by the window of the bank office, wishing he had told his father he was too busy to accompany him and cousin Matthew downtown for a meeting. "We must support each other!" Gavin had boomed, and so, as usual, Daniel acquiesced.

There was apparently some sort of trouble brewing with First Financial Bank of New York and the immigrant population, who were feeling increasingly discriminated against. *And justifiably so!* Daniel mused as he stared at the horses, carriages and wagons on the street below. It would never end. It would never go away. Those whose ancestors had come across the ocean on the Mayflower would always feel they had the unalienable right to lord their holy blood over the rest of the citizens who had dared to come in later years.

"One meeting isn't going to solve anything," Daniel muttered to his father, who stood by his side and had been chatting in a very animated manner to cousin Matthew.

His father turned to him absently and murmured, "Of course it will!" before turning back to his previous conversation.

Daniel shook his head and gritted his teeth in frustration. When would his father ever accept reality? The Irish would never be treated fairly, would never be allowed to socially rise above their own humble ranks.

The door was eventually opened and a businessman stepped through, looking very dapper and well dressed in an austere black suit, crisp white shirt and black bow tie. His dark hair was thick and styled off his forehead, his green eyes sweeping the room with a friendly gaze. He looked to be, Daniel noted with a fair amount of cynicism, about Daniel's age.

The young man bid everyone take a seat and be comfortable, introduced himself as Luke Birmingham from the First Financial Boston branch, and said he was there to see if he couldn't somehow help.

Daniel smothered a snort and sat next to his father. The room itself held close to fifty people, and was beginning get stuffy in the summer air. Mr. Birmingham moved to open one of the windows, apologizing for the uncomfortable feel of the room. Daniel's estimation of the man bumped up a reluctant notch at his solicitous behavior, but he attributed it to the fact that the man obviously wanted to lull them into a false sense of security.

"We're here today to address some of your concerns," Birmingham said, "but allow me first to tell you that I apologize on behalf of the bank that you find yourselves in a position to have to defend your rights. I am fully aware that this society is often harsh, and that while in theory you should never find yourselves discriminated against, the reality is often much different."

Daniel worked at keeping his mouth from dropping open. It wasn't so much the words, as the tone in which they were delivered. The man actually believed what he was saying! He must be Irish.

"I understand," Birmingham continued, "that many of your loan applications have been rejected due to terms 'undisclosed,' and that you are feeling it is because of your nationality or homes of origin that these rejections have occurred. It is my plan, over the next few days, to personally review each application and insure that such is not the case. If there are legitimate problems surrounding your applications that are at odds with bank policy, we will review further at that point and see if there aren't some other options or alternatives. Often the loans can be completed if you are willing to accept a slightly higher rate of interest, among other things."

There was a murmur of general consent around the room, and Birmingham then opened the floor for any questions. Many people wanted to know why their loans, personally, had been rejected, to which the man patiently repeated that he would be looking over those loans to see wherein the problems lay. He took a piece of paper and a pen, writing the name of each applicant who wanted his application reviewed, and continued to answer general questions concerning bank procedure for an additional forty-five minutes.

The question and answer period eventually drew to a close, at which point Birmingham said, "Are there any other questions I can answer for you today?"

Daniel raised his hand.

"Yes?"

"Are you Irish?"

The crowd laughed. Birmingham did as well, and when the laughter died down, he replied, "No, regrettably. My ancestors were British."

"Pity," Daniel answered, and couldn't stop the smile that tugged at the corners of his mouth.

"I agree." Birmingham smiled in return, and closed the meeting. People filed out in a mood much better than the one they carried in at the beginning, and a sense of hope seemed to fill the air. Daniel walked to the front of the room and extended his hand to Luke Birmingham.

"I appreciate your efforts," he said.

"Thank you. Are you here on your own behalf?"

"No," Daniel replied, motioning over his shoulder to Gavin and cousin Matthew. "I'm here with my father's cousin. His business loan application was rejected last week. He was hoping to open a pub."

"We'll see what we can do about that. And tell me your name?"

"Daniel O'Shea."

"It's a pleasure to meet you. Your cousin is fortunate to have such family support." Birmingham placed a few papers into a leather portfolio and turned to leave when a young clerk entered the room with a piece of paper. The clerk extended it to Birmingham and said, "A telegram for you, sir."

Daniel watched as the young man thanked the clerk and then scanned the small paper, his expression growing grim. Daniel was inclined to turn away and give the man his privacy, when Birmingham's face turned white and he leaned against the desk for support.

"Is something wrong?" Daniel asked, feeling sheepish at his question; something obviously was amiss.

"I . . ." Birmingham wiped at his forehead. "My mother has a sister who lives in New Orleans," he replied. "It seems that her husband was recently attacked over an article he had written for his newspaper . . ."

Daniel shifted uncomfortably. "I'm sorry to hear that," he murmured.

Luke shook his head. "My mother is thinking she'll go to New Orleans and help her sister bring him back to Boston to recover . . ." He glanced at Daniel with a fair amount of alarm. "I can't allow my mother to go to New Orleans now."

Daniel nodded, one brow raised. "I wouldn't let mine."

"I need to tell her to wait," Birmingham said, almost to himself, "and once I'm finished here, I'll go myself. I'm closer, anyway." He glanced at Daniel in embarrassment. "I'm sorry to involve you in this," he said as he made to leave the room.

"Think nothing of it," Daniel said, walking him to the door. "I wish you luck."

Birmingham nodded and offered his hand once again. "Thank you. I hope all goes well for your cousin's pub."

He was gone, then, and Daniel could only watch the hallway where his form retreated to the stairs, and then disappeared altogether, sincerely hoping that things worked well for Luke Birmingham and his mother's sister and family.

***

Luke reached the telegraph office and fired a message to his mother, angrier than he had been in a long time. In essence, his telegram told her that he would go, that he couldn't possibly sleep at night knowing she had ventured into Confederate territory alone, and what on earth was their father thinking by agreeing to such a mad plan?

He directed her to return any further messages that day to the hotel and he left the bank, frustrated and worried.

When his mother's return message reached him at the hotel, after he had dined for the evening, several pieces began to fit like a puzzle. The reason Elizabeth had decided to go to New Orleans on her own was because James was out of town, visiting one of the iron mines that was working double its usual load in order to produce more iron for the upcoming war effort.

Luke shook his head. It was so like his mother. If she hadn't alerted him to her intentions, James and Luke would both have returned home to find her gone. He again repeated his earlier message to her that he would go, as he was closer anyway, and she should inform his Aunt Jenny of the change in plans. He would have to forge papers under his cousin Ben's name, he supposed. Ben would be more legitimately allowed to travel the Confederacy than Luke would, even in light of the fiasco that had preceded Ben's hasty departure all those years ago. His actions hadn't been common knowledge beyond Bentley's immediate outskirts—Jeffrey and Sarah had gone to great pains to insure that much.

Luke's sleep that night was fitful. How on earth was he to review the loan applications he had pledged his attention to, and still be able to leave quickly to help his Aunt Jenny transport Jean-Pierre? He had obligations now to these good people in the city, and he didn't want to fail at keeping his word to do his best on their behalf. The thought of his uncle, however, had his stomach in knots. What was the extent of his injuries? Did he have a chance at a normal recovery? His mother's first telegram mentioned that Jenny feared for his life, which was the main reason for moving him to Boston.

Please, he prayed as he drifted in and out of sleep, help me find a solution!

The solution presented itself to Luke as he munched on a sandwich for lunch the next day after having spent the morning reviewing several loan applications. He needed someone already living in New York who was trustworthy and had the best interests of the immigrant population at heart, who could review the applications in his stead. Who better than an Irishman? An image of Daniel O'Shea's face swam in his mind, and he wondered if O'Shea might be amenable to such a suggestion. He seemed bright enough, although he would have to be interviewed to ascertain whether or not he was qualified. Luke shook his head on a momentary stab of doubt. Perhaps he wouldn't be interested; a man who spent time brawling, if the fading green bruise on his left cheekbone had been any indication, most likely would not be looking for professional employment.

Luke shrugged and finished his lunch in a hurry, making his way back to the bank and hoping to secure an appointment with the bank president, Mr. Strickland. The New York president turned out to be much like his brother, Luke's employer in Boston, both in opinion and appearance. They might as well have been twins, and Luke wasn't altogether convinced they weren't the same person.

As luck would have it, Strickland was free, and Luke was ushered into the man's office, which was a mirror image of his brother's domain in Boston. Luke had an eerie sense that he had already played out that scene, but shoved it aside. He stated the purpose for his visit, without preamble, explained his own personal emergency, and offered his suggestion for a solution in the form of one Daniel O'Shea.

Strickland sat in dumb silence for a moment before finding his voice. "I ask you to come here and help with these bloody Irish, and as a solution, you offer me one to place in my employ?"

"Yes, sir."

"Are you mad?"

Luke bit back a sigh. He should have known it wouldn't be simple. "Sir, if you'll forgive me for saying so, the rejected applications I reviewed this morning should have been accepted without question. They were rejected for the simplest of reasons—reasons overlooked in other cases. I'm not suggesting it's bank policy that denied these people their loans, but as far as I could personally ascertain, this branch is showing signs of gross discrimination. If you want to put things to right and maintain a good, working relationship with the immigrant population here, you need someone acting as a liaison between them and the bank. As a show of good faith, if you employ an Irishman, you're extending an olive branch, if you will, that will not go unnoticed."

Strickland paused, apparently warring with an inner struggle that finally burst forth. "I shouldn't have to cater to a bunch of groveling, struggling ingrates!"

Luke leveled him with an even stare. "If you would like to see your bank prosper, I suggest you make amends." He paused. "Tell me, sir," he said in an undertone. "What is it about them you so dislike?"

Strickland sat back in his chair, the light from the window glancing off his balding head. "They come in as a group, they multiply, they speak the same, they are *Catholic*—the next thing you know they're all voting the same way and we're in the minority! You come from good Protestant stock, boy, surely you understand! I shouldn't have to explain anything to you!"

Luke pinched the bridge of his nose with his thumb and fore-finger, but refrained from comment.

Strickland finally sighed. "I suppose your plan might work," he said. "Who is this O'Shea?"

"He was at the meeting yesterday. I should be able to locate him through his cousin. If he's interested, I can bring him in for an interview—if he isn't qualified for the position, we'll look for someone else."

"Fine."

Two days later found Daniel O'Shea sitting behind a desk in First Financial, reviewing previously rejected loan applications on a part-time basis, wondering how he had come to find himself in such a position. He wasn't a banker, that much was true, but when Luke Birmingham had come to him and presented him with the situation, he finally felt as though he might be able to make a difference. He cut back on the orders he was currently taking for his carpentry business and was able to manage both responsibilities, at least for the time being.

They had gone through two days of intensive training, and as Daniel reflected on his conversations and the tutelage of Luke Birmingham, one of the things that stayed uppermost in his mind was Luke's admonition that Daniel always be fair. "Some of these applications should be approved without any problems at all—your father's cousin's for example," he had said, "but there are others with some problems that the bank would not be able to address and realistically should not be approved. You mustn't be blinded by your loyalty to your countrymen. Remember to act so that your own integrity will never be called into question."

It was sound advice, and Daniel would do his best to remember it. He shifted through the stack of papers on his desk after bidding Luke a warm farewell and wishing him luck with his aunt and uncle, again shaking his head at life's odd twists and turns.

***

Camp Dennison, Cincinnati, Ohio
25 June, 1861

Ivar stood looking at the items splayed across his cot, knowing that they now comprised the bulk of his earthly possessions, and that he was soon to know them better than probably anything he ever had. Just that day, the men had been issued uniforms, arms, and accoutrements. In his possession were a simple leather kit that held sewing and writing supplies, a candle, a canteen, a powder flask for his rifle, and photos of his parents and Inger. Next to the assorted items lay a hand-made blanket on which was stitched his name and regiment. This collection of things was to be his life for the next three years.

A three-year enlistment.

Had he known that this would be the eventual outcome, Ivar wasn't so certain he would have gone into the enlistment office that fateful day. But as things had progressed at camp during the month, including a visit from General McClellan who had come to inspect the troops, word went around that Lincoln had extended the call and was looking for three-year volunteers.

Of course, a one-hundred-dollar signing bonus went a long way toward convincing many men that their time spent in the service of Uncle Sam was well worth it. Tempting as it was, though, he had been about to tell his commanding officers that he wouldn't be extending his own tour, when he had looked to his left at his friend, Mark Stephenson, who had a wife at home alone with five young children, and to his right at his other good friend, Jed Dietrich, who had a wife and seven children at home alone, and he knew his own desires would have to come second. If his two friends, whom he had known since they were young boys, were willing to sacrifice all that they had in defense of the country, then Ivar, with his one child and intensive family support could surely manage, as well.

And so three months had become three years. With a grim smile, he reasoned that if Berit hadn't left him when she had, she definitely would have by the time she received news of his extended enlistment. The plans for the following day involved boarding trains headed for Columbus, and from there, on to western Virginia. As Ivar surveyed the items across his cot, he wondered if he would ever see his home again. He shook off the sense of gloom and gathered his things, placing them carefully in his haversack. There was work to be done, and after all, work was always the answer.

CHAPTER 22

"The New Orleans Zouaves was composed of the most lawless and desperate material which that city could send forth. It is said that its colonel, with the approval of the Mayor of New Orleans, established recruiting booths in the different jails there."
—Mrs. Sally Putnam

***

New Orleans, Louisiana
30 June, 1861

Marie finished the school day with a sense of despair. If she was finished with work, then it was time to go home and join her mother at her father's bedside. He hadn't wakened for a month. Marie was beginning to wonder if he ever would. Jenny sat at his side, day and night, feeding him broth and caring for him as though he were an infant, and his physical body seemed to be thriving.

Still, he slept.

The doctors said that the severe blows to the head must have injured his brain, and they gave no real opinions one way or the other as to whether or not he'd regain consciousness. One physician had said his brain must surely be dead, and that Jenny should just stop feeding him and let him die a natural death. Jenny had promptly thrown the man from the house.

Marie was in the throes of internal despair. It hurt beyond words to see her strong, vital papa lying like a helpless child. She had known he would eventually find trouble because of his opinions, and it gave her no sense of victory to realize she had been right.

After the first week, Jenny had insisted that Marie resume her responsibilities teaching the children. "Your father would insist," she said, and brooked no further argument when Marie said she would rather stay home and help her take care of him.

"This is the last place you need to be, Marie," Jenny had said, her voice stern despite her own fear and worry. "When your father wakes up, I'll send word. Otherwise, you need to teach those children."

Jenny had been right; work became Marie's sanctuary. The world around her had fallen apart, and the children were the one bright constant. She felt as though she made a difference for them, and they adored her. They filled her with a sense of purpose and kept her from dwelling on her father, whose outcome was so frustratingly uncertain.

She couldn't even count on Gustav's irritating company anymore; the young man had up and enlisted! He was gone, off with a predominantly French regiment, drilling and preparing for the glory of war. He sent letters frequently, and they were filled with hopes of being able to shoot a Yankee or two.

When had things flown so crazily out of control? She gruffly cleared the lump in her throat and tidied her belongings, preparing to go home. There was a stack of paper and a book on one corner of the desk, and remembering its purpose, she placed the items into her carrying bag. Constance and Peter had missed school two days in a row, and she intended to go by their house on her way home to be sure all was well.

Climbing into her small carriage, she urged her horse forward and made her way down the dusty lane to the small farm where Constance and Peter lived. She secured her horse and walked to the front door, knocking firmly upon it and wondering if she might not instead find the children's mother outside tending to the animals. She didn't wait long before the door was opened and a worn-looking Mrs. Braxton appeared.

"Yes?"

"Mrs. Braxton? Do you remember me? I'm Marie Brissot, the children's teacher."

"Oh, yes. I s'pose you're wondering where Peter has been." The woman was frail and bone-thin, her face gaunt and weary.

"Well, yes, and—"

"I've had to keep him home 'cause I've been sick. I needed him to take care of things 'round here 'til I'm on my feet again."

Marie paused. "And you didn't need Constance to help as well?"

The woman's smile was fleeting. "Naw. That girl loves learnin' so much I hate to deny her it. Life's gonna' be hard enough for her, soon enough. Peter could take or leave school—Connie really seems to like it." Mrs. Braxton's expression turned wistful. "Wouldn't a minded it myself, when I was her age. My pa wouldn't hear of it, though."

"Can you tell me where Connie usually goes after school? Is she here? I have some papers she forgot to take with her. Oh, and these are for Peter," Marie said, handing the woman Peter's missed assignments, but retaining Constance's.

Mrs. Braxton took the papers and motioned with her head toward the back of the house. "She likes to roam the property. For all that we're poor, we got us a lotta land."

Marie nodded. It was a shame that nobody had helped the Braxtons manage the land so that they might start turning more of a profit. She would have to look into that. "Thank you, ma'am," she said as she stepped from the porch. "Do you mind if I look for Constance?"

"Not a'tall. Help yourself. She could be anywhere, though. That girls runs off any chance she gets." The woman closed the door and Marie stood gazing at the small, ramshackle house for a moment before making her way around to the back. Mrs. Braxton was correct—they did indeed have quite a substantial amount of land, she discovered, as she roamed the property looking for the young girl. There were several fruit trees in varying stages of death; Mrs. Braxton was obviously unable to keep up with the amount of work the farm required.

Marie passed a pen holding three pigs, two goats and five chickens. There was also a bedraggled-looking mule standing at attention inside a separate corral. She spied several outbuildings that proved to house old plows and farm implements that had long been rusted and unused.

Just as she was about to give up the search, she wandered past a small grove of trees that hid an old shed. Nearing the dilapidated old building, she heard a hushed voice inside that was most assuredly Connie's. Glad that she'd found the girl and wondering what it was that had kept her from coming to school unbeknownst to her mother, Marie pushed the small door to the shack open and poked her head inside.

"Constance?" Marie's eyes were blurred as they tried to adjust themselves to the darkened interior of the shack. She heard Connie's gasp of horrified surprise, and the rustle of a chair as she stood.

Marie finally came to understand the girl's horror. As the dimmed interior came into view, she saw Constance surrounded by what was presumably a family of five black folk. Constance had an elementary primer clutched in one hand—she had obviously been teaching the people to read.

Marie processed the information with a sudden sense of final comprehension. So that was why the girl was so curious about whether or not Marie believed everyone deserved an education. She had been speaking of other races.

Marie was not her mother's daughter for nothing. Jenny's Quaker grandparents had spoken of slavery and degradation in religious terms and brooked no argument when it came to the question of whether or not slavery was an institution sanctioned by God. In their view, it most certainly was not.

And thus, the generations produced a young New Orleans schoolteacher who felt everyone had a right to learn. She stepped forward into the small shack and waved a hand gently at Constance, who was so terrified that she looked on the verge of collapse. Marie's heart went out to the poor pupils, who looked very near the same condition, themselves.

"It's all right," she murmured quickly. "Sit down." She motioned to Constance and found one more vacant chair in the corner. It was rickety, but serviceable, and she swatted at the dirty seat once before sitting upon it and summoning a smile.

"So, is this why you've missed school the past two days?"

Constance swallowed visibly, her eyes large and liquid.

"You never told me you wanted to follow in my footsteps, Connie—I'm flattered."

"Please, ma'am . . ."

"Connie, I am not speaking flippantly. I think what you're doing here is not only brave, but commendable." She looked at the girl for a few moments, waiting for comprehension to register on the girl's face. Finally, it did.

"I thought you would turn us over to authorities," Constance breathed out on a sigh, one tear escaping and falling behind her spectacles. She wiped at it absently with one finger.

Marie shook her head. "I think I'm what people might call a misplaced Southerner. I live here, but I don't necessarily like the way things are."

Constance's pupils had yet to utter a sound. Marie took a closer look at them, taking in their grubby clothing, the lack of shoes, the looks of trepidation still apparent on their faces. "Would you like to introduce me to your friends?" she asked Constance.

"Yes." Connie drew herself together and cleared her throat. She pointed to the father of the family as though presenting a king. "This is Justis Fromere. He lives on the Fromere plantation, about one mile down the road."

Marie extended her hand. "How do you do? I'm Marie Brissot, Constance's teacher."

The man nodded and took her hand, his eyes huge. "Fine, thank you, ma'am," he murmured.

Constance then introduced Justis's wife, Pauline, and their three teenaged sons, Adam, Abel, and Noah. Marie shook hands with the whole family, each murmuring softly in return, eyes downcast. Noah, the youngest at fourteen, however, looked her straight in the eye and gripped her hand in a firm shake. "I's doin' fine ma'am," he said when she asked after his welfare.

Marie smiled. "I'm glad to hear that, Noah. And are you learning much from Constance, here?"

"Yes'm. We's already learnin' to read." Noah's expression was solemn, his eyes earnest. Marie swallowed past a thickening lump in her throat.

"Good!" She glanced at the others who were still staring at her as though she had just dropped from the moon.

"Constance, do you suppose you'll be coming to school anymore? There's much I'd still like to teach you."

"Oh, yes, yes indeed. I haven't left school—it's just that with Peter being home these past couple of days, it gave me more time to spend with the Fromeres—I usually only have one or two hours in the evening."

Marie studied the family, her brow creased. "Forgive me for asking," she said to Justis Fromere, "but how is it that you are allowed time to leave the plantation? Does your mistress ask for an accounting of your whereabouts?"

The family patriarch cleared his throat. "We's actually freed slaves, ma'am," he answered, his voice deep and rich. "We work on the plantation for pay. When we be needin' time to shop or go about town, we can, with permission."

Marie nodded. Free or not, however, the family undoubtedly encountered resistance from every corner. "Do you move about unmolested?" she asked, knowing the answer before it came.

Constance supplied the response. "No, they don't. They have even tried, on two occasions, to move north. They've been caught by slave hunters, and each time returned to Madame Fromere, who confirms the papers authenticating their freedom."

"So you've relinquished all hope of moving north, then?"

Pauline shrugged and ventured forth with a comment. "It's easier to stay with Madame Fromere. She's kind and pays us."

"But she's old, Miss Pauline," Constance interrupted. "What will you do when she dies?"

"That's why we's here," Noah stated firmly. "To learn, so we can leave."

Marie nodded. "I think that's very wise, Noah. Learning is the first step. It so happens that I know some folks up north. We'll see if we can't get you there, yet."

***

When Marie finally returned home, the handsome young man who stood at the door with his shirtsleeves rolled up and his bow tie hanging loose around his neck greeted her with a weary smile. The exhaustion clearly etched on his features was at odds with his bright greeting.

"Well, if it isn't my little cousin Marie!"

She threw her arms around his neck in relief. Finally! Some help. "Luke!" she said, torn between laughter and tears. "You made it so quickly! Only a week! I wasn't expecting to see you here for quite some time. You didn't encounter any Confederate trouble?" she asked as he drew her inside and closed the door.

"Very little. I've been pretending to be my cousin, Ben. Truth be told, I was expecting more. Seems everyone's too busy working their way north to pay much attention to me."

She sobered and moved toward the seating area of the parlor, motioning for him to sit next to her on the sofa. She clasped his hands. "So tell me, is it bad?"

He nodded. "Not so much yet, but I fear it will be. People are whipped into a frenzy, Marie, in every city I passed, whether Union or Confederate."

She nodded, her jaw tightening. "I suppose you've seen Papa?"

He nodded. "I've been sitting with him since I arrived, actually. Your mother has gone into the city to make some final purchases before we leave. Are you packed and ready to go?"

Marie withdrew her hands and glanced out the window. "Well," she sighed, "I've had a change of plans since my mother last telegraphed yours."

"What kind of change of plans?"

"The kind that requires me to stay here."

Her pronouncement was met with silence. She turned her gaze from the window and looked at her cousin, whom she hadn't seen in nearly ten years and didn't know at all as an adult. Her only memories of him were fun and carefree—he might well not be the lighthearted youth she remembered.

"Have you spoken with your mother?"

"No. She won't like it, but I'm almost hoping she'll be so consumed over Papa's welfare that she won't give it much thought."

He laughed, then, and a closer glance told her he was genuinely amused. "There's a war on, Marie. I'm sure she'll give it thought." He paused. "Why would you want to stay? If your father's life is in danger here, why is it you think you'll be safe?"

Marie shook her head. "I'm nothing but a disgraced, fallen woman, haven't you heard? People leave me alone because my diseased state might transfer to their own darling children. Besides, I have nothing to do with the newspaper. The locals here are afraid Papa will recover and print more inflammatory editorials. I, on the other hand, pose no threat to them as long as I don't write for the paper. Did Mama tell you what happened?"

Luke shook his head and settled back against the cushioned sofa. "Not in any great detail."

"Papa was thinking of printing an editorial for the paper that outlined the comparisons between Northern and Southern materials and possessions in terms of advantage. The numbers themselves are, well, damning, if you will, and Papa must have known it, because he printed only one copy of the article, probably for himself, and must have dropped it outside the newspaper office. Someone found it and the following day Papa was mobbed on his way home from work again. Only this time, the damage was much worse. He was all but left for dead on the side of the road. Michael happened upon him and brought him home, barely breathing."

" 'This time'? There were others?"

She nodded. "Once before, when he printed something unpopular." She sighed a bit before adding, "We've considered the risks. It seems insane to transport him such a great distance in his condition, but Mama and I both feel he needs to leave. He needs to be somewhere far, far away from these people."

Luke watched her quietly for a moment until she began to fidget under his regard. "I'm sorry," he said. "I'll do everything I can to help care for your father."

Marie tried for a smile that wouldn't materialize. "Thank you, Luke."

"Now why don't you tell me why you don't want to go to Boston."

"I can't leave the children. They have no one to care for them, really. Their parents are barely able to fend for themselves, let alone care for their little ones. I'm the only stable adult figure some of them have. And besides, there's nothing I can do . . ." Her eyes filmed over and burned with tears, and she frowned, shaking her head. "My parents have supported me all these years and never once have they suggested that I should be ashamed of myself or of my past mistakes. Now, my father lies helpless and I wish I could find solutions. Instead, I find myself unable to cope."

Luke nodded, but remained silent.

"I can't stand to be here," she whispered, "knowing he's so near death. It breaks my heart until I'm convinced it will surely fall from my chest. I find that I am better able to go about my life if I am thinking of something else—primarily the children. What would I do in Boston, Luke? Watch my father die? I can't help him, but I can help my school children."

Luke slowly nodded. "I can appreciate that, Marie, but your mother simply will not allow you to stay here unchaperoned."

At that, she laughed, and genuinely. "The townspeople expect it of me." She patted his knee and rose to begin dinner preparations for her mother. "I will take care of the details, Luke," she said. "Oddly enough, I truly feel I need to stay here."

CHAPTER 23

"There are but two parties now, traitors and patriots, and I want hereafter to be ranked with the latter."
—Ulysses S. Grant

***

Boston, Massachusetts
7 July, 1861

"Mother, I embroider—I do not make clothing."

"Camille." It came out as a sigh, in spite of Elizabeth's intentions to keep her frustrations under control. "You have never made your own clothing, true, but that doesn't mean you don't know how. Now we are going to finish these shirts, and I don't want to hear one more word of complaint."

"Can't we at least take these things over to Olivia's house and work with her? She and her mother are doing the same thing today."

Elizabeth's smile was strained. "I know. I spoke with Olivia's mother yesterday." In truth, Olivia's mother, Hortence Sylvester, made Elizabeth's head pound. The woman meant well, but she was a nervous thing, and couldn't stem the flow of high-pitched chatter that seemed to gush out of her mouth from an endless reservoir of inane social gossip. The thought of spending time sewing soldier's shirts with Hortence was enough to make Elizabeth yearn for a darkened bedroom and a cool cloth to cover her eyes.

"No, we'll just finish these here, and then we'll go downtown for a bit," Elizabeth told Camille and ignored the gusty sigh of protest. "I have some things I need to buy, and I thought we might pay a visit to Dolly and Abigail Van Dyke. Dolly has taken ill again."

Camille dropped her hands into her lap, clutching her sewing needle so tightly her fingertips were turning white. "Why must we visit them? Mother, those women are positively boorish!"

"And what makes them boorish, Camille?"

"They attend those wretched Society meetings! They're all fired up about abolition and Women's Rights—they are hardly ever invited to polite society events, and besides, they're new money."

Elizabeth stared at her daughter, trying to summon a reply. Where on earth had she gone so horribly wrong with this one? True, her other daughter ran around town pretending to be a man, but at least she possessed a brain. "Camille, *we* are 'new money.'"

"Well," the girl fumbled, grasping at straws, "we have a lot of it!"

"Camille." Elizabeth placed her own hands in her lap and strove for patience she wasn't sure she could summon. "Are you aware that I am an abolitionist myself? As is your father—he donates large sums of money to the cause? And Luke?"

"You're not as bad as Luke—he never misses a meeting! It's just so, so . . . gauche."

Elizabeth felt a stabbing pain behind her right eye. "Since when is it gauche to try to secure freedom for an entire group of people unjustly enslaved?"

"Olivia says that the Negro is happy with his lot in life—that the abolitionist rhetoric of the North is the imaginings of a bunch of do-gooders who have no idea how things really are. The Negro doesn't have the same intellectual capacities as the white man, and therefore slavery is a kindness. He might not otherwise be able to sustain his own life."

Now, the pain behind Elizabeth's right eye spread to the left, and beneath the pounding was fear. Her own daughter could not possibly be spouting such atrocities. Had she learned nothing through the years? "Do you know why the white man has assumed the African doesn't have sufficient intellectual capacities, Camille?"

The girl shook her head.

"Because slaveholders have made it illegal to educate slaves. It's against the law in slaveholding states. The slave can't very well learn and exercise those intellectual abilities if he's never taught, now, can he?"

"But Olivia says—"

"Olivia should never open her mouth! I can't believe the things she's infused into your brain, Camille! I ought to have been paying closer attention. What is it that's so fascinating about Olivia that you would discount everything you've learned from home?"

Camille flushed. "Olivia's always surrounded by handsome suitors."

"So are you!"

The girl shook her head. "Not like Olivia's. Mine are all young boys. Hers are men."

"How old are these 'men'?"

"Twenty-two, some twenty-three."

"So you're thinking that if you start sounding like Olivia you'll attract older men?"

Camille flushed again, maintaining a stony silence.

"Sweetheart, let me tell you something." Elizabeth set her sewing to one side and moved to sit next to Camille on the sofa. "There is nothing attractive about ignorance." She took Camille's hand into her own and smoothed her fingertips over the back of it. "I don't care what you hear from Olivia, from her mother, her sister, or anyone else who thinks they know best. I want you to remember this. *There is nothing attractive about ignorance.* Someday, presumably, you'll be married, and don't you think your husband would enjoy having a wife with informed opinions?"

"Men don't want wives with informed opinions!" Camille wailed. "They want someone pretty who can host a good dinner for their important friends!"

"Some men, maybe, but don't you want a husband who's at least a bit like your father? Someone who cares what his wife thinks and values that opinion?"

"There aren't any men out there like Daddy."

Elizabeth laughed and patted Camille's hand. "There are, sweetheart. You might just have to look for awhile."

"I don't have 'awhile.'"

"You're already approaching spinsterhood?"

"Olivia thinks so."

"I'm thinking Olivia should be banned from this house."

"Mother! She's my best friend!"

"Hmm. That's what worries me." Elizabeth held up a hand to forestall Camille's angry retort and said, "Tell me what you want more than anything else right now."

"A husband."

"Other than that. Something in my control."

"Mmm." Camille's brow wrinkled in a frown. Her eyes flickered, then, with something Elizabeth could have sworn was calculation. "Olivia's parents are going to D.C. to visit Mrs. Sylvester's sister, and Olivia told me yesterday that her brother, Nathaniel, asked if Robert and I can go along."

"Washington, D.C.? Camille, that city is a veritable fortress right now, surrounded by the enemy on all sides!"

"But you asked me what I want most right now—Robert and I want to go with them to D.C."

"I had rather hoped you would choose something that didn't have the potential for getting you shot!"

"Oh, Mother, you said it yourself! D.C. is probably the safest city on the earth these days. Nobody is foolish enough to try an invasion, not even Mr. Jefferson Davis."

"Well, I don't know—"

"Just say you'll think about it, all right?"

Elizabeth bit the inside of her cheek, deep in thought. She had hoped to bribe her daughter into doing something. She rose from the sofa and walked to the far wall, which was filled with bookshelves. Running her finger along the volumes on the middle shelf, she finally found the one she'd been considering.

"I will think about it, but in return I'd like you to do something for me. Do you promise?"

Camille nodded reluctantly.

"I want you to read this book, and when you're done, come and tell me and we'll talk about it."

"What is it?" Camille accepted the book from her mother and examined the cover.

"It's a narrative of the life of Frederick Douglass. He was a slave who escaped and now lives here in New England."

"I thought you said slaves weren't allowed to be educated. How did he write a book?"

"He learned how to read and write in spite of his masters' forbiddance. He learned from children off the streets, from anyone who would teach him."

Camille nodded. "All right, I'll read this. But remember, you promised to think about Washington!"

"And I will. I may not say 'yes,' however," she cautioned. "Will you still read the book?"

Camille twitched her lips, apparently recognizing her own bargaining power. "That hardly seems fair."

"I know. Maybe you'll just read it because you know your sainted mother wants you to, and because you love her so much, you'll do it for her sake."

Camille smiled in full, shaking her head. "You win. I'll tell you when I'm finished with it."

"Good." Elizabeth resumed her seat and picked up the shirt she had been working on. "Now, I thought you said that Olivia's sister was encouraging the lot of you to stay informed. Whatever happened with your newfound love for the newspaper?"

"I'm still reading it," Camille said, putting the book aside and picking up her own sewing. Her brow wrinkled in a slight frown. "I don't understand everything, though. Today the paper said Lincoln suspended habeas something or other. I don't even know what that is."

"The Writ of Habeas Corpus is the constitutional right that says a person can't be arrested and held under lock and key without just cause. It's something that a court can issue to demand that authorities release a person who is being held in custody. But the constitution also says that the government has the right, in times of trouble, to suspend it. To arrest people who might be a threat to the government—in this case, Confederate sympathizers who could cause real trouble."

Elizabeth watched as comprehension crossed Camille's features. "That's why some people are calling Lincoln a tyrant, then? Because he's now made it legal for people to be arrested and held without a firm reason?"

"Yes, that's why they are calling him a tyrant."

"Do you think he is?"

Elizabeth paused, her hands stilling for a moment. "No, I don't think he's a tyrant, but I hope people are very careful about how they use this power. Thus far, it affects only the area from Philadelphia to Washington—especially Maryland."

"Why was the judge unhappy with it?"

"The judge?"

Camille made a motion with her hand. "The old one—the one who swore Lincoln into office."

"Oh, yes. Taney. He told Lincoln that the president doesn't have the right to suspend habeas corpus, but Lincoln says that since the constitution doesn't exactly say which government branch has the power to do it, that he can, given the circumstances surrounding it." Elizabeth resumed her sewing with a smile at Camille. "Are you still confused, or does it make sense, now?"

"It makes sense. I'll have to tell Olivia. She didn't understand it, either."

Elizabeth wasn't surprised.

***

"I brought it up with Mother," Camille told Robert later that night in the hallway by his bedroom door.

"You did?" Robert's face was flushed with excitement. "What did she say?" He opened his door and grabbed her arm, pulling her into the bedroom.

"She said she'd think about it," Camille answered with a scowl, rubbing at her arm. "She didn't promise to say 'yes.'"

"Well, why not?"

"Robert. Surely you didn't think she'd readily agree to allowing us a vacation in the midst of what could very well turn into a battle ground?"

"I don't know!" Robert threw his hands into the air in frustration and began to pace the length of his spacious bedroom.

Camille wrinkled her nose in distaste as she surveyed her brother's domain. "Robert, it looks like a military convention in here." There were drawings and photographs of Army hardware, and books on war heroes and military strategy sprawled and stacked in every corner. A thought suddenly struck her, and she said with a fair measure of alarm, "You're not thinking of running away from the Sylvesters in D.C. so you can enlist, are you?"

Robert glanced at her while he continued to pace. "No," he said, heaving a sigh. "I did consider it, but I'm not clever enough, and Father would catch me and thrash me to within an inch of my life. I'll just have to hope the war lasts long enough for me to legally enlist."

"Aren't you worried about getting shot?"

"Are you daft? I won't get shot!"

"Hmm. Well, anyway, there you have it. We'll have to see what she says after she's had some time."

"But the Sylvesters leave in a week!"

"I know. That gives me one week to convince her." Camille turned and opened the door. As she entered the hallway, her ears perked up at a sound at the front door. Her mother was squealing in surprise. Elizabeth never squealed.

Robert was on Camille's heels as they made their way to the balcony overlooking the front foyer. "Hey, Luke's back!" Robert said, as they watched their brother maneuvering a wheeled contraption, carrying a man who appeared to be sleeping. "Oh," Robert added in a hushed tone, "it's Aunt Jenny and Uncle J.P."

Camille looked aside at her brother in annoyance. "You call him 'Uncle J.P.'? His name is Jean-Pierre."

"I know that. Last time we saw them, he said I could call him J.P."

"The last time we saw them, you were four."

"Exactly. I couldn't say 'Jean-Pierre.'" Robert shoved a lock of hair from his forehead.

Camille shook her head and walked to the staircase, muttering something under her breath about how it was a miracle people in polite circles even accepted her, given that she had such odd siblings. Robert followed her and they made their way down the stairs to Elizabeth, who held her sister in a tight embrace.

"Oh, Jenny," she was saying. "It's wonderful to see you, but such trying circumstances! We'll take good care of you all." She went over to Luke, who was working with Griffen to move the wheeled contraption through the foyer.

"Is the main floor guest room ready, then?" Luke asked his mother after she kissed his cheek and called him a "good boy."

"Yes," Elizabeth answered, linking her arm through her sister's and propelling them toward the hallway.

They paused when they caught sight of Robert and Camille, both of whom Jenny wrapped in a warm embrace with an exclamation of surprise over how they'd grown. "And Marie sends her regards," Jenny told the pair.

Elizabeth started in surprise. "She's not here?" She glanced behind them at the door. "I just assumed she was still coming in from the carriage!"

Jenny sighed. "No, she's in New Orleans." She shook her head. "It's a long tale—I'll explain it when I think I can do it without crying. Basically, she feels she needs to be with her students." Jenny's eyes welled with moisture, and Elizabeth brusquely took her arm, and led them again toward the bedroom.

"Say no more," she said to her sister. "We'll talk about it when you're ready."

Camille and Robert stood to one side while Luke and Griffen propelled the chair that contained their unconscious uncle.

"He looks terrible," Robert said in a whisper.

"Well of course he does!" Camille snapped. "He was attacked!"

"That was over a month ago," Robert answered in annoyance. "I'm not talking about the bruising—it's hardly noticeable. I'm talking about the fact that he won't wake up!"

Camille's gaze followed the last of her older brother as he made his way toward the guest room. It was troubling, she had to admit. To be beaten so badly that your body still lived but the brain refused to awaken? She shuddered in spite of the heat of the day that still lingered in the house. "Mother will make things right," she murmured. She then thought of something else. "And in the meantime," she added, turning to Robert, "she may be so distracted that we'll be able to go with the Sylvesters to D.C."

"I hope you're right," Robert said as he climbed the staircase to return to his bedroom. "We may not get another opportunity to go."

***

Anne Birmingham sat in her father's study four days later, watching him as he leaned against the hearth, staring at the empty fireplace. "You can't keep ignoring me," she said quietly.

He cleared his throat gruffly. "I'm not ignoring you, Anne."

"You speak to me in monosyllables. You hardly acknowledge my presence. Sometimes I feel invisible if we're in a room together. Was it really so heinous? All I was doing was writing a silly newspaper column."

He shook his head and finally looked up at her. "It's not that, Anne. At first I was shocked, I'll admit. And you must admit as well, it is odd."

She nodded her agreement.

"But just when my temper had cooled and I had almost found a sense of pride in your daring, your mother told me of your plans to move to Chicago." He was silent, then, venturing nothing further.

"You don't approve of Chicago either?"

"The timing is bad, Anne. Imagine yourself in my position for just a moment! How am I to feel about my daughter moving to Chicago in the middle of a war?"

"Chicago isn't so far . . ."

"It's at least three days by train, and that's under optimal circumstances!"

Anne was quiet. If her father only knew the truth . . . She tamped down on a prickle of guilt. "I'll be fine. You know Isabelle personally, and I've often heard you speak highly of Allan Pinkerton, so you can't be harboring reservations about my employment."

"No, no, I don't." He moved away from the fireplace to sit next to her in a chair. "I will miss you, though. Dreadfully." James took her hand and pressed her knuckles to his lips. "You're going to do this, aren't you? There's nothing I can say that will convince you to stay here with your mother and me?"

"I'm nearly twenty-three years old. How long would you have me live under your roof?" she asked with a gentle smile.

"Luke still lives here, and he's older by two years! I can't *make* him leave!"

She laughed. "Luke will leave as well. Eventually."

James sighed. "I know. I didn't imagine you moving away from home alone, however. I always envisioned that you'd have a husband to . . ."

"Take care of me?"

He nodded.

"I don't need it." She cast him a sidelong glance of sympathy, not intending to offend his sense of convention.

He shook his head, almost imperceptibly. "Neither does your

mother. But she lets me anyway. There's a bit of advice for you, Anne-girl," he said, tapping the back of her hand with one finger. "Let your husband take care of you on occasion, even if you don't need it."

She smiled a bit. "I'll remember that."

"Now then, tell me your plans."

"The day after tomorrow, I leave for Washington, D.C. I'll meet up with Isabelle, and from there we'll go to Chicago."

"So it's settled, then."

"Yes."

"You'll take care of yourself?"

"Of course." Anne watched with eyes that burned as her father placed one more kiss on the back of her hand before rising and leaving her alone in his study. Her throat ached as she watched his retreating form, wondering if she wasn't making a huge mistake. The thought of what lay before her flickered through her mind and she remembered the restlessness that had spurred her into action in the first place. Shaking her head at her reluctance, she rose and went to her bedroom to make final preparations for her departure before she was tempted to change her mind.

Elizabeth and Jenny sat in the solarium at the back of the house, as they had much of the time since Jenny's arrival, speaking of the years they'd spent apart and mulling over what the future held in store. Jean-Pierre's condition remained unchanged, and Jenny was growing gaunt with worry.

"There is a specialist," Jenny said, "who lives in Philadelphia. One of the surgeons in New Orleans told me about this man. He supposedly is an expert on illnesses involving injuries to the head, but is in such high demand that he's rarely accessible."

"Hmm," Elizabeth murmured. "Philadelphia, you say? I wonder how this man would feel at a personal invitation. He's reputable, I suppose, being in such high demand . . ."

"Yes, so I was told. The only problem is that I don't feel right about moving Jean-Pierre again, and I don't want to leave him for an extended period of time, either.”

“James and I would be happy to make the trip, Jenny—you needn’t leave.”

“I couldn’t let you, Lizzie. I’ve imposed so much already.”

“Nonsense. It’s been like the old days, having you here with us again. Let me speak to James and see what his schedule is like this week. He mentioned business in New York, and truth be told, I had wanted a bit of a vacation, myself. I was planning on accompanying him on his next trip, and Philadelphia is close enough that we can visit this doctor of yours and see if he won’t help.”

“I would so appreciate it! I have his name, but not his address . . .”

“James and I know a few people in Philadelphia. We can find him, I’m sure. Oh, look,” she said as James passed by the door, “there he is now. She motioned for her husband to join them in the room, and repeated the conversation she had had with her sister. He was amenable, of course, so the plans were set to leave two days hence.

What they didn’t know, however, was that Robert was outside the door, listening to the plans as they were laid. A grin split his face ear to ear as he walked quietly away from the door and up to his bedroom.

***

“It’s all a matter of timing . . .” Robert muttered as his parents’ coach pulled away from the drive two days later. Anne had left at daybreak, James and Elizabeth were on their way to the train station, and the time had come for Robert and Camille to pay a visit to the Sylvesters.

The coach ride was a quiet one. Camille sat in her finest day dress, a matching bonnet of soft yellow and green framing her face. She chewed her lower lip and looked pensively out of the window while Robert sat across from her, nervously tapping his foot.

“You ought to have let me just ask her,” Camille finally muttered. “She might well have said yes, and then we wouldn’t have to worry about what they'll say when they find out."

"If they find out."

"*When* they find out." Camille blew out a breath in exasperation. "Robert, they will find out, you know! Mother sees Mrs. Sylvester quite frequently." She paused. "Do we really want to do this?"

"Oh, Cammy, yes, we do! Just think of it! Aren't you bored to tears with Boston? I am!"

The look on his face was so earnest and eager that Camille didn't have the heart to deny him his fun. *You don't have to go with him,* asserted a voice in the back of her mind. No, it was true, she didn't have to, but truth be told, she desperately wanted to experience something new.

By the time they reached the Sylvesters and explained that their parents had made a last-minute trip to New York but had given their children permission for the trip to D.C., Camille had convinced herself that it wasn't really going to be much of a problem. Her mother, after all, hadn't actually said *no.*

"We'll leave early tomorrow morning," Mrs. Sylvester told them. "We'll send a carriage around for you and meet you at the train station."

"Won't it be just wonderful?" Olivia squealed as she walked Camille to the door. They were saying their good-byes after the brief visit. "All those fantastic men in uniform!" The last she added in an undertone, casting a glance over her shoulder at her parents, who were engaged in conversation with Robert and Nathaniel.

Camille nodded her agreement with a bright smile, her reservations continuing to ebb. It was no problem at all, really. And maybe Robert was right—maybe James and Elizabeth wouldn't ever find out, and nobody would be the wiser.

CHAPTER 24

"The Privileges of the Writ of Habeas Corpus shall not be suspended, unless when, in Cases of Rebellion or Invasion the public Safety may require it."
—*The U.S. Constitution concerning habeas corpus*

***

Washington, D.C.
19 July, 1861

"You were right, Belle. This city looks like a garrison." There were guns stationed on every corner, it seemed, and soldiers filled the capitol in more numbers than Anne or anyone else in recent history had ever seen. She stared, wide-eyed, trying to take it all in. There were many different companies of soldiers about town, usually dressed like each other, but often differing from those of other companies and regiments. There was a sense of camaraderie—of family—about the groups. Anne knew this came from the fact that they had probably all grown up together, lived side-by-side or down the street, and now were defending their country together. It would be that much harder on them, she mused with a slight frown, when they fell.

"It does indeed. Probably didn't look like this the last time you were here, did it?" Isabelle asked with a grin.

"No, it didn't. How much longer will you be here?"

Isabelle shrugged. "Until Lincoln says it's time to go home. Or until Pinkerton thinks we need to go back to Chicago, but he's kept us busy here—"

"Who's still here, then? You, Pinkerton . . ."

Isabelle nodded. "And Kate Warne and Timothy Webster."

"Are you still trying to infiltrate sympathizers?"

"Yes. The frightening thing is that there are so many it hasn't been a difficult challenge to find them. Ah, here we are, home again," Isabelle said as the two made their way into the hotel lobby and up the stairs to her room.

"Now that we've had a good, healthy lunch," Isabelle said as she unlocked the door and stepped inside, "what is it you need me to do?"

"I need you to cut my hair off."

"Oh, Anne." Isabelle sighed. "Well, I suppose we must. I don't suppose you have some good shears?"

"I do." Anne walked to the suitcase she had deposited in the room earlier in the day and rummaged about until she produced a black bag. She handed it to her friend, saying, "Everything a good barber needs is right in here."

With a raised brow, Isabelle took the bag and opened it, peering inside. "Did you raid a barber shop before getting on the train?"

Anne laughed. "I did some shopping," she admitted. "I visited the finest barber shop in downtown Boston and told them I was on an errand to buy supplies for a passing regiment—that I needed the best available for our faithful boys. The proprietor directed me to his supplier, and I bought that," she finished, motioning to the bag Isabelle held in her hands.

"When do you want me to do this thing?"

Anne shrugged. "There's no time like the present."

"Now? Do you have any other clothing with you other than dresses?"

"Actually, this dress I'm wearing is the only one I brought with me, and I'll be leaving it here with you. My only other clothes are the basic soldier's uniforms I made before leaving Boston."

"Let's hope your future regiment approves of your color choices."

"I chose basic blue—it seems to be regulation, except for a few unique companies," Anne said, gesturing toward the window, which afforded them a fine view of the numerous troops she had seen upon her arrival. "Any other embroidery—company or regiment name, for instance, I can add later."

Isabelle nodded. "All right, then," she said and retrieved a sheet from the linen closet, spreading it on the floor and dragging a chair to sit atop it. "Have a seat, dearie." She patted the back of the chair with one hand and then dove into the barber bag, pulling out a wickedly sharp-looking pair of scissors. She snapped them open and closed twice in rapid succession. "Speak now or forever hold your peace."

"Do it."

***

Washington, D.C.
20 July, 1861

"You say you're a newspaper man? And you have no preference as to which regiment you'd like to join?" The harried enlistment clerk pushed his spectacles farther up on the bridge of his nose and regarded Anne with a hawk-like stare.

"That's correct."

"Infantry? Artillery? Cavalry?"

"Infantry."

"All right. There are plenty of regiments stationed right here in the city—some from your hometown of Boston, in fact. I suppose we could put you in one of those . . ." As the young man began shuffling papers about on his cluttered desk, Anne pursed her lips for a moment.

"Actually . . ." she said, and tried not to wince as he glanced up in irritation.

"Yes?"

This man was her ticket out of Washington, D.C. She wanted to move farther south, farther away from Boston and the all-too perceptive eyes of her shrewd parents. She wanted to join with a regiment that had potential for southern movement, not one that was likely to stay put and guard the capitol.

"I was hoping for something away from the city—something perhaps farther south?" she suggested, allowing herself to slip comfortably back into the role she had perfected as "Adam Jones." The male intonation, mannerisms—they came rushing back to her like old friends, and with her newly cut hair, she felt more the part than she ever had.

"Farther south, farther south . . ." The clerk continued to rustle through papers, and just when Anne was beginning to despair that the clerk would ever find his way through the mass of documents and troop rosters, another young officer approached him from an inner office and handed him a piece of paper.

"I'm busy!" the clerk snapped.

The officer shrugged. "Colonel said you need to file this with the other regimental information on Ohio."

The clerk grabbed the piece of paper with a curt "Fine," and set it aside. He glanced back at it, seemingly as an afterthought, his eyes widening as he read the contents. "Well, here we go then," he said and gestured to Anne. "This is perfect. A regiment, farther south, and they've had a measles outbreak that has left many of their men ill. They could use another strapping young lad, I'm sure."

He began processing a mountain of paperwork that made Anne's head swim. When he finally motioned for her to sign her name to her enlistment form, she nearly forgot which name she was using. After the slightest pause, she wrote Aaron Johnson where the clerk indicated, and she then produced a paper that stated she'd been examined by a physician in Boston and had been pronounced healthy. Isabelle had secured the form, and Anne hadn't asked how.

The clerk filed her health report with her other papers and offered her a brief, irritated salute. "Welcome to the Army, Private

Johnson. You're to report to the 7th Ohio, currently stationed in Weston, Virginia. You can make the bulk of the trip by train. I suggest you head to the station—with all the trouble getting in and out of the city lately, it may take you some time. If you're lucky, the tracks have been repaired."

Anne nodded her thanks and made her way out of the building and into the bright light of the noonday sun. She ran her hand over her short hair, loving the feel of freedom she experienced at the lack of cumbersome curls and heavy clothing. Ah, yes, it was bliss to be a man, she mused with a smile as she walked the short distance to Isabelle's hotel. She would say her good-byes to her friend, and then she was on her own.

***

"I have never seen so many military men in my entire life!" Olivia's squeal of delight elicited stares from people who passed by on the crowded streets of the capitol city.

Nobody's ever seen so many military men! Camille found herself wanting to say. She found Olivia's scatterbrained exuberance annoying, and the feeling was surprising. She couldn't remember a time when she'd actually looked at Olivia and found her scatterbrained. It must be Elizabeth's influence, stretching from afar and reaching out to choke her about the throat. Camille shook her head at the image and also at the flicker of unease she had experienced the last few days whenever she thought of her mother and father. Robert, the fool, was oblivious to her distress. He was on the same level of ecstasy at the heavy military presence as was Olivia. She was tempted to ask her brother if perhaps he, and not she, was the one in the market for a husband.

In truth, Robert's exuberance had her worried. Camille found herself less and less occupied with studying the soldiers for potential husband material and more concerned with keeping an eye tightly focused on her brother. It would be just like him to try something foolish, and if he slipped away to enlist, not only would she never forgive herself, her parents would probably have her jailed. The writ of habeas corpus had been suspended, after all, she mused with a wry smile. Her mother could have her locked away indefinitely without legal recourse.

"What are you smiling at?" Olivia whispered in her ear. "Did you see someone you like?"

Camille glanced aside at her friend. Had Olivia gone mad? The way she was ogling the men was going to have the entire city thinking she was a woman of loose morals. "If you don't calm yourself, your mother is going to lock you in the hotel room!" she hissed.

"Posh! My mother is too distracted. She can't wait to see Aunt Helena."

Well, that much was true, Camille had to admit. Hortence Sylvester was almost beside herself with the anticipation of seeing her sister. She had been chattering about it so much, and so consistently, since leaving Boston, that Camille was ready to clap her hands over her ears. And Camille was one who favored chatter!

And so they were on their way to Mrs. Sylvester's favorite restaurant, to meet Aunt Helena. Camille glanced behind her, wanting to make sure she still had her brother in tow. Ah, good—there he was, lagging along behind the group with Nathaniel, gawking at the military hardware present everywhere in the city and the multitudinous crowds of soldiers that lined the streets and stood at attention, guarding various government facilities. Camille gritted her teeth. It was an opportunity of a lifetime! She should be enjoying herself and the unlimited prospects for flirtation. And her mother wasn't even there to tell her not to act hoydenish! Yet all she could do was stew over her foolish brother and hope he didn't try anything silly.

They passed near the train station and Camille shook her head—it had taken some time to get into the city, and she wasn't looking forward to the energy it would take to get back out again. Things were running more smoothly now that there were troops guarding the rail lines, she had heard, than shortly after Sumter, when D.C. had sat unprotected on all sides. Still, it was an effort to come and go, and she wished she could just blink her eyes and find herself back in Boston when the time came.

She jostled against a woman and Olivia grabbed her arm, trying to steer her out of the way. She cast a glance back over her shoulder and murmured a quick apology to the woman she had bumped, only to see a face she was sure she recognized. Camille narrowed her eyes, trying to put a name to the woman. She was accompanied by a young soldier—why he must be barely eighteen!—who was slight of frame and maybe a couple of inches taller than Camille. She shook her head again. If Robert saw that boy, she could only imagine what he'd say. "If he can enlist, why can't I?" She hoped he wouldn't see the pair.

She turned around and continued moving forward at Olivia's urging, again trying to remember where she knew the woman she had bumped into. It plagued her as they continued on their way to meet Olivia's aunt. She mulled it over, much as a dog would do with a bone. She hated it when she recognized a person and couldn't remember from where!

They finally reached the restaurant, and lunch progressed amidst many effusive hugs and tears. Camille learned that Aunt Helena actually lived just outside Baltimore, and wasn't it such a disgrace the way things were progressing! Lincoln behaving like a tyrant and allowing Baltimore's mayor, (the mayor!) to be arrested, along with the police chief and held without any formal charges.

"Lincoln can't do that," Olivia gasped into her soup, outraged.

"Yes, he can," Camille replied. "He suspended the writ of habeas corpus."

"Well," Olivia's father sniffed, finally offering a comment after days of letting his wife do all his talking for him. "Personally, I agree with Justice Taney. Lincoln doesn't have the right to suspend it."

Camille swallowed. How far, exactly, did she want to venture into this conversation? All she knew, really, was what her mother had told her. She shrugged. What did she have to lose? What would Mr.

Sylvester do to her? Make her wait outside while the rest of the family finished lunch?

"Actually, the constitution doesn't exactly say who has the right to suspend it," she said, throwing caution to the wind.

Olivia's mother and father stared at her, their spoons poised midair. Aunt Helena's lips were pinched in tight disapproval, and Olivia herself looked as though she couldn't believe Camille would dare contradict her father, regardless of how slightly.

Robert must have sensed her unease. "She's right—Lincoln argued that since the constitution doesn't specifically say who has the right to suspend it, that any of the three branches can." He shrugged and glanced at Camille, whose face was burning at the rude response she had received. And why shouldn't she share what little she knew on the topic? The Sylvesters were acting as though their opinions were carved in stone, the only valid ones at the table!

Robert laughed and dug his fork into his food. He elbowed Nathaniel and said, "But then, look at what happens when a woman starts to read the newspaper. She starts to think she knows about the world at large." His quip greatly pleased the male members, at least, of the luncheon party, and they guffawed together, the mood lifting.

Camille shot a hot glance at her brother, who shook his head almost imperceptibly at her, warning clearly written in his expression. She finished her lunch in stony silence, wondering why she cared. It wasn't as though she was out to win an argument, or was really even worried about the outcome one way or another. She supposed that her pride rankled because she felt she was right in her defense of Lincoln. The constitution *didn't* say, and as president, Camille figured he had as much right as anyone to act in what he felt was the country's best interest.

That must be it, she reasoned as she continued her meal. When a person felt she was right about something, and was then basically ridiculed, that person had a right to be irritated. One thing was for certain; she didn't like the look of Olivia's father. She never had, really. He didn't carry a pleasant countenance, and he let it be known often that with the exception of his oldest, married daughter, he felt the female members of his household held little more intellectual capacity than young children. Actually, Camille had to admit, he wasn't so very different from many others of her acquaintance. But it wasn't how *she* had been raised.

She thanked her lucky stars for a good father, and then wondered if, when he discovered her and Robert's escapade, he would allow them to live to see Christmas. She shook her thoughts aside and finished her meal, rising with the rest of the group to venture back out into the heat of the day.

It was only as they neared the hotel where they were staying that Camille remembered, in a flash, where she had seen that woman she recognized at the train station. It was Anne's friend, Isabelle Webb. Anne was supposed to have met Isabelle in D.C. and then traveled to Chicago with her. Isabelle had obviously been on her way to the station, presumably to go out of town; so where was Anne?

She mentioned it later to Robert, who shrugged. "She was probably already at the station, or maybe right behind Isabelle," he said, distracted with the photos of the Union's latest weaponry that Nathaniel was shoving in his face. "It was very crowded at the station—we probably only just missed seeing her."

CHAPTER 25

"There is nothing like it this side of the infernal region. The peculiar corkscrew sensation that it sends down your backbone under these circumstances can never be told. You have to feel it, and if you say you did not feel it, and heard the yell, you have NEVER been there."
—*Union veteran, on the "Rebel Yell"*

***

Bull Run Creek, Virginia
Early morning, 21 July, 1861

Richard Birmingham stood in the trenches with the rest of the troops from the 2nd South Carolina along the Bull Run creek. It was all he could do to stay awake; the past three days had seen changes in weather and position, defending the trenches and watching as Brigadier General Bonham's scouts ran back and forth, in and out of the woods, relaying messages to the commanding officer as to the approaching enemy's positions.

Bonham himself was often seen in the company of Brigadier General Beauregard, and when Richard had caught a glimpse of the man who had gained such glory for himself at Sumter, his first inclination had been to rush over to the man and remind him that HE, Richard Birmingham, had been present with him at that wondrous event. When he moved to do so, however, one of his fellow Palmetto Guards had eyed him with disdain, saying, "We were all there, Birmingham, and if you think you're going to find yourself climbing into Beauregard's good graces by running over there and yapping at him, you're more dim than I thought."

The rebuke had stung, but Richard made a note of it. Someday, he would repay every person who dared make a fool of him. As for the present, the Yanks were coming, and Richard had been completely wrapped in enthusiasm at first, wanting his first real taste of battle. To his disappointment, however, it was taking awhile to materialize. They had been sitting in the rain for three days, and he was growing weary of the wait.

The first bit of good news had hit just a few hours before at two-thirty in the morning; a rumbling to the left front of the artillery wagons signaled that someone was approaching. Shortly before daylight, it was confirmed that it was indeed the enemy. Bonham had then made good use of his field glass, seeing Union troops in large numbers moving along the Warrenton turnpike toward the stone bridge.

As the information was eventually communicated to the troops in the trenches, Richard had felt a surge of adrenaline unlike anything he'd experienced. Finally! The only problem now was that the longer they were forced to wait, wait, wait, the sleepier he became. His energy level was flagging in the face of a long, sleepless night. He would be ready, though, by the time the bluebellies made an appearance. He'd blow 'em back up North to where they came from.

"Who's commanding 'em?" came a question from a soldier somewhere off to his left.

"McDowell," was the derisive response from Edwin Cornwell, the young man who had insulted Richard earlier. "He's thinking he can send us packing like McClellan did with Granny Lee's men in Philippi."

Richard hated to agree with Cornwell on any matter, now that he had been personally insulted by the sharp tongue, but the tone in which the young man spoke was in complete accord with his own feelings. The farmers located in Virginia's upland western counties were pro-Union, and had resisted the Confederacy every step along the way. Lincoln had sent McClellan to rid the areas of Confederate presence, and Robert E. Lee, with whom everyone had been so impressed, had been unable to convince his men to hold their ground. Richard had seen with his own eyes the newspapers that ridiculed Lee and called him "Evacuating Lee" and "Granny Lee."

It was true! And where was the backbone of his supposed men? To flee before Yanks—it was disgraceful. Well, now McDowell was on his way to meet Beauregard and the true men of the South, Richard reasoned. They'd give him what-for!

***

Camille stared at the grand procession, of which she, Robert and the Sylvesters were a part as they moved along in their open carriage toward the little town of Centreville, Virginia, near a railroad center called Manassas Junction. It was early morning, nearly nine o'clock, and they were almost there, following closely on the heels of several thousand Union troops who had been amassing for several days in preparation for moving on toward Richmond. The Northern papers, and even Lincoln himself, had expressed an urgency to move quickly and take the Confederate capitol at Richmond, Virginia, that the war might quickly be resolved and the misbehaving Southerners whipped back into shape. The Confederacy had troops lined along a creek called Bull Run, and there they stood, defending the quickest route to Richmond.

The procession following the Union troops was nearly as grand as were the soldiers themselves! Camille looked about herself with eyes wide—at the regimental bands that played "Dixie," of all things, and the soldiers who stopped periodically and broke ranks to pick blackberries and fill their canteens.

"This war business doesn't seem to be so bad after all," she murmured to Olivia.

"I know!" Olivia's eyes were shining. "And just think of the parties we'll see in D.C. tonight after we send the rebels home with their tails between their legs!"

Camille suppressed a smile. "I thought you were more or less a Rebel sympathizer yourself, Livvie," she said.

"Well," the girl answered with a wave of her hand, "I might as well support those I have the easiest access to. I'm not likely to spend much time with the Confederates."

Camille turned half an ear to the conversation transpiring between Mrs. Sylvester and her sister. "Can you believe the cost of these picnic supplies?" Hortence was saying in an outraged tone. "The wine and hamper of food cost three times its normal price! Those French cooks are making a profit on our national pride! You should have seen all the people who had purchased supplies like these in order to watch the engagement—the cooks and hotel keepers will be able to retire on today's earnings alone!"

Aunt Helena agreed. "But it's not as though you don't have the money."

Hortence glanced at her sister in slight irritation. It was gauche to mention finances, but as the Sylvesters's financial matters were above par, of course, it was acceptable in cases of such obvious compliment. "That's true, dear," she said, patting Helena's knee.

Camille glanced toward the side of the carriage, where Robert rode astride a fine-looking horse. Next to him on his own mount was Nathaniel, and riding slightly in front was Mr. Sylvester. Robert sat proudly in the saddle, and Camille knew he was wishing for all he was worth that he were part of a cavalry instead of a mere civilian spectator.

The crowd of civilians and politicians eventually slowed and dropped back approximately three miles from the Confederate lines, settling in and making themselves comfortable for a grand show. There were politicians in the crowd, and more newspaper reporters than Camille had ever seen in one place. *Anne should be here*, she mused.

The Sylvester women made themselves comfortable in the carriage, which Mr. Sylvester situated under a large tree, Hortence eventually dispensing some of the fare from the overly large picnic basket she had acquired at "three times the cost." Many of the other followers were spreading blankets on the ground, looking for shady spots in which to enjoy the spectacle. The music played on, the sun shone hot. With Washington, D.C., to her back approximately thirty miles away, and the beautiful, rolling hills of Virginia before her, Camille could almost believe she was on a fantastic holiday, completely devoid of strife and all talk of war.

***

Robert dismounted and secured his horse next to Nathaniel's, his eyes scanning the creek under the warm, morning light. *Ah, to be one of them!* he thought to himself as he watched the Union troops move into position in the near distance. It was ridiculous to be observing from so far away, back with the women and old politicians. He wanted a better view! He would miss it if he wasn't careful.

He glanced at Nathaniel, who had apparently been reading his thoughts. "Maybe we should go for a little walk," Nathaniel said in a loud voice to Robert.

His father overheard, and said, "Fine, Nathaniel, but stay close."

"Close is relative," Nathaniel muttered to Robert as they walked casually away from the party revelers and toward the creek. "All we want to do is watch, anyway, right?"

"Right!" Robert grinned at his friend, wishing for all the world that they weren't only fifteen years old. Life was cruel that way, sometimes. He was mulling over that hard fact when before them, in the distance, he and Nathaniel saw the troops crossing the creek. There was noise, then, muted and sounding like little more than small pops of what they knew must be gunfire. The soldiers before them laid down, and Robert ran forward, hoping to obtain a better view. Nathaniel was quick on his heels, and before long, the boys were close enough to hear a shouted command: "By the left flank—march!"

As the Union soldiers crossed a wide field, Robert glanced up and spied, not far off, Union cavalrymen. They were situated toward the back of the formation, apparently awaiting orders to move to the front. Robert gestured toward the mounted troops, and with a grin, Nathaniel nodded and the two ran closer to the horses and men. As they ran, the sounds of gunfire toward the front lines increased, and Robert glanced to his right, finally feeling a trickle of unease snake its way down his spine.

"We best stay back," he panted to Nathaniel, when they had reached the back lines of the cavalry.

"Are you afraid now?" Nathaniel asked him, apparently astonished. "We didn't come all this way to 'stay back'!"

"Fine, but we don't want to get in their way," Robert said. There were trees behind them, and they stayed along the edge, while still commanding a clear view of the mounted soldiers. Not far to their immediate left, a surgeon's tent was being hastily erected. Robert glanced at it, not really registering the fact that it would be used for men who were wounded or dying.

The minutes stretched on, and as the boys watched, fascinated, the first of the wounded began being transported from the front lines to the back of the formation. Robert looked in amazement as several of the mounted troops glanced quickly away as the wounded passed by. Were they men or were they men? They couldn't look at a wounded fellow comrade?

"I'll be . . ." Nathaniel breathed and elbowed Robert in the ribs. When Robert glanced at him in question, he motioned to a man on horseback who apparently hadn't looked away quickly enough and was vomiting from the saddle at the sight of the wounded being carried to the surgeon's tent, which was now filling with people.

Robert edged, in stunned fascination, toward the surgical tent, his eyes taking in the sight of torn and missing limbs, protruding bone, his ears registering the groans of the wounded. As he glanced again toward the battle scene itself, which had seemed to take on a life of its own, he saw the field dotted with blue uniforms that lay prostrate upon the ground, not moving.

Dead, that fast? How could it be? He heard retching sounds beside him and looked quickly at Nathaniel, who had apparently watched a bit too closely as a surgeon had removed the shirt of a soldier who had received a severe shot to his abdomen, tearing his flesh apart in a way Robert had certainly never witnessed before. As they watched, jaws open, the boy gurgled incoherently for a moment before falling slack against the surgeon who was attempting to save him.

Before long, the stream of wounded was continuous, and Robert felt his head swim at the gore. Never in his wildest imaginings could he have conjured such images of death and torn flesh. He hadn't known the human body could be mutilated in such ways! In all of his readings on military history, he had glanced over the messy details with an eye of dismissal, preferring instead to dwell upon tactics and maneuvering, mercy and chivalry. The sight that now greeted his roiling stomach was almost too much to bear.

Robert turned his back and gave Nathaniel the privacy he needed to continue emptying the contents of his already-empty stomach; the boys had been too excited for breakfast. When Nathaniel was finished, Robert glanced at him and said, "I think we should go back to your parents."

Nathaniel nodded. "I've seen enough."

It took the boys a bit longer to return to the "encampment" than it had to reach the battlefield. Their pace was considerably slower. By the time they reached the Sylvesters, other newspaper correspondents had been shuttling back and forth in an effort to gauge which side held the current advantage. They continued doing so over the next few hours, and close to the noon hour, the general consensus was that McDowell's troops had driven the Confederates left, and were pressing their advantage.

The crowd cheered and waved their handkerchiefs toward the battlesite, lifting their champagne glasses in salute. All across the "picnic area," elated Washingtonians cheered that the war was all but won, that the Union army was victorious and 'Jeff Davis' would be hung from a tree.

Robert watched the proceedings with a dull sensation in the pit of his stomach. He sat under the tree, next to the Sylvesters' carriage, with Nathaniel at his side, looking deathly pale. He wondered if his own complexion matched his friend's. He had never seen a man's stomach ripped open before. It wasn't an experience he cared to repeat. *I suppose,* he mused with a sense of defeat, *that that makes me a coward.*

He glanced up at the carriage and saw Camille's gaze focused on his face, her brows drawn in a slight frown. She was distracted, however, when Olivia bent to whisper something in her ear. She turned to her friend with a comment, her attention redirecting itself elsewhere. It was just as well. He had all but bullied Camille into taking this trip—he couldn't very well admit to her that it had been a mistake.

Two newspaperman approached their small party, speaking with each other and writing notes on paper with hands that seemed to shake. Robert knew he couldn't have written anything down at that moment if his life had depended on it. Mr. Sylvester flagged the men over and asked them what they knew.

"McDowell has rallied the troops," one said, "telling them they've won a glorious victory. Some of our boys are walking over the battlefield, picking up Confederate swords and bayonets as souvenirs."

A young boy of seven or so, overhearing the men speaking, ran up to the one and said, "Is it bloody?" The excitement in his young eyes reminded Robert of how he had felt that very morning.

The newspaperman grimaced. "I should say so," he said, speaking more to Mr. Sylvester than the child. "It's the most amazing thing I've ever seen. We watched through our field glasses—the Confederates are lying all over the field and in the creek, some with arms and legs blown off, some dead, others just lying there bleeding to death, unable to even crawl away." He shook his head, and Robert noticed the man's face was as pale as Nathaniel's. "They were lifting their hands, looked like they were begging for help—I saw some Union soldiers offering drinks of water to the dying Confederates . . ."

Robert stood and mumbled an excuse to Nathaniel about needing to stretch his legs for a bit. He moved away from their shady spot, feeling the intense heat of the approaching noon hour as it soaked through his warm overcoat. He removed it and sought relief from the heat in his shirtsleeves and vest. Glancing back at the battlefield, he could only imagine how hot it must be for those in the fray.

If this was victory, he decided, it felt hollow.

***

Camille glanced at her brother, who had moved off into the distance. He had been acting strangely ever since his return from his "walk" with Nathaniel, and she wondered at it. "Let me see that thing," she said to Olivia, who was examining various specta- tors through the spyglass.

"Not yet," Olivia whispered, waving a hand absently at Camille. "I see a very handsome man just over there!"

Camille glanced in the direction Olivia was looking and scowled. "Olivia, I can see him just fine without the spyglass, and as a matter of fact, he looks very much to be spoken for. Now let me have it!"

"Oh, very well!" Olivia slapped the spyglass into Camille's outstretched palm and continued to scrutinize the object of her quest through squinted eyes. "That may be his sister, you know."

"Nuzzling his neck?"

"Well, how gauche to behave so in public!" Olivia sniffed and turned her attention elsewhere.

Camille, meanwhile, fastened her gaze upon the battle scene before her and looked carefully at the furious blend of blue and gray. There was so much movement it was nearly impossible to

follow, until her gaze fixed upon one, lone soldier who lay prostrate on his back, his gray uniform a profusion of red. The sight
might not have affected her terribly until she realized that the
man was attempting to wave weakly for help with an arm that no
longer had a hand attached. She stared in unblinking dismay at
the sight, until he was eventually trampled by a mixture of
soldiers from both sides of the battlefield. When the melee
cleared and she spied the young man one more time, he was as
still as death.

As still as death . . . Camille dropped like a stone into the
carriage seat behind her, her grip on the spyglass suddenly slack. It
dropped to the floor of the carriage with a loud *clank.*

"Camille, you'll break it, and it cost Father a pretty penny!"

She hardly heard Olivia's admonition. Her thoughts were with
the young boy lying prostrate on the hill not three miles hence,
and the mother and father he would never again embrace.

***

Richard Birmingham had finally been able to fire his gun! He
had actually been close enough to the Yankee lines that he had
dropped at least two of them on his own. His company was
ordered to pull back again, and defend the left flank. He swallowed his disappointment, and wished he were toward the center,
where Thomas Jackson stood with his troops.

Those about him were beginning to show signs of despair as
the calls to fall back increased. The Union had a slight advantage
in terms of number, and it appeared as though McDowell and his
men might win the day. Richard ground his teeth in frustration.
Nobody would miss him, he knew, if he slipped toward the center
of the eight-mile Confederate line along Bull Run creek and spent
some time with Jackson and his men.

He did so, running quickly with his rifle in hand. The
adrenaline flowed through his system, giving him energy despite
his physical fatigue. He hadn't slept for over twenty-four hours,

or eaten in at least ten, but he took comfort that the enemy hadn't, either. He wondered if Thomas Jackson was feeling weary, as well. By all accounts, Jackson was an eccentric sort who highly valued his health and his digestive system. Some called him a hypochondriac and wondered at the fact that he often extended his right arm above his head and held it there for many minutes. He never did explain why, but there were those who wondered if he wasn't doing it to "establish equilibrium," *whatever that meant*, Richard mused as he ran to find the man and his regiments.

Jackson was deeply religious and often dispersed Sunday School material to his men. He didn't drink or smoke, and had yet to show evidence of a sense of humor. He was, however, a brilliant military mind, and he absolutely hated Yankees. Richard figured that made the man his new best friend.

As Richard neared the center of the line, he passed a General who was apparently trying to rally his men. He shouted to the troops, hoping to rouse their ire.

Richard approached a young private who stood, uncertainly, off to one side. "Who is that?" Richard asked the boy, motioning with his rifle toward the General.

"That's General Bee," the boy answered. "He doesn't want us to leave."

Richard looked at the private in disgust. "And why would you? Are you a coward?"

"No!" Two spots of color appeared on the boy's cheeks. "But have you seen those men out there?" he asked, motioning toward the field. "If they make it back at all, they're usually missing limbs!"

They're not fast enough, Richard mused. He had stood right in the volley of fire and hadn't been hit. He turned his attention to General Bee, who was still calling out to his men. "Look, there is Jackson with his Virginians, standing like a stone wall!" He shouted for all he was worth. "Rally behind the Virginians!"

Richard cocked a brow. Was it meant to be a compliment or an insult? He supposed, since the man was trying to infuse courage into the frightened men, it was intended to be a positive remark. He shrugged, and left the young private to his own devices, moving onward toward Jackson's regiment that was "standing like a stone wall."

It was nearing late afternoon. Both sides were exhausted from the day's fighting. As Richard stood observing the proceedings, word came that fresh Confederate troops had just arrived by train, and the order eventually came from Beauregard to counterattack. He listened, heart pounding, as Jackson shouted, "Charge, men, and yell like the furies!"

The air about him was rent with a shrieking, high-pitched scream, and Richard joined his own voice to the fray, running forward into battle with his rifle raised high.

***

Camille stood near the carriage, bone-weary and wishing the Sylvesters would pack up their things and head back to D.C., when she heard a shrieking, screaming sound that made the hair on her neck prickle. Slowly, she looked toward the battlefield to see an ocean of different shades of blue and gray moving toward them. She dropped her jaw, her brain slow to process the fact that the battle was apparently coming right toward them.

"Uh . . . uh . . ." she said, waving a hand at Hortence Sylvester, who, herself, stood rooted to the spot, clutching her sister's arm. Closer and closer the armies loomed, until suddenly thousands of Union soldiers were tearing across the "picnic" grounds and down the dusty road at breakneck speed, their eyes wide with fear, faces showing a raw emotion that Camille had never seen before.

She spun about, finally spurred into action. "Run," she said to the Sylvester women, who were all staring open-mouthed at the sea of humanity coursing toward them. Where was Mr. Sylvester? Camille looked about wildly for the man, frustrated when he didn't appear. Her brother suddenly rushed her from behind, however.

"Cammy," he said, grabbing her arm, "we have to run!"

"We should take the horses and carriage!" Mrs. Sylvester finally screeched, comprehension dawning on her drawn features.

"There's no time! Look!" Robert shouted and pointed down the road. There were items strewn about everywhere as the soldiers stepped on, crunched, or hurled impediments in their paths.

Robert pulled on Camille's arm with such force she was sure she would have bruises. She, in turn, pulled on Olivia's dress, and the three of them began to run. A glance over her shoulder showed her that Nathaniel was doing his best to galvanize his mother and aunt into action.

They ran for all they were worth, Robert, to his credit, keeping pace with the women who had cumbersome skirts to deal with. As Camille began to run short of breath, they veered off to the right, hoping to avoid most of the crush. A man Camille had met earlier in the day, who had introduced himself as Albert Riddle, an Ohio congressman, was standing in the middle of the road, shouting to the retreating Union troops. She watched in amazement as he stood his ground, rallying the men with assurances that they could prevail, if they would. And when nobody seemed inclined to listen, he resorted to name-calling, and finally, threats.

His pleas were unheeded as the stampeding mob proceeded on foot to Washington, D.C. The soldiers that Camille and Olivia had eyed with such admiration the day before were now exhausted, filthy, bloodied, and ravenously hungry. Many of them had blackened lips from the powder of the cartridges they had bitten off as part of the procedure for loading their weapons. In all, Camille looked at the lot with her heart full of grief. They had been so handsome, and now they were terrified, much as she herself was.

Robert continued to urge them forward, Camille's breath coming in short gasps and Olivia clutching her side. "I can't run anymore," Olivia moaned.

"You'll have to," Robert retorted. "Look."

Wave after wave of the enemy progressed toward the area where they had been eating their picnics and cheering the soldiers, not even hours before. In the distance, Camille spied Nathaniel and his mother and aunt, moving along without the benefit of the carriage, which had been smashed against the side of the tree. The horses were nowhere to be found.

Olivia gasped in outrage. "Those Rebels wouldn't take women as prisoners of war!"

"We don't know what they'll do, unfortunately," Robert announced, again beginning to run, pulling his sister along by the arm, "and I don't want to be on hand to observe it."

"But they're *gentlemen*," Olivia cried out as she also began to run again, allowing Camille to pull her forward to keep pace. "I can't believe this is happening!" she gasped.

"Don't speak, Olivia," Camille gritted. "You'll waste your breath."

***

Richard Birmingham stood close behind the officers as they conversed, following the aftermath of the bloodiest battle most of the soldiers had ever seen. Jefferson Davis himself was on site, reviewing the day's activities with "Stonewall" Jackson and Pierre Beauregard. Richard kept a careful distance, but was unwilling to give up such a marvelous opportunity to hear firsthand what the Confederate president had to say.

His first comments were full of praise for the commanders and the men who had accomplished such an effective rout of the enemy. He balked, however, at Jackson's suggestion that they pursue the enemy right into D.C. and end the whole thing immediately. Apparently Davis didn't feel confident in the ability of the troops to rush the heavily fortified capitol, and elected to wait.

The men eventually made their way toward the home of Wilmer McLean, a Confederate loyalist who had offered the use of his home to Beauregard as his Manassas headquarters. "McLean has decided to pack up his family and move, now that his house has been shelled," Richard overheard one of the men tell the others. "Says he and his family will be safer in Appomattox Court House . . ."

The reply was lost to Richard, who now had to admit that he couldn't very well follow the generals and president back to headquarters. In fact, it was probably high time that he find his own regiment and company. As he wandered slowly back over the hills, he passed a farmhouse that had been caught in the crossfire. He stopped, watching with detached interest as a figure was carried from the house, draped in a sheet.

"Who is that?" he asked a soldier who was standing nearby, also watching and looking as exhausted as Richard felt.

"The old woman who lived in the house. She was too ill to move, apparently, and got caught by shells from both sides. Completely blew one of her feet right off."

Richard shuddered involuntarily, for the first time that day feeling a tremor of distaste. Didn't seem right that an old woman should die in her own house, shelled to death. He walked slowly back over the fields, shaking the sense of gloom that had suddenly dampened what had otherwise turned out to be a very nice day.

One thing was for certain. He liked killing Yanks.

CHAPTER 26

"Today will be known as BLACK MONDAY. We are utterly and disgracefully routed, beaten, whipped by secessionists."
— *George Templeton Strong, reacting to the outcome at 1st Bull Run*

***

Glenville, Western Virginia
22 July, 1861

Anne had been with the 7th Ohio for one day, and it was all she could do to write quickly enough. She scribbled notes in her notebook about the beautiful terrain, the miserable weather, and mostly, the people. The men of the regiment, and more specifically, those in Company B with whom she had the most contact, were from a wide variety of backgrounds and experiences. They were lawyers and teachers, farmers and blacksmiths, each bringing their own perspective to the service in which they were engaged.

She hadn't really known what to expect on arrival, but quickly learned that despite the rainy weather and limited rations, morale was generally high. The great majority of the men in the regiment had signed on for a three-year term of service, but most hoped the war wouldn't last that long.

Camp life consisted of drills, drills, and drills, reconnaissance missions, rain, rain, and more rain. The makeshift tents leaked horribly, of course, and when she had once muttered something about wishing they had barracks, she was informed that the barracks back at Camp Dennison in Ohio had eventually flooded out as well. She was doomed to be wet either way, it seemed.

The men had been friendly to her, and very curious when she introduced herself as a "war correspondent" from Boston. Given the fact that she was a "newspaper man," most were willing to share their impressions with her, and in return, she promised to show them her finished articles before sending them off to Jacob Taylor in Boston. "Provided I can find telegraph lines, that is," she told them. It was proving to be a challenge; she had known from the start that she would be unable to carry her own telegraph equipment and lines like other reporters and news groups did. They could regularly send messages back home to their editors because they had entire wagons full of equipment to construct their own telegraph lines wherever they set up camp. Anne was a one-man show, however, and would have to make do however she could.

The new name had been a bit of a challenge. She was used to being called "Adam Jones," but "Aaron Johnson" was still unfamiliar. To her knowledge, however, nobody suspected her secret; they merely assumed her to be the young man she told them she was. That her breasts were wrapped so tightly with linen she might as well have been wearing a modified corset undoubtedly aided her appearance. More than one soldier had commented on her youth—they must think she was a sixteen-year-old runaway—but for the most part they gave her a cursory glance, if anything, and left her alone.

Word had reached the regiment by now of the horrible Union rout at Bull Run. Anne's first emotion at the news was regret that she'd not stayed in D.C. one more day—she had missed one of the biggest reporting opportunities of the war, thus far, but then she hadn't really had a choice. Orders were orders, and once she had enlisted, she had been obligated to join her regiment as soon as possible. She shook her head, remembering accounts of hundreds of observers who had gone to the scene of the battle hoping to be entertained. Who was that stupid? *Well,* she amended ruefully, *you wanted to be there too, Anne.* She turned her attention again to her notes, trying to organize her thoughts into a concise article she could send off to Jacob the moment she found access to telegraph lines.

***

Ivar Gundersen sat just outside his tent, enjoying the brief lull in rainstorms, and watched young Aaron Johnson, the newspaper reporter, wondering how long she thought she could maintain the charade. He had pegged her as a woman from the first moment he laid eyes on her. She was far too beautiful—her cobalt blue eyes large and luminous in a face delicate of feature and quick to smile—and he was amazed that nobody else seemed to know. Certainly, if they did, they would send her packing for home.

He shrugged a bit, figuring her business was her own, and he actually had to mentally salute her efforts, despite his initial reaction that she blended well with others of her gender who were so adept at deceit. It wasn't his business and he knew he wouldn't interfere, he mused, as he shot cursory glances at the young woman. He forced himself to be discreet, and turned his gaze off into the distant, rolling green hills. His curiosity was rabid, but if people caught him looking a little too intently at Aaron Johnson, there would be trouble. The soldiers in his Company would probably shoot him with his own gun.

He tamped down on a smile and brought his attention back into focus as Major Casement approached and told him and several others milling about that they had orders to move on to Bulltown, a distance of approximately thirty miles. They would leave the next day. Ivar took the news in stride, wondering if the weather in Bulltown was any better than in Glenville.

***

New York, New York
24 July, 1861

Daniel O'Shea walked back to his small office on the second floor after having a brief meeting with the bank president, Mr. Strickland. Luke Birmingham had told him that the man might not always be what most people might consider warm, but that Daniel should receive whatever the man told him with patience. "That he's making concessions toward the immigrant population at all is a small miracle in itself," Luke had said.

Daniel had snorted. "He's doing it to keep his bank on solid ground."

"Well, whatever the reason, your cousin will receive his loan, correct?" At Luke's pointed expression, which he had followed with a slight grin probably meant to soften his words, Daniel had acquiesced and muttered that he would hold his tongue.

It was certainly taking an effort on his part, he mused, as he reached his desk. Strickland looked at him with a distaste he didn't even bother to conceal, but to his credit, he was working amenably with Daniel and others who had been treated unfairly with regard to their loan applications. It was a start, he supposed with an inner sigh.

He rummaged about for a moment, straightening files and preparing to leave for the day. He had quite a substantial order pending and needed to get home to his shop so that he could complete the bureau with its ornate mirror by the time his customer needed it. He paused in his movements when his hand brushed over a small object he had stashed in his desk drawer. He pulled it out, unwittingly, and glanced again at the daguerreotype of a young woman with rich, dark hair and beautiful features.

Daniel shook his head, knowing he needed to mail the thing back to Luke Birmingham. The image was of Luke's cousin who lived in New Orleans. When Luke was on his return trip home with his aunt and uncle in tow, he had stopped and invited

Daniel to come by their hotel room so that they might quickly review Daniel's progression with the bank. They had visited, discussed business and then enjoyed a nice meal together in the parlor of the hotel suite, with Luke's unfortunate uncle resting in the adjoining bedroom. His aunt had risen periodically to check on him, her features drawn. In spite of her obvious worry, however, she had been a gracious hostess to Daniel and had even shown him a picture of her pride and joy, the daughter who had opted to stay behind in New Orleans.

The following morning, Daniel had remembered something he had forgotten to ask Luke, so he stopped by the hotel suite on his way into the bank. Luke and his relatives had already left, and housekeeping was cleaning the rooms. When he asked after his friend, he was told that they had vacated a good two hours earlier, and had left behind a personal item on one of the nightstands. It was the picture of Marie Brissot, Luke's cousin. He immediately offered to send it to Luke, and when the young maid had resisted, saying it was hotel policy to take care of such matters, he had turned on the charm that his mother always said he possessed in spades, but rarely used. No harm would come to the piece, he cajoled, and he knew Mr. Birmingham well—he could easily send it to him as he had other items he needed to mail to the man as well.

The maid eventually weakened and let him take the picture, and he had kept it in his desk drawer ever since. Every time he took it out with the intention of putting it in the mail to Luke, he looked at it, studied every detail of it, and then placed it back in the desk, reasoning that he had time and could always mail it later. It really wasn't well done of him at all, and he knew it. Poor Mrs. Brissot was probably missing her daughter horribly, and worrying about her as well. She would be missing the daguerreotype and would want its safe return.

Later, he promised himself, carefully closing and locking his drawer as he made his way out of the bank to head for home.

***

New Orleans, Louisiana
24 July, 1861

Marie gazed at Constance, feeling troubled and torn. "I don't know, Connie," Marie told the girl. "I just . . . I don't know."

"But you said they deserve an education! You said!"

"Of course I did, and I meant it!" Marie took the girls' hands and tugged, taking a seat in one of the vacated student's desks and motioning for Constance to sit next to her. "I meant every word. I just never said that *I* would be the one doing the teaching."

"But I can't do it like you can," Constance said. "I've tried, and yes, they're learning, but I can't help but think it would be so much better if you were their teacher."

Marie sighed. "It works well in theory, Connie, but I'm afraid reality might prove to be a bit different. Do you know what would happen to them if people saw them coming here for school?"

"I didn't mean for them to come here! I meant for you to come to *my* place."

Marie was silent, her mind whirling. If she were caught educating blacks, her fate could well turn out to be worse than her father's. She would be lucky if they didn't string her from the nearest tree. Yet how could she express these reservations to a young girl who was willing to risk her own life and limb that others might have a better life?

"May I think about it, Constance, and we'll discuss it again tomorrow?"

Constance looked crestfallen, but she nodded. Her eyes contained a flicker of something that looked for a brief moment like disappointment, and it made Marie wince. She shook her head in frustration and pulled the girl forward for a quick hug. "I'm scared," she whispered.

"So are they," Constance whispered back. "I told them sometimes you have to be brave to get what you most want."

It simply wasn't fair for any person to put such pressure on another! Marie walked from room to room in her house, looking desperately for something to clean. She held a dust rag in one hand and began swiping it over every surface she could find in the library—never mind that she had just cleaned thoroughly the day before, and with her parents gone, nothing was ever amiss or out of place anyway.

Constance had taken on her own battle when she started teaching the Fromeres, and it was none of Marie's business. She approved, she even supported the endeavor, but never had she said that she wanted Constance's cause to be her own. She had seen the work of the locals upon her own father for crimes that they perceived necessitated harsh penalties. She didn't want to envision herself on her bed, unable to awaken.

She dusted the house until the sun went down, and found that she had moved past the dinner hour without realizing it. It didn't make a difference, anyway, because she wasn't hungry. She wondered if she'd ever be able to eat again. Standing in the front parlor, she looked out into the dark street and considered her life. She was alone, by choice, in an environment that had nearly killed her beloved father. She had no protection whatsoever, aside from a shotgun that belonged to her father. She was considering teaching a black family, for whom her heart ached, yet such action might well mean the end of her life as she knew it.

Where was that gun? She looked first in her parents' bedroom, the study, the library, the conservatory, the parlor, and even the kitchen. It was nowhere to be found. Did her mother take it with her? No, she had helped her mother pack—she would have remembered seeing the gun.

It must be at the newspaper office. She walked outside, heedless of the late hour, and readied her horse. Winston, the aging groom, appeared from his small room at the back of the stables as she was hefting her sidesaddle onto the horse. "Let me help you with that, miss!" he called.

She smiled and worked with him to buckle the requisite straps and secure it into place. Stepping into the stirrup and preparing to mount, she paused when Winston cleared his throat.

"Miss," he began, "I told your mother that I would keep a lookout for you, and I reckon she wouldn't want you riding around the city late at night. Are you sure you know what you're doing?"

"I do know what I'm doing, Winston, but I thank you for your concern. I have to go to the newspaper office for something. I'll be back shortly."

He nodded reluctantly and stood in the shadows until she turned around at the end of the drive to give him a little wave. He looked worried and drawn, and she was sorry for his distress, but she was so agitated she couldn't keep still. She urged the horse faster and made her way into the heart of the city, her thoughts focused on the retrieval of her father's firearm. If she had it in her possession, she might not be so afraid. The streets were still busy with people coming and going, and she was at once nervous and comforted by the hustle and bustle. If there were people around, she was probably safe. Yet, if there were people around, perhaps she wasn't.

Reaching the newspaper office, she tied her horse in the stable and let herself in the back door, knowing she'd find Michael working late to have the morning edition printed and delivered on time. Sure enough, there he was, and his face registered enormous surprise when he caught sight of her.

"Little Marie, what are you doing out tonight? *Sacrebleu,* but your parents would have the fits if they knew!"

"I know, Michael," she said, planting a quick kiss on the old man's cheek. "That's why we won't ever tell them!"

"Child, why are you here? It isn't safe for you here." He took her by the shoulders and looked deeply into her eyes. Marie returned his earnest gaze, her own eyes burning at the familiar lines in his face, the weathered skin, the gray hair that was turning to white and the bushy white eyebrows to match.

"I came looking for my father's shotgun, Michael. It's not in the house. Have you seen it?"

"Do you have need for it, Marie? Has someone threatened you?"

No, but I'm about to do something that might well see me hanged. I thought I'd try to protect myself, first. "Nobody has threatened me. I'd just feel safer if I had it in the house."

Michael nodded. "It's in the back office, with your father's other things."

"Is it the only one you have here?"

"No. I have two more in a chest in the office closet. I'll be fine."

She nodded, and after giving the old man a quick hug, made her way toward the back of the large room, past the press and other equipment, and into her father's office. Seeing the small room made her throat thicken with tears that she smothered by quickly going about her business and locating the shotgun, unlocked, in her father's carrying case. If only he had had the gun on his person the night of the attack, he might have been able to ward them off! It would have been only a deterrent, however—her father was a pacifist, and she knew as surely as the sun set that he wouldn't have killed anyone.

She, however, had no such compunctions. Had she been with him that fateful night, she would have pulled the trigger on any who dared lay a finger on her father. Taking a shaky breath, she pulled the gun from its resting place and ran a hand down the long barrel. It provided her with a measure of security, and even if she never had to use the thing, it was a comfort just knowing she had it.

Marie looked about the office one final time before opening the door to leave. When she did so, she heard loud voices coming from the front of the building. Rushing out of the door and down the hallway to the main room, she hurried back to Michael to find him surrounded by several men. It was dark in the room—apparently they had extinguished the lamps, and some were wearing cloths to cover their faces.

"We saw her come in here," one man's voice rang out in a threat to Michael. "You can't hide her forever!"

"I'm telling you, she left!" Michael's voice shook with fury. "Haven't you people done enough? I told you there would be no more inflammatory articles printed from this press! I insist that you leave, or I shall have you all arrested!" Michael's French accent became more pronounced with each word he uttered.

"I forgot to get something, and I just came back, Michael," Marie said aloud and walked further into the room, hoping to cover Michael's lie. "Is there anything I can help you with, gentlemen?"

The apparent ringleader of the group stepped toward her, his face entirely in the shadows, but lit slightly from behind by the gas lamps glowing outside on the street. "Someone saw you leave your house, Miss Brissot, and come here to the office. There are those of us who'd like to know what your intentions are concerning this newspaper."

Marie shook her head slightly, fighting a smirk. She recognized the man's voice, although he was clearly trying to disguise it. He was her neighbor, three doors down, who owned one of New Orleans' textile mills—one of those few the South actually possessed. Her own neighbor was spying on her! She didn't know why she was surprised. *Several* of her own neighbors had probably been responsible for beating her father senseless.

"I merely came to visit Michael, and to retrieve some of my father's personal belongings from his office."

"Maybe we should take a look at that office and see what Jean-Pierre left behind!" shouted a voice from the back of the crowd. There was a chorus of agreement from several of the other men in the room, and Marie grew uneasy at the tangible rise in energy level.

"You will *not* go into my father's office! This is private property, gentlemen, unless you've forgotten, and you have absolutely no right to be here! My father is no longer a threat to you, *thanks* to you—not that he ever was!"

"What are you hiding back there, missy? Something we might wanna take a look at? The old man got more articles he wanted printed?"

Marie squinted toward the back of the group, trying to identify the voice. It wasn't one she recognized from her own social circle, and it sounded coarse, rough. "There is nothing of interest in his office!" she shouted, holding her left hand toward Michael, who moved to intervene. Clutched more firmly in her right hand was the gun she held hidden down behind her skirt. "You have robbed my father, quite possibly, of the ability to ever write another article again as long as he lives! You can congratulate yourselves, gentlemen, that you may well have gotten away with cold-blooded murder." Her voice shook and she willed herself not to dissolve into tears. There would be time enough for that later, and thankfully, her anger level had risen to a point where she didn't even fear for her own safety.

"You could be tellin' us whatever you want, there, you French filly! I'm gonna see for myself, and who's gonna stop me? The old man, here?" The rough man pushed his way forward through the crowd, and Marie watched in growing rage when some of the men picked up on his mania and began swarming toward her.

She whipped the gun from behind her skirts and pointed it straight up, firing a shot into the ceiling that resulted in a cascade of debris. *"You will not take another step, or I will blow you back out the front door!"* Marie screamed, noting with detachment that she sounded nothing like herself. She sounded like a woman crazed.

She pointed the shotgun toward the body of men that had retreated like sheep, some stumbling over themselves in their haste to clear their way out of her path. "You will leave this office, and leave it in peace! Michael is nothing like my father—he has nothing to prove to the lot of you, and he has assured you of this! Indeed, in the time my father has been *out of commission*, Michael has printed only pieces guaranteed to soothe your bloody Southern pride! So go ahead! Believe you will win your stupid war! Send your sons off to fight, send the sons of the poor off to fight while you stay at home drinking your wine! Do whatever you will, but *leave me and mine alone!"*

There was hushed silence as her voice ceased; yet it still echoed through the rafters and smoke still drifted from the gunshot. They slowly backed out of the door, one at a time, until the last of them had gone. Marie eventually lowered the weapon until the barrel pointed at the floor, and stared dumbly at the now-vacant room.

Michael moved to quickly lock the front door and draw the shades, then lit a lantern. He approached Marie, his face wet with tears, and enfolded her in an embrace that was her undoing. The sobs arose then, great heaving gulps that would surely never cease. She didn't even have enough strength in her limbs to return his hug.

She eventually sank to the floor, Michael joining her, and the two of them sat thusly in silence for a moment until Marie's sobs quieted. Michael retrieved a large, gingham-checked handkerchief from his pocket and handed it to her, wiping at his own eyes with the back of his hand.

"*Ma chère*," he finally said. "You were *tres magnifique*."

"Beasts, all of them," Marie mumbled into the handkerchief. Michael chuckled, and she glanced at him in angry surprise. "They're not?"

He held up his hands as if to ward off attack, and said, "Dear Marie. All of the people of New Orleans? They are all monsters? Think back on your life, child. So many people here in this city have made your life rich and full, and have done the same for your parents, too. Only a few of them are 'beasts.'"

"Oh, Michael," she whispered. "I think I'm the only person in the whole of the South who believes this war is madness! People are thrilled! They think the Confederacy is the most wonderful thing!"

Again, Michael chuckled and drew an arm close about Marie's shoulders. "*Non, chérie.* You are not the only one. There are many, many others who are frightened." He gave a little squeeze. "It will all be over soon. You will see. And now," he said, glancing about the room, "I have a mess to clean."

Marie glanced, chagrined, at the results of her handiwork. "I'll help. I hope the equipment isn't ruined."

"It's fine." He laughed out loud, then, and Marie felt her cheeks warm, her mouth tugging into a reluctant smile. "How I wish I could have seen their faces, little one! You had them running for the hills!"

Marie and Michael worked side by side in comfortable silence, punctuated periodically by general comments as they cleaned the mess Marie had made. When they finished, Marie helped Michael with his printing duties for the morning's edition, and when they finally left the shop tightly locked in the wee hours of the morning, Michael saw her safely to her home.

Marie glanced in derision at her neighbor's house, three doors down where he was innocently sleeping. Michael followed the direction of her gaze and heaved a small sigh. "I cannot leave you here alone, *chérie*. Will you come home and stay with Matilda and me?"

Marie shook her head gently and placed a hand on the old man's arm. "I'll be fine."

"I worry, Marie."

She kissed his weathered cheek with a soft smile. "I say my prayers, Michael, every night."

Once she had seen to the comfort of her horse and made sure the house was secure, Marie prepared for bed and glanced at the clock in her bedroom, wearily counting the few hours of sleep she had ahead before she would need to be at the school.

She kneeled at the side of her bed, her white nightgown flowing around her in billowed waves, her dark hair standing out against the material in stark contrast. She hadn't lied to Michael—she did pray, and every night, as her good Christian mother had taught her to do.

Dear Father, she began in a quiet whisper, *please, I need Thy help. My parents are far away, and I may never see my father again . . .* A tear seeped from behind her closed eyelids. She thought she had exhausted the tears in the newspaper shop. *I am afraid for my life, and I am about to embark on something that will undoubtedly place me in greater danger than ever.* She took a deep breath, still whispering her prayer as though afraid the walls would hear and betray her. *I want to help the Fromeres, and I need Thy protection. My father has enemies—enemies that are now mine. Please, please send Thy angels to be with me! To guard me, Michael, the shop, Constance and the Fromeres—bless us all, wilt Thou, Father? Truly, truly I know that with Thy help I cannot fail . . .*

The tears fell in earnest, and she finished her prayer, wiping her face with one of her mother's lacy handkerchiefs, inhaling the perfumed scent and missing her mother so much it hurt. Why had she stayed behind? What had she been thinking? She should have gone to Boston where she would have been safe. There was nothing for her in New Orleans—nothing that meant anything anymore.

As soon as the self-pitying thoughts materialized, an image flashed into her brain—an image of a young, black family who had sat in the confines of a run-down shack and gazed at her, first in horror and despair, and then finally in hope. The image melted into another that contained the young faces of her school class; faces that undoubtedly would never receive an education if it weren't for her time and compassion. Those children didn't pay for her services—she provided them from the goodness of her own heart, and they needed her.

She climbed into bed, no longer doubting her resolve to stay behind, and suddenly felt as though she were no longer alone. As she drifted off into sleep, the thought again materialized in her tired mind.

With Thy help, I cannot fail . . .

CHAPTER 27

"I found no preparations whatever for defense . . .Not a regiment was properly encamped, not a single avenue or approach guarded. All was chaos, and the streets, hotels, and bar-rooms were filled with drunken officers and men absent from their regiments without leave—a perfect Pandemonium."
—General George McClellan on the condition
of Washington, D.C., following 1st Bull Run

***

Boston, Massachusetts
14 August, 1861

Griffen opened the front door of the Birmingham mansion to a young man who looked so like the one who currently sat in the comfort of the breakfast room that he blinked his eyes, trying to make sense of the vision.

"I don't know if you remember me," the man said with a tired smile, "but I'm Benjamin Birmingham."

"Of course!" His identity finally registered and Griffen shook his head, opening the door wider to admit the young man. "Master Luke is dining. Will you follow me?" He led young Benjamin to the parlor, instructed him to wait, and then went to fetch Luke. The butler shook his head again as he walked, marveling at the similarities between the cousins. They had grown into men, and he acknowledged that it meant he was aging, as well. He glanced at the back of his gnarled, pale hand marked periodically with liver spots, and nodded slowly. He had become an old man.

He sighed. It had been a good life. All in all, he had no regrets. He tapped on the door to the breakfast room, and informed the family that there was a visitor waiting to speak with them in the parlor, smiling at the happiness he knew they would all shortly experience.

Luke glanced up at Griffen's pronouncement. He was just finishing the last of his eggs and sausages, and said to Elizabeth when she asked Griffen who the visitor was, "I'll get it, Mother." He rose and tossed his napkin lightly in his chair and smiled briefly at his parents and his aunt as he left the room.

His long strides ate the distance through the breakfast room and across the large foyer into the parlor, where he spied a man roughly his own height and build, who stood looking out the window. "Yes?" he said, moving closer to the man whose back was still to him. "Can I help you with something?"

The man turned, and Luke sucked in his breath. "I hope so," the visitor replied. "I've come an awfully long way to see the world's most ardent abolitionist."

Luke crossed the room in two strides and grabbed Ben, wrapping his arms about his shoulders in an enormous hug, slapping him periodically on the back and fighting the embarrassing tears that flooded his eyes. He pulled back and looked at his cousin, gratified to see the same emotion reflected in Ben's face. He stared in amazement for a moment. People had always told them how much they looked alike when they were young, and he had even seen it himself, but not as much as he did now. The dark hair, green eyes, the strong, chiseled features were a mirror image of his own.

"Mercy," Ben drawled then, and Luke smiled at the one difference between them. "I have a double." He laughed and gave

Luke another quick squeeze. "I can't tell you how good it is to see you, Cousin."

"Likewise! And you made such good time!"

Ben nodded. "The travel went well—no problems or difficulties."

"And is the city as you remembered it?"

"For the most part. But it's grown!"

Luke nodded and with his arm about Ben's shoulders, he propelled him toward the door. "You must come and see Mother and Father. They'll be thrilled."

The exclamations of surprise that greeted the pair when they stood in the doorway of the breakfast room confirmed Luke's statement. Elizabeth leaped from her chair and made her way to them, throwing her arms about her husband's nephew in unabashed affection. "You made it in one piece!" she exclaimed, framing his face between her hands. "And how handsome you are! My, my, Benjamin. You've grown into a man."

By this time, James had reached the doorway as well and clasped Ben's hand between both of his in a warm shake. "Welcome back," he said, his voice gruff. "We've missed you, Ben."

Ben nodded, his eyes stinging. "I've missed you all. It's good to see you again."

Elizabeth led him to the table and motioned for one of the attending servants to place a plate of food in front of the weary traveler. They all resumed their seats and began peppering Ben with questions, all of which he answered around mouthfuls of food. He hadn't eaten so well in weeks.

"Now," he said when the minor interrogation had ceased, "tell me where everyone is! Where is Anne?"

There was a slight pause before Luke answered, "She's gone to work for Allan Pinkerton in Chicago."

Ben glanced at his aunt and uncle. "You don't approve?"

Elizabeth shrugged in apparent dismissal, but her creased brow was at odds with the casual reaction. "Anne is a grown woman, and she'll do as she pleases. We weren't thrilled with her timing, however."

"And how are Robert and Camille?"

At that question, the silence was more prolonged. James's face took on the expression of a thundercloud and Elizabeth's grim smile was anything but jovial. James finally replied, "Robert and Camille will be fortunate if they ever again see the light of day."

"Oh dear."

Luke shook his head. "They went to D.C., unbeknownst to anyone in the household, and were on hand at Bull Run three weeks ago."

Ben's fork clattered against his plate and his jaw went slack. Luke nodded, and said, "They've been barricaded in their bedrooms ever since their return. The folks have yet to decide their final fate." Luke gestured toward his parents with a slight smile, meant to ease the moment.

"Dare I ask about Jimmy?"

James finally laughed. "Jimmy is doing well, thankfully. He is content to follow his parents' counsel, for the time being, at least."

Elizabeth nodded. "He is enjoying school, and is quite a good artist. He's a good boy."

Ben turned to his aunt's sister, who had remained largely silent throughout the exchanges. "I'm sorry to hear of your husband's condition," he said to Genevieve Brissot. "How is your daughter faring these days?"

At that, Jenny gave a short laugh and the spark of real humor Ben saw in her eyes surprised him. "It seems we're all destined to give you less than positive news, Ben. Marie stayed behind in New Orleans to teach her students and take care of the house while we're gone, and I worry myself sick about her. I still find myself amazed that I let her convince me it was a good thing." She pointed her fork at Luke. "*You* should have been my voice of reason, young man." She softened the remark with a shake of her head and a wink. "I must lay the blame somewhere other than my own shoulders."

"I'll take it, Aunt Jenny," Luke said. "She was convincing though, wasn't she?"

Jenny shook her head and sat back in her seat, dabbing at the corner of her mouth with her napkin. "That she was. She always has been. That girl has a mind and will of her own."

Elizabeth snorted lightly in agreement. "Must run in the blood. Marie has cousins that could match her will for will."

Luke regarded Ben over his drink later that night in the quiet of the family parlor. "So what are you thinking you'd like to do?" He asked, once they had caught up on years of lives lived apart.

"I was thinking seriously of enlisting," Ben admitted. "Have you given the matter much thought?"

"I have." Luke leaned back in the comfortable chair and propped his feet on a nearby footstool. "In fact, I'm thinking I have little excuse for not enlisting. I'm working at the bank because I enjoy it and I'm trying to build a career, not because I really need the money. My inheritance from father will see me well into my dotage, so it's not as though I work because I have to. If anybody ever had the luxury of taking time to do something honorable, it is I."

Ben nodded. "I've thought the same thing. I did have much of my own inheritance in different accounts by the time I left home, and I've saved almost every penny I earned for the last five years, so I do have a bit of a buffer. I don't leave behind anybody who needs my support, financial or otherwise, and the thought that I ought to be enlisted in the cause just will not leave me in peace."

Luke pursed his lips thoughtfully and ran a finger along the rim of his glass. "There's talk of forming a cavalry regiment right here in Massachusetts and I'm wondering if that isn't something we could do well. Would you be interested in joining a cavalry?"

"Absolutely. I even have my own horse to contribute to the cause. I left him in the livery just in town."

Luke glanced up in surprise. "You could have left him here in our stables. Why did you leave him in the livery?"

Ben glanced away, sheepish. "It's been so long, Luke, since I've seen you and the family—I feel as though I'm imposing enough without adding another horse for your groom to look after . . ."

"That's just plain ridiculous, Ben. Your being here is never an imposition, and I know I speak for Mother and Father both in saying that. First thing tomorrow morning we'll go and retrieve your horse. Once we do that, we'll go and look into the details on the formation of the 1st Massachusetts Cavalry."

Camille sat upstairs in her bedroom, looking into the mirror on her vanity table with her chin cupped in her hand. Her hair was curled and looking glorious, for all the good it would do her. The face that stared back was glum and depressed.

It had been nearly a month since the disastrous visit to D.C., and Camille still lived the details of Robert's and her return home as though it were a fresh occurrence. It had taken so long for them to leave D.C. that Mr. Sylvester had sent a telegram, unbeknownst to Camille and Robert, to James and Elizabeth to inform them that they were safe, the children were safe, and they would be home as soon as they could procure tickets for the train ride home.

The scene that had greeted Robert and Camille was beyond her wildest, worst imaginings. Her parents had sat them both in the parlor, after nearly collapsing upon them when they reached the front door, and had then proceeded to give them the most heart-wrenching tongue lashing Camille had ever received.

It wouldn't have been so bad had they merely been angry. They had been terrified as well, and hurt. Elizabeth had begun her chastising with a firm voice that spoke of the level of her distress, only to eventually dissolve into tears. That was something Camille had seen happen only one other time in her life, and it had been when the family received news that cousin Ben had been all but run from his home on a rail.

James had tried to pick up the pieces where his wife had left off, pacing back and forth in front of the empty hearth, but was too overcome with his own emotion to venture much farther than Elizabeth had. Her parents' reactions were Camille's undoing. As if the trauma of the event itself hadn't been bad enough, the situation was compounded tenfold by the obvious grief her parents were experiencing.

"But we're well, Mother," Robert had murmured in a small voice, looking dangerously close to tears himself. "We weren't hurt, and we took care of each other, and we'll never do anything like this again."

"That's right, you won't!" James again found his voice. "Neither of you are setting foot outside this house for at least a month unless your mother or I request your presence with us!"

And so, they sat. Truthfully, Camille mused, as she continued to study her face in the mirror, it was a justifiable punishment, and both she and Robert knew it. They had spoken together on a few occasions since their return, but they were both recovering from the trauma of witnessing the battle and ensuing mayhem and hadn't been able to effectively voice their thoughts.

Camille turned her head at a soft knock upon the door. Opening it, she found Robert standing on the other side, looking pale and drawn. She opened the door wider to admit him and followed him wordlessly when he sat on a chair in front of the small fireplace that was positioned on the far wall of her bedroom.

She sat in a chair opposite his, and looked at his face, feeling suddenly very old. Her heart ached for her brother, and that was a new occurrence. They had never been close; but suddenly they had a bond that was almost too ghastly to remember, yet try as she might, she couldn't forget it.

As though reading her thoughts, Robert said in a hoarse voice, "I dream about it."

She nodded, clasping her hands in her lap and leaning on one of the armrests for support. "I do, too." She paused for a moment. "Were you scared, Robert?"

"Terrified." He admitted it without embarrassment. "I thought we might be shot. At the very least, trampled to death—first by our own, and then by the enemy."

Camille nodded again, but said nothing.

"I . . . I . . ." Robert fumbled, searching for words. "I pushed you into it, Cammy, and I want you to know I'm sorry for that. We should never have gone, and you said as much before we left. I wish I had listened to you."

She waved a hand. "It's not your fault, Robert. Had I truly not wanted to go, I would have stayed home."

"Have you heard anything from Olivia?"

"Only that she and her mother are still confined to their sick beds. They're so upset they can't even leave their bedrooms, apparently."

Robert snorted lightly and said, "It's a good thing they didn't venture too close to the battlefield, or they'd be dead now from apoplectic fits. I can't even begin to tell you how gruesome it was."

Camille glanced into the hearth. "Do you still want to be a soldier, then?"

Robert shook his head, dropping it in shame. "I don't have the stomach for it anymore. It didn't take much to prove it to me, either. All I saw was the first few minutes of battle and I was running for the safety of camp like a mongrel. I am such a coward."

"Stop, Robert! There's nothing cowardly about wanting to preserve your life, or protect it from such a gruesome end." She paused. "I looked through the field glasses, myself, you know."

He glanced up in surprise. "You did?"

"I did. I watched a man die. I see him every night when I close my eyes to go to sleep. I don't think he'll ever leave me in peace."

"Oh, Cammy, I'm so sorry. Is that why Olivia has been so sick then? Did she look through the spy glass, too?"

At that, Camille laughed out loud. "No," she said, sobering. "Olivia didn't see anything bloody. She's probably still trying to recover from having to walk fifteen miles before we were finally picked up and given a ride back into the city." An image of D.C. on the night of July 21 flashed through her mind, and she flinched. It had been a nightmare. People walked about as though in a daze. The

Union loss had been a devastation Lincoln could ill afford, and the people were crushed. They had been so sure it would end at that sluggish creek, and the Confederacy would be suitably chastised.

They had sat that night with the Sylvesters, in the hotel, listening intermittently to first, Mrs. Sylvester, and then Olivia, as they cried and sobbed and ranted about having witnessed such barbaric and cowardly behavior. When they had finally been able to leave the hotel and head for the train station, the journey had taken twice as long as it might have otherwise, for Olivia and Mrs. Sylvester had to be all but carried from hotel to carriage, and then carriage to train station.

Camille would have liked to have been carried, herself, but one look at Robert's shocked, haunted expression told him he would be of no use to her; most likely, he needed to be carried, as well. She had pulled herself together, taken a deep breath and pretended she was her mother. Elizabeth would walk onto a train platform of her own volition or die trying.

As for the other picnic revelers who had been nearly trampled to death upon their return to the city that fateful night, they looked as though they had fought the battle themselves. One observer had gone back to the scene the next day and remarked upon the miles of strewn picnic supplies, canes, hats, bonnets, and parasols littering the road. It was bizarre, unprecedented, and had caught the entire Union by surprise.

"I saw your bedroom the other day," Camille said. "Where are all of your military pictures?"

"I put them away for awhile." Robert scowled. "I can't have them around. I don't know what I'll read about from now on."

"You don't have to give up your military passion just because you witnessed one awful battle."

"Well, it's a little bit of a challenge to visualize a military without soldiers in it. And I can't visualize soldiers anymore without seeing one whose innards were blown open and then who died right in front of my face."

Camille winced.

Robert shrugged. "Maybe sometime later I'll get my things back out. I put them in a trunk in my dressing room."

"You could start learning about something else, perhaps."

"Like what?"

"Oh, I don't know. You could become a wastrel like Mr. Sylvester and spend all your time at the men-only clubs downtown."

He grinned ruefully. "Did you hear Mother when they came by the day after we got home?"

Camille shook her head. "I had barricaded myself in here."

"She gave Mr. and Mrs. Sylvester a tongue lashing like I've never heard. She even berated them for taking their *own* children to D.C. at a time like this, let alone someone else's. If I hadn't been so upset, I might have laughed."

He stood to leave. "I think I'll go sit with Uncle J.P. for awhile. Aunt Jenny says she thinks it helps if people read to him." He glanced at Camille when he reached the doorway. "Uh, Uncle Jean-Pierre, I mean," he mumbled.

Camille's heart broke a bit. "It's alright, Robert. You can call him Uncle J.P."

CHAPTER 28

"A reckless and unprincipled tyrant has invaded your soil. Abraham Lincoln, regardless of all moral, legal, and constitutional restraints, has thrown his Abolitionist hosts among you, who are murdering and imprisoning your citizens, confiscating and destroying your property, and committing other acts of violence and outrage, too shocking and revolting to humanity to be enumerated."
—*General P. G. T. Beauregard*

***

Charleston, South Carolina
14 August, 1861

"And now those bloody Yanks have passed their so-called 'Confiscation Acts'!" Stanley Charlesworth said with vehemence around a mouthful of lamb. "That means those Union soldiers can confiscate the property, *any* property of Rebel slaveholders!"

Sarah Birmingham signaled a servant to refill Stanley's wine glass. The man usually mellowed a bit after his second or third glass. Truly, she agreed with his sentiments, but he was so obnoxiously loud with his comments that it made her head pound. "How are you enjoying the meal, Stanley?" she asked.

"What? Oh, splendid, splendid. And another thing, that Lincoln had better think twice before prolonging this thing any longer! Did you hear? He and those buffoons that call themselves senators have passed an income tax to finance the war! Those Northerners love their money, I tell you. They will not long support a conflict that is going to pilfer away at their bank accounts."

"Very true," Jeffrey offered, raising a glass in salute. "I'm sure you have the right of it, Stanley."

"All this talk of war," Clarice Charlesworth sniffed. "One would think there is nothing else to discuss these days!"

The entire table glanced at the girl, eyebrows raised for a moment, before the conversation again resumed around her. "Well!" she said as Calista elbowed her in the ribs. "Aren't you tired of it?"

Stanley turned to Jeffrey. "I hear Davis is thinking of sending representatives to Britain on our behalf. Surely you'll be among them?"

Jeffrey shook his head briefly and took a sip of his drink. "I don't think so, Stanley. It's a bit more involved than I would like to be."

"You must be mad! As I live and breathe, Jeffrey Birmingham, I will never understand you. Why would you not want to be a part of this?"

"Well, for one thing, the ports are blockaded. And even if the emissaries happen to get through the lines, there's no telling how far they'll make it into open seas before one of the Union naval ships overtakes them."

"They wouldn't dare!"

Jeffrey shot Stanley a dry look that he tried, a moment too late, to disguise. "This is war, Stanley. Of course they'd dare."

"So you're afraid of being caught then, is that it? Surely the cause is worth any risk!"

"Perhaps *you* should give it a try, Stanley," Sarah interjected. "I'm sure with your vast knowledge of the state of affairs these days, you would be more than adequate representation for the Confederate States of America."

"Don't I wish I could! I don't have near the audience with Jeff Davis that your husband has, however, madam. Were I him, I would try it as quick as a flash."

"Hmm." She forked a delicate new potato topped with a creamy hollandaise sauce into her mouth and refrained from further comment. Sarcasm was lost on the man, and always had been. *Why* she had to ask herself again, did they always have the Charlesworths over for dinner?

The meal eventually drew to a close and the men retired to the library to enjoy a glass of port together while the women made their way into the conservatory. Sarah and Heloise Charlesworth discussed matters befitting plantation mistresses while the two Charlesworth daughters took turns at the pianoforte, causing Sarah to wish she had removed the thing from the room before their dinner guests had arrived.

"And where are Charlotte and William tonight?" Heloise asked.

"They are in town for the week," Sarah answered.

"And Emily?"

"Emily is ill."

"Oh dear, nothing serious, I hope?"

Definitely serious. Emily was beginning to make John Brown look relatively tame. Well, Sarah amended, it wasn't as bad as all that, but Sarah could feel energy churning inside that girl that would certainly lead her places that Sarah didn't want to contemplate. "No, just the headache."

"Ah. And what do you hear from Richard?"

"He is still with Kershaw, drilling with the regiment. He was successful at Manassas—didn't sustain even so much as a scratch, which came as a relief, of course."

"Oh, Sarah, you must be so proud of your son!"

"Yes, I am. I am proud of my son." It was funny, though, that the image that materialized in her brain wasn't of Richard.

Finally, the Charlesworths took their leave and Jeffrey and Sarah stood at the door, watching the carriage disappear down the long, dark drive and into the night. "Do you enjoy their company?" Jeffrey asked his wife.

She sighed. "Not especially."

"Is there a reason we dine with them so frequently?"

Sarah laughed, then. "I was wondering the same thing myself. I suppose because we've always done it. It's tradition."

He shook his head as they walked slowly into the foyer, toward the staircase. "We may want to consider changing that particular tradition. I find myself increasingly less patient with that whole family as the years go by."

Sarah placed one foot on the bottom stair. "We'll allow some time to pass before inviting them again. And what are your plans for next week?"

"I'll be here, mostly. I've had enough of Richmond for the moment."

"Did you see Richard before you left?"

"I did. He was well, eager to fight."

Sarah nodded absently. "I hope he doesn't . . ."

Jeffrey waited for her to finish. When she didn't, he said, "—make any enemies?"

She nodded again. "He does seem to have that particular talent."

"That he does."

Sarah began climbing the stairs, preoccupied with thoughts of her youngest son.

"Sarah?" Jeffrey called when she had almost reached the top.

She turned. "Yes?"

His mouth suddenly felt dry and he couldn't fathom what it was he wanted to say to his wife. She waited patiently. *Do you love me at all?* he wanted to ask. "I don't know how all of this business will end," he finally murmured. "Things may change irrevocably."

Sarah moved a few steps back down to better hear him. "Do you believe our new government will fail?" she asked, for once without guile. She might find her husband lacking in strong character, but one thing at which he was excellent was an uncanny ability to read people's intentions and personalities.

He sighed softly. "I don't know, Sarah. I simply do not know. I think we will hold strong for a time, perhaps, but I do not see how we can sustain this conflict for very long. The Union will not give up, and quite simply, their resources outmatch ours at least two to one in every possible area."

Sarah nodded. "I know. I've thought about that, myself." She paused. "How do you think Bentley will be affected?"

"Well, hopefully not at all, but it's impossible to know for sure. We don't have the same leverage as the cotton plantations, but we still generate a significant amount of revenue. Davis thanked me personally for our latest donation before I left Richmond."

Sarah nodded again, her gaze distant. "I would hate to see my whole life destroyed," she murmured. "I have lived all of my years in the walls of this home. I would defend it to my last breath."

"As would I. Even should the conflicts extend this far south, which I almost doubt they will, we will not go down without a fight." Jeffrey watched as Sarah gave him a fleeting smile and turned, again climbing the stairs and disappearing around the corner.

It was true, he mused as he walked slowly to his study. He would defend Bentley because it was also his life. He had sold himself to Bentley and was committed. He may not agree with the wisdom of the Confederate leaders or the way in which they were conducting business, but one thing was for certain: there was no turning back. If the Union proved victorious, the Southern way of life would be in for dire changes. Sentiment throughout the Confederacy was at a current high following the resounding victory at Manassas Junction, but Jeffrey was holding his optimism in reserve. One conclusive battle did not a victory make.

***

Summersville, Western Virginia
14 August, 1861

Anne strolled through camp with two unopened letters in hand. She had finally received correspondence from home, as well as from Isabelle, who was still with Pinkerton in Washington. She was anxious about the letter from her parents, hoping it wouldn't contain any evidence that suggested they thought something was amiss.

She finally found her tent and crawled inside, sitting on the hard earth, grateful it wasn't raining, for the moment at least. The regiment had traveled from town to town over the past few weeks, largely by foot, covering a distance of roughly eighty miles. Once Anne's sore limbs had become accustomed to the constant marching, she found she was adapting well to regular exercise.

The rain, however, was another issue. She had seen more rain in the region of western Virginia than she wanted to think about. Camp life was utterly miserable—everything was wet, and only two days earlier, the camp had been moved to higher ground for sanitary reasons. She was beginning to think that the prospect of life in the desert wasn't a poor idea.

Opening the first letter, she read with misty fondness her mother's familiar handwriting. Everyone was well, except for Camille and Robert, who had nearly gotten themselves killed at Bull Run. Anne's mouth dropped open in surprise and she hastily read over the lines again. She shook her head at first, a reluctant smile appearing on her lips, and before she knew it she was laughing out loud. *Camille* of all people, witness to a battle?

It really wasn't funny, and Anne found herself wondering why she couldn't stop laughing. Perhaps it was the absurdity of the very thought that her younger siblings had not only left town without their parents' permission, but had also gone to a city that was in virtual lockdown, thinking to find a pleasant vacation. Anne could see it as clearly as day; Camille had undoubtedly been wooed at the thought of potential husband material, what with all the soldiers milling about the capitol, and Robert had probably been hoping for a chance at military glory.

Anne read the rest of her mother's letter with interest. They were expecting Ben to materialize any day, and were anxious to see him, and Anne's Aunt Jenny had brought her husband from New Orleans, hoping he would recover from a beating—something about an article he was going to print in his newspaper. She pursed her lips. Anne hated it when bad things happened to good people, and Jean-Pierre and Jenny were definitely good people.

She folded the letter and placed it in her knapsack, and then opened the seal on Isabelle's missive. She scanned the page, which began *Dearest Aaron*, smiling at Isabelle's usual cynicism and wit, and read with interest the information her friend shared on the state of affairs in military leadership. General McDowell, after his failure at Bull Run, or Manassas, as the Confederacy was calling it, was replaced by General George B. McClellan.

> *Lincoln seems to think the Army of the Potomac will be better served by McClellan, but I must tell you, Aaron, I despise the little man. To make matters worse, Lincoln has not offered any kind of security position to Pinkerton, so Pinkerton is now McClellan's head of the secret service. He works directly with McClellan, now, and I thank all things holy that Pinkerton has allowed me to continue surveillance around Washington and does not ask that I work directly with the General.*

Anne nodded, a smile upon her lips. Belle would do it, without a doubt. McClellan had better hope he led his armies on to continual victory, or he would be verbally accosted by one of Pinkerton's finest.

I shall be interested, the letter continued, *to see what you think of the little irritant, should you ever come in contact with him. He has a substantial number of men under his command, and you may well find your regiment attached to McClellan's Army of the Potomac at some point, so beware.*

I believe he has the Union's best interests at heart—certainly his own, which include aspiring glory for saving the Union, so I do not think his actions will be of detriment to us. I must grudgingly admit that he has given the troops a confidence they had most assuredly lost following the disaster at Bull Run, and they look to him as their undisputed leader. He has drilled and trained them to perfection, and they appear to be quite a powerful fighting machine. The men refer to him affectionately as "Little Napoleon," a comparison he glories in and encourages. However, I find him a most officious, aristocratic little beast.

And THEN we have the issue of John C. Fremont, Lincoln's leader in the western territories. I asked Kate Warne for her impressions of the man, and she admitted to finding him handsome, but we both agreed with the President's recent reaction to the man. It happened following a Union defeat in Missouri; without consulting Washington, Fremont, (who Kate says plans to win the Presidency from Lincoln in '64), declared death to all enemies found behind Union lines and freedom to all Missouri secessionists' slaves.

Lincoln, of course, was furious. The President and the senators make policy. Generals do not. And Lincoln has been maintaining a hold on Missouri only by the merest of strings! To free the slaves of that state at this point will be tantamount to shoving Missouri right into Confederate hands. While the sentiment of freedom for the slaves is noble enough, it is my opinion that Fremont sought more for his own glory than anything.

Here's a bit of gossip for you—did you know that Fremont considers himself quite the showman? He surrounds himself with displaced European nobility and a personal guard of Kentuckians that all stand over five feet, eleven inches. Lincoln calls him the "damndest scoundrel that ever lived, but in the infinite mercy of Providence . . . also the damndest fool."

Anne finished the letter, mentally stashing away the information she always obtained from her correspondence with Isabelle, and placed the paper alongside the other one in her knapsack. She stretched as much as the small confines of the tent would allow, and stepped out again into the sunlight. She spied a passing soldier, a man who was in her Section, who had been friendly to her from the start. "Mark," she called. "What have you heard on the reconnaissance parties?"

Mark Stephenson joined her with a quick smile. "Nothing

yet, but we should hear word soon. They were supposed to be back today."

They stood, chatting for a moment outside Anne's tent, when a young private rushed by, his face flushed. "What's the word?" Mark called out to the young man.

"Captain Sprague and his reconnaissance party were captured by the Rebels!" the private blurted, clearly upset. He ran on to spread the word, and Anne watched his retreating form, dread settling into her stomach like a lead ball. Thus far, the regiment had seen minor picket action, but no one had been hurt. This new development was entirely different.

Mark turned toward Anne, his expression strained. "And so it begins," he said. "I had hoped . . . well, I had hoped . . ."

Anne knew what the man was trying to say. They all had hopes that a few minor skirmishes would scare the Rebels back home and the whole of it would be over. Now, the enemy had captured some of their own. It was sobering. As always when events around her began to churn, Anne's fingers itched for her pen and paper to record comments and impressions of other people. That way, her own anxieties often took on a lesser role because all of her efforts were concentrated on listening, observing, and good writing.

She dashed into her tent to retrieve her notebook and pen, and quickly emerged, her thoughts already swirling. In her absence, Mark had been joined by Ivar Gundersen, a man Anne hadn't been able to draw two words from, in spite of all her attempts at conversation. He had to be the most intensely private person Anne had ever met in her life. He joked with the men, he laughed often, he spoke fondly of surface details about his family back home, but when it came to his thoughts on people, the war, religious views, *anything* that required personal, sometimes private insight, he offered maybe one or two words and then closed up tighter than a clam shell.

Anne had to admit that it wasn't just his views on the war that held her interest. She also found him strikingly handsome. He had a thick head of honey-blonde hair, piercingly blue eyes, firm facial features, and a muscular frame that was evidence of his farming profession. She supposed that his manner, which she ofttimes would describe as aloof, added to his appeal.

He nodded once to her now, and she glanced at him for a moment, wondering what he thought of the recent goings-on about camp. It couldn't hurt to ask. "Has Mark told you about Captain Sprague and his men?"

"Yes, he just told me."

"It's eerie, isn't it?" Mark interjected. "We were on reconnaissance ourselves, only a couple of days ago. Those men could very well be us."

Anne nodded, a twinge of unease skittering down her spine. It was true, and she hadn't thought of it that way. Turning her attention to her paper and pen, she scribbled a few notes.

Ivar gestured to her paper and said, "Writing an article to send back to Boston?"

Anne glanced up in surprise. It was the most he had said to her since their first introduction. "Yes, actually, I hope to send something soon, or I may just find myself unemployed."

He smiled a bit at her quip and then said, "Doesn't this Rebel-capturing business bother you quite a bit?"

"I'm sure it bothers me as much as everyone else." What, exactly, was he trying to say? Why should it bother her any more than anybody else? All of her senses immediately went on alert.

He must have noticed the change. "I mean, you're young, and . . . well, young." He closed his mouth, looking a bit sheepish.

"I'm not so young that I don't know what I'm about," she said, relaxing a bit. She must be overreacting. She'd have to stop doing that, or people would become suspicious. "But yes, it does bother me. Makes me more wary, I suppose."

It wasn't long before they were joined by Jed Dietrich who, Anne had pieced together not long after her arrival with the regiment, had been good friends with both Mark and Ivar back home. They were all kind, good men, and she enjoyed their company.

"Crazy business," Jed said with a shake of the head as he approached the small group. "I hope those bloody Rebels treat them well."

"We can hope," Mark growled in return, "but what are the odds they'll behave like gentlemen? They're waging war on their homeland, after all."

Anne continued to scribble on the paper, snatching the men's quotes as quickly as they were uttered. They were used to her frantic writing by now, and while they teased her a bit, for the most part anymore they seemed to forget she was doing it. She moved slightly away from the group, perking her ears at other conversations that peppered the camp.

She walked slowly, writing and eavesdropping as the men of the regiment expressed their dismay over the capture. These were comrades, friends, fellow soldiers—along with anger and concern over the prisoner's conditions, she heard a very real element of fear.

She was struck by one very significant thought as she slowly made her way through the tents and groups of people; these men were not professional soldiers. She had pondered on that before, but suddenly it took on a whole new meaning. It was one thing for professionally trained men, who had chosen the military as a career, to face such an awful prospect as capture by the enemy. It would be terrible for them, to be sure, but generally speaking, a soldier who was thus by profession was a man who had chosen that vocation—who knew of the risks and relished his work anyway. These men whose company she currently enjoyed were not soldiers by choice, per se. They had joined the army to defend their country, but given a lifetime career option, they had all chosen something different.

These were schoolteachers, businessmen, and farmers. Many of them had never even shot a gun as a means of providing a meal for the dinner table. Life was not as it had been for their predecessors a mere hundred or so years earlier. Society had progressed—most in the cities and towns purchased their food from stores; they didn't have to go into the woods and hunt it down.

And now, here they were, all of them together, toting weapons and drilling as soldiers. Anne marveled at such at thing. Those men had probably never dreamed as children that one day they would be fighting their own countrymen, on what had once been, and still was, according to Lincoln, United States soil.

As Anne walked back to her tent, she spied Major Casement who was walking about, talking with the men. She approached him, and heard him saying, "We've received orders to move to Cross Lanes."

"How far is that, Major?" one of the men asked.

"Roughly seven miles. We'll leave at 10:30 in the morning."

Anne absorbed the information, and when she reached her tent, she found her three friends still standing there. She told them what she'd heard, and they all nodded.

"More marching," Mark sighed. "When this war is finished, I'm not walking another ten feet unless I have to. I'll ride my horse from the house to the barn, see if I don't."

They all laughed at the image, and Jed added, "And I won't even think of eating any more hardtack. I may use a stack of it as door stoppers, but it won't come near my lips."

"Speaking of which," Anne commented with an inner grimace, "isn't it nearly dinner time?"

Ivar nodded. "I've found it much more palatable to soak it in my coffee before trying to eat it," he said. "Took young Sam's advice."

"The hardtack?"

"Yes. I nearly broke a tooth the first time I tried to eat it."

Anne could commiserate. Her jaw had ached after attempting her first hardtack meal. It was a simple biscuit made of flour and water, and Anne had decided that if she threw it just right, she might be able to kill someone with it. She had even recommended it as possible ammunition to Major Casement, who had laughed and told her he appreciated her attempt at humor. She hadn't had the heart to tell him she was half serious.

"Actually, we should probably be grateful we've got it," she muttered to her friends and moved to enter her tent. They grumbled in agreement and left to retrieve their own food. There had been a few days since Anne's arrival when supply lines had been interrupted and they had gone without any food entirely. By the time they were finally fed, she had looked at the hardtack as though it were the most blessed thing in the world.

Movement in the morning might just be a good thing, she mused as she readied her meager fare and went outside again to find Mark, Jed, and Ivar. Often when the regiments passed through towns, the locals went to great efforts to provide them with a wonderful meal, rousing band music, and lots of warm support. It was a huge boon to tiring spirits, and it just might help them forget for a moment that some of their number were now sitting in enemy hands.

CHAPTER 29

"I find myself in a new and strange position here. President, cabinet, General Scott and all deferring to me—by some strange operation of magic I seem to have become THE power of the land. I almost think that were I to win some small success now, I could become Dictator, or anything else that might please me . . ."
—General George B. McClellan, to his wife on his arrival in D.C.

***

Boston, Massachusetts
4 September, 1861

"You've enlisted? You're leaving?" Strickland's voice had risen in level and was now nearly a squeak.

"Yes, sir. I leave in roughly a week. Of course, I would be thrilled to still hold a position here at the bank when I return, but I understand you'll need to replace me in the meantime."

Strickland opened and closed his mouth like a fish out of water. "But we have plans for you! You can't just leave—you fixed the New York branch, and my brother and I had planned on promoting you . . ."

"I appreciate that, sir, but I feel my country needs me."

"Bah! The country already has thousands!"

It took some doing, but Strickland eventually accepted the fact that Luke was serious. He followed him to his desk, however, and talked incessantly about all he was giving up while Luke placed his belongings in a small packing crate.

"Sir," he finally said to the man when he was ready to leave, "I appreciate the opportunities you've extended to me here. I hope that on my return, you'll still have need for my services."

Strickland blustered and stammered, but shook the proffered hand and followed him to the front door of the building. "Please change your mind," was his final, pleading parting shot.

Luke turned back and smiled. "I can't. I'm sorry."

He made his way to his small, open carriage and placed the crate inside, climbing in and taking the reins in hand. His next venture was one he was looking forward to probably less than the one he had just completed. When he finally drew his carriage to a stop in front of Abigail Van Dyke's home where she lived with her mother, he took a deep breath and stared at it pensively for a moment.

Yes, most assuredly, this would be harder. He had become very fond of Abigail of late, and they had been spending a considerable amount of time together, often before or after Society meetings. Of all the women he had spent time with, this was one for whom he had developed some strong feelings. He had hopes of winning her total affection, of soon purchasing a home of his own and convincing her that she would be happy in said home, by his side as his wife.

Abigail was unpredictable, however, and that was part of her charm. He never quite knew what she was going to say from one moment to the next. She was pretty, with a sizeable inheritance, and those two factors combined insured a considerable line of suitors that were quite regularly camped out on her doorstep or in her parlor. She had turned much of her attention, however, on Luke, and that fact had put a spring in his step and a *thump* in his heart.

He secured his carriage and walked the short distance to the front door of the charming red brick home. It was an old colonial house that had served Dolly's family for years, and the women took great pride in its origins. Upon reaching the front door, he raised his hand to the knocker and paused, feeling a slight pang at what he was about to say to the woman to whom his heart was rapidly falling victim.

He stiffened his resolve and knocked upon the door, smiling at the servant who opened it and placed him in the front parlor with instructions to wait while Miss Abigail was notified of his visit. He was unable to sit, and so he slowly paced down the length of one wall, across the next, and so on until he had walked the circumference of the room. He continued his small journey and was on his third trip around when Abigail appeared in the doorway, a slight flush on her cheek and a bright expression about her eyes. Luke's heart skipped a beat, and he realized that if there was really any one thing to keep him from going through with his enlistment, this was it.

They exchanged pleasantries, and Abigail sat upon a divan, patting the spot next to it. He took it, and looked at her carefully, wondering where he should begin.

"Something's amiss," she finally said, her expression growing guarded.

"Well, I don't know that 'amiss' would accurately describe it, but yes, I do have something of import to tell you."

Abigail accepted the news of his enlistment with a blank expression, her eyes finally growing distant. She stood and walked to the windows then, looking out into the street without comment. He stood as well, and moved behind her, wishing for all the world that she would say something so that he might have an indication of her feelings.

"I suppose I knew it would come to this," she murmured without turning around. "As ardent a supporter of the Society as you are, you couldn't long stand by and not do your own part to right this country's biggest wrong."

"I wish the Union's motives were that noble," he answered quietly. "The goal of the war is not to free the slaves."

"I know. And I suppose preservation of the Union is a noble enough cause," she quipped, her tone dry, "but I wish . . . I wish . . ."

"Time will tell. In the meantime, I must go with my cousin. I wanted you to know because—" He put his hand on her shoulder and turned her slightly, wanting to read her expression. "Because I have grown enamored of you, Miss Abigail Van Dyke, and I had hoped to deepen our association."

He waited a heartbeat while she absorbed his words, her expressive face giving away little until she finally offered him a slight smile. "I would not have been offended by such a notion, Mr. Birmingham."

"And how do you feel about correspondence from afar?"

"Well, as I do know how to write, I would be more than happy to exchange correspondence with you."

"Abigail—" He stopped, unable to ask her that which he most wished to. *Please don't become involved with anyone else while I'm gone—will you wait for me to return and marry me? Live with me for years here in Boston until we grow old and die?* "I will miss you," he finally murmured, his hand lifting of its own accord to trace the line of her cheekbone.

When her eyelids fluttered closed, he acted without thought and leaned forward, touching his lips to hers in the most feather-light of kisses, his brain barely registering the fact that if her mother entered the room, he might have some explaining to do. She softly returned his kiss, looking almost disappointed when he drew back.

Luke drew a shaky breath. "I would be most honored if you would write to me, then," he whispered.

"What is the length of your enlistment?"

"Three years. God willing, it will not last so long."

Abigail nodded, her eyes clouding. "I will miss you, as well, Luke Birmingham. Will you come by once more before you leave town?"

"Yes. Without a doubt."

***

New York, New York
4 September, 1861

Daniel O'Shea lit a lamp in his workshop to combat the waning outdoor light and continued planing the long piece of wood lying on his worktable. It had been months since he had worked so long into the evening. More often than not, he stopped at dinnertime and worked afterward for possibly another hour before locking the doors to his shop and walking the few feet to his small home; or, on weekends, making his way into the city for his weekly round of fights.

Lately, however, Daniel had had much on his mind. The bank work was rewarding, and he was doing good for his people, but it truly wasn't his passion. While he loved being part of a process that brought good folk to the realms of the respectable working class, he hated being imprisoned behind a desk. He much preferred the work he did with his hands in his shop.

Then, too, there was the small matter of a certain daguerreotype he still held in his possession. The image of Marie Brissot filled his consciousness every day, and try as he might, he couldn't bring himself to put the thing in the mail and send it back to its rightful owner. He called himself the worst sort of cad—Jenny Brissot surely wanted it back—but he couldn't bear to part with it.

He must be going daft, Daniel reasoned as he continued working on the long piece of wood, smoothing it to perfection, the sweat pooling between his shoulders and forming on his hairline. He impatiently shoved his forearm across his forehead, wiping at the beads that threatened to fall into his eyes. Who, after all, kept a picture of a total stranger and then looked at it daily, wondering what it would be like to meet that person in the flesh?

Daniel wondered if Marie missed her parents. He reckoned she must like being a schoolteacher since she had stayed behind for that very purpose. He wondered if she was in any danger from the men who had attacked her father. He wondered many things about the mysterious young woman, but would never know the answers because he was thousands of miles away and furthermore, she didn't know he even existed.

He had her address; Luke had scrawled it on a piece of paper for Daniel before he had gone to fetch his aunt and uncle. "This is my final destination," Luke had said. "If you don't hear from me for more than a month or two, you'll know something probably happened. Then I suppose you're on your own," he had finished with his mouth quirked.

It couldn't hurt, really, to write the girl a quick letter and ask after her welfare. Perhaps then, if she responded that all was well, he could put her out of his thoughts once and for all. "Feisty," was the word Luke had used to describe her. It was odd, Daniel mused as he ran a finger along the smooth edge of the piece of wood, that he should find himself so enamored not only of a woman he'd never actually met, but one who was apparently so unlike his late fiancée. Alice had been blonde and demure. This Marie, by all accounts, was opinionated, of strong character, and olive complexioned with dark hair and eyes.

It was nearing midnight when Daniel finally left his shop and bathed in the hipbath he'd purchased years ago for Alice. He dried off, readied himself for bed, and almost as an afterthought, drew a piece of paper from the small secretary that was situated in a corner of his front parlor. Dipping his pen in an inkwell, he sat at the little desk and began writing. The words flowed quickly, though he hardly knew what he was writing, and he glanced up, realizing he had filled a page with correspondence to a young woman living nearly a world away.

He glanced over what he'd written, tempted to tear the thing into pieces. Instead, he replaced his pen and ink and rose to retire. Maybe someday he'd actually put the letter into the mail.

***

Charleston, South Carolina
4 September, 1861

It was with a small measure of alarm that Emily read the note she found on the floor just inside her bedroom. *Come tonight—I need to discuss something with you. R.*

Emily knew that "R." It was Ruth. Ruth would never have written a note for her to find that someone else might have accidentally come across, unless something dire was afoot.

She left her bedroom and made her way around the house, trying to look casual, but wanting to talk with Ruth immediately and put her curiosity, and her worry, to rest. She couldn't very well ask where the woman was; ever since her discussion with Sarah over Mary and her child's paternity, things had been decidedly strained between Emily and her mother.

After looking for quite some time and not finding the older woman, Emily gave up on her search for Ruth, contented herself with the knowledge that she would speak with her later in the evening, and instead climbed the stairs to the third floor to visit Clara. When she reached Clara's room, she stood outside the open door for a moment, watching the young child.

Clara was ten years old, and beautiful. Most of the world didn't even know the girl couldn't hear—not even a little bit. But she spoke with her hands, using a combination of signs Emily had taught her, and a small chalkboard on which she "conversed" when she was trying to express something beyond her signing capacities.

Rose was with her, as always, and the two were inseparable. Rose was the very image of her sister, Mary, and possessed every inch the same intellect and quick mind. Emily had taught Clara and Rose side by side as little children, and still devoted four hours a day to their learning. Sarah had originally hired other teachers for Clara, hoping someone could communicate with the child, but when Emily had realized that the teachers were not only impatient with the little girl, but cruel in their punishments, she told Sarah she wanted to do the task herself.

Sarah had been dubious, at first, but Emily proved she had a bond with her little sister; and because Clara trusted her, she was able to learn faster and more thoroughly from her than someone else. Emily had also taught Rose, alongside Clara, and she had found a purpose in her life throughout the past five years that almost filled the void left by her brother. Almost.

When Clara spied Emily in the doorway, her face brightened and she signaled, "You've come back?"

Emily nodded. They had finished their lessons before lunch so that the girls could spend the day exploring outside, but Emily was suddenly loathe to be apart from them. The girls were sweet, and funny, and they didn't know yet that life was cruel. Rose would discover that fact for herself soon enough, if she hadn't already, and in some ways Emily wished she could just keep them up here, in this suite of rooms, forever—protecting them from pain.

A deaf child and a slave. They were two of a kind.

"Let's go outside," Emily signed and said aloud at the same time, helping Clara continue to read lips, which was something she actually did quite well, and was improving upon daily. "We can look for birds' nests again."

The girls both brightened and stood, replacing their tea set in its proper cupboard and tidying their other toys. Rose lay her small black doll on the bed she slept on, which was next to Clara's, but a good two feet shorter. Emily shook her head slightly. Rose didn't know it, but she was actually lucky. Not only was she still allowed to sleep in the main house, even though she was nearing the age where she could realistically begin working, but she was also allowed a bed. Most other slaves who were companions to white children were given pallets on the floor.

"Hmm," Emily muttered to herself. "Lucky indeed."

Rose glanced at her as she smoothed a hand over her dress and tightened the bow at the back of her pinafore. "Pardon?" she asked Emily.

"Nothing. Are you ready?"

"Yes. Do you think we'll find three like we did last time?" Rose asked, hand signing as well for Clara's benefit.

Clara shook her head with a bright smile. "No," she signed emphatically. "I think we'll find four this time."

Emily smiled in spite of herself. Clara—ever the optimist. There were lessons to be learned from the child, if Emily could only make herself.

"Come in," Ruth beckoned to Emily later that night after she knocked softly upon the door of the shack.

Emily entered, curiosity nearly eating her alive. "What's wrong?" she asked, glancing first at Ruth, then at Mary, who sat in a chair mending a dress that had already seen too much wear. Next to her, on the floor, was a large tub filled with water where Ruth had placed some of her clothing to soak before she scrubbed them.

Ruth chuckled and pulled a chair aside for Emily to sit next to Mary. "Nothing's wrong," she said, and folding her arms, she leaned back against the small wooden table. "I just figured it's time you and I had a little talk."

Emily folded her hands in her lap, suddenly feeling very much like a small child. It had been years since Ruth had approached her in such a tone. "Very well," she murmured.

Ruth laughed out loud, then. "Don't look as though I've just taken away your very best friend," she said. "In fact, that's what I'm trying to avoid."

Emily glanced at Mary in mild panic. "What do you mean?"

"I mean, Emily, that you are like a combustible powder keg these days," Ruth murmured, her tone gentle. "I see much of Ben in you, child, but I fear that your temper, if allowed to continue to run unchecked, will wreak havoc not only for you but for Mary and Rose, as well."

Emily sat silent, absorbing Ruth's words.

"It's not as though I don't appreciate your spirit, Emily. The good Lord knows you're one of very few white folk who see the world as it was meant to be seen. But I'm afraid that if you continue to sass your mother, she'll not allow you any more contact at all with Mary, or me, and she might even become worried enough to separate Clara and Rose. Or she could sell us all on a whim, you know. Sarah is afraid of you, Emily, I can see it in her eyes."

Emily's own eyes widened in surprise, and then burned as tears threatened, but she held them at bay. "I didn't realize I was endangering you three," she murmured, her face warm.

"Oh, sweet girl," Ruth said and she moved to Emily's side, pulling her close. "Truly, I fear more for you than anyone. I don't want you doing anything rash—anything that will convince your mother that she needs to send you away, somewhere. We would miss you dreadfully."

Emily nodded, her head rubbing against the worn material of Ruth's dress.

"You know, Emily, your mother's really not so awful," Mary interjected, still mending her own clothing.

"Don't you dare tell me you're grateful, Mary!" Emily moaned, sniffling and running a finger under her nose.

Mary dropped her hands in her lap, an exasperated expression covering her face. "Emily, I *am* grateful, as much as I'm frustrated. Do you have any idea how different things are on other plantations? Children run about barefoot and wearing only a shirt, if they're lucky, until they're twelve years old! The slaves are stacked deep into the cabins with no beds or cots, and they're always ill. What Ruth and I have here is practically a mansion!"

"Mary! My parents will not let you leave! I don't care how nice your home is—if you can't leave, it's a prison! You work your fingers to the bone in my mother's house, day, after day, after day, and you are not paid for your work. You're offered instead clothing that wears itself out before it's replaced and food that is a mere pittance of what we consume up there." Emily jerked a thumb in the direction of her own home.

"Emily," Ruth interjected, "we are the last people on God's green earth to defend slavery, but I hear stories of our people on other plantations, the Charlesworth's even, and I thank the stars above that our lot is not as bad as theirs. And so, we will bide our time. And in the meantime, girl, you keep your head about you. Will you promise?"

Emily nodded.

"You can do so much good, and I know you will. But if you rush all crazy-like before stopping to think, you won't be of any use to anyone, least of all yourself. So slow down, curb your tongue, and *think*."

CHAPTER 30

"Because it has the largest purse."
—Baron Rothschild, London banker, on
why he felt the North would win the war

***

Boston, Massachusetts
15 September, 1861

Robert Birmingham pushed aside his schoolbook on mathematics and rose from his chair, stretching stiffly. It was nearly bedtime, and he found himself almost looking forward to it. He was tired. He felt he'd aged a hundred years since his and Camille's ill-fated vacation to Washington, D.C. It had been nearly two months, and by some measure of kind Providence, at least the nightmares were beginning to recede.

He felt he had lost a part of himself, somehow, and he supposed that to be the nature of the melancholy that had settled into his system and held him tight in its grasp. Ever since he was young Jimmy's age, he had collected books and toys that were military in nature, and fascinating in the utmost to him. He had spent recent years making a study of military strategy and tactics, learning with fascination about the lives of historical and current military heroes.

And now? Robert glanced about his bedroom, and the places where many of his favorite items used to sit. He shoved his hands deep into his pockets and sighed. Truth be told, he missed his books, pictures, posters, and figurines. It seemed a mockery to him, however, to continue to enjoy them, knowing full well that the young boy he had seen die before his very eyes, would never again feel his mother's warm embrace or embark upon a life of his own and someday retire with the genteel grace of the elderly.

Robert opened his door and walked down the hallway, descended the front stairs and slowly wandered the main floor, wishing for some sort of distraction. He and Camille had been relieved of their confinement, with the swift promise that should they ever again attempt such foolishness, they'd find themselves locked in Boston's finest jail. He shook his head. As if they'd ever again *want* to attempt such foolishness.

Camille had changed, as well. She was but a shade of her former, chatty self; she read the newspaper at breakfast with the rest of the family and spent little time with many of her former friends, choosing instead to be near Elizabeth. Robert should have been happy about that, he supposed, but he felt responsible for the shift in Camille's character, and it bothered him. Just once he'd love to hear her say something stupid and carefree so he could assuage himself of the guilt.

He walked past his father's open study and glanced inside to see James and Jimmy, their heads close together, bent over the massive desk. Robert ventured into the room for a closer look, only to find that his father and brother were maneuvering Robert's old Revolutionary War figurines about on the polished surface.

He felt his face pull itself into an involuntary grimace, and he turned to leave the room when his father noticed his presence and called to him, motioning him closer. "Come and sit with us, Robert."

Robert did so, reluctantly. He watched for a few moments without comment as his brother shoved the little figurines back and forth across the desk, making quiet gunshot noises with his mouth as he did so. Jimmy never said much, and it was anyone's guess as to what went on in his young head. Lest the child grow to believe as he had, that war was something glorious, Robert said, "It's not really all that fun, Jimmy. People look quite ugly after they're shot."

James glanced at him pensively for a moment and then said to Jimmy, who looked confused, "Would you go to the kitchen, Jimmy, and ask Cook if she won't make a snack of cheese and crackers for us to enjoy? You wait there and bring it in when it's ready."

Jimmy nodded, tossed an enigmatic glance at his brother, muttered something indiscernible under his breath, and left the room.

"Robert, I should have addressed this with you weeks ago, but your mother and I were so shocked when you first came home, and even more so when we heard other firsthand accounts of what actually happened—well, I was angry and afraid . . . I didn't feel quite up to discussing it."

Robert sat staring at the figurines on the desk, many of which had been tipped onto their sides in mock battle.

"I've heard the servants gossip about the fact that you've completely stripped your room of your former favorite possessions."

Robert nodded, once.

James drew a deep breath and took one of the "redcoats" from the desk, rolling it absently between his hands. "I know you saw some very ugly things, son, and I can't tell you how much I regret that, for your sake. I'm not very good at this sort of thing—if you would like to tell me about it, that would be fine."

Robert shook his head, unable to meet his father's direct gaze.

"That's fine too." James sounded almost relieved, and Robert nearly smiled at that. "Sometimes I think it's a man's best bet to try to forget things he'd rather not think about. I do think though, Robert, that you are in the very best of positions to continue your interests in the military."

Robert glanced up in surprise. James was no fan of war or the military; that much was common knowledge. "What do you mean?"

"I mean that now you've seen what war is really about. You know that it isn't all about glory, it's also ugly. But knowing that gives you good perspective. It's an unfortunate fact of life that war is sometimes necessary. And in my opinion, war is probably something that is just around the corner for every nation. As long as it's a looming threat, a country must be prepared for it, and must be lead well. Seems to me that a man who studies strategy and tactics, and yet knows that it's not something to be entered into lightly would be a man to be admired."

"Are you suggesting I pursue a career in the military?"

"I'm not suggesting anything, especially at this point—and heaven forbid the war is still on when you're old enough to enlist. But if there's one thing I've learned about life, it's this: it's a fortunate man indeed who can make a living doing what he feels passionate about. For me, it was business and industry. For you, Robert, it has always been military and heroes. Your interest in these things has been a source of pride for me because you have continually found fascination with heroes who were noble and good. If you were bloodthirsty and murderous, I might be leery of your intentions."

Robert shook his head a bit. "I don't know that I can make myself like it again."

"Well, the decision is yours to make, but I just want you to know that it's alright if you find that some of your former hobbies again become interesting."

"I do miss it," Robert admitted, taking one of the colonial statuettes from the desk and examining it. The Revolutionary War set had been created by one of Boston's finest craftsmen, and had been a gift from his parents for his tenth birthday. How he had loved those toys! He had played with them for hours on end, and as he had grown older and made a serious study of the war, he had maneuvered the pieces through recreated battle scenes.

Jimmy eventually reappeared with a large tray full of crackers and cheese. He set the tray on the desk after shoving some of the figurines aside with a sweep of his arm, and the three munched their snack in comfortable silence. "Robert," James said as he swallowed a mouthful of food, "why don't you tell Jimmy how armies are organized. He asked me about it earlier, and I can't remember."

Robert glanced at his father. "You can't remember?"

James shrugged, an innocent expression on his face.

Robert wanted to laugh. James never forgot anything. He had a mind like a steel trap, and when Robert had first shown an interest in the military, it had been his father who had taught him the basics. "All right," Robert sighed, leaning forward. "Jimmy, the basic military unit is the regiment. A regiment consists of roughly a thousand men, who are then divided into ten groups of one hundred, called companies. Does that make sense?"

Jimmy nodded, his mouth full of food.

"Each company is further divided into two platoons, which are then divided in half again into sections, containing roughly twenty-five men each."

Jimmy nodded again, trying to swallow his crackers. He coughed, and a few crumbs flew from his mouth to speckle the oak desk. James rose from his seat. "I'll be back with some drinks," he said, and disappeared.

When Jimmy stopped coughing, Robert continued his lecture. "Now, three or four regiments are combined to form a brigade, roughly three to four thousand men. Three or four brigades combined then form a division, and three or four divisions combined form a corps. So by the time we reach the corps level, we have roughly fifty thousand men. Does that make sense?"

Jimmy's eyes were crossing by this time, and he gratefully accepted the glass of juice his father handed him upon returning to the room.

"And then," Robert continued, "five or more corps combined create an entire army. Do you follow?"

"I think I'm still back on the regiment," Jimmy admitted.

James laughed out loud, and Robert couldn't blame him. A reluctant smile tugged at his own lips, and he shook his head.

Jimmy was quiet, true, but when he spoke he often surprised his family with his wit.

"Well," Robert sighed, "it's alright. You probably don't find it as interesting as I do anyway." And it was true, he realized. He still found it interesting, despite the blood and dismembered body parts that swam about in his memory. As he finally rose and bid his father and brother goodnight, he figured that maybe it wouldn't be so awfully bad if he retrieved just one of his books from the chest in his dressing room. Perhaps the one on General Washington . . .

An hour after his older brother had left the study, Jimmy's father finally told him that he needed to get some rest and that it was time for bed. Jimmy asked if he could take one of the figurines with him to his bedroom, to which his father replied that he could take the entire set, if he wished.

Jimmy carefully packed the set into its case and carried it upstairs to the quiet solitude of his bedroom and went about preparing for bed after placing the set on his desk. Once washed, and dressed in his nightclothes, he took one of the colonial soldiers from the set and climbed into his bed, clutching his drawing pad and pencil as well.

He made himself comfortable under the covers, and by the light of a lamp that still burned on one of his side tables near the bed, he began to sketch the figurine. Drawing was Jimmy's passion, just as he knew soldiers were Robert's. Iron was his father's passion, and the family was his mother's. For some fool reason, Camille's passion seemed to be men, and that caused Jimmy to shake his head slightly in confusion. Anne's passion had been a secret wish to be a boy, apparently, and Luke's passion was the slaves.

They all had a "passion," it seemed. He had stood for long moments outside the door earlier that night, listening to his father talk to Robert and internalizing every word. Jimmy didn't like to talk, but he listened extremely well. He took everything people said and mulled it over, choosing that which made sense and filing the rest away for later definition. He didn't have many friends, because he was so quiet, but he found he didn't mind that so much. As long as he had his pencil and paper, he was able to make sense of the world.

Before long, the little figurine materialized on the page before him, and Jimmy continued his sketch, shading and adding depth until the picture was the very image of the small statue. He sat back and held it, arm's length, for inspection. Well, he mused, it wasn't perfect, but it was close.

Words, he found, didn't always make sense. But drawing did.

***

Gauley Bridge, West Virginia
30 September, 1861

Anne turned exhausted eyes upon the small picture of a Revolutionary War colonist soldier that she had just pulled from a small package sent from home. Her mother had sent a letter, as had her father, and they hoped all was well with her in Chicago.

She ran a finger along the picture Jimmy sent, her eyes burning. *It's only because I'm tired,* she told herself sternly. *It's not because I wish I were home.* If she said it enough, she just might believe it. It had been a month, now, and she could still feel the panic.

The regiment had been moved from town to region, marching, marching, interminably marching until she felt sure she would be walking in her sleep for the rest of her life. And then, suddenly, at a little place called Cross Lanes, the 7th Ohio had been attacked by Confederates under General Floyd. They had been badly beaten, and the various companies scattered between Gauley Bridge and Charleston, West Virginia. The regiment, when it was eventually reconnected, again resumed camp at Gauley Bridge, amidst rainstorms and loss of morale because of the fighting.

Anne herself had not been witness to the bulk of the carnage. Her company had been one of the first ordered back to Gauley Bridge, and she had missed the severe fighting that many of the others experienced. She watched in fascinated horror as many of the men dealt with having their first taste of battle, or "seeing the elephant," as was the common term. They looked shocked, as though the world had suddenly fallen out from beneath them. Many were quick to recover, shoving the fear far below the surface and continuing with their daily routines as though nothing had happened. Others, however, continued to walk about as though in a daze, a haunted expression never quite leaving their eyes.

Little Jimmy was improving as an artist, Anne mused, as she continued to study the picture. She remembered the model for the image well; it was one of Robert's Revolutionary War figurines. How he had loved that set as a young boy! He was obviously now sharing with Jimmy, if the youngest had taken to sketching it.

Anne swallowed past a lump in her throat and folded the paper, placing it back into her knapsack with the others she had received from home. She felt her heart leap a bit when she thought over the news her mother had shared—that Luke had enlisted with their cousin, Ben, and was now a member of the 1st Massachusetts Cavalry. They were currently training and would be mobile soon.

It was one thing for Anne, herself, to be in possible danger. It was quite another to think of her brother facing combat possibilities. As much as she told herself he was a big boy and could take care of himself, she knew she would worry anyway. She gathered her knapsack in her lap and wrapped her arms around it, shivering from the constant drizzle, and weary to the bone of being cold and wet.

***

Ivar watched the young private from his vantage point outside his tent and shook his head. She had gumption, he had to admit.

But why, why would a woman be marching far from home with a military regiment that had already seen action, and would likely do so again and again? Why wasn't she home, thinking about getting married and having little babies? When he had met Berit, it was all she could talk about—that and life in the big city. Of course, he mused wryly, she hadn't been happy once the deed had been done, either. She had said what she thought he wanted to hear. She had been miserable single, and then miserable married.

Ivar walked over to young "Aaron," and when she glanced up, she smiled and moved over a bit on the log she sat upon to give him some room. He sat next to her and motioned to her knapsack she still held in a chilled embrace. "You've received mail from home?"

She nodded. "Letters from my parents and my youngest brother."

"I hope they are well."

"They are. My mother sends news that my oldest brother has enlisted, however."

"Does this come as a surprise?"

She sighed. "I suppose not. But he was so established, and had a job at a bank in Boston that was showing such promise . . ."

"But then, we've all left things that show promise, haven't we?"

She nodded. "I suppose we have. I just worry."

Ivar looked about the camp in its soggy glory and thought of his warm, comfortable home in Ohio. "I have a daughter," he told the young woman, wondering why he felt compelled to talk to her. Perhaps he was wishing someday she'd admit to him she was a woman. How *he* knew, exactly, he couldn't be sure. It constantly amazed him, however, that nobody else seemed to see it.

She glanced at him in surprise. "Oh, you do? How old is she?"

"She's two years old. Almost three."

The woman followed his gaze and studied the tents, and soldiers milling about, most of them writing letters home or playing card games wherever they could find a relatively dry spot. "I'm sure you must miss her. And her mother."

"Her mother has been dead nearly as long as the child has been alive."

"I'm sorry to hear that."

Ivar wished he could say the same, and then mused that probably his eternal soul would be damned that he wasn't more Christian in his love for his deceased wife. "Mmm," he finally answered the woman, and ignored her questioning gaze. "So," he said, diverting the conversation, "how did you begin writing for the newspaper?"

She sighed a bit and tried to get comfortable on the hard, wooden log. "Well, I had always enjoyed writing as a child, and as I grew older and eventually graduated from school, I made a portfolio of my writings and approached the editor of the local paper one day with my work in hand. I suggested he might benefit from having someone about town who could collect gossip or any other interesting tidbits that would create an interesting side column. He agreed to try my services for a trial run, and much to my delight, the arrangement became permanent."

"You must enjoy it, then."

"Very much."

"And was it your idea to enlist?"

"Yes. I told my editor that I'd like to try something new."

"He obviously agreed."

She nodded. "He had some concerns . . ."

"About your young age, of course."

She glanced at him sharply, then relaxed at his bland expression. At least, he hoped it was bland. He might have tipped his hand a bit too soon. "Of course," she finally murmured.

She was intriguing. What kind of woman wanted to go into battle merely to have a firsthand view from which to write? And she looked so young. "How old are you?" he asked on impulse.

"Eighteen."

She had answered quickly, and then casually averted her gaze, focusing on a pair of men who were laughing loudly over their card game. The response was too quick, or her aversion too casual; there was something he couldn't quite put his finger on, but now he would have wagered his entire meager army pay that she was lying about her age as well as her gender. Which meant she was either older or younger than eighteen. Could she really be younger? Impossible. Her parents obviously believed her to be somewhere safe, although how she accomplished the feat of receiving and sending mail to them he had no idea, but he would bet that she must then be older.

"Did you leave a sweetheart back home?" he asked, closely watching her face.

"No. Just my immediate family."

"Ah, well, I suppose there'll be time for that when this is all over."

She nodded, her expression carefully blank. She took a deep breath and smiled. "So," she said, turning the focus of her attention fully on him. "Tell me about your family."

Ivar shared the basic details of his immediate family history, of his parents' immigration and their lives in the States. "My father has slowed a bit because of an accident several years ago," he said, then broke off abruptly, feeling he'd shared enough on that account. His father's condition was his own business, and Ivar felt his pride rankle at the mention of Per's weakness. He wouldn't want the world knowing his physical strength was waning.

"Was there an accident on the farm?"

He nodded once, curtly. She must have sensed his closure, for she didn't broach the subject further. Instead, she focused on his mother. "She sounds like an admirably strong woman, from the way you've described her."

"She is. She could tackle any task, perform any job. Pity that women aren't allowed more freedom to pursue employment in which they might excel, wouldn't you agree?"

"Most assuredly." The vehemence in her voice was all the confirmation he needed that his suppositions had been correct, had he been in doubt. She was a woman, in a man's clothing and a man's haircut, doing a man's job. Ivar thought of the older brother she'd mentioned and wondered what he would think if he knew.

Ivar knew one thing for certain, however; he was glad she wasn't *his* sister. He'd have thrashed her.

***

Camp Brigham, Readville, Massachusetts
30 September, 1861

"I hear tales of other regiments who are doing nothing but marching, and I almost feel guilty we're mounted," Ben muttered to his cousin one day after a particularly long drilling session.

"I know. Have you seen the articles in the paper? The *Boston Examiner* has an in-the-field correspondent who says they've marched in so much rain they'll likely never be dry again." Luke brushed his horse carefully and saw to it that its oats and hay were in place before they retired to their own quarters. "Our lot here seems relatively simple."

And in truth, it had been, although both men had gone to bed so tired each night they felt sure they'd sleep forever. Each day was remarkably the same; they drilled, and then drilled, and then drilled some more. They studied field formations and battlefield communications; they worked with their mounts to assure smooth and effective movement as a body. What time wasn't spent drilling was spent in the care of the animals or letter writing to loved ones back home.

Luke glanced at his cousin, wondering what the man was thinking. It had been ages since he'd mentioned his family in South Carolina, and he knew Ben couldn't be as impartial to their welfare as he was content to have Luke believe. There was talk, although it was supposedly just rumor, that their regiment would eventually receive orders to head south.

As it currently stood, the regiment had been divided into three battalions of four companies each. Each battalion could possibly receive differing orders, and it was anybody's guess as to whether or not they would move south or stay to defend Washington. McClellan was supposedly going to eventually move on Richmond if Lincoln had his say—that scenario was also an option.

How would Ben react returning to his homeland after all these years? Was he still so embittered over all that had happened just before he left that he would welcome the opportunity to swoop down and wreak vengeance like a dark angel? Luke might never know, because Ben certainly never broached the subject, although there was a look in his eyes, at times, that gave a glimpse of the anger that simmered just beneath the surface.

Well, perhaps it was time to discuss it. "Have you given much thought to Bentley these days?" he asked casually as they splashed water on their faces and tried to clean up a bit before bedtime—at least as much as the primitive conditions would allow.

Ben grimaced. "Only every day," he said. "I think of them every day."

"And what will you do if we are forced to march against them?"

"Well, I don't imagine it will be as though I'll be ordered to burn my own home to the ground—instead I suppose I envision a battlefield setting, perhaps . . ."

"Yes, against your former neighbors, perhaps even—even . . ."

"Even my family?" Ben glanced at him askance as he dried his face on a small hand towel.

Luke winced in sympathy.

"I've thought of it," Ben admitted quietly. "Before I left, Emily sent word that Richard had enlisted and is serving somewhere in Virginia."

"Do they know you're here?"

"No. I don't want them to know. It will be the ultimate betrayal. At least for my parents, and Charlotte and Richard. Something tells me Emily would applaud me from the rooftops."

Luke grinned. "She's probably not the same, fiery little carrot-top I remember."

"No," Ben laughed. "I think she's now a fiery *big* carrot-top." He slowly sobered, and his smile faded. "I worry about her constantly."

"Do you think she's volatile?"

Ben nodded. "I do. I only hope she can keep her head about her."

Luke entered the barracks and made his way to his cot, attempting to make himself comfortable on it and perhaps do some reading before he went to sleep. "Have you heard from Joshua in the past years?" he asked Ben, who was again fishing about in his knapsack for his "Mormon Bible," as Luke liked to call the small volume of scripture. Ben had told Luke that he liked to read it each night to "stave off the rage."

"No," Ben said, finally extracting the little book. "The only way I've been able to communicate with him is through Emily, and that was veiled, at best. There was no way to come right out and ask how things were going for all of them, for Joshua, Ruth, Mary and Rose. I never knew who would end up reading the letters I sent home, although they were addressed specifically to Emily, and I didn't want her getting into trouble on my account."

Luke nodded. "He sure was a good man, wasn't he?"

"Joshua?"

"Yes."

"Indeed, he was a good man. God willing, he still is. I hope to see him again one day."

"As a freed man?"

"As a freed man."

CHAPTER 31

"Teach the rebels and traitors that the price they are to pay for the attempt to abolish this government must be the abolition of slavery."
—*Frederick Douglass*

***

Boston, Massachusetts
16 October, 1861

Camille sat in Olivia's front parlor, sipping her tea and nibbling on a small cake. Try as she might, she couldn't make herself focus on Olivia's chatter, which frustrated Camille more than the chatter itself. What on earth had happened to her? She didn't know who she was anymore! Olivia had returned to her former self, recovering (finally!) from her fit of vapors over the debacle at Bull Run, and was as intent as ever on finding a suitor worthy of her hand.

Camille, however, was distracted. Her thoughts swirled daily with the news she read each morning and the discussions the family engaged in around the table, and she felt as though some strange creature had invaded her brain and taken over her thoughts. She was no longer content to think only of herself, and it made her angry. Which was, she supposed, a form of self-absorption in itself, and so she tried to content herself with that much, at least.

The war, the war! She was sick to death of the war, and wanted it to go away. The problem now was that Anne had moved to Chicago, and Camille missed her, in an odd way, and Luke and Ben had enlisted, leaving her to worry over their welfare. She had seen with her own two eyes what could happen to a man on a horse in the midst of a battlefield, and she couldn't shake the feeling that what she had witnessed at Bull Run was but a precursor of things to come.

And then, there was Robert. He was slowly, ever so slowly coming back around to his former habits, but the boyish enthusiasm for life was gone. He was serious, now, and she would have given anything to hear him laugh in his old, silly way. She should have asserted her authority as the older sibling and put her foot down! She should never have allowed him to talk her into the D.C. holiday—then he would still be happy and she would only care about finding a husband. Instead, she was now becoming a woman of opinions, and it was most vexing.

"My mother says those abolitionist societies are going to be our downfall," Olivia confided in a conspiratorial whisper. "It's fortunate for you that Luke enlisted. Now you won't have to deal with that embarrassment any longer. Mother says they'll get what's coming to them, and in a big way."

Oh, do shut up! she wanted to say to Olivia, as her friend switched topics and began babbling on and on about the dinner party she was planning for the Christmas holidays. Camille rubbed her forehead with her fingertip, placing the teacup back in its saucer and mulling over the fact that she was starting to think like her mother.

That thought alarmed her, and she rose quickly, murmuring to Olivia that she had to be on her way, that she had forgotten an appointment at some such place and must hurry. Calling outside for her carriage, she quickly climbed into it and ordered the driver to take her home, leaving a baffled Olivia in her wake, sputtering incoherently.

It was one thing to find comfort in Elizabeth's strength, and to try to mimic it on occasion. It was quite another to *think* like the woman, for goodness sake! Her mother was a veritable blue-stocking! If she hadn't come across James Birmingham when she had, she'd likely be an old maid!

"Oh, heaven help me," she moaned aloud as the carriage clattered down the street. "I'm becoming intelligent."

It was only as she neared her home that part of Olivia's babbling penetrated her fog-enshrouded panic. What had she said? Something about the abolition societies? Camille's pretty brow creased in a frown. Had Olivia heard tales of threats against the Society?

Camille ventured quickly into the house, only to find her parents both gone—her father at his offices and her mother on errands. She paced in the foyer for a moment and was working herself into an emotional fit when Robert crossed the balcony above on the way to his bedroom.

"Robert!" she called with some relief. "Come down here at once!"

He made his way down the stairs, frowning. "What is it?"

"You must come with me!"

"Where?"

"To see Abigail Van Dyke."

Robert's face showed surprise. "Luke's lady friend?"

"Silly, she's not his 'lady friend'—you make her sound like a light skirt."

Robert shrugged. "Well, she's a lady, and she's his friend . . ."

"Oh, anyhow! There's nobody else home, and I don't know who else to warn. I think the Sylvesters may know something about an intended attack on Luke's Abolition Society."

"Why not go directly to Garrison?"

"Because he's a busy man, and I don't want to interrupt him."

"Camille, don't be a ninny! If there's a problem facing the Society, he should be the first to know!"

"He scares me! He's intimidating and intelligent, and I think he would find me ridiculous! I've only just recently begun to recognize the plight of the slave!"

Robert stared at her. "So?"

"So I'm going to the Van Dyke's instead. *They* can tell him if they wish!" She grabbed his hand and dragged him toward the front door.

"Why do you need me along?" he asked, glancing with longing to the second floor, where he had a new book awaiting him in his bedroom—this one a tactical analysis of the Mexican War.

"Because those Van Dykes are bluestockings!"

"And you're afraid they'll think you ridiculous as well?"

"Oh, Robert!" she finally wailed. "I don't know! Just come with me!"

In the end, he figured he owed it to her to acquiesce. After all, it was his fault that both he and Camille were rooting about for identities that seemed to have deserted them.

***

"Once again," Dolly Van Dyke said as she placed her teacup in its saucer. "Tell me exactly what Olivia said."

Camille was flustered. Dolly Van Dyke was intimidating, and surely thought her an idiot. "She said that I was lucky Luke isn't around anymore to be an embarrassment to the family with all of his abolitionist talk, and that the Society would get what's coming to them, or . . . something."

"Do the Sylvesters have a severe aversion to the Society?"

"Oh, yes. They think it's abhorrent that educated people would espouse the virtues of racial equality. They think slavery is a favor to black folk."

"Mmm. Now I know why I dislike that woman so much," Dolly muttered in obvious reference to Mrs. Sylvester. "Do you think they have it within their power to cause real trouble for the Society?"

"Well, they have plenty of money."

"Mrs. Sylvester's sister has a reputation for causing trouble within the Society, remember, Mother?" Abigail interjected from her position next to Dolly on a divan. "She lives in Baltimore and causes Mr. Garrison all sorts of ruckus when she's in town visiting, or when he's on the lecture circuit in her area."

Robert straightened in his seat. "Her sister?" He glanced at Camille. "We've met her."

Dolly's eyebrows shot up in surprise. "Is she in town?"

"No, but we went with the Sylvesters to D.C. in July—the primary focus of their visit was to see 'Aunt Helena.'"

"Ah, yes, I remember Luke saying something about your vacation," Abigail murmured.

Camille's face flushed hot. "He needn't have spread it all around town," she muttered under her breath.

Abigail laughed. "Oh, he didn't. It wasn't as though he announced it at a Society meeting. And don't be embarrassed. I admire your fortitude."

Camille glanced at the young woman, trying to assess her sincerity. It seemed genuine enough, and the smile was friendly, so Camille allowed herself to relax a bit. "It wasn't such a very good idea after all," she admitted, "and we didn't think Aunt Helena was so fantastic, did we, Robert?"

Robert shook his head. "She whined like a mule."

"It's true," Camille nodded. "It's gauche of us to speak ill of the woman, but her company was most tiresome. Now that you've told us more about her, I wonder if the Sylvesters didn't have an ulterior motive for their visit."

"What could it have been?" Abigail asked.

"I don't know." Camille pressed her lips together in thought.

"Were there periods of time when they conversed alone, out of earshot?"

"Oh, most assuredly," Robert answered. "They were like two hens that couldn't stop clucking long enough to draw a breath. They talked apart from the rest of us, and with us, as well."

Dolly glanced at Abigail. "We need to tell Lloyd."

"Lloyd?" Camille asked.

"Mr. Garrison. In fact, we have a meeting tonight. Will you attend with us, the both of you?" Abigail offered.

"Oh, no, we couldn't . . ." Camille and Robert both stammered on top of one another.

"Oh, but with Luke gone, it would be so nice to have other young Birminghams in his stead!" Abigail's smile was engaging, her eyes alive and friendly, and Camille didn't have to wonder long why Luke had become so enamored of the woman. But really, it was too much of a stretch. It was one thing to read Frederick Douglass's autobiography and find sympathy for him and his people. It was another thing altogether to risk ostracizing herself from her dearest friends by attending a Society meeting.

"Truly, I cannot," she said quietly, hoping the formidable Van Dyke women would understand, but knowing they probably wouldn't.

"It's all right," Dolly answered, her eyes kind. "Perhaps next time. I do think the both of you would find it interesting. Please consider coming along at some future date."

Camille heard Robert breath a soft sigh of relief that matched her own at the temporary reprieve. "We will consider it," she said, answering for the two of them and standing to leave. "At any rate, we thought you should know there may be mischief in the air."

"And we thank you for passing that along," Dolly said as she and her daughter walked them to the door. "Take care, won't you, and say hello to your mother and father for us."

The ride home in the carriage was quiet, Camille lost in her thoughts and Robert in his. When he finally voiced his musings, Camille wasn't surprised to find they reflected her own. "Do you think you'll ever attend a Society meeting?" he asked her.

She sighed. "I don't know. If I do, I can rest assured that all my friends will disassociate themselves from me."

Robert nodded. "And yet, there are many in our circle who are avid Society members. It just seems there are a select few who ardently oppose it."

"And those are the very people to whom I am closest." Camille frowned and looked out the window at the passing trees, whose leaves had fallen to the ground. "Why don't you want to go?"

Robert shrugged uncomfortably, his gaze following hers out the window. "It's too much."

"Too much what?"

"Too much pain. I've read Frederick Douglass's autobiography as well, you know."

Camille glanced at him in surprise. "Oh? When?"

"Last year. Luke made me. And then he thrust several slave accounts on me—papers the Society publishes—and was hoping to eventually start taking me to his meetings, I think."

"So why didn't you go?"

"I don't like to think about it. They do horrible things to those people, Camille. The slaveholders and other Northern sympathizers who have an economic interest in the survival of the system try to suggest that slaves are treated well and are happy. It's usually just not true."

Camille had begun to surmise as much herself, but was again confused at the disparities between what she was learning, and what she thought she knew. "Look at Aunt Sarah, though," she said, again watching the trees. "Once when we were small and at Bentley on holiday, one of the little slave children was sick and I saw Aunt Sarah care for the child herself. She was as tender as she would have been with her own."

Robert laughed. "In that case I find myself unimpressed. Aunt Sarah is not very tender with her own. She was more tender with *us*, I think, than our cousins."

"She expects more from them," Camille answered absently. "She expects perfection from her children, and she probably feels coddling them will produce weaknesses."

"Well, whatever the case, just because she is kind to her slaves doesn't mean it's a good system."

Camille smiled. "You're sounding like Luke."

Robert nodded. "Maybe so. I don't suppose that's such a bad comparison."

CHAPTER 32

"Man clutched at man, and the strong, who might have escaped, were dragged down by the weaker . . . One officer was found with $126 in gold in his pocket; it had cost his life.
—Randolph A. Shotwell, Confederate witness at Ball's Bluff

***

Ball's Bluff embankment, near Leesburg, Virginia
21 October, 1861

Finally, finally! Richard Birmingham stirred in anticipation at the prospect of another massacre. It was true, Confederate troops had clashed with Union soldiers off and on since Manassas, but in Richard's opinion, skirmishes and picket action didn't count.

He stood at the top of a one-hundred-foot high embankment that overlooked the Potomac, approximately thirty miles upriver from Washington. On the other side of the river sat Maryland, and the word was that upwards of fifteen hundred Union troops would soon be on their way across, attempting a reconnaissance mission.

Richard glanced down the narrow cowpath, the only possible means of reaching the top of the embankment, and smiled. The idiot Yanks were walking straight into a nightmare and wouldn't realize it until it was upon them. As if to underscore his thoughts, a voice behind him yelled, "Birmingham, get back here!"

He scowled and turned from the edge of the embankment and went to join the rest of the troops hidden and lying in wait. There were four regiments in all, thousands more than the estimated number of Union troops soon to be gracing the shore. The voice calling him back into place was that of Edwin Cornwell, the very same man who had called him a fool that day at Manassas, and hadn't stopped since.

Richard glanced at the young man's face, satisfied in the extreme with the fresh bruise that adorned Cornwell's eye, encircling it like a raccoon mask and so swollen the eye itself was almost shut tight. That had been Richard's doing, and he hadn't even had to strike the man himself.

Cornwell was too mouthy for his own good. He had belittled Richard one too many times. Last night, after Cornwell had mockingly questioned Richard's paternity, drawing plenty of laughter from the other troops, Richard had gone to his section leader and confessed, in quiet tones, that he had seen Private Cornwell looking at the leader several times, and in a very intimate way. It was none of Richard's business, to be sure, but he was a man, after all, and he figured a fellow man would want to know if one in his section had dubious and perverse intentions.

His tale had worked like a charm, and the angry section leader had charged Cornwell without even stopping to question whether Richard's carefully planted allegations were true. By the time the dazed and bruised Cornwell was able to defend himself and clear his good name with the section leader, he had already been beaten to a pulp. The section leader would always wonder now, however, as would the other men of the company who had been on hand to witness the scuffle and ensuing exchange of heated words. Yes indeed, Richard had done his work well.

Although the men hidden in the densely wooded area were hushed, there was a hum that vibrated from one soldier to the next, an expectation and nervous excitement that had them working hard to be still. Time passed—to Richard it felt like hours, and finally one of the lookouts came rushing back into the woods, hissing, "They're at the base!"

Slowly, very slowly, the troops to the near edge of the embankment cautiously emerged from their hiding spots, guns at the ready, to ambush the surprised bluebellies. The wait wasn't long at that point. The first few blue-shirted soldiers appeared at the top of the cliff, followed by a steady stream that crowded after the first few.

The signal was given, and shots were fired, catching the Union soldiers completely by surprise. One of the first to fall was a colonel, shot dead in the forehead. Richard watched as the man fell, and his subordinates rushed to carry him back the way they had come. The soldiers still coming up the embankment who saw their comrades hauling the body of the colonel back down immediately panicked, and began retreating without a direct order to do so.

Meanwhile, the crowd of blue gathered atop the embankment had scurried back as far as they could without falling over the edge, and when they realized that those on the fringes of the crowd were falling like flies from the Confederate guns, they moved, screaming and scrambling en masse to the edge of the embankment. It wasn't long before panic sent them all over the edge, falling onto those who were still climbing the narrow path, unaware of the full measure of the chaos and melee transpiring above.

Richard skirted toward the edge of the embankment, off to the left side, careful to stay out of the line of fire and managing to fire off a few shots of his own while he watched the blue mass of bodies as they fell down the embankment, crushing their fellow soldiers, some inadvertently skewering themselves on upturned bayonets.

By now, the blueshirts still standing atop the cliff were being rounded up as prisoners, and Richard's fellow comrades gathered alongside him to witness the carnage below. He glanced at the faces of the Confederate soldiers who watched, wide-eyed and disbelieving at the mess. His gaze again fell to the base of the hill, where the three boats that had transported the soldiers across the river were situated. Two of the three were bombarded with panic-stricken young men who, in no time at all, swamped the vessels, causing them to sink like stones.

The water was filled with screaming, thrashing, wounded, and drowning men. When one would surface, two others took hold in an attempt to save themselves, eventually pulling all three under. Richard glanced to his left where Cornwell stood, openmouthed, the bruise on his face showing in stark relief against the pallor of his skin. "Sweet God Almighty," the young man whispered, and crossed himself. "Never in my *life* . . ."

Richard had to agree. Never in his wildest dreams could he have imagined such a rout. It would go down as a huge Confederate victory, and that was a mighty good thing. All in all, it had turned out to be a profitable day for Jeff Davis's boys. This would be one worthy of writing home about. As Sarah had been harping at him to let her know how his days were filled, he supposed she might like to hear about this one.

***

Charleston, South Carolina
28 October, 1861

"Richard escaped unscathed," Sarah said as she read from a letter she had only just opened. "He says it was an unbelievably ridiculous sight, watching all of those Union soldiers hurl themselves down the side of a one-hundred-foot embankment."

"I suppose the alternative was much more appealing," Emily remarked dryly as she plucked a book from a shelf in the library.

"Oh, posh, Emily," Charlotte scoffed. "Those bluebellies are cowards! They proved it at Manassas Junction, and here they go again!"

"Does Richard say where he'll be camping next?" Jeffrey asked as he poured a drink for himself and one for his son-in-law. William took it from him with a murmur of thanks and stared pensively out the window.

"No." Sarah shook her head and silently finished reading the letter, handing it to her husband with a grim expression, keeping her private thoughts to herself.

"What do you hear from James Chestnut?" Charlotte asked her father as she settled into a window seat and took up her embroidery.

"Well, it's not supposed to be common knowledge, but Mason and Slidell have made it successfully out of Havana on an English mail packet, the *Trent*."

Charlotte glanced up from her sewing. "I didn't know they had left," she said.

Jeffrey nodded. "They slipped out of port on a blockade runner the night of October eleventh. If all goes well, they'll be granted an audience with Queen Victoria herself, and will be able to convince her to officially recognize the Confederacy and aid our cause."

Charlotte's brow wrinkled in a frown. "Father, you could be on the *Trent* yourself this very minute and you know it! Why did you not pursue a diplomatic mission like that, for heaven's sake? You well know it would have been yours for the taking!"

Jeffrey's lips formed the ghost of a smile. "I'd rather be close to home, my dear, but I thank you for your vote of confidence."

"I just don't understand it," Charlotte muttered and returned to her sewing.

Emily flipped through the pages of her book, listening to the surrounding conversation with half an ear. James Mason and John Slidell were old acquaintances of her father, both former lawyers and senators, apparently handpicked by Jeff Davis to bend the ear of a queen.

She shook her head and glanced about at the room and its occupants. *What a nice, happy family,* she mused. *All we're missing is the prodigal son and the rapist.* She opened her mouth to say so, with the express purpose of antagonizing everyone in the room, when Ruth's voice rang loudly in her ears.

Slow down, curb your tongue, and think, the wise older woman had told her. It was frustrating to curb one's tongue when it seemed to have a mind of its own. For Ruth, however, Emily would do just about anything.

"Is there danger of the *Trent* being intercepted?" William was asking her father.

"I suppose there's always the danger, but the *Trent* is a British vessel. If the Union were to interfere with her passage in any way, it would be a flagrant violation of international maritime law. Lincoln might as well declare war on England, as intercept that ship."

William raised his glass in salute to his father-in-law and said, "It's a delight to be associated with someone on the inside. Just think of all the things we know that nobody else does!"

Jeffrey chuckled and muttered a self-deprecating reply while Charlotte scowled at the pair of them and Sarah moved closer to one of the large windows that overlooked the spacious lawn to the back of the house. Emily watched her mother, whose face was drawn and was obviously in deep thought. For a moment, she pitied her greatly. In all of Emily's sixteen years, for her birthday had just come and gone—and quite unremarkably, at that—she couldn't remember a time when Sarah had been carefree or jovial. She was always, always serious. Perhaps it was the feelings of responsibility for Bentley, or her driven determination to see that at least some of her children were successful in life—whatever it was, it had not made a happy woman out of Sarah Matthews Birmingham.

For one insane moment, Emily wanted to put her arms around her mother's thin shoulders and squeeze. Thankfully, the impulse passed, and Emily rose from her chair, bidding a curt farewell to those in the room and walked to her bedroom, book in hand.

Something tickled at the back of her mind and she couldn't quite determine what it was about the past few moments she was trying to retrieve. She skipped mentally over the conversations, dwelling for a moment on the *Trent*. What was it William had said about the whole thing? That they were a lucky family to be privy to confidential information because of Jeffrey's connections to the Confederate government?

Emily stopped in her tracks in the middle of the staircase, her heart ceasing its rhythm, and then resuming with a tremendous *thud*. Of course! Of course! Why had she not seen it before? Ruth had planted the seed by telling her to slow down and think, and William, in his bumbling way had given her the spark of an idea that just might give her a purpose—a way to make something good happen.

Emily propelled herself up the rest of the stairs on legs that trembled from the excitement. She reached her bedroom, slamming the door behind her and rushing to stand before the full-length mirror in the corner that she usually bypassed due to a lack of interest. Pulling her hair free of the childish braids she had worn ever since she could remember, she fluffed her fingers through her hair and pulled it to the back of her head, taking careful stock of her features.

It was manageable, she supposed. Her face was passably pretty—at least her mother used to tell her that when she was little and hadn't developed her adolescent mean streak. The hair was darkening to a shade of rich medium-auburn and was thick and full. She was maturing into something tall and graceful, not the gangly thing she had been ever since childhood, and she was filling and curving in all the right places.

Funny—she'd never seen a need for it before. Truthfully, she hadn't *had* a need for it before. She was at the brink of adulthood, with a brain that was years ahead of its time, and it was time to put those assets to good use. She would soften her approach to the family, keep her ears perked, start attending social functions with her parents and Charlotte as she should have been doing for over a year now, and she would absorb *everything*.

When the time was right, she would take what she was learning, and share it. With the Union.

Emily was going to become a spy.

***

Cleveland, Ohio
8 November, 1861

"Put your leg up on this pillow," Amanda said to her husband as he sat reading the paper in the small parlor.

Per chuckled even as he allowed his wife to make him more comfortable. "You're going to spoil me, good lady," he said to Amanda and smoothed a strand of hair that hung loose at the side of her face.

"No, I'm going to keep you alive with us for a long time to come."

"Amanda, I've told you I'm not going anywhere," he said with a wink.

And I don't believe you, Amanda thought, and seeking to distract herself, motioned to the newspaper her husband still held in his hands. "What does the newspaper say today?" she asked after retrieving a tray of small, open-faced sandwiches and tea she had placed on the sideboard. She dispersed the contents as Per glanced at the paper once more before folding it in his lap and accepting the small china plate on which his goat-cheese sandwich was prettily arranged.

"Apparently one of our Union ships, the *San Jacinto,* fired two shots across the bow of the *Trent,* a British mail steamer. They boarded her and captured two Confederate emissaries who were on their way to make an appeal to the Queen of England."

"Where are they taking the captives?" Amanda asked.

"Boston."

"This could cause trouble with England."

"Yes, it could. But apparently the Union sees it as a great act of nobility on the part of the captain of the *San Jacinto.* He's being lauded as a hero. We need it after that disgraceful episode with the Quaker guns."

"The Quaker guns?"

Per nodded. "McClellan was afraid to advance on the Confederates surrounding Washington, D.C., because of the reports of all the 'guns' they supposedly had trained on the city. When the Confederates pulled back toward Richmond and abandoned their holdings, McClellan's men discovered that the 'guns' were actually large logs, painted black to look like guns."

Amanda stopped chewing. "We were held at bay by logs?"

Per laughed, and then slowly shook his head. "Yes, we were held at bay by logs. The paper also says Lincoln is still upset over the loss at Ball's Bluff, and is mourning the loss of his friend."

"Who was his friend?"

Per glanced at the paper he still held in his lap. "Colonel Edward Baker," he answered. "It says he was one of the first to the top of the hill at Ball's Bluff and was killed instantly. He had been a close, personal friend of the Lincolns. They even named their second son after him."

"He must have grieved when he heard the news," Amanda murmured. "Poor man."

Per nodded. "One of Lincoln's friends is quoted here as saying that the president clutched his heart and staggered down the street as though the weight of the world were on his shoulders."

"I worry about Ivar," Amanda murmured, and Per nodded silently. It was nearly impossible to ignore the fact that he was gone. They cared for little Inger day and night, and she was a constant reminder to them of her father.

"He'll be alright," Per said. "He's a Viking, you know."

Amanda laughed, and it warmed his heart. "That's true," she said. "He has fierce, fighting blood in his veins."

"That's right. If anyone gives him trouble, he'll just lop off their heads."

Amanda took a bite of her sandwich and washed it down with a sip of tea. "They really weren't so bad, you know, the Vikings. They were colonizers."

"Mmm hmm." Per shook his head. *You should tell that to the poor monks whose villages they "colonized,"* he thought with a fond grimace.

The front door burst open and Inger came bouncing into the house from the front porch. "I saw the moon!" the child squealed in delight. "And it's not even night time!"

Amanda gathered the little girl into her lap and kissed her soft cheek. "Did you look through Bestemor's telescope?"

"Yes!"

"And did the moon look big?"

"This big!" Inger held her little hands in the shape of a circle. She spied the sandwiches on the tray and made a dive for the coffee table.

"No," Amanda said and set the child next to her on the sofa. "We use our manners. I will get a sandwich for you."

Amanda handed the child a plate and sandwich, watching in amusement as Inger ate the food with relish. Amanda shrugged and said on a sigh, "Well, I suppose we have time to work on that."

CHAPTER 33

"One war at a time."
—*Abraham Lincoln*

***

New Orleans, Louisiana
15 November, 1861

Marie sniffed the paper she held in her hand, missing her mother. The letter smelled of her perfume.

Ma chère Marie,

How I miss you! I pray for you every day, my sweet, and hope this letter finds you healthy and whole. There is much going on these days, it seems, yet nothing remains changed with your father's condition. Your aunt and uncle have employed the services of a very qualified physician—went all the way to New York, in fact, to find the man, but still your father sleeps. I pray that the next letter I send will contain better news on that score.

As for life in the North, we are privy, here, to much information. Your Uncle James has influential friends, both in business and government, and they are full of news each time he meets with them. This affair over the British steamer, the Trent, has the English queen in quite a tizzy. She is demanding the release of the two Confederate emissaries, and I'm sure you've heard in the local papers, (not to mention your father's!) that London is all but calling for war. The South, as I understand it, is elated. Has this been your experience? Are our countryfolk ecstatic over this turn of events?

At this, Marie nodded. People in New Orleans were indeed ecstatic over the prospect of war between England and the Union. The United States could not possibly hope to conduct and finance two wars at the same time, and the fact that Britain was so outraged with Lincoln and the North surely meant that the Queen would soon officially recognize the Confederacy and fund its efforts to gain independence from the mother country.

Secretary of State Seward has been urging President Lincoln to consider that war with England may be just the thing to unify the Northern and Southern states, but by all we have heard here, Lincoln is resisting such a notion. I cannot help but believe him to be in the right of it. War with England is not going to mend what has been broken. As it stands now, the two Confederate emissaries are still being held prisoner here, but I believe it will not be long before Lincoln sets them free, if only in the hopes that cooler heads will prevail . . .

Marie finished the letter and folded it carefully, placing it in the small, wooden box in the parlor where she had begun storing all of her mother's letters. She had hoped for better news about her father, but would apparently have to continue to hope, because the reality was still a depressing one.

She checked her image quickly in the ornate oval mirror near the front door, tucking a stray hair behind her ear and smoothing her eyebrows into place. She left her home, locked the door behind her (and felt a stab of anger over the fact that it was a necessity), then climbed into her waiting carriage, and urged the horse onward toward Constance Braxton's farm.

It was a Saturday, and as had been the custom for several weeks now, the Fromere family had finished their work early in the day and were free to spend the afternoons in Constance's run-down shack, taking lessons from their instructor, Miss Brissot. Thanks to an overabundance of dense undergrowth, once Marie was far into Braxton property, the carriage was hidden not only from the surrounding roads but from the humble Braxton home, as well. Poor Mrs. Braxton was so consumed with keeping her children fed that she was little concerned with the comings and goings of her older two offspring as they spent their time in the dilapidated outbuildings dotting the property.

Marie felt a surge of affection for the Fromere family as she quickly made her way down the dirt road that led to the farm. They were so bright and eager to learn, and Marie had felt such a sense of accomplishment in the past few weeks over their progress. She was as proud of them as she had ever been of any of her students, perhaps a bit more so because she knew that for these good folk, it was forbidden for them to learn.

When she considered the family's potential, individually and as a unit, she marveled at the idiocy of the legislation that made it illegal for those of African descent to be educated. The slaveholder was perpetuating a myth that had existed for generations—that the slave didn't have the intellectual capacity for learning. It was a farce, Marie realized as she halted the carriage near the shack and secured her horse. The slave learned as well as a white person. The problem for the slaveholder, she mused grimly as she walked toward the shack, was that if his slaves became educated, they might then find a way to escape from the system that held them bound. The economy of the South would then collapse, and those living in splendor might find themselves in the same squalor as their servants.

The Fromeres greeted her in their usual solemn and respectful manner; Noah, the youngest son, still the only one of the family willing to meet her gaze with frank openness. Marie unpacked the supplies that she brought with her each session, and doled out the chalkboards and readers to each family member. Constance attended their informal meetings when she wasn't helping her mother, and she currently sat with the family, acting as an aid to Marie.

"You are all doing so well," she praised the Fromeres two hours later as they paused for a moment to stretch their limbs and eat a light snack. "Are you enjoying the lessons?" she asked Pauline.

"Oh, yes'm," the woman answered. "We look forward to this time each week."

"And befo' long," Noah said, "We's gon' be readin' big books."

"Absolutely you will," Marie agreed. "I'll find some for you to take home next time I see you. You must take care that nobody sees them, however."

"Yeah, like that Bussey fella'," Abel commented quietly.

Marie's ears perked up. "Has someone been giving you trouble?"

"Someone always been givin' us trouble, Miss," Pauline answered somberly.

"Who's Bussey?"

"He's the son of a plantation owner 'bout thirty mile away. He don' believe we's freed folk." Noah scowled.

Marie studied the solemn faces of the beleaguered family. "There has to be a way to get you north," she murmured. "Do you want to leave?"

Justis cleared his throat. "This life be the only one we've known, Miss, but we sho' would like a chance to start somewheres fresh."

Marie nodded. "I should tell you, though, that there are those up north who are just as nasty to black folk as are people down here. You may face resistance wherever you go. I should think, though," she added, thinking of Luke's avid abolition commitments throughout his life, "that there are many who would be willing to help you in the New England area. Perhaps not everyone, but more than you'll find here."

They nodded their agreement.

"In the meantime," Marie continued, "we're going to work hard on your reading and writing skills, and on your spoken English—the more you sound like the people with whom you're trying to live, the more readily you'll be accepted." *I hope,* she silently added. "And do your best to stay away from this Bussey, and others of his type. Let's just keep you out of trouble as much as possible."

Constance caught Marie's arm as the lesson finished and the Fromeres quietly took their leave. "I want you to know how grateful I am, Miss Brissot, that you're doing this for them," the young girl said. "Someday I want to be a teacher just like you."

Marie ran a hand over the girl's hair and affectionately tugged on the braid that hung down her back. "You already are a teacher, Connie."

When Marie returned from school early the following week, she found a letter waiting for her, postmarked from New York. Curiously, she studied the envelope for a moment as she absently set aside her satchel containing her school supplies, and eventually took a seat at the dining-room table.

She opened the letter and unfolded it, gazing curiously at the scrawled writing that adorned the whole of it. Glancing at the bottom, she spied a name she didn't recognize. With a shrug, she drew her eyes to the top of the page and began reading.

Dear Miss Brissot,

You don't know me, and in fact you must find it odd to receive mail from a stranger, but I must tell you that I have met your mother and greatly admire her. My name is Daniel O'Shea, and I am a business associate of your cousin, Luke Birmingham. I had the opportunity to spend some time with Luke and your mother as they traveled north for Boston, and your mother spoke fondly of you.

I suppose I am writing to you now to pass along your mother's well-wishes, although you've surely heard from her by now, and to tell you that I personally find your strength and determination to stay behind very brave. You must love your students, and they are fortunate indeed to have your instruction.

Marie read the rest of the letter, which told her briefly about its writer, his life and family. He closed by expressing fond admiration for Luke and considerate wishes for her continued health and welfare. She looked up from the letter and out the window at the setting sun, stunned that a stranger would take the time to pen her such a kind letter.

Who was he, this Daniel O'Shea, that he would be so impressed by her family as to take a personal interest in her life? Glancing down again at the neat script, she experienced a small stab of envy that this stranger had seen her parents even more recently than she had.

"Well, Marie," she finally sighed aloud into the quiet stillness of the home, "you could very well have gone with them." No, she admitted, she couldn't have. Her place, for whatever the reason, was in New Orleans. She closed her eyes, mentally touring the city and surrounding countryside—the hustle and bustle within the city limits, and the peaceful, languid bayous and waterways. The profusion of trees and flowers, the humid feel of the air that was such a part of her life. Truth be told, she couldn't imagine a place she would rather live. The setting itself was so beautiful it made her throat ache. And the rich Arcadian culture with its French influence was a reflection of who she was.

She opened her eyes, thinking of the people who had beaten her father, who hated people like the Fromeres and would gladly see them forever in captivity, to serve their own selfish purposes. Well, she mused with a sigh, the place itself was wonderful. Some of the people were not. She supposed such was the case wherever one went.

Shaking herself out of her momentary reverie, Marie retrieved a paper and pen, and again sat at the table. What to write? "Dear Mr. O'Shea, you may want to limit further correspondence with me, because although I'm sure my mother neglected to mention it, I am generally known in these parts as Hester Prynne, and I wear a scarlet 'A' upon my chest regularly as befits my station in polite society . . ." Smirking, she shook her head and twirled the pen back and forth in her fingers.

Dear Mr. O'Shea, she finally wrote:
Your letter was very kind, and I thank you for taking the time to write to me . . .

***

New York, New York
25 November, 1861

"Danny Boy, I tell you if I were your age, I would enlist with the Navy!" Gavin boomed over dinner.

"I'm busy here," Daniel said. "Between the bank and my carpentry, I don't have time to run off with the Navy."

"Son, you have no sense of patriotism."

"This isn't my country."

"Oh, Daniel," Brenna finally interjected, "this *is* your country! You don't even remember Ireland!"

Daniel sighed. He truly didn't want to discuss it. He felt absolutely no compulsion to serve a country that would rather he had stayed across the ocean and starved. "I have too much to do," he repeated.

"I'll bet they pay well," Gavin said.

Daniel snorted his laughter. "I can guarantee that whatever they offer to pay me won't be as much as I'm making now. Besides, are you trying to get rid of me?"

"No, Danny, I'm not trying to get rid of you." Gavin was quiet for a moment, thoughtfully chewing his food. "I want you to feel like you belong here," he admitted. "I want this country to mean something to you."

"Da, I can appreciate that, but I don't think this place will ever mean to me what it does to you."

Later, in the quiet of his home, Daniel studied the image of a young woman living thousands of miles away. He wondered if she had received his letter, and assuming she had, he wondered if she must think him insane to write to her. His thoughts swirled together, snatches of the dinner conversation coming to the fore.

The Navy—Gavin wanted him to enlist with the Navy. Well, that was a fine thing. Daniel shook his head with a short laugh. The only way he'd ever enlist with the Navy is if it offered him guaranteed passage to New Orleans.

With a reluctant sigh, he finally gathered his jacket and made his way out into the night, hitching his horse to the wagon and going into the city to meet with a man he'd been avoiding. He figured he owed it to Smitts to at least explain why he had been absent from the weekend fights ever since taking employ at the bank. He was working hard each day, trying to make a difference for people whose lives were changing because of his efforts, and he didn't want his own conduct or appearance to detract from that.

The tavern was unchanged, as always, and a surprised roar of the regulars greeted him at the entrance. Daniel shoved his way through the crowd to Smitts, who was standing behind the bar. "Just wanted to let you know I'm retired, now," he shouted to be heard above the ruckus.

Smitts leaned forward, his bloodshot eyes open wide. "You can't quit! I've made arrangements! For weeks now, there've been bets placed on you and my new find!"

"I'm sorry. I just can't do it anymore." He offered his hand to the man behind the bar, but Smitts made no move to take it. Instead, his eyes darted to a point just to the right of Daniel's ear. Daniel felt a prickle of unease settle along his spine and he turned, but too late. He was spun from behind by a man who stood easily a foot taller than his own six-foot-three. The pummeling that followed was a blur. Because Daniel had been caught by surprise at the first, the initial blows to his head left him stunned and barely able to put up any fight at all. He dimly registered the noise of the crowd, growing more faint with each passing moment. It wasn't long before he couldn't hear anything at all.

It was impossible for Daniel to tell how much time had passed when he finally awoke again. He painfully attempted to open his eyes and take stock of his surroundings, but only one eye would cooperate, and then only partially. The smell of a fire permeated his senses, and his blurred vision showed him a small room, rough wooden planking on the floors and a fire in a small hearth. At his side was a woman he was sure he knew—the purple dress was the last thing he saw before he again surrendered to the dark, the pain in his head and midsection fading in the face of his oblivion.

His stomach was on fire. It was Daniel's first conscious thought when he again awoke, and he couldn't decide how to remedy it. Forcing his eyes open again, and still only one eye cooperating, he saw the small room wherein he lay, this time with the aid of the light that entered through a window facing east. Casting his gaze downward to his burning abdomen, he spied a wrinkled hand applying a salve of sorts to a cut that spanned from the side of his waist and across his belly to the lower rib on the other side.

Looking up in panic, he tried to sit, only to be pushed back onto the bed by hands that were attached to arms encased in the purple dress.

"Lavender," he gasped. "What . . . what . . ."

"Ssshhhh," the woman whispered, "you'll be fine, Danny. Just let the man care for your cuts."

"Who?"

"This is my friend. His name is Jones—he's a bit like a doctor."

Like a doctor? Daniel winced and tried to sit up again. "I think I should go home," he mumbled against Lavender's straining arms.

"Lay still, boy," the man growled. Daniel took a good look at Jones and wasn't comforted in the least by his appearance. He looked like an old sea dog—thin, wizened, with a grizzle of stubble on his chin and a patch covering one eye. "I know what I be about."

Daniel coughed, and with it felt a rising sense of nausea that he was sure was about to humiliate him. He lay back down upon the bed and tried to focus his thoughts and bring to the fore exactly why he was with Lavender and her sailor and not in the comfort of his own home.

"What happened?" he whispered when the coughing passed.

"Ah, lovey, you were done for, that's what. Smitts hired the giant to fight you, and told all his customers he was a sure win. They all placed bets against you, and Smitts told the big oaf to beat you however he had to. I heard him say it weeks ago. Only you never came."

"I've been busy . . ."

"And Smitts has been boiling mad. And o' course none of us know where you live, so he could only wait for you to show up. After the giant finished with you, I paid young Johnny to help me drag you here to Jones."

Daniel sighed and winced in pain as Jones secured a bandage to the cut. "I'd like to know when Smitts decided knives were part of the fight."

Lavender clucked her tongue. "Poor dearie. You best stay clear of Smitts for awhile. His giant was giving him a bigger portion of the winnings. I think he'd a been happy with you dead."

Daniel shook his head, regretting the movement as he did so. He was bound to have gotten a good beating sooner or later, but he had rather expected that it would be a fair fight. Smitts hadn't seen the last of him. He turned his head toward Lavender as Jones stepped away from the bed, having completed his task. "I can't believe I slept through the whole night—I best be getting home for Sunday dinner," he said. "My mother will worry."

Lavender's brows shot up in surprise. "Sunday? Dearie, it's Monday morning—you slept right through Sunday dinner."

Daniel shoved himself upright on the bed in shock, grabbing his head and midsection at the protesting pain and fighting a wave of nausea.

"Sit still, boy, you wanna mess up me handiwork?" Jones shouted at him, moving to shove him back down onto the bed.

"Lavender," Daniel choked, "you must get my shirt! I have a job at the bank . . . my mother must be sick with worry . . ."

Lavender appeared, carrying a bloody rag with sleeves. "Here's your shirt, lovey, but it's a bloomin' mess! You can't wear it like this. Wait!" she said, running through a doorway to the left of the hearth. "I have something else," she called, and came back carrying a coarse, tan work shirt that had seen better days but was in much better condition than the fiasco that was what was left of Daniel's former shirt.

He thrust his arms into the sleeves as the woman held the shirt for him, and fumbling with the buttons that stretched the material a shade too taut across his chest, allowed her to help. She pushed his fingers aside and deftly fastened the garment, covering the profusion of ugly dark bruises that peppered his midsection around the bandage. She smoothed her hands over his shoulders, and ran a hand through his disheveled hair as well. She murmured an apology when he winced in pain at her ministrations and said, "Danny, we cleaned off the blood, but boy-o, you're not your usual pretty self. You best go straight home."

"I can't, Lavender, I have a job at a bank here in the city—what time is it?"

"Half-past ten."

Daniel cursed and shoved himself off the bed, staggering a bit before gaining his equilibrium. "I don't suppose you have my horse and wagon?"

"Yes, out back, but . . ."

"Lavender, thank you for your help. I won't soon forget it." Daniel limped toward Jones, who stood off to one side, eyeing him in dubious scorn.

"You shouldn't be outta that bed," the little man wheezed.

"Thank you, as well. I will pay you for your care." Daniel stumbled from the small house and taking stock of his surroundings, followed the wall of the building to the back where, true to Lavender's word, his horse and wagon awaited him. Lavender rushed out behind him and shoved him lightly aside when he attempted to harness the horse to the wagon. He thanked her again for her help, cursing his own vulnerability.

He painfully made his way down the street and across town, hoping against hope that Strickland would give him some time to go home and clean himself up, maybe even give him the day to rest. It was not to be. When he finally reached Strickland's office, Daniel was met with disgusted fury.

"How can you *dare* to come into this establishment not only late, but looking like the hounds of hell?" Strickland quivered. "You may consider yourself terminated, Mr. O'Shea!"

"But sir, please, I can explain . . ."

"Get out of my office!"

"Please!"

"Shall I have you escorted?"

Daniel looked at the man once, hard, before finally turning on his heel and holding his head high as he made his way to the stairwell, clenching his teeth against the pain with each step. The frustrated rage he felt as he made his way down the stairs and out into the bright sunlight had his head hurting so much he felt it would surely explode before he made it home.

It's my own fault. I should never have gone back into that tavern, should never have been fighting in the first place. Daniel finally maneuvered the wagon out of the bustling city and toward the countryside, clenching the reins, grateful his horse seemed to know the way home. He dreaded seeing his mother and father. They must be worried sick by now, wondering where he was. He saw them every day on a regular basis, and they would surely have noted his absence yesterday. He was beginning to feel much as he had as a child when he knew he had broken the rules and stayed away from home too late.

When he reached his parents' home, he was dismayed to find them gone. Assuming they were probably out looking for him, he made his way down the hill to his own small home. Once there, he unhitched the horse and went inside, passing the large mirror his mother had placed above the mantle years before when he built the home. His face was utterly unrecognizable. It was no wonder Strickland had exhibited such disdain; however, as Daniel thought of his abrupt dismissal the anger again surfaced. He felt the weight of the applicants whose paperwork he was to have supervised, felt the pain of their loss because of Strickland's prejudice, and he tightened his hands into fists, moving forward and placing them on the mantle.

He rested his forehead on his hands and took deep, even breaths, only to realize that it caused him intense pain. It was amusing, he supposed, that the only part of his body that didn't hurt were his hands. His hands were usually the first to experience pain—they had been broken numerous times, yet this time he had been caught so completely by surprise that he hadn't even had the chance to fight back.

It was too much—it was all too much. He sank to the floor, taking stock of his life. He had been fighting for years—fighting the thoughtless children who said and did cruel things, fighting a system that, although theoretically designed for his success, seemed determined to have him fail. He had been fighting the pain of his brother's death for over a decade, and he supposed that was at the crux of it all. Colin had been his best friend, his playmate, his confidante, his *brother*, and he missed him so much he felt the tightening in his chest at the very thought. Daniel slowly rocked back and forth, his fists pressed against his swollen eyes, as if pushing hard enough would heighten the physical pain enough to take away the pain in his heart.

I must get away, I must get away . . .

He thought numbly of his father's suggestion that he enlist in the Navy, and for the first time, it was the only prospect in his life that looked even slightly appealing.

He registered the tapping on his front door, the sound of his parents' voices, and their exclamations of dismay at the sight of their twenty-seven-year-old son, large and full of life, rocking himself on the floor. "I'm sorry," he groaned as he felt his mother's arms encircle his shoulders and his father's hand upon his knee.

"It will be all right, Daniel, my boy," he heard his father murmur. "It will be all right."

CHAPTER 34

"Students have all gone to war. College suspended. And God help the right."
—*Registrar's journal, Centenary College*

***

Boston, Massachusetts
27 November, 1861

"I'm not altogether certain about this," Camille muttered to her mother as they sat in the downtown Boston meeting hall for an American Anti-Slavery Society meeting.

"It's fine," Elizabeth whispered in response and patted her daughter's hand. "It's high time you attended. I should have been bringing you all along."

Camille glanced about at the Society members, surprised to see many of her family's social circle, much as Robert had suggested. The bulk of those assembled, however, were respectable middle-class folk—largely of Quaker or New England Puritan heritage, her mother had said earlier. They were God-fearing people who lived and died by the oath that slavery was an abomination and should be immediately abolished.

The origins of formal anti-slavery societies had begun years before, had started small and had eventually grown in numbers that exceeded 160,000. It was a small minority of the thirty-two-some-odd million combined population of the Union and Confederacy, but it was still an impressive number.

Camille's Aunt Jenny sat on the other side of Elizabeth, and on Camille's immediate left was Abigail Van Dyke, with her mother, Dolly seated next to her. Presently the meeting began, and Camille focused her attention on the balding man of nondescript stature who stood before the crowd, speaking in a firm voice that rang with authority.

Yes, most assuredly, William Lloyd Garrison intimidated her, Camille decided. It wasn't as though he were rude, or arrogant, but he was a man who clearly knew what his life was about, and that life had been built around seeing the abolition of slavery come to fruition. He was married and the father of five children, who all supported the cause and believed in it.

"You needn't look at him as though he'll swoop down and carry you off to the gallows," Abigail whispered in Camille's ear.

Camille glanced askance at the other woman, who was smiling. "I don't think that," she whispered back. "I'm just afraid he'll look into my eyes and discover me for the fraud that I am."

"Do you not believe in the abolitionist cause?"

"I do, I just am not so . . . so . . ." Camille waved a hand about at the people seated around them. "So fervent about it, I suppose."

Abigail patted Camille's hand but refrained from further comment. After a few moments more, she leaned in close again and subtly pointed to a man who was seated two rows ahead of them, off to the left. His profile was visible to them, and Camille glimpsed a strikingly handsome face.

"That's Jacob Taylor," Abigail whispered.

"Who?"

"Your sister's editor."

Camille glanced at Abigail in surprise. "Anne's?"

"Yes, when she was posing as Adam Jones—Jacob was her employer."

Camille shook her head. "Did Luke never keep his mouth shut about anything?" she muttered under her breath, and received a jab in her ribs from her mother's elbow. Elizabeth followed the gesture with a shushing sound, and Camille scowled at her.

Abigail's shoulders shook with suppressed laughter. "He only told me the good things," she whispered. "I'm sure the severe family skeletons are still in the proverbial closet."

"I don't think so," Camille whispered back. "There's not much more to tell!"

The meeting continued with speeches from long-time members, and was concluded with some remarks delivered by one of the most eloquent speakers Camille had ever been privileged to hear. She had been whispering again with Abigail and missed his name.

He spoke on the conditions of slave life, of the natural inclination for the human spirit to crave freedom, and of the necessity to see that such atrocities did not continue further. As he talked, some of the turns of phrase and thoughts expressed began to sound familiar, and when he finished speaking, she turned to her mother amidst the thunderous applause and said, "Is that *him?*"

Elizabeth was clapping her hands and turned to Camille, her eyes glistening. "Who?"

"Is that Frederick Douglass?"

Elizabeth nodded with a misty smile and turned her attention back to the front of the crowd. The reception that followed the meeting consisted of Society members mingling and speaking of Society business, the current state of affairs, and general gossip. She caught snatches of conversation as she made her way to the front of the room with her mother, Aunt Jenny, and Abigail.

"McClellan is dragging his feet!" one woman said as they passed. "He is whipping his army into shape for nothing! He's creating a fine-tuned machine that he's not willing to use!"

It wasn't an original opinion; Camille continued to read the papers daily and knew that the great majority in the North were disgusted by McClellan's refusal to move on the Confederacy. His excuse was that the enemy numbers were vastly superior to his own—facts which often proved erroneous. More often than not, his troops greatly outnumbered those of the enemy, yet his caution led him to believe the opposite. His reluctance to move into action was exacerbated by his Secret Service aid, Allan Pinkerton, Anne's new employer. Pinkerton had been relying on information that was proving to be false, greatly exaggerating the numbers of the enemy, especially those not only on the other side of the Potomac, but surrounding Richmond as well.

Camille had asked Anne in a letter sent only a week before what she knew of the faulty information Pinkerton was relying upon. Now that she was making a concerted effort to be an Informed Woman, Camille found her curiosity had no bounds, and wasn't it just so convenient to have a sister employed by the very man who was making a laughingstock of the president's pet general? She found herself awaiting Anne's reply with interest.

The talk continued swirling about the room in a similar vein—the war being the focus of every conversation. How long would it last? Would the states ever again form one body? Did the Southerners deserve to be part of the Union again? Would emancipation ever be an official policy of the war?

Camille soaked in all of the bits and pieces, absorbing the information and analyzing the people who were speaking, placing them into categories according to their appearances, tone of voice, and gesture. Some made her smile, others made her scowl in derision. By the time they finally reached the front of the room, her head was swimming with the external stimuli.

Her mother was speaking to someone, and when she pulled her forward to meet the man, her tongue froze to the roof of her mouth and she was momentarily stunned. He smiled gently at her, his soft brown skin covering a face that was intelligent and perceptive. "It's a pleasure to meet you, Miss Birmingham," he said.

"Ffff . . . Fred . . . Mr. Douglass!" she stammered. "I'm . . . It's such an honor—I've read your book! It was amazing," she blurted, knowing that when she left for home, she would curse herself for yammering like a fool.

"I appreciate the compliment," Frederick Douglass replied, taking her hand and holding it gently between his own. "I'm glad you're in attendance here tonight," he added. "It's always nice to welcome new faces."

"I . . . I . . . my brother was usually . . . that is, he's enlisted now, but we thought we would come tonight..." *Oh, I am the veriest idiot.*

"Yes, I know your brother, and I'm so glad you have come in his stead. Please do join us again, won't you?"

Camille nodded dumbly and stared at the man, his aging, kind face, the black suit and snowy white shirt, tailored to perfection, and the coarse black hair that was turning to white. She thought back on the things she'd read in his autobiography about his years as a slave and felt her eyes smart. Clearing her throat gruffly, she smiled when he warmly pressed his hands against hers and moved on to another who was clamoring for his attention.

"Excuse me," she mumbled to her mother and Abigail, who called after her as she rushed through the throng of people toward the door. She reached the inner door of the auditorium and walked through it, standing in the foyer for a moment and attempting to catch her breath. One lone tear escaped and trailed a path down her cheek, and she brushed at it impatiently.

Crying? When was the last time she'd cried, for heaven's sake? She hadn't even cried after Bull Run. But here he was, in the flesh, and he had escaped an awful life of bondage and created a life for himself that was full of purpose and meaning, and he was so eloquent it took her breath away.

"May I offer you this?" someone at her elbow murmured. She turned to find Jacob Taylor, Anne's former editor, holding a snowy white handkerchief and extending it in her direction. She took it with a mumbled "thank you," and dabbed at her eyes. She folded it carefully and handed it back to the man, flushing to the roots of her hair.

"Are you well?" he asked, his frank brown eyes assessing her entire form.

"Quite," she sniffed. "I've just met Frederick Douglass, only to stammer and yammer and make a complete cake of myself."

Her companion laughed. "He often has that effect on people."

"It was most embarrassing."

Jacob Taylor leaned against the doorway with his shoulder, his hands buried deep in his pockets. He stood a good foot taller than she, and looked down upon her with the same assessing eye as he had when offering her the handkerchief. "I noticed you in the crowd," he said, gesturing with his head. "You like to watch people, don't you."

She cocked a brow. And what business was it of his if she did? "Perhaps."

"You're like your sister that way."

"Anne?" Camille laughed. Nobody had *ever* compared her to Anne.

"Yes. She's a people-watcher too."

"Well, it might have been a little less embarrassing for the family if she'd kept her dress on while doing it," Camille stated, her tone flat.

Instead of being offended, Jacob tipped his head back in laughter. When he subsided, he said, "Oh, come now. Nobody knows of her escapades *but* the family. Anne told me that the only others outside who knew were your groom and her friend who works for Pinkerton."

"And now the Van Dykes. Luke couldn't keep it to himself, apparently," Camille muttered, glancing back into the crowded room.

"Dolly and Abigail are not gossips," Jacob said. "You needn't worry it will travel any farther." He eyed her speculatively for a moment. "Would it be so very bad if it did? Are you not even a little bit proud of your sister?"

Camille opened her mouth to say no, and was surprised. "Yes, I suppose I am. It was very brave of her. It was also very stupid."

"You would never do the same thing yourself."

"Never."

"Do you write? Do you enjoy writing?"

Camille paused, her brow wrinkled. "I don't suppose I've done enough to judge one way or the other. I write letters—that's the extent of it."

"Would you ever consider it, do you suppose?"

She frowned up into the prying man's face. "Why, sir, is that any of your concern?"

"Well, miss, let me say this—if you are even *half* of the people-observer that your sister was, you probably have remarkable insight. Should you ever decide you'd like to try your hand at writing, I hope you'll call on me. And now," he said, motioning again with his head toward the crowded room, "you'd best make an appearance. We've not been formally introduced, and I would hate for your reputation to suffer for being seen in private conversation with a confirmed old bachelor."

Camille eyed him, one brow cocked. He wasn't exactly what she would term *old*, but he did present a valid point. It wouldn't do at all to be seen with him unchaperoned. She thanked him for the use of his handkerchief and walked slowly back into the room, conscious of his eyes upon her back as she moved to find her mother.

CHAPTER 35

"You might as well attempt to put out the flames of a burning house with a squirt-gun. I think this is to be a long war—very long—much longer than any politician thinks."
—*William Tecumseh Sherman*

***

Charleston, South Carolina
4 December, 1861

"Well, what do you think?" Emily asked as she turned a slow pivot before Ruth and Mary. They stood outside in front of Ruth's and Mary's shack, in the darkening, cool December night. Emily was dressed in a gown of forest green that dropped to the edge of her shoulders, showing an expanse of delicate skin, with a nipped waist that flared out over the large hoops and petticoats that were all the rage.

Her thick red hair was piled in curls atop her head, a few strands left down to softly brush against her neck. The flush in her cheeks betrayed her excitement, and her green eyes glittered with barely suppressed energy.

"Oh, mercy, child," Ruth breathed. "What's happened to you?"

"I'm doing it, Ruth! I've slowed down, I'm using my head, and I'm going to make a difference."

"And how are you going to do that?"

"I'm going with my father tonight to the Chestnuts' Christmas ball. Mother is under the weather."

Ruth drew her brow together. "I'm not following."

"I'm just going along to smile, to pay my respects to the Confederate royalty, and listen for all I'm worth. Then, should the opportunity ever arise to *pass along* the things I've overheard . . ."

Mary suddenly grabbed Emily's arm. "You're going to *spy*? Emily, are you insane?" She glanced first in one direction, then another, and pulled Emily with her to the steps of the shack. With Ruth coming along behind, the two of them hustled Emily inside the shack and closed the door.

"Emily," Ruth said firmly. "I told you to think. Not to be crazy."

"Oh, Ruth, it's the first sane idea I've had!"

"Is this what you've been so secretive about the last few weeks?" Mary's voice was strained.

Emily nodded. "I told Mother I want to start taking more of an active role in my life as a Matthews-Birmingham. I said I've always had an avid interest in politics, which is true, and I'd like to accompany father to his formal functions whenever he has the time and feels inclined to let me follow along."

Ruth's eyes clouded. "You are so like your brother, child, I can hardly believe it. The next thing you know you'll be moving out west too, because your parents and the neighbors are ready to string you from the nearest tree. What you're contemplating is treason, you do realize that?"

"Ruth, it's not treason to me, because I owe no loyalty to this current sham of a government. The Confederate States of America has waged war on the United States, and I am loyal to the Union. I am loyal to a president who thinks the enslavement of an entire people is a heinous thing." Emily's eyes were bright and filmed over with tears she blinked impatiently back. "It's not treason. I'm going to try, in my own way, to right a hideous wrong."

The women with her were silent, and Mary sniffed, wiping her fingertips against her face. When Emily leaned forward, Mary's arms encircled her in a warm embrace, and she whispered in her best friend's ear, "I'm so afraid for you."

"Don't be," Emily whispered back. "There are worse things."

She embraced Ruth as well, and kissed the older woman on the cheek. "I love you, Aunt Ruth," she murmured. "I always have."

They were interrupted by a knock on the door, and Ruth immediately tensed. Emily backed behind the door, and Ruth opened it a crack, only to heave a sigh of relief. She opened it wider to admit Joshua, who stepped inside. "I came to see if you . . ." He stopped short when he caught sight of Emily. His eyes traveled her form from the top of her head to the hem of her dress that swept along the crude wooden floor.

"What on earth are you about?" he asked when he finally found his voice, although when it came out, it was beyond strained.

"Don't you think it's time I took my place in genteel society, Joshua?" she asked.

He was quiet for so long, Emily decided he wasn't going to answer her.

"I suppose I thought you'd stay around here forever," he finally admitted. "You are certainly old enough. Girls are married at your age . . ."

She laughed and slapped him on the arm with the fan she held clutched in one gloved hand. "Don't be ridiculous," she said. "I'm not out to find a husband—perish the thought! I'm on a clandestine mission."

"Emily's going to spy!" Mary choked out in hushed tones.

"Spy?"

"Oh, spy is such a dramatic term. I'm just going to hone my listening skills. I must run, though, or I'll miss the carriage. Father said he was leaving in ten minutes, and I'm sure it's been at least that."

Muttering a curse in regard to the corset that was cutting off her breath, Emily turned, opened the door, and blowing her friends a kiss she then disappeared into the night. Joshua stared after her with his mouth hanging open. "She's plumb crazy," he finally mumbled. "That girl is going to get herself killed."

"Mmm. Maybe not." Ruth, too, watched the retreating form of her young mistress.

"How can you say that?" Mary asked, her eyes filling afresh with tears. "She *is* crazy!"

"No, child. I do believe this is the first sign of rationale I've seen in that girl. She took my advice. She's finally *thinking*." Ruth wandered out on to the front step, calling back over her shoulder that she needed to check on one of the sick children three doors down, and that she would be back before long.

Joshua closed the door behind her and followed Mary to the chairs situated near the table. "Are you all right?" he asked her, noting her drawn face.

"I'm worried about her. I hope she knows what she's doing. Crazy, crazy," she muttered.

Joshua shook his head. "And here I thought she was pursuing something simple, like potential suitors."

"Ha. That girl will avoid marriage like the plague, you mark my words."

"Has she told you as much?"

"Yes! She thinks marriage is little better than enslavement."

He laughed. "How can she say that when her parents have a marriage that points to the very opposite? At least for *Mrs.* Birmingham."

"Theirs is the exception, not the rule. Jeffrey and Sarah Birmingham are oddities."

Joshua nodded. It was true enough. He glanced at the girl he assumed was his half-sister, wishing things could be different for her. "When you're courted, Mary, I will only let the very best near you." He smiled and lightly mussed her hair.

She leaned forward, placing her head in her hands. "The only man I'll ever be interested in will never court me," she mumbled.

"Oh? And why is that?" As though it mattered, he reflected. Slave marriages weren't considered legal, and the terminology at the end of the service often stated, "until death or distance do you part." A slave marriage was null and void should one or the other of the parties be sold. The sanctity of marriage was not extended to black folk, yet they were expected to reproduce and supply the master's fields with new generations of slaves at every opportunity. The hypocrisy of the church-going slaveholder rankled Joshua.

Mary glanced up as though surprised she had spoken her thoughts aloud. "Oh, just because," she said, her expression uncomfortable.

Now his curiosity was piqued. "Who is he, Mary?"

"Nobody." She stood and went to the window.

He followed her, wanting to know what she was thinking but not wanting to pry. In the end, his curiosity won the battle. "You must tell me," he cajoled. "I'm your brother, after all."

"Somebody far away."

He closed his eyes. She could be referring to a slave on another plantation she had met either at the market or while running errands. Somehow, though, he knew it wasn't. "Ben."

When she didn't respond, but instead touched her forehead to the windowpane, he knew his response had found the mark. He closed his eyes, hurting for her. It seemed they had more in common than mere blood. "I'm sorry," he whispered, because even if Ben were still at Bentley, he could never have courted Mary, even if he had wanted to.

"It's all right," she whispered in return and accepted the squeeze he placed on her shoulders. He kissed the top of her head and let himself out of the door, looking in the direction of the mansion. Doomed, both of them. For the object of *his* affection was not in a position to accept whatever suit he might be able to provide, either. The young girl with the key to his heart had just run off into the night to use her father for his influential contacts and was risking the hangman's noose by flirting with treason.

It was a sad thing to realize that the one person whose company he most enjoyed in life was forever out of his reach. It was cruel, and painful, and he winced as he made his way to the stables to bed down in his humble quarters, wondering what life would have been like had he been born into it with skin just a shade lighter.

***

Ruth glanced down into the face of the young woman. "Any day now, Nellie, and you'll be holdin' yourself a squealin' bundle."

"Can't come soon enough. I'm beat," Nellie muttered as Ruth ran her hands along the distended abdomen. "I mopped like a crazy woman today, hopin' to speed it along."

"You mopped? Nellie, I told you to dust."

"I know, I know, it's just that . . ." Nellie's face took on a look of instant panic. "I left a bucket and mop in the massah's study!"

Ruth cocked a brow. "When?"

"Just afore dinner! The mistress—she'll have me whipped! Her bein' so grouchy and all with Massah Richard bein' off to war . . ."

Ruth cast the young woman a glance over her shoulder as she stood and left the shack. "I'll fetch the bucket and mop, Nellie, and the mistress is not going to have you whipped." She shook her head as she left the slave quarters and walked back out into the dark of night.

Ruth entered the mansion and padded her way down the hallway to Jeffrey's study, noting the dimmed lights throughout the house. Sarah had probably already turned in for the night. The house was quiet. As she entered the study, her eyes adjusted to the low glow of the single lamp that still burned and she located the bucket and mop Nellie had left near the hearth.

She retrieved them and was nearly to the door when a soft voice said, "Won't you stay for a chat, Ruth?"

Ruth spun around, her heart hammering in her chest, to see Jeffrey seated behind his desk in the shadows, a glass of bourbon in one hand. "I thought you were still out," she scolded lightly, knowing Jeffrey wouldn't find her insolent. He had never taken issue with the slaves, ofttimes leaving Ruth with the impression that he regarded them as more than the property the rest of the world believed them to be.

"I'm taking some time alone for a moment," he said, and then chuckled. "As if most of my time isn't spent alone!"

She refrained from comment. It would hardly do to tell the man that if he had wanted a lifetime of cozy company, he had married the wrong woman.

Jeffrey twirled the liquid in his glass, watching it swirl before taking one last swallow and placing the glass lightly on his desk. "You and I are similar, Ruth."

Again, she remained silent.

"We are both slaves."

His comment stung, and she wondered how he possessed the nerve to say such a thing to her. To equate his station in life with hers? He could leave anytime he chose. True, he'd be without any material possessions, but at least he had the option to leave Bentley and begin a life elsewhere. He knew very well that she could not.

"I've offended you."

Silence.

"Ruth, I know you to be a woman of enormous intellect. You may speak your mind with me."

"Forgive me then, sir, but I find your comparison between our lives odd."

"Do you not see it? You are a slave here because of your skin. I am a slave here because of what lies beneath mine. Or rather, what I lack beneath mine. I do not have it in me to leave, Ruth. I am a coward." He leaned forward in his chair, bracing his arms on his desk and murmured, "At least you tried."

She stiffened slightly at the reminder. "I do not think the mistress would approve of this discussion, Master Jeffrey."

He waved a hand. "Of course, Ruth, you are correct. But I do wish for you to know that I think you are an admirably strong woman. You're a kind and compassionate woman—truly the kindest I have the privilege of knowing. I hope that someday, when we all find ourselves on the other side, you will take a few moments of your time in heaven and visit me in hell."

The man had obviously treated himself to more than his customary single glass of whiskey. Ruth smiled a bit in the darkness. "You speak foolishly, sir. I doubt you'll find yourself in hell."

He looked up at her, his eyes bleak. "Will you stay with me here for awhile, Ruth? Sit and talk with me for a spell?"

She shook her head. In truth, she could think of nothing more dangerous. Warning bells sounded in her ears and she remembered her mother's face as she was wrenched from her arms and sold because the master had found too much favor with Lily. "The hour is late, Master Jeffrey," she said a bit stiffly. "Good night."

She turned and left the room.

***

Camp Brigham, Readville, Massachusetts
4 December, 1861

Ben lay in the unyielding cot, under a scratchy blanket, and shivered. It was cold, and he was tired of being cold. He was also tired of being tired, and the daily routine hadn't varied for weeks. There was a positive side, however; the cavalry regiment was improving daily, the drills were becoming secondhand, and they were learning to work as a unified body.

He didn't regret enlisting, but he was weary, and he wished for an uncomplicated life. He also wished they were somewhere warm. There was continued talk of Southern movement. As much as it caused him untold anxiety, he'd have given anything to be in his warm bed at Bentley, if only for a moment. It didn't take long, though, before he remembered all the others who were outside in shacks, in beds not so warm, for even though South Carolina was known for its balmy, year-round warmth, there were months where the temperatures dipped and the humidity intensified the cold.

So many ghosts, so many memories floated about in his head, offering him little rest. He turned first to one side, then to the other until he finally heard a voice ask softly in the darkness, "You can't sleep either?"

"No."

"What are you thinking about?" Luke whispered, obviously trying to keep from disturbing the rest of the men in their barracks.

"Home."

"Hmm. Me too. I was just wishing I could hear Robert's and Camille's daily arguments at the breakfast table."

Ben smiled into the darkness. "They are entertaining, those two."

"They are. They're closer, it seems, since their holiday in D.C. I suppose witnessing battle has a way of drawing people to common ground."

"In that case, we ought to be a lot closer before this whole ordeal is through," Ben chuckled. "I confess, I'm not much looking forward to battle."

"You know, there's talk of eventually moving toward Hilton Head. Are you, that is, will you . . ."

"Will I be comfortable being so close to home?"

"Yes?"

"Probably not, but I don't see there's an alternative. At any rate, I knew what I was getting myself into when I decided to fight against my birthright. I approach it with my eyes open."

"If we are anywhere near Bentley, will you try to see your family?"

"How can I, Luke? I've already disgraced them; now should I show up on their doorstep in a blue uniform?"

"Yes, but to be so close . . ."

Ben sighed. "I'll think of a way to see some of them. I don't think my parents care to see me at all, and Richard is somewhere in Virginia, fighting the likes of me—I don't suppose I have to worry about running into him. Richard and I never did see eye to eye on anything. I'd like to see Emily, though, and Clara, Joshua, Mary, Ruth, Rose . . ." His voice trailed off into the night, and he drifted into a troubled sleep.

Luke turned onto his side and thought of the letter he intended to write to Abigail in the morning. Apparently, she was attempting to coerce Camille into becoming involved in Society functions. He wished he could be there personally to see it. He, too, fell into a sleep that was intermittently disturbed by dreams of an uncertain future and wistful memories of the home he'd left behind.

***

Boston, Massachusetts
4 December, 1861

James Birmingham sat in his study, nursing a glass of brandy and thinking over a conversation he had had earlier in the evening with an influential senator. "You're a brilliant businessman," he had been told. "You could have a military position of some importance, should you show the slightest interest."

James had demurred, using his business as his excuse. "I need to stay here," he had said. "My contribution to the war effort is tied directly to my iron. I am of more use to the Union here at home."

It was true, he mused now, hours later. He needed to stay put and continue to run his business so that the Union would have what it needed in terms of raw materials to be converted to weapons and supplies. Underneath, however, was an undercurrent of unease. If the war lingered, and the Union armies continued encountering disastrous situations like the two major routs that had already occurred, it wouldn't be long before he might find himself under pressure to serve in a military capacity.

If only he possessed Robert's obsessive interest in the military, he might find the prospect more appealing. But he didn't, and what would he do if called upon to lead men into battle? He was a businessman, for heaven's sake! He made his living manufacturing iron!

Well, he mused as he took another swallow of the amber liquid, if it should come to that, he would pray that Robert would be of an age to accompany him. What kind of man wanted to take his son into battle with him? The kind of man who realized his son had an exceptionally uncanny ability to absorb details, sort facts, and plan strategy. James figured it probably meant he was a fool for daring to risk his son's well-being, but he also recognized Robert's brand of brilliance. It was an asset he couldn't afford to overlook. Probably, though, he was worrying over nothing. The war would soon be finished, and the world would again be righted.

Nothing to fear.

CHAPTER 36

". . . The sun rises, but shines not . . ."
—*Walt Whitman*

***

New Orleans, Louisiana
15 December, 1861

The sky was dark and full of stars, and as Marie looked out of her bedroom window on the second floor, she wondered if her mother was looking at the very same stars at that very moment. Her latest letter from Boston indicated that her father's condition remained unchanged, and her mother was beginning to despair that Jean-Pierre would ever recover.

It made Marie angry. To give up hope would be to abandon the very thing that sustained her from day to day—the hope that her family would again be together and whole. That, combined with the optimism she found in the Fromeres and in her young students, kept her afloat.

The world around her was chaos. New Orleans was surrounded on the coast by Union fleets, and blockade runners were constantly trying to maneuver their way past those Union ships in an effort to communicate and trade with Britain. The city was tense with the knowledge that the Union was steadily attempting to take control of the Mississippi, and had effectively blockaded nearly every Southern port down the Atlantic and around into the Gulf.

Michael was keeping her father's newspaper running, and had calmed the fears of those who had ruined her father's life, insisting they had nothing whatsoever to fear from the *New Orleans Herald*. Since the incident when Marie had shot a hole in the ceiling of the newspaper offices, she and Michael had been blessedly unmolested.

Unable to settle down for the night, she rose from her bed and padded over to the small desk situated in the corner of her bedroom. She decided to write to her new pen-friend in New York. She had created a fairly regular correspondence with Daniel O'Shea over the past month and found it soothing to pour her heart onto the paper and send it off to a person she'd never met—a person who always answered back with interest and with his own unique perspective, without knowledge of her past or any preconceived notions of her character.

Daniel didn't side with either country—he wasn't pro-Union or Confederate. He seemed to be a bit adrift, rooting about and searching for a place that would welcome him with open arms. Marie shook her head. He may spend a lifetime looking, then, because she doubted there was a place on earth entirely free of prejudice.

Dear Daniel, she wrote,

I am unable to sleep. I am worried again, over things that are completely out of my control. The city has begun preliminarily celebrating, if in an understated fashion, the one-year anniversary of South Carolina's secession and the birth of the Confederacy. My father's condition remains unchanged and I fear my mother is losing faith. I am busy here with activities that occupy my thoughts late into the night until I am certain my brain will shut down of its own volition, which it often does and then I fall into a fitful sleep.

Marie set her pen down on the desk and stretched, only to be alarmed at an insistent knocking on her front door. Her heart pounding, she flew from her chair and thrust her arms into the sleeves of her housecoat, grabbing the rifle from under her bed as she ran toward the door and down the stairs. She quietly ventured toward the dining room window, which offered a clear view of the front verandah. Waiting for her eyes to clearly define the two figures standing at her door, she narrowed her focus until with a surprised cry, she moved to the front door and opened it, allowing her midnight visitors entry.

"Constance and Peter, what on *God's green earth* are you doing here?"

"Oh, Miss Brissot," Constance sobbed, "the Fromeres are in trouble! That Bussey boy raised a ruckus in town and blamed Noah for it, and now there are folks looking for the whole family, saying that they're no good and shouldn't be considered free blacks, and . . ."

Marie locked the door and drew the children into the parlor, making sure the heavy drapes were drawn before striking a light to one of several kerosene lamps situated about the room. "Now, Constance, what kind of 'ruckus' did the Bussey boy cause?"

"He beat the mayor's son unconscious! Peter saw him do it!"

Marie glanced at Peter, who nodded, his face alarmingly white. "They won't believe me, though," Peter rasped. "I tried to tell the mayor himself, but Bussey denied it when the mayor confronted him, and now they're saying Noah tried to kill the boy."

"Does the Bussey boy know it was you who told on him?"

"I don't think so."

Marie rubbed her forehead. "All right. Where is Noah?"

"He's in the shed where you teach the family," Constance cried. "They're all there! The mayor's friends said they'd go after the whole family!"

"Does your mother know about this?"

"No," Peter answered. "She thinks we're in bed."

"All right. Wait for me here." Still clutching her gun, Marie ran up the stairs and into her parents' bedroom. Rummaging through her father's closet, she found an old pair of work trousers and a white shirt, both of which she quickly put on, rolling the pant legs until they hit her ankle and stuffing the shirt into the waistband. She then ran to her bedroom and donned her most serviceable pair of practical boots and an overcoat. Again taking the gun in hand, she went downstairs and out the back door, pulling the children along with her.

She quietly readied a team of horses and harnessed them to the one large carriage her family owned. It was a closed vehicle, thankfully, and if she could make it to the Braxton's farm and back again undetected, they all might survive until morning.

The trip to the farm was quiet. Marie stashed the children inside the conveyance and told them to stay down, although there were drapes over the windows that made it impossible to see inside. She rode atop, guiding the team of horses with a practiced hand, grateful for good animals that responded to her touch.

The moon was full, giving plenty of light for the journey, but Marie almost wished it weren't. She would have liked the comfort of total darkness that would have hidden her from prying eyes. She eventually reached the Braxton's farm and drove undetected around back to the shed, halting the carriage as close as she could manage against the dense undergrowth.

Marie approached the old building with Constance and Peter on her heels, knocking softly at the door and identifying herself. She ventured inside to find the faces of her friends so drawn in fear that it tore at her heart. "You must come with me," she told Justis and Pauline. "I have an empty house, and you'll be safe there. My parents are gone—there's nobody but me."

Pauline began to quietly sob and Marie drew the woman into her arms, fighting a sting in her own eyes and mentally cursing when the tears dislodged themselves and trailed a path down her cheek. It would do the Fromeres no good if she couldn't hold herself together, and she swiped at her face, releasing the woman and saying, "Please, I beg you, do not argue with me. You must come with me right now. I will take care of you until we can get you safely out of New Orleans."

"Maybe it's not as bad as all that," Pauline murmured, drying her own eyes, clutching a small bag of belongings in front of her.

"Oh, dear lady, I'm afraid it is. Noah has unwittingly made some very powerful enemies. I know of them firsthand." She looked to Justis. "Will you come home with me?"

He nodded slowly, and wordlessly extended his hand, clasping hers tightly. "Thank you, miss," he whispered.

"We must hurry," Marie said and motioned for the family to follow her out to the carriage. When she had the Fromeres safely situated inside with the curtains fully closed, she turned to Constance with a brief hug and said, "Now you go back to bed. They'll be safe with me."

Constance sobbed against her shoulder and Marie held her thin frame as it shook. Pulling back, she held the girl's face in her hands and said, "You be strong, now. Go home with Peter and help take care of your mother. All right?"

Constance nodded and allowed Peter to take her arm, and the two of them walked toward the house. Heaving a huge sigh, Marie climbed to the top of the carriage, released the brake, clicked to the horses, and began the short journey home.

The carriage traveled down the country lane, twisting and turning, making its way toward the city. Marie had neared the edge of a dusty road, densely populated with trees, when she heard voices. She pulled the horses to an immediate stop.

". . . can't have just disappeared!" one young man was saying. "Where would they have gone?"

"We'll find 'em," another answered. "Bloody Nigra thinks he's as smart as a white boy! Says he even knows how to read!"

Marie held her breath as a pack of teenaged boys crossed the other side of the lane roughly twenty yards away, headed in the opposite direction. She prayed for all she was worth that the horses would be still. One small snort, or jingle of the harness, and they would be discovered.

Mercifully, divine Providence smiled upon her and the horses remained blessedly silent. There was not a sound or movement from inside the carriage, and large clouds moved to cover the bright light of the moon. Mouthing a word of thanks toward heaven, Marie waited until the boys were long gone before continuing her journey home.

She reached the stables at the back of her home without incident and unhitched the horses, seeing them into the comfort of their stalls. She then opened the door of the carriage and smiled at her guests. "We're home," she whispered, her heart again constricting at the eyes wide with fear, set against their dark faces.

She led the Fromeres in through the back door and locked it securely behind them, taking them directly upstairs and showing them what accommodations were available to them. "You must use my parents' bedroom," she said to Pauline and Justis, who stared at her as though she had sprouted another head. "It's right in here."

"We can't possibly, miss!" Justis murmured.

"I insist. I shan't sleep well if you don't," she said, hoping to guilt them into accepting her offer.

"And you boys," she said, walking out into the hallway, "will use these two rooms. This one here is a guest room, and there are two twin beds. The room across the hallway is mine, and there's one bed in there. I'll just move some of my things downstairs to my father's study. There's a small bed in there and we often used that room as an extra guest room when people came to visit, so it will suit me just fine."

Abel spoke up then, catching Marie by surprise. The quiet boy rarely said anything at all. "We can't take your room, miss. It just wouldn't be right."

"Nonsense, Abel," she said with a wave of her hand as she retrieved her nightdress and a few personal articles from the bedroom. "Truly, it's not an inconvenience for me, and besides, you're all safer up here. Please," she said, pausing to look at all of them, "I insist. Truthfully, I've been lonely. It'll be nice to have the company."

They stared at her in shocked silence, as though they couldn't take in the swift turn of events. "Miss," Justis finally said, "someday, if not in this life, then in the next, we will repay this kindness."

"It's my pleasure, Mr. Fromere."

After fixing a quick snack of simple sandwiches and milk for her guests, Marie left them to ready themselves for bed. She eventually heard the footsteps upstairs cease, and she made herself comfortable in her father's study. After washing her face and changing back into her nightdress for the second time that night, she sat upon the small bed and took stock of what she'd done.

Her breath quickened, her skin grew hot, and her eyes blurred with the stress of the evening. Just when she felt sure she'd collapse from fear, a calm peace stole over her heart and mind. The impression came swift and reassuring.

I will not fail thee . . .

***

Green Spring Run, Virginia
16 December, 1861

Anne shivered in the cold as the members of the regiment finished setting up camp for the night. It was only temporary—they would be marching again by morning, at least another sixteen miles before they reached Romney, where they would presumably remain for the rest of the month.

They had just traveled a distance of roughly 220 miles by rail, and to say she was tired would have drastically understated her condition. The past several weeks had seen activity she never imagined she would encounter. Earlier in November, General Rosecrans had ordered Colonel Tyler to send five hundred men to General Benham at Loop Creek for temporary duty. Anne's company had been one of those assigned, and the escapade had had its share of adventure.

Following several miles of marching, they existed for several days on their new assignment with very little to eat—nothing but coffee and hard bread— and the weather began turning extremely cold. The order had eventually come to pursue Confederate General Floyd's men, which they did, to a place called McCoy's Mill, where a heavy skirmish took place and ended in a rout of the Confederate soldiers.

Her eyes had been opened once and for all, Anne realized as she now dumped her belongings in the large tent she would share with Ivar, Mark, and Jed. She had thought herself immune to things like rabid fear and disgust. Watching the men die, however, was an experience she knew she would never forget. The sounds of their last cries for help would be forever seared into her memory. Upon their own retreat, she and Ivar had stopped to offer a drink of water to a young man in a gray uniform, lying in a pool of his own blood, his final breaths coming out of his mouth in a mist against the cold air.

They were eventually reunited with the rest of the regiment after finishing their temporary duty, making their way back through four inches of snow, camping overnight on one occasion without shelter or food. Her feet had been numb, which was actually a relief, after a while. Numb was better than pain.

Afterward, as they ventured into the month of December and its requisite troop movements, the travel by rail had been a blessed respite. Because many of the rivers in the area had become flooded from the heavy snow and rainfall, crossings by barge were also a necessity, and one for which Anne was grateful. Her feet were blistered and sore, and any movement she was permitted without walking was a gift.

She sighed and looked around the tent, grateful for the shelter, flimsy and temporary though it was. Her pack lay open on the ground, and she reached inside it, glancing over the notes she had only just telegraphed to Jacob Taylor when she was at the train station. Her writing was saving her life, she realized as she glanced down at the paper. It was the one thing that kept her from deserting and running back home. She was cold and miserable, and her dreams were haunted at night by the bloody faces of dead men. If she hadn't felt her responsibility to deliver news from the field as she'd promised, it would be altogether too tempting to go to her commanding officer and simply tell him she was a woman.

She glanced at her last letter from her mother that was sitting at the top of her knapsack, sent via Isabelle's sister in Chicago, and felt her eyes burn from missing her more than she'd ever imagined she could. Shaking herself slightly, she murmured, "Pull yourself together!" and decided to venture outside with her canteen for some water. Provided there was a good water source close by, she might be able to quench her thirst.

She left the tent and stepped out into a blast of wind, shivering and pulling her overcoat firmly closed, clutching it with her fist. After asking around a bit, she found that sure enough, the river running parallel to the campsite was good for drinking. She filled her canteen with the icy water, thinking she must be an utter fool, yet when she took that first drink and felt the dry, parched ache in her throat recede, she was glad for the river.

Anne slowly walked back to the tent, exchanging tired greetings and comments with the other troops, trying for a smile but feeling as though she might just have bitten off more than she was able to chew. It was worth it, though, and she knew it. She picked up her pace a bit, lifting her chin and glancing at the darkening night sky. She was out here, and she was doing it! Had she stayed home, she would have regretted it for the rest of her life. She was not about to be beaten!

Feeling much better, and ignoring her aching feet, she lifted the flap and entered the tent. As she glanced up and took stock of what was happening, her head began to spin and her heart thundered in her ears. Ivar was standing over her knapsack, his hands in his pockets, his eyeglasses upon his face, glancing down at the letter that lay atop her belongings in clear view for all to see. She cursed her stupidity a thousand times over for being so weary that she forgot to be cautious.

There was her mother's neat handwriting on the letter that sat face up, slightly unfolded and visible to Ivar's curious eye. Anne put her hand at the throat of her overcoat, clutching it closed with a fist and willing herself to breathe evenly.

He finally turned to her with an inscrutable expression and said, "'Anne.' It suits you much better than 'Aaron.'"

HISTORICAL NOTES

Fact or Fiction?

One of the tasks facing a reader of historical fiction is that of discernment. The reader must try to decide which of the myriad of details in the book actually happened, and which is a figment of the author's imagination. The following is my attempt to help the reader understand where there may be disparities between my work and actual history. While I tried my utmost to stay as close to the truth as possible, there were instances wherein I was forced to bend reality a bit so that I could have witnesses to certain important events.

The Regiments

One such occurrence is in Chapter 32, where Richard Birmingham is witness to the Union disaster at Ball's Bluff. In reality, as far as my own research shows, the Palmetto Guard, or 2nd South Carolina Volunteer Infantry, in which Richard is enlisted, was not on hand for this particular battle. It was a battle of significance, however, and when looking over my cast of characters, I had to work with who was on hand and was in closest proximity to that particular region. The 7th Ohio, with Anne and Ivar, was close, but Richard was closer, and so the reader views those scenes through his eyes, although in truth, the 2nd South Carolina wasn't actually there.

The Newspapers

While the bulk of the information the public received in the 1800s was disseminated through newspapers, and people were well informed, albeit sometimes in an exaggerated or biased fashion, the newspaper was a staple and there were papers all over the country.

The newspapers I focus on in this book, however, are my own creations. The *Boston Examiner* that Anne writes for, and the *New Orleans Herald*, Jean-Pierre Brissot's paper, are fictional. I wanted to be able to share events with the reader at the time the characters learned of them, and by using these fictional newspapers, I was able to put into them that which I felt was necessary not only for plot movement but also as a means of historical exposition.

To my knowledge, there wasn't actually furor in New Orleans over a newspaper editor writing inflammatory editorials that resulted in bodily harm to him. Jean-Pierre's exploits are entirely figments of my own imagination.

The Banks

Luke Birmingham works at a bank in Boston called "First Financial," and also ends up working briefly with that bank's New York branch, attempting to aid immigrants with their discrimination complaints. In truth, those banks are fictitious, and Luke's (and subsequently Daniel O'Shea's) battles for fairness on behalf of the immigrant population are also my own creations. There were biases and troubles between differing ethnic backgrounds and peoples, to be sure, but this particular issue is my own doing.

The Slaves

My account of the Birmingham slaves, while possibly not entirely reflective of the majority of slaves or slave life at the time, was crafted that way for a purpose. It was illegal, yes, to teach slaves to read or to educate them, but several accounts that I have discovered show that upwards of five percent of the slave population was actually literate. While five percent is a low statistic, it's still five percent, and I wanted my characters in this story to be part of that statistic.

I also chose to create these early African Americans as literate and articulate to prove a point: that even in the midst of a society that felt slaves did not possess the intellectual capacities equal to that of the white man, they did indeed excel, and their thirsty minds absorbed information like sponges. Not only did they learn, they also survived and lived to tell the tale.

For any who might believe that such a thing could never have happened, that slaves living in the South before and during the war could never have risen to any kind of literate or articulate brilliance, I need only point such a person in the direction of Frederick Douglass as proof. I am in awe of the man and his brilliance, not only with his insights of the world into which he was born, but with his mastery and unparalleled command of the English language. I marvel at his spirit and his strength.

Abolition and Women's Rights

By the time the Civil War began, the Abolition groups, largely located in the New England area, saw membership upwards of approximately 160,000 members. In contrast to the combined Northern and Southern population of roughly thirty million this is indeed a small minority, but 160,000 people is still somewhat significant. It was this minority who believed that the goal of the war, from the outset, should have been freedom for the slaves, and who were loud and uncompromising in their demands that the phrase "all men are created equal" become a reality.

As for the women, there were also Women's Rights societies in full swing, demanding the right to vote and work to earn wages equal to men's. The famed Women's Rights meeting in 1848 in Seneca Falls, New York, was a momentous event that spearheaded societal change, allowing women to enjoy today what they were denied a century ago. If it seems that some of the female characters in this book were too "modern" for their time, I need only to point to these real, historical women on whose shoulders the modern woman stands.

Women Enlistees

Much myth and speculation have surrounded the subject of women who fought as men in the Civil War, and bits and pieces uncovered through the decades point to upwards of four hundred women, both sides inclusive, who enlisted, fought, and even died as men. In many cases, the gender of these women wasn't discovered until they were dead and ready to be buried.

But how would they have conducted bodily functions without being discovered? Surely a person couldn't hide her gender while living in such close quarters with others? I have encountered sources that suggest that it may not have been as impossible as we might think. The times were different then—men were often private and went off by themselves to take care of things considered personal, so it wouldn't have been strange for a woman, posing as a man, to disappear for a few moments to conduct her business.

There were women during this time period who were forward thinkers, just as there have been women who have been years ahead of their respective days in all eras through the ages. For those who would suggest that a woman could never enlist, live, and fight with men and get away with it, I must remind us all that truth is often stranger than fiction, and that which seems the most unbelievable did occur. *See photo on page 455.*

Tidbits

Chapter 13 details the firing upon Fort Sumter. I have placed Jeffrey and Richard Birmingham with General Beauregard at Fort Johnson when the firing began. Edmund Ruffin, the fire-eater who is credited with firing the first shot of the war, was actually on Morris Island. In order to create a cohesive scene viewed through Jeffrey Birmingham's eyes, I combined locales so that Jeffrey sees Ruffin firing that "first" shot, although Ruffin was, in reality, not with Beauregard at Fort Johnson.

The telegraph lines were strung through the Salt Lake valley in 1861, but not quite as soon as I lead the reader to believe. In January of 1861, I have Ben Birmingham reading a telegram sent by his cousin, Luke. The telegraph actually reached Utah later that year.

In Chapter 24, just before the 1st Battle of Bull Run, Mrs. Sylvester's sister makes reference to the fact that Lincoln's suspension of the Writ of Habeas Corpus is an "outrage," and that the jailing of the Baltimorean mayor is also an outrage. The date that I have her down as saying this was July 20. In reality, the mayor of Baltimore and several others of that city's politicians were not actually jailed until September. Those influential people in Baltimore called a special legislative session wherein Lincoln feared they would vote to secede, leaving D.C. surrounded by the enemy on all sides. He jailed those who had influence over such an outcome and kept them locked up until new, stalwart Unionist legislators were voted into office.

BIBLIOGRAPHY

Axelrod, Alan. *The Complete Idiot's Guide to the Civil War.* New York: Alpha Books (Macmillan), 1998.

Ball, Edward. *Slaves in the Family.* New York: Ballantine Books, 1998, 1999.

Bowman, John S. *The Civil War Day by Day—An Illustrated Almanac of America's Bloodiest War.* Greenwich: Dorset Press, 1989.

Davis, Kenneth C. *Don't Know Much About the Civil War.* New York: Avon Books, 1996.

Davis, William C. *The Soldiers of the Civil War.* New York: Quadrillion Publishing, 1993.

Davis, Burke. *The Civil War, Strange and Fascinating Facts.* New York: Wings Books,1980.

Douglass, Frederick. *Narrative of the Life of Frederick Douglass, An American Slave.* New York: Dell Publishing, 150th Anniversary Edition, 1997; Introduction copyright, Henry Louis Gates, Jr., 1997.

Hackwell, Grace-Marie Moore, owner and creator. "1st Regiment Massachusetts Volunteer Cavalry http://hometown.aol.com/Shortyhack/1st mass.html.

Hardman, Larry, owner and creator. "7th Ohio Volunteer Infantry, USA." http://www.ehistory.com/uscw/features/regimental/ohio/union/7thOhio/index.cfm. Copyright 1999.

Kelly, Brian and Petrea. *Latter-Day History of the Church of Jesus Christ of Latter-day Saints*. American Fork: Covenant Communications, 2000.

Lyman, Darryl. *Civil War Wordbook, including Sayings, Phrases and Expletives*. Pennsylvania: Combined Books, 1994.

Mayer, Henry. *All On Fire—William Lloyd Garrison and the Abolition of Slavery*. NewYork: St. Martin's Griffin, 1998.

McPherson, James M. *Battle Cry of Freedom*. New York: Ballantine, 1988.

McPherson, James, and Mort Kunstler. *Images of the Civil War*. New Jersey: Gramercy Books, 1992.

Miller, William J., and Brian C. Pohanka. *An Illustrated History of the Civil War*. Virginia: Time Life, 2000.

Moore, John Hammond. *A Plantation Mistress on the Eve of the Civil War—The Diary of Keziah Goodwyn Hopkins Brevard, 1860-1861*. Columbia: The University of South Carolina Press, 1993.

Oates, Stephen B. *The Whirlwind of War, Voices of the Storm, 1861-1865*. New York: HarperCollins, 1998.

Varhola, Michael J. *Everyday Life During the Civil War: A Guide for Writers, Students and Historians.* Ohio: Writer's Digest Books (an imprint of F & W Publications, Inc.), 1999.

Ward, Geoffrey C., Ken Burns, Rick Burns. *The Civil War.* New York: Knopf, Inc., 1990.

GLIMPSES OF
THE CIVIL WAR

PHOTOS FROM CIVIL WAR REENACTMENTS
BY AL THELIN

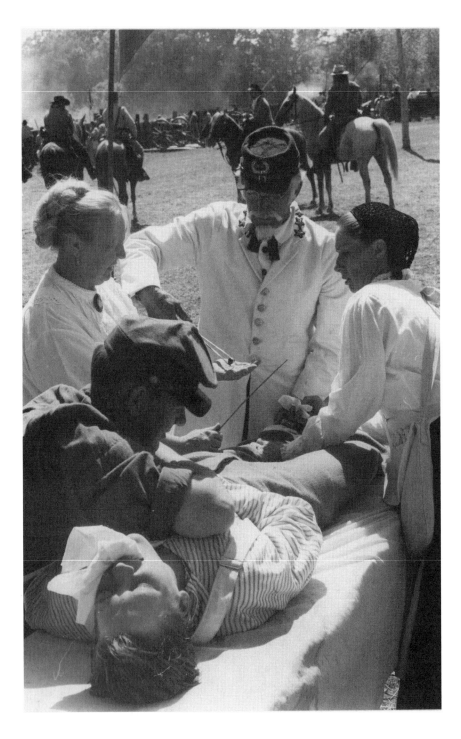

ABOUT THE AUTHOR

A graduate of Weber State University, N.C. Allen has enjoyed a successful writing career for a number of years. She has proven herself a gifted and prolific writer whose versatility has earned her a large and loyal readership.

She enjoys spending time with her family, reading, traveling, and learning of other times, people, and places. She and her husband, Mark, live in Ogden, Utah, with their two children.